THIS BOOK
IS IN THE CARE OF

_____

_____

"A wildly imaginative, wonderfully irreverent epic that shines with wit and wisdom—and features excellent instructions on how to cope with Thwaps, Fangs, and the occasional Toothy Cow."

—ALLAN HEINBERG, writer/co-executive producer of ABC's
Grey's Anatomy, and co-creator of Marvel Comics' *Young Avengers*

"Andrew Peterson, a natural storyteller in the oral tradition, has nailed the voice needed to translate a rip-roaring tale to the written page."

—DONITA K. PAUL, author of *DragonSpell, DragonKnight,*
DragonQuest, and *DragonFire*

"Peterson deserves every literary prize for these fine books. It is obvious that his musical talents have been put to good use as his use of words, plot, and narrative read like a well-scored film script. Amazing— thrilling and well worth reading again and again."

—G. P. TAYLOR, *New York Times* best-selling author of *Shadowmancer*
and The Dopple Ganger Chronicles

"So good—smart, funny, as full of ideas as action."

—JONATHAN ROGERS, author of *The Charlatan's Boy*

"[The Wingfeather Saga] is a welcome feast of levity—and clearly a labor of love. Andrew Peterson has awakened my inner eight-year-old, and that is a very good thing."

—JEFFREY OVERSTREET, author of *Auralia's Colors, Cyndere's Midnight,*
and *Raven's Ladder*

"An immensely clever tale from a wonderful storyteller."

—PHIL VISCHER, creator of *VeggieTales*

Also by Andrew Peterson

The Wingfeather Saga

Music

Carried Along

Clear to Venus

Love and Thunder

*Behold the Lamb of God: The True
Tall Tale of the Coming of Christ*

The Far Country

Resurrection Letters Vol. II

Counting Stars

Light for the Lost Boy

For Children

The Ballad of Matthew's Begats

Slugs & Bugs & Lullabies
(with Randall Goodgame)

Sea Dragons. A Desperate Quest.
And the Final Battle for the Shining Isle.

The WARDEN and the Wolf King

ANDREW PETERSON

THE WINGFEATHER SAGA BOOK FOUR

RABBIT ROOM
— PRESS —

THE WARDEN AND THE WOLF KING © 2014 by Andrew Peterson

Published by
RABBIT ROOM PRESS
523 Heather Place
Nashville, Tennessee 37204
info@rabbitroom.com

Cover design by Brannon McAllister
Cover illustration and map © 2011 by Justin Gerard
Illustrations © 2014 by Joe Sutphin
Edited by Pete Peterson and Jessica Barnes

ISBN 9780988963252

First Edition
Printed in the United States of America
14 15 16 17 18 — 6 5 4 3 2

This one's for you, Dear Reader.
You're almost home.

"I dreamed of a song—I heard it sung;
In the ear of my soul its strange notes rung.
What were its words I could not tell,
Only the voice I heard right well,

A voice with a wild melodious cry
Reaching and longing afar and high.
Sorrowful triumph, and hopeful strife,
Gainful death, and new-born life . . ."

—George MacDonald, 1842

Contents

Contents

Contents

Part Four: Anniera

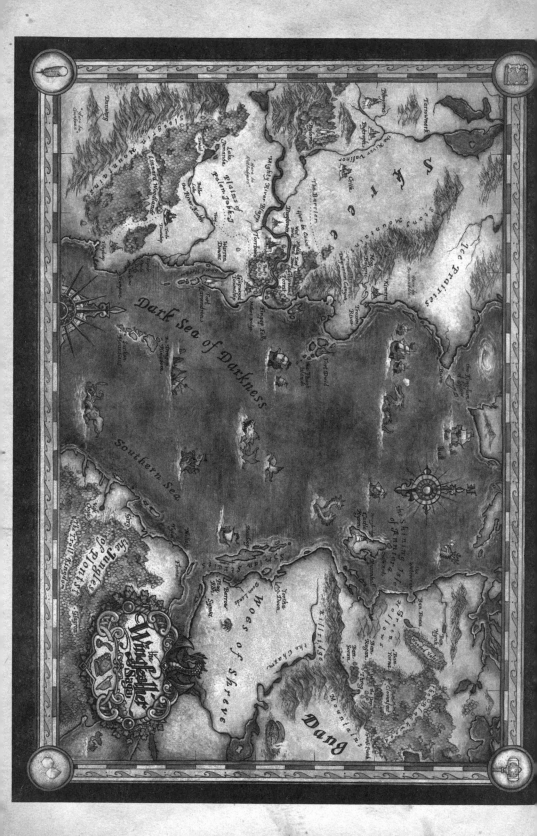

Part One:

THE GREEN HOLLOWS

In the Fourth Epoch, in the year 435, during the peaceful reign of Lander Wingfeather and his wife Illia Finley of the Green Hollows, a girl was born. Her elder brother Olmer would be the Throne Warden, and the girl was to be the High Queen of the Shining Isle. Her name was Madia, and her beauty was renowned in the free lands of Dang. When she was a young woman of marrying age she paid a summer visit to Ban Rona in the Green Hollows, where King Lander and Queen Illia often sailed when the wind was warm. There they attended the Bannick Durga and spent the days in happiness while the Hollowsfolk reveled in gamery. Of all the pleasures of Ban Rona, young Madia most enjoyed stealing away from the games at the Field of Finley to the cavernous halls of the Great Library.

There she met a bright young man named Bonifer Squoon.

—From *The Annieriad: The Fall of the Fourth Epoch*

As compiled by Oskar N. Reteep, esq.

Appreciator of the Strange, the Neat, and/or the Yummy

Chief Librarian, Historian, and Book Smeller of the Great Library of Ban Rona

1

The Slog of War

What happens next?"

"How am I supposed to know? I've never been in a war."

"But we've been here for three hours at least. And we haven't eaten a thing."

"Look, all I know is we're supposed to sit here and be quiet until the tribes are finished pledging—or whatever it's called. And we're all hungry, but at least *you* don't get cold."

"How many tribes are left?"

"You can count."

"Wait, how many tribes did we start with?"

"Kal, can you just find some way to be interested in what's going on? Mama said this hasn't happened in decades. And they're here for *you*, after all. The least you can do is show some interest. Shh! Here comes a tribesman."

Janner and Kalmar sat on a wooden platform overlooking the Field of Finley, now covered with snow. These were the fields, Janner remembered, where many years ago Podo Helmer had won the heart of Wendolyn Igiby by competing in the games of the Bannick Durga against the roughest and rowdiest of the Hollowsfolk. But there were no games today. Today was about war. Which meant boredom.

That morning, Nia had woken the brothers in their bedroom at Chimney Hill with the reminder that the day of tribute had come, and that as High King and Throne Warden of Anniera, their presence was required. After a quick breakfast prepared by Podo and Freva, Nia presented the brothers and their sister Leeli with formal attire.

Leeli got a white dress lined with burble fur and a gray speckled coat that fell about her like a blanket. It was held around her shoulders by a silver brooch in the shape of a beaming star. When Leeli emerged from her bedroom with the dress and robe on, her hair draped over one shoulder and her cheeks burning with the hope of her own beauty, the boys were speechless. Podo, who was wearing an apron and clopping one-legged around the table collecting dirty dishes, looked up and whispered, "Mother moonlight, she's pretty."

The brothers got no such compliments, but they felt handsome in their royal clothes. Kalmar needed no coat since he was already covered with silvery brown fur. Instead he wore a black leather vest lined with blood-red fabric, fastened down the front with shiny silver buttons, each of which bore the Annieran dragon—the same insignia Janner had seen on the Uncle Artham's journals back in Glipwood. Nia draped a black cloak over his shoulders and fastened it at the neck with a silver sun. She tried to put a crown on Kal's head—not an official Annieran crown, she told them, but something she had commissioned from a smith in Ban Rona, a circlet that would at least make him look kingly enough for the ceremony. But after several failed attempts to secure it over his wolf ears, which constantly twitched, Nia decided to forego the crown, much to Kalmar's relief.

Finally, Janner was given a black coat of polished leather, with boots and gloves to match. When he pulled the gloves on and wiggled his fingers, he

noticed on the back of each hand the same Annieran dragon stitched into the leather with crimson thread.

"Here," Nia said as she draped a black cloak over Janner's shoulders. He noticed when she drew near to fasten his brooch—which was in the shape of a crescent moon—that instead of looking up at her, they were eye to eye. "When did you get so tall?" Nia asked quietly. She adjusted his cloak and her hands lingered on his shoulders. "You look like a Throne Warden. Tall and handsome and humble. Keep an eye on Kalmar today. This ceremony is exactly the kind of thing he loathes."

Janner glanced at Kal, who was hunched over the table, brushing crumbs from breakfast into a little pile, then licking them up.

"Kalmar!" Nia snapped, and he jerked upright and wiped his hands on his cloak.

"Kalmar!" Nia said again, and he grabbed a napkin from the table and cleaned his hands and cloak with a nervous laugh.

"Kalmar!" Nia said, snatching the napkin from him. He hadn't noticed that it was soiled with sweetberry jam—jam that was now smeared all over his new cloak and his hands, which he absentmindedly wiped on his vest.

"Out!" Nia ordered.

Janner bustled Kalmar and Leeli through the door, where Oskar N. Reteep waited with the sled hitched and ready. Kal bounded into the wagon.

"In the words of Chancho Phanor, 'You three look magnificent! Is that sweetberry jam?'" Oskar pointed at Kalmar's cloak.

Somehow, even though his face was covered in fur, Kal's cheeks seemed to flush as he reached down and lifted Leeli in behind him. Janner clambered up the other side.

"It's going to be a fine day, Jewels!" Oskar clicked the horse into motion and pulled his scarf over his mouth. He was already a big fellow, but the many layers of coats, cloaks, and blankets made him look enormous. All Janner could see of the old man was his bright red nose and spectacles peeking out from between the scarf and his cowl; the rest of him was a mountainous pile of blankets.

After an hour of riding through the snow they crested the hill and saw what seemed to be the entire population of the Green Hollows gathered around the perimeter of the Field of Finley. Out of the silence of the long ride came the sudden racket of the multitude, the whinny of horses, the snapping of many flags in the wind. The aroma of campfires mingled with that of meat roasting on spits and the odor of horse manure. Each tribe had erected its own main tent and surrounded it with smaller ones, between which were wagons, horses, and campfires. Thousands of Hollowsfolk stood in groups around the fires. Others had struck up games and were rolling in the snow or chasing one another out beyond the tents.

But the center of the Field of Finley was immaculate, a smooth circular blanket of white as long and wide as an arrow shot. Not a single footprint marred the snow, though the path around it was muddied with traffic. At the section of the field nearest the road, a platform had been erected, and a man standing beside it raised a hand in greeting when he saw the Wingfeathers. Even at a distance Janner recognized the tall, bearded figure of Rudric, Keeper of the Hollows.

Janner felt a tug of grief. Rudric hadn't meant to kill his father, Janner knew that, but it didn't make the pain or the awkwardness disappear—for either Janner or for Rudric, who had scarcely been seen at Chimney Hill in the months since Esben's death. Rudric was a good man, and Janner liked him, but he had become an emblem of his father's absence. Janner couldn't imagine how Nia must feel—Nia, who had been in love with Rudric up to the very day that Esben returned.

Oskar grunted. "Right. Well, as some author surely said somewhere, 'We'd better get on with it.'" He drove the sled down to the platform and greeted Rudric.

"Oskar. Good to see you," Rudric said. He extended a hand to Leeli, who took it after a slight hesitation and allowed him to lift her out of the wagon and lower her gently to the ground. Then Rudric nodded a greeting to Janner and Kal, though he only met their eyes for a moment. "This way, Wingfeathers. It's going to be a long day, but this is important if we're going to be an army worthy of battle."

Next to the platform was a tent with two Durgan Guildsmen standing guard at the entrance. Their black hoods were pulled low over their faces and their arms were crossed. When Janner and his siblings followed Rudric inside, the guildsmen nodded a silent greeting first at Rudric, then at Janner and Leeli. It was hard to tell if it was his imagination, but Janner didn't think they acknowledged his wolf brother.

He didn't have time to think more about it because as soon as he entered the tent he saw twelve tribesmen and as many tribeswomen standing at attention. They were gathered around a long table beneath the iron branches of a chandelier aflicker with candles. Janner could tell it was meant to resemble the great tree of Ban Rona. He couldn't help noticing the irony that only a few months ago Nia had declared *turalay* and put her bloody handprint on the tree in order to save Kalmar from the very people who were now pledging their allegiance to him.

Rudric took his place at the head of the table and gestured at three empty seats. "Welcome, clans of the Hollows." Rudric nodded at the children. "Welcome, Jewels of Anniera."

Then, at once, everyone in the room sat. The Wingfeather children looked around in confusion, then plopped into their seats.

The men at the table all looked like typical Hollows men: barrel chests, long moustaches and beards, faces and hands that bore knots and scars from years of hard work and harder play. And though their clothes differed in color and cut, they all wore a mixture of burly furs and leather that was well-groomed and threaded with patterns and emblems. The women, on the other hand, could not have looked more varied. Some of them were slim and feminine, like Nia, while others, somehow no less beautiful, hulked like the men. Some wore bright dresses and had swords slung over their backs, others wore plain cloth but had their hair arranged in looping braids. Some were even burlier than the men, with whiskers and warts as ugly as Olumphia Groundwich's. They sat beside what Janner assumed to be their husbands and it seemed likely that they had administered the wounds that led to many of the men's scars—and yet most of the couples were, in fact, holding hands.

"For those of you who have not yet laid eyes on him," Rudric said, "I present to you Kalmar Wingfeather, High King of the Shining Isle."

Every eye in the room appraised Kalmar without a shred of sensitivity. Most of the faces wore their wariness and distaste plainly, though a few gave him sincere smiles and nods of greeting. Janner noted with pride that Kalmar sat up straight and met their eyes.

"Hello," he said, clearing his throat. "I'm not sure what to say except, uh, that I'm glad you're here. I don't know about you, but my life has been pretty messed up by Gnag the Nameless. Somebody has to stop him or he's going to basically take over all of Aerwiar and turn everybody into—into—" He glanced at his claws and furry hands. The tent fell painfully silent. Kalmar drew a deep breath and held his Fang hands out for all to see. "Into this. Somebody has to stop him. And it doesn't seem like anyone but the people of the Green Hollows are brave enough to fight back. So like I said, I'm glad you're here. That's all." He hid his hands under the table and slumped back in his chair. "Oh, I forgot." Kalmar sat up again. "This is my sister Leeli. She's a Song Maiden. And my brother Janner is the Throne Warden. We don't know what we're supposed to do, but we want to help."

Leeli stared around the table at the Hollowsfolk as if daring them to speak against her brother. After a pause, the clan chiefs and chieftesses grunted their approval and banged on the table with heavy fists so long and loud that Janner thought the table would break.

Rudric quieted the assembly and explained the order of the day, which, as it turned out, would be unbearably boring for all three of the children. Beneath the twelve clans of the chieftains and chieftesses there were many separate tribes, and the heads of each tribe, each in their turns, were to come before Kalmar and pledge allegiance to the Shining Isle and its boy king. One clan leader at a time, they marched before the platform on the field. They gave accounts of their clan histories, including tales of greatness in various battles over the centuries, going all the way back to the Second Epoch, each leader taking care to describe his or her clan's particular strengths and weaknesses. After an hour or so of what amounted to boasts, tall tales, and bravado, the clan leader would bow, parade his flag first before his chief, then before Kalmar, then mount it beside the Annieran flag.

Oskar took copious notes. Leeli had brought her songbook and practiced whistleharp fingerings, Janner struggled valiantly to pay attention, and Kalmar did his best to stay awake.

The ceremony droned on for what seemed like an eternity until the head tribesman of Ban Soran swaggered before the platform. He was a wiry fellow who wore no shirt despite the bitter cold. His chest and face were painted with crimson stripes, and he all but snarled when he spoke.

"My name is Carnack, and I pledge nothing to a Fang of Dang."

2

Janner's Pledge

Oy," said Rudric under his breath. "I was afraid this might happen."

"What happens if he won't pledge?" Janner asked. Rudric didn't hear him because he was whispering something to the chieftain of Ban Soran.

"What's going on?" Kalmar asked with a yawn.

"Didn't you hear what that guy said?"

"I wasn't listening."

Carnack had planted himself in the snow before the platform with his fists on his hips and his nose in the air. Rudric stood and addressed him. "Carnack of Ban Soran! I haven't seen you for a while. Your chieftain tells me you've been patrolling the southern foothills of the Killridges. Is that true?"

"It is," he said with a snarl.

"Then you have seen Fangs, have you not? And you have fought them?"

"Aye. And they've killed my kinsmen. Evil they are, through and through, and I'll not bow to one today or ever."

Rudric glanced at Kalmar, who was paying full attention for the first time. "Then what is your challenge, Carnack?" Rudric asked.

"No challenge, Keeper. I'll fight in your war. I just don't want to pledge my clan's blood and bone to a Fang of Dang. If I fight, I fight for the Hollows, not for a monster."

Janner saw the chieftains and chieftesses shifting uncomfortably. The whole point of the ceremony was to unite the clans under the Annieran flag. Carnack was a splinter in that unity—and a splinter could easily grow into a wedge. Carnack's chief, Horgan Flannery, addressed his tribesman.

"Carnack, ye fool! Seven tribes have pledged without incident. Why must you be the sore tooth? Do it in the name of the Shining Isle if not its king. We have a long history with that kingdom, and I mean to preserve it."

"Come, Carnack." Rudric held out a hand. "For the sake of our strength."

"No." Carnack folded his arms and looked away. "I pledge nothing to no Fang."

Leeli put her whistleharp away and leaned over to the boys. "Kal, this would be a good time to do something."

"But what?"

"You could fight him," Janner suggested. "That seems to be how Hollowsfolk work stuff out. See?" He pointed at Rudric, who was barely restraining Horgan Flannery from leaping off the stage and pummeling Carnack.

"Look at that guy!" Kalmar whispered. "He'd destroy me."

"No he wouldn't," Leeli said. "You're stronger and faster than any of these people."

Kalmar sighed and shook his head. "I hate this stuff."

In one swift motion he leapt from the platform and landed just a few feet in front of Carnack. There was a gasp from Rudric, Horgan, and the rest of the chieftains. Carnack sprang into a fighting stance and backed away, sword in hand. For the first time that day, the perfect snow of the Field of Finley was marked with footprints.

But Kalmar drew no sword, for he had none to draw. Nor did he circle the warrior as if he wanted to attack. He merely stood before him in the snow, his black cloak hanging about him like a shadow.

"What's your game, wolf?" Carnack spat.

"I don't have a game." Kalmar spread his hands to show that he held no weapon. "I just want Gnag the Nameless to lose. Don't you?"

"I do," said Carnack after a pause. His sword dropped a few inches.

"Janner, the flag," Leeli whispered, pointing at the Annieran flag behind them.

He understood in an instant what she meant. Janner removed the Annieran flag, then helped Leeli to her feet. The Throne Warden and the Song Maiden stepped down from the platform and joined Kalmar on the snow. Carnack looked at the three children uncertainly. Conscious of the eyes of every warrior present, Janner planted the Annieran flag in the snow and knelt, pulling Kalmar down with him.

"If you won't fight for the Shining Isle," Janner called out so all could hear, "then let it be known that the Shining Isle fights for you." He stared at the snow and waited for some response. All he heard was the flutter of the flag in the cold wind.

"What say you, Carnack?" asked Horgan finally.

"Aye," Carnack answered.

Janner heard the thunk of Carnack's sword returned to its scabbard, then he looked up to see the tribesman stomping back to his tents, head bowed with what might have been humility.

Kalmar raised his eyebrows at Janner and Leeli as they made their way back to the platform in an uncomfortable silence. Rudric affirmed them with a quick nod as they took their seats, and for the rest of the afternoon the ceremony languished on without further incident. By the end of the day the people of the Green Hollows and the remnant of the Shining Isle had officially locked arms in alliance.

At dusk, when the tribe leaders and their regiments marched around the field to a medley of Hollows tunes such as "Hound and Horse and Chicken, Too," and "Rounder's Reel," and the ever-popular "Grouncing as We Nibble as We Go," even bare-chested Carnack led his tribe proudly by and raised a hand in salute to Kalmar, though Kalmar didn't notice because he was busy licking sweetberry stains from his vest.

"A fascinating day!" Oskar declared when the parade was over. "Thank you, Rudric, for allowing me to watch."

"Of course, Oskar. Well done, Wingfeathers. I apologize, Your Highness, about Carnack's defiance."

"'Your Highness' means you, Kal," Janner said, nudging his brother out of his sweetberry hunt.

"Huh? Oh! Don't worry about it. I can hardly blame him. I hate the way I look, too. When can we eat?"

Rudric smiled. "Your work here is done, children. It was good to see you." A look of sadness came into his eyes, then he turned away to speak to the chieftains.

The ride home was quiet, except for Leeli's snickering at the volume of Kalmar's growling stomach. Oskar grew oddly anxious the nearer they drew to Chimney Hill, and when they crossed the bridge and rounded the ascent to the house Janner knew something was amiss. No lights burned in the windows. No lantern flickered on the porch. If not for the smoke rising from the chimney the place would have looked deserted.

"Where is everybody?" Janner asked.

"I don't know!" Oskar said, too quickly. "I mean, I'm sure there's a good reason the house is dark. I mean, I don't know! Ah! Here we are."

Janner turned to his siblings, but they were studiously looking away. When he turned back to Oskar he saw that the old man had already heaved himself from the sled and slipped inside the dark house.

"Why in Aerwiar is he acting like that?" Janner asked. But Kalmar and Leeli shrugged as if nothing were amiss and climbed down, leaving Janner alone in the sled. "Hello? What's going on?"

Janner muttered to himself as he entered the house after his siblings, annoyed at their mysterious behavior. He smelled dinner, but why were the lanterns shuttered? By the red glow of the fire in the hearth he saw Podo reclining in his favorite chair, but the rest of the room was dark. Oskar and the others were nowhere to be seen, and if they hadn't been acting so weirdly, Janner would have suspected that there was some true danger at hand. But if not danger, then what?

"Hello?" he said to the dark room. "What's going on?"

Then Janner heard a snicker behind him, and a gruff voice said, "Get him."

Before Janner could utter another word, he was tackled from behind.

3

The Thirteenth Muffin

As Janner was pulled to the floor and jabbed from every angle he finally put a name with the voice he heard: Guildmaster Clout. But why in the world would Clout be here? And why would he ambush Janner in his own home? And why, above all things, would he and several other voices be laughing while they poked Janner in the ribs and legs and gut?

"Happy birthday, laddie," roared Podo, and at once the main room of Chimney Hill was flooded with lamplight. The cluster of bodies that had tackled Janner dispersed and left him dazed and blinking on the floor. Janner saw not only Clout, but eight of his fellow Durgan Guildlings dressed in black, and grinning. Kalmar howled with laughter and Leeli beamed. Nia emerged from the kitchen with a platter piled high with honeymuffins, then placed it on the table, which was heavy with steaming food.

"It's my birthday?" Janner asked, which only made everyone laugh harder.

"I had a feeling you'd forgotten," Nia said. "Things have been too busy lately to keep track of the days, let alone the dates. So yes. It's your birthday. Your *thirteenth* birthday."

At last, a smile spread over Janner's face. He brushed himself off and greeted his fellow guildlings with playful punches. "Larnik! Brosa! How long have you been here?"

"Long enough to want to eat a henfoot," Brosa said.

"Let's eat," said Kelvey O'Sally. "My dogs are aching for the scraps."

Janner hugged Podo and his mother, remembering Nia's comment about how tall he'd grown. How had he forgotten his birthday? He had asked her about it weeks earlier, but with his Durgan training, his T.H.A.G.S., his winter chores, and his anxiety about the coming war, the last thing on his mind was his birthday.

The meal was a combination of his favorites: spice roasted shadhaunch, butterfire biscuits, hogpig gravy, pumpkin soup, soakbeans, and herder's meatpie. But even better than the food was the joy he felt in the presence of his family and friends: Guildmaster Clout, Larnik and Brosa, Morsha MacFigg, Churleston James, Joe Bill, and Quincy Candlesmith, along with two of the O'Sally brothers: Kelvey and young Thorn (who sat quietly beside Leeli). Janner had been in class and played countless games with these friends, but they had never before gathered at Chimney Hill for a meal. The fact that they had done so in his honor filled him with gladness. They ate and ate, Podo regaling Janner's friends with the most embarrassing stories he could think of.

"Like the time ye got yer head stuck in the yard gate!"

"That never happened," Janner said.

"Did it not?" Podo said, taking a greasy bite of shadhaunch.

"It was a wagon wheel," Janner mumbled, feeling amidst the laughter that he had never eaten so much in his life.

"Can we get started with the honeymuffins now?" Podo asked, rubbing his hands together with glee. "It's me favorite part."

Nia smiled and passed the platter of muffins to Janner with a roll of her eyes. "We might as well get it over with."

"Mama, these look good, but I'm stuffed," Janner said with a sigh as he passed the tray to Brosa, who pushed it back toward him with a devious smile. "Aren't you having one?" Janner asked.

"Nope."

"Those are fer you, lad," Podo cackled. "Every last one of 'em."

Janner looked around the table and was met with nothing but grins, even from Nia.

"It's a Durgan Guild thing, son. Sorry."

Janner counted the honeymuffins with mounting dread. There were thirteen. He had just stuffed himself with dinner, and now he was supposed to eat a platter full of sticky sweet muffins? "Do I have to?"

"Welcome to Ban Rona, guildling," Clout said, leaning back and tossing his napkin onto his plate. "This is my favorite part, too."

By the time he had finished the fifth muffin, Janner was ready to lose his meal and Podo was ready to lose his composure, snorting gleefully every time Janner wiped the sweat from his forehead. The rest of the party had commenced to pleasant chatter among themselves, but always with an eye on Janner's progress. He was enjoying his birthday less with every bite. When he swallowed a dangerous burp he pushed away from the table thinking that the joke had played itself out. But Nia of all people stopped him. "Where do you think you're going?"

"But there are eight more. Eight!"

"Then you'd better get busy," Morsha MacFigg said with a snicker.

"Oy. We all had to do it when we turned," Quincy Candlesmith said.

Janner paced the room for a few nauseous minutes then sat back down and forced four more muffins down. Podo watched with gleaming eyes, hardly able to contain himself. "Ah, this is the life, lass. Watchin' yer grandson grow up before yer very eyes."

Unable to believe he was doing it, Janner at last lifted the thirteenth honeymuffin to his lips. Hot bile rose in his throat and he decided he would never eat again. No one at the table spoke, and he had their full attention as he bit into the gooey dessert. He figured it was only because he felt so ill, but the final muffin, the one at the bottom of the pile, seemed to taste different. After he swallowed the first bite everyone at the table stood and began clearing their dishes.

"Wait, that's it?" Janner said, barely noticing the way he slurred his words. The room was spinning, and he began to suspect it wasn't just that he had eaten too much. "What was in that last muffin?" he mumbled.

"That's your birthday present," said Clout. He took the muffin from Janner and helped him to his feet. "Nia, do you have his pack?"

Janner tottered but felt Clout's strong hand on his elbow.

"Good luck, Janner," said Brosa.

Kalmar whacked him on the shoulder. "See you in a few days, old man."

"Be careful," said Leeli with a kiss on his cheek.

"What's going on?" Janner asked, though it sounded more like, "Whazzzzgoingnnnn?" His knees buckled and Clout eased him to the floor.

Clout sat on his haunches and looked Janner in the eye. "You're thirteen, lad, and one of the finest Durgans I've seen in a long time. You'll be fine. Help me out, guildlings." Janner felt himself lifted by several hands. Someone pulled his arms through the sleeves of his winter coat while someone else placed a heavy pack over his shoulders. He was afraid, but whatever they had put in that last muffin made the fear seem distant. Nia hugged him, Podo clapped him on the back, and the next thing he knew he was outside in the freezing air being lifted onto a horse in front of Guildmaster Clout.

Out of the night rode a figure that Janner dimly recognized as Rudric. He was surely uncomfortable being so close to Chimney Hill, and Janner felt an impulse to try and make him feel welcome, but his lips wouldn't move. Rudric handed Clout something—a sword?

"Make sure he gets this, Clout. It was mine when I was a lad, and I want him to have it if that's all right."

"Oy, Keeper," Clout said with a nod. "A fine gift."

Then Rudric nodded at Janner and rode away. Janner wanted to say thank you, or at least wave, but his arms were as useless as his mouth.

"There's nothing to it," Clout said as he repositioned Janner and clicked the horse into a trot. The last thing Janner heard as he drifted into unconsciousness was his guildmaster's voice: "You just have to find your way home. We'll be waiting."

When Janner woke, it was early morning. He was lying under a blanket in a snowy wood beside the embers of a dying fire, and he had no idea where he was.

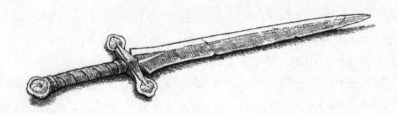

4

Blindplopped

The white sky, visible beyond the gray skeletal trees, was brightening in the east, but the sun hadn't yet broken the horizon. Frost covered Janner's blanket, and the wind had blown a little drift of snow against his pack. He sat up and shook his head, trying to remember how he had come to be there. As the previous night came back to him he realized how terribly cold he was. A violent shiver began in his stomach and coursed outward to the tips of his fingers and toes. Thankfully there were enough stray branches that Janner was able to resurrect the fire. He pulled off his gloves and warmed his hands, but he knew that unless he found more wood the little fire would weaken again.

He studied his surroundings, still trying to piece together the strange ending to his birthday party. The fire crackled at the center of a clearing no bigger than a tent. The trees were tall and thin, crowded with bramble and brush, making it impossible to see whether he was in one of the little stands of applewood that dappled the prairie hills or a deep forest farther south and west. He was glad to be in the trees, because he could hear the frigid wind and see it raking the treetops. But the more he woke, the more annoyed he felt that his friends and family had left him alone in the wilderness. Someone had said it was a Durgan tradition—well, what a ridiculous tradition! Not only did Clout—he remembered now that it was Guildmaster Clout who brought him here on horseback—abandon him, he had somehow covered his tracks to make it even more difficult for Janner to find his way home. The snow between the trees appeared untouched by anything other than thwaps and a few birds. Clout, a master of sneakery, would have had no problem disguising his tracks, had he left any in the first place.

Janner spent several minutes collecting firewood and soon had a healthy blaze to warm his bones. When his body stopped trembling he set his attention to his supplies. He found beside his pallet and pack an unstrung bow and a quiver of exactly thirteen arrows. "Ha ha," he grumbled. The bow was lashed to a sword and a dagger, comforting weapons for a boy alone in the woods.

The sword. Rudric! Janner unwrapped it and drew it from the scabbard. He admired the stout blade, nicked but sharp and gleaming in the early light. The leather of the hilt was dark and smooth with years of use, and it fit his hand perfectly. "Thank you, Rudric," he said as he sheathed it.

His backpack, the same one his mother had made for him in Skree before they had escaped Uncle Artham's treehouse, was bursting at the seams. He felt a familiar satisfaction at the way the worn leather had lost its stiffness. He and this pack had survived gargan rockroaches, the Stranders of the East Bend, and even a voyage across the Dark Sea of Darkness—and they both had scars to prove it. He unbuckled the flap and several little bundles of rations wrapped with paper and twine tumbled out, along with an envelope bearing his name. Janner tore open the envelope and unfolded a letter.

Janner,

Your mother tells me that you escaped a factory full of slaves, traveled alone across Fang territory, and found your family in a city built under the ice. You should have no problem with this little test of your Durgan abilities. Every guildling undergoes a similar trial of skill and strength, though it must be said: not every guildling's birthday is in the dead of winter, and some aren't ready for blindplopping until their fourteenth or fifteenth year. But you're more than ready. Too bad for you. You've been taught sneakery, hunting, tracking, orienteering, and combat. There's no reason you shouldn't be able to figure out where you are, find food, and make your way home—unless of course you encounter a toothy cow, of which there are few in the Hollows. Also, keep an eye out for grobblins, especially in the winter. But you'll be fine. Just be wary of skonks, because of course they attract the spike-eared vargax, which is only vulnerable in the middle paw—the MIDDLE paw, mind you.

I have full confidence that you'll make it home without incident. Unless you see the ridgerunners. I forgot about them. They're getting braver these days, coming into the Hollows in little bands—likely scouting for the Fangs. But don't worry about them. They probably won't kidnap you.

Now, you should probably know that when a guildling is blindplopped, as you have been, there is no guardian. No one is watching over you, ready to rescue you as soon as things get difficult. I'm not training flabbits here— I'm training Durgans. Defenders of the Hollows. That means you're on your own. Of course, if you don't show up at Ban Rona for a week or so, we'll send out a search party to bring you home, though there probably won't be much of you left. Your mother grew up here; she knows how it works, and she's given me her full permission. I expected to have to talk her into the blindplop, but she agreed without hesitation. That should make you feel some pride, boy.

One last thing you should know. By the time you read this, you'll be feeling hungry. That's because you've been sleeping for two days. It may seem like your birthday party was last night, but it wasn't. You're farther from home than you know. A two-day ride could put you pretty much anywhere in the Green Hollows. Have fun!

Guildmaster Clout

P.S. I forgot about the cloven. Don't let them eat you.

P.P.S. Also, I noticed a thork nest in the stand of trees near where I left you. They're usually docile, except at sunrise. And don't build the fire too high! That just makes them angry.

Janner slipped the letter back into his pack and held very still. He heard a snap, but couldn't be sure whether it was the fire or a thork in the trees. Clout had taught him that ears work best when eyes are shut, so he closed them and held his breath, listening so hard that he could hear his own heart. Then he had the awful realization that there was something breathing in the trees. And it was behind him.

5

Thork Whacking

Janner gulped. *Thorks.*

What was a thork, anyway?

He sifted through the pages of memory, trying to picture the creature. He knew he had read about thorks in Pembrick's *Creaturepedia*, but he couldn't recall anything specific. *You're about to find out exactly what a thork is, right down to its eating habits,* he thought. *Just as soon as you turn around.*

The creature behind him must have sensed the inner tension in Janner, because in the moments before he sprang, the breathing stopped and he heard some movement. With a prayer to the Maker, Janner spun around with a shout. Before him in the snow stood a hairy creature with a long tongue dangling out of the side of its toothy mouth, watching Janner calmly. Janner froze, the point of his sword only inches from the creature's snout.

The thork looked strangely like a dog. One of Leeli's dogs, in fact—a big, brown and white hillherder with droopy eyes.

"Baxter?" Janner said, lowering the sword and breathing a sigh of relief.

The dog barked and wagged its tail. Attached to Baxter's collar was a small tube with a cap at one end. Janner scratched behind the dog's ears as he removed the tube and slid a parchment from it.

Dear Janner,

Happy birthday! I asked Baxter to keep you company. I'd hate for you to be all alone in the cold hills without anyone to talk to. He's not supposed to help you find your way home, but if anything really bad happens you can send him back for help. All you have to say is "Get Leeli," and he'll come straight to Chimney Hill and lead us to you. Hopefully you're not reading this out loud, or he'll already be gone.

Love,

Leeli

"Thanks, Leeli," Janner said. At the sound of her name, Baxter cocked his head and looked at Janner expectantly. "Thanks! I said, 'thanks.'" The dog relaxed and licked his hand.

Janner checked for thorks again, then sheathed Rudric's sword and fastened the scabbard and dagger to his belt. Beneath the parcels of food and dried fruit (and one honeymuffin—the sight of which made him nauseous) were matches, a flask of oil and several strips of torch cloth, fishing line and a few hooks, some salt, a canteen, and his journal. He was glad Nia had thought to include it. It had only been a few minutes since he woke and already he felt less alone and more capable of finding his way back. Not only that, Leeli had given him the (somewhat unfair) advantage of Baxter's tracks in the snow. All he had to do was follow them out of the woods and back to Ban Rona. He felt a little guilty until he remembered that he was still two days' journey away, which was hard enough to do alone.

And then, as Clout had predicted, his stomach growled.

Janner tore the wrapping from one of the parcels and bit into a hunk of dried hogpig meat sandwiched between two pieces of crumbly bread. It was cold, but it was delicious—and at least it wasn't the honeymuffin. He took a swig of water from the canteen and threw another stick on the fire. The sun was still below the horizon, but the sky was lightening rapidly, which gave the air an illusion of warmth.

Then Baxter barked. Janner turned around to look and almost spat out a mouthful of hogpig. Baxter was looking up into the trees at several whitish blobs squirming along the trunks. If the trees were candles, these things looked like cabbage-sized drops of wax running slowly down. Thorks? When Baxter barked again, one of the featureless blobs opened a mouth as wide as its body and hissed. Its teeth, of course, were long and needle-sharp. As far as Janner could tell, the things had no eyes, no feet, no fur—only mouths. Thorks were white, moist blobs with teeth. At least they didn't look fast enough to be dangerous.

Janner drew his sword and waited at the base of one of the trees. When the thork was low enough, he whacked it so hard that bits of bark flew from the tree. He hit the thing square in the center, and the blow nearly split it in two. But the white mass reshaped itself, snapped its teeth, and continued its descent. Janner whacked it again, and this time the mass split in half; some of its goo stuck to his sword when he pulled it away. But the thork squirmed itself back into one blob, clacked its teeth together, and crept on.

As Baxter growled and bounded from tree to tree, Janner saw a thork drip to the snow then ooze its way toward the dog's rear leg. He jumped behind Baxter and struck the blob, slowing it but doing no damage.

A quick look overhead told him that there were hundreds of the blobs descending from the trees surrounding the fire. If he didn't get out soon he'd be trapped. Janner shoved the food back into his pack, rolled up his blanket and pallet, and grabbed the bow and quiver.

"Come on, Baxter!"

The dog leapt over three of the thorks already squidging through the snow.

Janner didn't think to follow the dog's tracks, nor did he have time to be sure he had collected all his belongings, but he had to go. He squirmed around one tree where a blob crept by at chest level and backed into another where a thork snapped at his pack. He weaved through the trees, jumping over some thorks and ducking under others, looking back now and again to be sure Baxter was faring well. After a few minutes of hard running, Janner and Baxter burst from the line of the forest and tumbled into the snow.

When he had caught his breath, Janner stood and brushed himself off, making sure they had left the thorks behind. The sun had crested the horizon and it gilded the wintry hilltops stretching away for miles. It was beautiful country, and the vastness reminded Janner not only that he was far from home—but that he was lost. Whichever way Baxter had come into the woods to find him, it wasn't here. And there was no way Janner was going back into those woods to find the trail. Part of him was glad, because it meant the test was fair again, and with a prayer of thanksgiving for Leeli he sat next to Baxter, relishing the sun's warmth as he finished the breakfast the thorks had interrupted. He was surprised to realize that, alone in the bright snowy morning, he was happy.

This was different than his trek through the Stony Mountains with the Fangs lurking around every corner, not to mention the burden of shame he had felt for losing his brother in Dugtown. He was a year older now, he had trained for months with the Durgan guild, and he doubted he was in any real danger from Gnag the Nameless here. Otherwise Guildmaster Clout wouldn't have blindplopped him, not with a war brewing; Nia wouldn't have allowed it.

He had nothing to worry about. He was well provisioned and well equipped. He was healthy and warmly dressed—even warmer with Baxter leaning against him. Janner looked out at the vast landscape, quiet but for the twitter of a few birds in the branches and the whisper of the prairie wind, and was delighted by the solitude. The knowledge that many miles away he was watched for by his friends and family gave him a lonely sort of peace.

The sun warmed the left side of Janner's face. That meant he was looking southeast. He closed his eyes and imagined the map of the Green Hollows hanging on the wall at the Great Library; he had seen it a hundred times, and it came to him easily. The line of forest (if he was where he *thought* he was) lay at the eastern edge of the Hollows, in the Outer Vales. The woods stretched away on either side, but on the left it hooked inwards again and followed a ridge into the distance.

"That's southeast," Janner said aloud. He squinted his eyes and thought he detected in the haze of horizon the hint of snowy peaks. He was pretty sure those were the Killridge Mountains. If that was true, then the forest at his back was the western sweep of the Blackwood.

The Blackwood? Surely Clout wouldn't have left him there—unless he was far enough north that there was little danger of encountering a cloven. Or maybe there was plenty of danger, and that was part of the point of the blindplop. Either way, Janner was pleased that he had at least oriented himself. He knew more or less where he was.

So what now?

If he bore southward he would eventually run into a road that led to Ban Rugan, where he could get better directions and some warmth. That shouldn't take more than a day, should it?

"I'm not getting any closer by sitting here," he said, patting Baxter on the shoulder. "Let's go, boy."

Janner heard another snap of a twig in the trees but figured it was a thork, or a thwap, or even a diggle of some sort, so he didn't bother to turn around. It didn't occur to him that it might have been a ridg-erunner.

Janner never made it back to Chimney Hill.

6

The Houndry Corps

On the morning Janner set out from the forest, Leeli harnessed her four fastest dogs to her sled for the short ride to the Guildling Hall where she was to meet the O'Sally boys for an orientation training session. A passel of puppies had just been weaned and they were ready to begin their journey into doghood under the guidance of what Leeli and the O'Sallys had named the Houndry Corps.

The moment war had been declared, the mood in the houndry had changed. Before, Leeli had delighted the O'Sallys with her quick mastery of dogspeak and she had spent most of her time teaching the pups the basic behaviors ("sit," "lie down," "come," and "dance"), but now she and Thorn spent most of their days running drills with the sleds so that the dogs would be quick to understand and obey in the heat of battle. Biggin O'Sally had told her that war hounds were traditionally used to transport weapons, supplies, and information to the front, after which they would transport wounded and dead to the rear for either medical attention or burial.

"'Tis a noble calling on these hounds, lass," Biggin had said, the pup in his arms wagging its little tail. "Many will die, but not without meaning. They die for their friends, and that's the next finest thing to life itself."

The thought didn't calm the trouble in Leeli's heart. Winter was ending.

Every morning for weeks now she had taken her crutch under her arm and made her way through the snow to the kennel at Chimney Hill. Podo had made her a new crutch that had at its foot a sort of snowboot, which kept it from stabbing through to the frozen earth every time she leaned on it. Instead of "Lizardkicker," Podo had merely carved Leeli's name along the shaft, and she had noticed with a pang of sadness that the letters were sloppy and uneven—a big difference between that and the bold, sure hand that had carved her nickname back in Skree.

Today, when she stood on the front stoop and breathed the cold air, looking out on the view of the Green Hollows from Chimney Hill, she didn't bother bidding her grandfather goodbye because he had fallen back to sleep as soon as breakfast was finished. Podo seemed to be aging suddenly, just as winter seemed to be turning to spring all at once. Only a week ago the drifts had been pristine and thick as cotton, and now mud seeped through the ruts where her sled passed. The snow-packed road down from Chimney Hill was darkening, and she knew it would soon be a sloppy mess, impassable by her sled.

Leeli fastened her crutch to the sled and eased herself into the kneeler. She made a series of clicking sounds with her tongue that set the dogs heaving. When she got to the base of the hill and crossed the stone bridge to the main road to Ban Rona, she reined in the dogs and looked to her right. Every day for three days she had watched the snowy lane, praying to the Maker that she would see Janner and Baxter strolling home, but there had been no sign of them. Nia assured her that though it might take a few days, Janner was more than capable of finding his way home, but Leeli detected the worry in her mother's eyes. That was why she had sent Baxter.

Leeli steered the dogs left and let them run. She sped up the road to the first hard turn, then veered the sled away from the road and into an irresistible slope of untouched snow. The dogs yipped as if to thank her for the gift, and the Song Maiden of Anniera laughed in answer.

They sped together, the girl and her dogs, faster than any horse and sled could have gone, and arrived at the houndry only minutes later in a spray of snow.

As Leeli climbed out of the sled, she felt a welling anxiety in her heart and knew its source. It wasn't just that Podo's time was coming—it was because spring meant war. And war meant death, and pain, and terror. She had seen enough in her nine years to know that even if the Hollows-folk were victorious against Gnag the Nameless, victory would come at a terrible price. She had heard Janner's and Kal's friends in the Durgan Guild talk about the coming war with a sort of relish, as if they looked forward to the fighting. Nia had explained that it was only their way of mocking their fear, of establishing their defiance of it. It wasn't that they would prefer war to peace, she had said, but that they knew they must fight, and if they must, then they would rather face it sooner than later.

But Leeli had come to cherish each day at Chimney Hill, each meal with her family, each visit to the houndry, each hiss of sled on snow, each speeding trip through the streets of Ban Rona, each kind face that greeted her. The mud beneath the snowmelt and the scrape of stone on her sled's runners was as sad to her as the deepening wrinkles on her dear Podo's face. How terrible was the truth that it was unstoppable, no matter how earnest her prayers.

When she had unharnessed her dogs and sent them to the houndry (there was a dog-sized entrance at the rear of the building), Leeli pushed through the front door and discovered Thorn O'Sally on his hands and knees trying to coax a puppy from beneath a bench. Several adult dogs were nosing their way between his arms, trying to get the puppy themselves.

"Back, girls!" Thorn said, shooing the dogs away. He changed his voice to a pleading falsetto. "Here, puppy! Come to Thorn, lad. That's it. Ow!" He jerked his hand out and sucked on it. "Leeli, this stubborn pup won't come out fer nothing. Took a whole haunch of hogpig from the table when I wasn't looking, and now it won't come out."

As soon as the other dogs saw Leeli they barked and bounded toward her. She scratched their ears with one hand while she limped across the hay-strewn floor. "Thorn O'Sally, bested by a puppy."

"Oy, I'm afraid so. Look at this!" Thorn showed her three red punctures in his hand.

"Which puppy is it?" Leeli leaned her crutch against the bench and knelt.

"Take a guess," Thorn muttered as he plopped onto the bench with a huff, nursing his pride as much as his hand. "Frankle's been trouble since he was littered, and it's only getting worse. The other dogs are starting to take a dislike of him, too."

Leeli peered into the shadows and saw the three-month-old puppy curled up against the rear wall guarding a hogpig bone with its front paws. She looked into its eyes and saw fear. Fear and strength. The two together could twist into the kind of blackness that would make it a mean dog, suited for little but a collar and a rope. The strength wasn't a bad thing, but the fear coiled around it meant trouble. And she knew the only way to save the dog from itself was to unravel the fear enough to cut it away.

She clicked her tongue and hoped Frankle understood her meaning: "I'm your friend. Eat your meat."

"What are you doing?" Thorn asked. "Where's my hogpig haunch?"

"You can have my lunch if you're still hungry. There are bigger things at stake than your belly, you know."

Thorn looked at Leeli like she was crazy. "Like what?"

Leeli tucked her hair behind her ear and beckoned for Frankle's mother, Yora, to come near. Yora nuzzled Leeli's chin till she laughed. "Which is more important, a good lunch today or a good dog for the next fifteen years?"

"Ask my stomach," Thorn grumbled. Leeli removed a henmeat sandwich from her satchel and offered it to him. He shook his head and stood. "That's all right. I like hogpig better."

Thorn crossed the houndry looking as pitiful as a wet dog. Even when he was pouting, Leeli liked him. From the very beginning he had treated her not like a weak girl with a bad leg, but like a friend. It was the children at school who deferred to her or tried to be too nice who got under her skin. Kindness was fine; it was pity that raised her hackles. Thorn opened the pens where the rest of the puppies were yipping for their training session with Leeli. She tore off a hunk of her sandwich and held it discreetly under the bench until Frankle gingerly took it.

"Let's get started," Leeli said as she grabbed her crutch and stood. She made a series of clicking sounds and the rowdy puppies tumbling about at Thorn's feet immediately formed themselves into a line and sat at attention, tails wagging so fast that they raised a cloud of dust. Leeli glanced behind her and saw with satisfaction that Frankle's muzzle and front paws had emerged from under the bench. She thought she detected a wagging tail, too. Good. The knot was loosening.

Just as Leeli turned back to the puppies, the front door of the houndry flew open. Biggin O'Sally stood in the doorway, panting.

"Princess Leeli," he said. "Come with me. Now."

"What's wrong?"

"I don't know. I was out in the practice field with the pack when Rudric sent Doffer with a message that we should to get to the Great Tree as soon as we could. Said things were real bad."

His face was so grave that Leeli didn't bother to correct his grammar. "What does that mean?" Leeli demanded.

Biggin O'Sally shook his head as he lifted Leeli into his dogsled. "I know what I *think* it means." The dogs sensed his fear and whined, pulling at the harness in their eagerness to run. Biggin looked at Leeli before he spoke, and Leeli saw the word in his eyes before he could give voice to it.

"War."

7

The Call of the Moonraiders

Biggin took the reins and turned to his son, who stood in the doorway with a look of shock on his face. "Thorn! Find Kelvey and suit the battlehounds. When you've finished with that, get the messenger dogs ready and send them to Green Hill Press on Cherry Lane."

But Thorn's feet were frozen. He and the puppies looked equally dismayed.

"Now, boy!"

Thorn jumped and stammered, "Yes sir," then bustled the puppies back into their pen.

The houndmaster shook the reins and whistled. As the dogs barked and lunged forward, Leeli had the terrible feeling that this was the last time she might see Thorn, or the houndry, or the dogs she loved so much. Biggin's fear meant that something unforeseen had happened, and she was afraid to ask what it was.

The Hollish army was supposed to invade Gnag the Nameless's stronghold, not the other way around. She couldn't imagine how the Fangs could make it past the sentries at the Watercraw, or the lookouts stationed on the edges of the Green Hollows, or even past the ships that scoured the Dark Sea of Darkness for sign of a Fang invasion. The grim look on Biggin's face—his moustache was drawn so low it looked like it might fall off—told her not to ask.

The sled hissed through the gates of the Guildling Hall and down the hill to Ban Rona. When they arrived, it seemed that the whole city was crammed into the Great Hall, just as it had been for Kalmar's trial many months ago, except that this time everyone was eerily silent.

When those at the back of the crowd saw Leeli, they parted so she could pass. She unfastened her crutch and Biggin lifted her from the sled—something she would never have allowed her brothers to do. Leeli and Biggin made their way forward until the enormous branches of the Great Tree were visible over the heads of the crowd. When at last she saw the platform at the base of the tree, her eyes strayed to the dark handprint where her mother had sealed Kalmar's freedom.

Kalmar and Nia stood on the dais beside Rudric and several other Durgans fitted in black uniforms. Each of the Durgans had a bow drawn, its arrow trained on a figure standing in their midst. A Grey Fang. It towered over them, taller and more muscular than any Leeli had ever seen. It was arrayed in armor and wore a blue cape; its fur was a shade brighter and longer than most, which added to its striking appearance. Indeed, the beast would have looked regal but for the hideous snarl on its face and the way its eyes burned with contempt for every soul in the hall. An empty scabbard hung from its belt.

The Fang turned toward her and sneered. Its voice was as deep as thunder. "The Song Maiden. I cannot understand why the Nameless One frets over such a foul little thing."

"Careful, Fang," said Rudric evenly. "If you want us to hear what you have to say, you'll have to be alive to say it."

"What's happening?" Leeli said, hurrying to Nia's side.

"This beast," Rudric said so all could hear, "was captured at the Watercraw. It claims to come with a message from Gnag the Nameless, and its lack of arms compels us to listen." The Keeper of the Hollows placed a hand on the handle of his warhammer and faced the Fang. "And *our* possession of arms compels it to speak."

The Fang rolled its eyes. "Even without a blade I could widow most of the wives in this hall. Enough with your blustery talk."

The Durgan bows creaked threateningly, but Rudric raised a hand. "Let the monster talk. I want to know what empty threats he and his master have for us. Go on, Fang."

"I've come to offer you peace." The Fang said the word "peace" with a hint of mockery. "Gnag the Nameless has no interest in the Green Hollows. He only wants the Jewels of Anniera. Give up the three children and avoid this war. That is his offer."

"You can't be serious," Nia said.

"That's what I thought, too," said the Fang with a chuckle. "We Fangs are all so . . . *excited* about this war. We would hate to miss it. Now give me your obvious answer and I'll be on my way."

Leeli wondered if it would be better for her and her brothers to give themselves over. Wouldn't it save the lives of many in the Hollows? Even if they fought the war and defeated Gnag, victory would surely come at a terrible price.

"Never," said Nia.

"Fine, then!" boomed the Fang with a wicked smile. "You think your children are more important than all the children in this city and all the rest of the cities in the land. I expected as much—from an Annieran. As did Gnag. Are you Hollish fools in agreement, then? Are you willing to die with your families just to save the Wingfeather children? Do you even know why Gnag wants them? Perhaps he's merely lonely in the Castle Throg and wishes to be delighted by the company of these three *talented* children. Is that worth the sacrifice of your offspring?"

Leeli glanced at Kalmar. He was looking at the floor, ears twitching, no doubt thinking the same thing she was. Leeli saw in the faces of the Hollowsfolk a great struggle. They hadn't asked for this war. They had been getting on quite peacefully before the Wingfeathers appeared. There was some truth in the Fang's words. Perhaps it was time to give up. If there was some chance that she and her siblings could save the Hollows, shouldn't they do it?

"Never," repeated Nia.

"I should add," said the Fang with a sigh, "that we have you surrounded. We know you've been gathering for war and all that nonsense. We've mustered the troll cities of the southern jungles. We've conscripted the Pirates of Symia and they're waiting in the straits for orders to advance. Oh, and the Wanderers of the Woes have united under Gnag's rule. They needed little persuasion. Not only that, the Woes have made such wiry fighters out of those humans! Gnag hardly needed to Fang them. But he plans to—and with scorpions, no less! They'll be beautiful. I'm sure you'll meet them soon enough—if you refuse this offer, that is."

The Hollowsfolk shifted on their feet. Even Rudric looked unsettled. Fang Scorpions? Leeli shuddered to imagine it. And if she and her brothers merely said, "Yes," and went with this Fang to whatever fate Gnag had for them, it would all be over.

"Why does Gnag want us?" Kalmar said in a voice that seemed very small.

The Fang cocked its head and studied Kalmar without mockery, without its sneer. "That's a good question, young one." Leeli was horrified at the tone of affection in the Fang's voice. It was as if it considered Kalmar an ally. "Why don't you come with me and find out? I can tell you there's such *strength* in Gnag's army.

You know that. *You* of all people. You and I could outrun, outsmart, and out fight this city entire. Save them and save yourself. Come with me, Fang."

"I don't want more strength," Kalmar said. "Strength has only ever gotten me in trouble—at least the kind you're talking about."

"What other kind is there?" the Fang said with another roll of its eyes.

Leeli limped forward on her crutch. She pulled her hair from her face and stood as tall as she could, which wasn't very. "Stop talking to my brother."

The Fang bared its teeth at her.

"Aye," said Rudric. "Go back to Gnag and tell him that if he wants the Jewels, he'll have to come and get them."

"If we don't get him first," Kalmar said, stepping to Leeli's side.

The Fang looked around the crowded hall before bursting into laughter. It was an awful sound. The Hollowsfolk cowered before it. Leeli's cheeks flushed with annoyance at the people of Ban Rona, a people supposedly renowned for their strength all but quaking in their britches before a single Fang. She knew it was more than just the Fang they feared—it was the loss of their families' lives, the destruction of their homes. But their lack of resolve made Leeli angry.

She pulled her whistleharp from her coat and played "The Call of the Moonraiders," an old Hollish fighting song the O'Sally brothers had taught her. Its melody was fierce and stirring from the first notes, and in seconds the Hollowsfolk found their strength. They pumped their fists in the air and shook the boughs of the great tree with their voices.

> *Ride like the moon in the starfield*
> *Silver and fine, silver and fair*
>
> *Deep in the heart of the darkness*
> *To shatter the night, to scatter and scare*
>
> *The moon, round as a warshield*
> *Sail the heavens and scale the sky*

Now we dagger the darkness,
Ruin and doom, Moonraiders fly!

The Fang's ears flattened and it snarled, first at the assembly and then at Leeli, who stared unflinchingly at the beast as she played. The Fang covered its ears and writhed as if the melody were a poison in its brain. Finally it could bear the song no more and it flung itself at Leeli.

The Durgans loosed their arrows. Leeli screamed. The furry hulk raced toward her as arrows thunked into its hide. Leeli curled into a ball, waiting for an impact that never came.

She opened her eyes amidst the cries of alarm and saw Kalmar standing between her and the Fang, sword drawn. The Fang was dead, headless and prone. Seconds later it crackled into dust and clumps of fur that lifted gently into the air, along with cheers from the Hollowsfolk.

Leeli wiped her eyes, which were leaking against her will, and hugged her brother. Her heart was troubled, and she could see the same in Kalmar's eyes. "People are going to get hurt. Because of us."

"People are going to *die* because of us," he said.

Leeli didn't have time to sort out what she was feeling because Nia wrapped them in a hug. "That was perfect," she said. "The Hollowsfolk needed to see that. They won't give you up for anything now."

That was what Leeli was most afraid of.

Rudric kicked the empty Fang armor. "Well," he said. "I guess Gnag has his answer. War it is."

Someone outside screamed. Leeli heard the pounding of feet on the roof of the hall. Through the tall windows she saw shapes in the sky, like a flock of wheeling buzzards. Then with a piercing shriek a creature burst through the leafless branches of the great tree and alighted on a limb.

And so on the seventeenth day of Threemoon, the first winged Fangs descended upon the Hollows and the second battle of Ban Rona began.

8

Territory Dispute

Janner walked over hill and valley, trudging through snow that came up to his shins. The effort warmed him so much that he removed his jacket and rolled up the sleeves of his shirt, happy to feel the bright sun on his skin even as his breath fogged the air. Baxter tailed him part of the time but spent most of the journey exploring. Janner spotted him every now and then as a dark speck on some distant hilltop, nosing through the snow after a hidden rodent or trotting into a valley to investigate a scent or sound. But at regular intervals Baxter would appear at Janner's side again, either for his assurance of Janner's presence or for Janner's assurance of his.

When the sun rode high, Janner's hunger demanded his attention so he began looking for a place to stop and eat. He came upon a stand of brush, crawled between the branches, and discovered a frozen creek at the bottom of a cleft in the earth. The snow around the bushes was marked with a multitude of tiny, graceful footprints, probably from flabbits and starbirds seeking water and whatever winter worms could be found in the shadows. Janner slipped down to the ice and broke the surface with his boot heel. He straddled the creek and dipped his canteen into the water and waited as it gurgled full, trying to keep his hands dry. Baxter peered down at him and yipped.

"Don't worry, I'll get you some. Then we'll eat," Janner said.

Then, to his great annoyance, his foot slipped from the icy rock and splashed into the water. He shook his boot and sighed, dreading how cold his foot would be once the water seeped through. When he looked up again, Baxter was gone.

"Baxter?" Janner capped the canteen and slung it over his shoulder, then scrambled out.

The lonesome stand of brush in the lonesome field of snow was no longer lonesome. Baxter was struggling in a net surrounded by ridgerunners—more than twenty of them, by Janner's estimation. They looked like a regiment of children bundled in white furs and leather, out for a day in the snow—except for the slings, spears, and daggers they wielded, and the wicked smile on every face.

"You're in our territory, boy."

"What?" Janner suddenly felt cold again. "I'm sorry, sirs, but I don't think so. I was at the edge of the western woods and have been walking southeast for several hours. Ban Rugan is just a few hours away."

Of all the ridgerunners, he found himself talking to one in particular, though it wasn't the one who had spoken. Instinct told him he was their leader. He was a few inches taller than the others, and he had a narrow face, even for a ridgerunner. He seemed to be trying to stare through Janner's skull and into his brain. The others were merely scowling, but this one studied him with an intensity that gave Janner the shivers.

"Your territory begins at the Killridge Mountains." Janner pointed east at the ridges that rose from the white horizon. "And those mountains are a *long* way from here."

"A long way, indeed," said the ridgerunner. "Such has our territory been expanded by Gnag the Nameless. All of the Hollows, in fact, are under our dominion now."

"Fruit!" one of the smaller ridgerunners cried, with a shake of his spear. The others nodded sagely.

"The Green Hollows isn't yours just because Gnag says it is." Janner knew he should have felt afraid, but he didn't. "And that dog isn't yours, either. Let him go."

The main ridgerunner folded his arms, shrugged, and said, "Let the dog go."

Janner was as stunned as the ridgerunners. "Really?" he asked.

"Yes. We're here for fruit, not prisoners. We'd have to turn around and drag you back to the camp, and that's four days from here. I don't see any harm in letting a little boy and his dog go free." Baxter squirmed out of the net and ran to Janner's side as the ridgerunner stepped forward and extended his hand. "My name is Nizzik. Have you any fruit?"

Janner shook his hand warily. "Mine's—Janner." He searched Nizzik's eyes for any hint of recognition and saw none. "Uh, yeah. I have a little." Janner dug through his pack and gave over a handful of dried xynocks and the last few slices of apple. He also insisted that they take the honeymuffin.

"Honey isn't fruit," he said, sniffing it. "But it's close. I thank you."

"You know, the Hollowsfolk aren't just going to let you have their winter stores."

"Why not?" asked one of the ridgerunners. "Gnag said we could have it all."

Janner had a hard time keeping a straight face. "But Gnag doesn't have any say in what happens in the Hollows. The war hasn't even been fought yet."

The ridgerunners muttered to one another and shook their heads.

"What?" Janner asked.

"That's not what we were told." Nizzik looked perplexed. "The Grey Fangs at the borderlands informed us that the new army would invade Ban Rona today. They promised a quick victory. The war should be over by now. That's why we came."

Janner felt a knot tightening in his stomach. "What do you mean 'new army'?"

The ridgerunner smiled. "You'll see."

He had to get home. He had to get home *now*.

"Come on, Baxter," Janner said. He jammed the food back into his pack, slung it over his shoulder, and ran, heedless of the amused look on the ridgerunners' faces.

An hour later, he happened upon the troll.

9

A Fang in the Dungeon

What is it?" someone cried.

Kalmar hardly had time to study the winged creature because Rudric had already put an arrow through its chest. It fell to the ground, exploding in a cloud of dust. But seconds later another of the monsters crawled through an opening high above and along a thick tree limb.

"A bat," Kalmar said to himself. "It looks like a bat."

The creature looked exactly like a bat, in fact, except for the long arms and legs, not to mention the armor and sword. Its wings were retracted along its back as it crawled nimbly on the underside of the limb. It was covered in a light brown fuzz that was thin enough to reveal the veiny muscles of its forearms and calves where there was no armor. But the creature's face was the most hideous. Its nose was turned permanently upwards as if, as Kal had been warned many times by his mother, someone had slapped it on the back while it was pretending to be a pig. The bat creature's eyes were milky white and a few sizes too big, like its pointed ears. Its wrinkly face seemed to be stretched in an eternal, evil grin. It was no surprise that its teeth were many and sharp.

As Kalmar watched, the claws of its hands and feet retracted, and it swung down with a screech, spreading its leathery brown wings wide to glide to the floor. Several arrows thudded into it as it flew, and it burst into another brown cloud of dust as it hit the base of the tree.

"Gravy!" Oskar cried. "They're everywhere!"

Three more Bat Fangs appeared and flapped about near the ceiling, dodging arrows and screeching. One of them spotted Leeli and dove for her. Kalmar dashed to his sister and yanked her out of the way just as the creature sped past.

"Get her out of here!" Nia grabbed Kal's shoulders and thrust her face into his. "Kalmar, take her. No one here is as fast as you. Go."

Kal nodded, lifted Leeli into his arms, and raced through the shouting throng for the doors that led to the dungeon. Outside he could see the Hollowsfolk beset by hundreds, perhaps thousands, of the Bat Fangs; the Great Hall afforded no shelter because there were now several of the beasts circling overhead and more slinking through the upper doorways and windows. The Great Tree was infested. The only safety he could imagine was down in the dungeon, where they might find a place to hide.

When he got through the iron door he swung it shut and eased Leeli to the ground. He could see her blinking and remembered that her eyes took some time to adjust to the sudden darkness, even with the lanterns flickering on the walls.

He heard someone—or some*thing*—rattling the handle and leapt back just as the door opened a crack. The racket of battle poured into the hallway again and a bat-like face pressed itself through the opening, hissing. Kalmar punched it and tried to push the door shut again, but a fuzzy brown arm reached through, clawing at the air. Its long yellow fingernails scraped at the iron. Kal rammed the door with his shoulder again and again, so hard that he half feared and half hoped the thing's arm would fall right off. With a final heave, he slammed the door and shuddered at the sight of three bloody fingers protruding for a moment before turning to dust. Leeli slid the latch and locked the door, squinting her eyes shut at the terrible scraping and beating on the other side.

"Mama's out there," she said.

"So is Oskar. And Rudric. But Mama told me to get you out of there. This is the best I could come up with."

Leeli grabbed Kalmar's arm. "Where's Grandpa?"

"Probably still asleep at Chimney Hill."

"We have to find a way out." Leeli started down the hallway, and Kal trotted beside her. "I need to get to the houndry."

"Leeli, those *things* are outside. They have the place surrounded. Besides, this is a dungeon—there not being a way out is kind of the point. Thorn will be all right."

"It's not Thorn I'm worried about," she said. "It's Janner. He's trying to get back here, remember? I need to send a dog to warn him."

"He's probably safer than we are right now. Even if he's close he'll be able to see what's going on from a distance. He'll be all right. He's a Durgan now." Something crashed into the door and made them jump. "Come on," Kalmar said, taking one of the lanterns from the wall. "We need to find a place to hide."

Then Kal stopped in his tracks. He felt an odd shiver in his belly and the fur on his back rose. He smelled something. Something rotten and sweating, and it smelled familiar. It smelled like—

"Kal, what's wrong?"

"Huh?" he asked over his shoulder.

"You were growling."

"Sorry. Just—just scared, that's all."

But it was more than that. He hadn't been in the keep of the Great Hall since his first night in Ban Rona, months ago, when the Hollowsfolk had beaten him and locked him away because of his Fangness. Seeing the damp, stone walls with fuzzy tree roots snaking through them recalled that terrible night and the hopelessness he had felt—and a certain creature in the cell next to his own. *Nuzzard*, he thought. That was its name. The Fang from the dungeon. It was still alive, still breathing and sniveling in the dark. Worst of all, it smelled like *him*. Like Kal.

He felt a familiar wave of dizziness, and shook his head to clear it. He had felt that same sensation, that of falling into a sudden sleep, when he had stolen the hens and hogpiglets for Esben months ago. Kalmar hadn't told anyone, but some nights he still woke up out in the snowy hills without remembering how he got there. It was getting harder and harder to keep that dizzy fog from taking over.

Something banged on the door again, but this time he heard voices, too.

"Open the door!" It was Rudric.

"Stay here," Kal said, backing Leeli against the wall a little way down the corridor. He sprinted back to the door, drew his sword, and yanked back the lock.

Oskar, Guildmaster Clout, Nia, and a host of others poured through. Rudric stood outside, batting at the air with his hammer. Several Hollish warriors flanked the onrush of bodies, battling the Bat Fangs overhead to keep them at bay as the corridor filled.

Kalmar leapt through with his sword drawn, but when he looked up he froze. The Great Tree crawled with hundreds of the beasts—Bat Fangs and Grey Fangs, too. They shook the great limbs and squealed like rats. More of them wheeled about, circling the trunk of the tree as if reveling in their victory. One of them grabbed Kal by the arm, snapping him out of his shock. He beat it back with his sword, then fought alongside the Hollowsfolk until the last of them were through the door.

"Is that everyone?" Rudric bellowed.

"Everyone in the Keep, at least!" shouted Nibbick Bunge. "Shut the door! More are coming!"

Just before the door slammed, Kalmar watched with horror as one of the last of the warriors was jerked off his feet and lifted, screaming, out of sight.

Rudric jammed the lock into place and pressed against the door, panting, while the Fangs pounded and scratched. "Help me!" he ordered, and several other men, women, and even a few children pressed against the door.

"Kal! Where's Leeli!" Nia spun him around and looked at him frantically.

"She's all right. She's fine." Kal took Nia by the arm and pulled her down the corridor to where Leeli waited among the others.

Nia squeezed them both tight. "Janner's out there," she said. Kal had never seen her so upset. She was usually calm in the face of great danger, but she wasn't merely afraid, she was angry—at herself. "I can't believe I let them blindplop him. I should never have let him out of my sight. This is my fault."

"Mama," Leeli said, "this is Gnag's fault. Not yours. Like Kal said, Janner might be safer than we are." Nia put her face in her hands and shook her head. "We're the ones who are stuck in a dungeon, surrounded by monsters."

"Maybe you should have blindplopped us too," Kal said.

"Next time, please just blindplop us all," Leeli said with a smile, and Nia laughed a little through her tears.

Rudric pushed his way through the crowd. He was sweaty and covered in flecks of blood that wasn't his own. "Are you three all right?"

"Yes, thank you," Nia answered without looking at him. Rudric nodded awkwardly and moved away to check on the rest of his people. Kal and Leeli watched him go, then looked at one another sadly.

"In the words of Erwail in Quarvue Cloodge's excellent animal tale *Squirrel Gets Away*, 'Are we trapped in here?'" Oskar jiggled his way toward them with the First Book under one arm, as always. He had three claw marks on one of his cheeks.

"I think so," Kalmar said. "I can smell Fangs outside. Too many to count." He smelled people in the Great Hall, too. Lots of them. People who hadn't made it, who had died because of him and Leeli. He hated the thought of it.

After a few minutes one of Rudric's men gave orders that everyone was to spread out, and then he informed Nia that they had an open cell reserved for the Wingfeathers to rest in. They followed him down the long, dark hallways, past cells where the wounded were being tended to and where folk were arguing over what to do next. The soldier waved them into a cell, bowed, and stood guard outside. Kalmar and Leeli sank to the floor beside Nia while Oskar paced, all of them listening to the soldiers making plans and blocking doors and windows while the bats screeched on and the wolves howled.

Leeli rested her head on Kalmar's shoulder and held her whistle-harp to her lips without playing. He knew she was thinking about Janner. In a way he couldn't explain, Kalmar believed his brother was safe.

It was another thought that troubled him, a thought reawakened by the scent of Nuzzard, the crazed Fang. It was a thought that had troubled him ever since he had first been held in this very dungeon: what if he became like the Fang that drooled in the darkness just a few cells away? What if he hurt someone he loved? As hard as he tried he couldn't ignore the thing's scent, the constant reminder that it lurked somewhere deep in the dungeon, and it filled him with great fear. Worse than that, he knew that there was a mad Fang locked away inside of him, too, a monster sniffing at every crack, always looking for a way out.

As if in answer, from somewhere in the darkness the maddened Fang loosed a mournful and soul-chilling howl.

10

The King's Decision

We need every arrow in Ban Rona," said Rudric. "Unless we can grow wings like Artham Wingfeather, the only way to fight those flying rats is to shoot them down."

Kalmar, Leeli, and Nia sat on the cold stone floor of the biggest cell, watching the Keeper of the Hollows command his men. He sat on his haunches in a circle of warriors. Guildmaster Clout, Danniby, and Nibbick Bunge were among them, stroking their beards and grunting assent.

"Sooner or later we'll come to the end of them—Gnag the Nameless can't have an endless supply of Bat Fangs," Rudric said.

"But neither do we have an endless supply of arrows," Bunge said with anxiety in his voice. His wife and son, Grigory, had been in the Keep, but they weren't in the dungeon. He hung his head. "There are so many of them."

"Keep strong, Nibbick," Rudric said with a hand on Bunge's shoulder. "Remember, when the Fangs turn to dust, our arrows are no worse for the wear. We'll need the best archers in the city aimed at the sky, and the quickest runners in the city collecting arrows from the ground."

Kalmar tried to listen, but his brain was filled with the sharp, unsettling odor of the Fang in the dungeon. Rudric had invited the soldiers into the Wingfeathers' cell to discuss strategy in case Kalmar had any ideas, and Kalmar was doing his best to pay attention—not because he had any opinion about strategy but because he wanted to show them that he cared, that he was trying. *Pay attention. Listen. That's what Janner would do.*

"What about the tribes at the Field of Finley?" Danniby asked. "There's no cover out there. They'll need our help."

"Oy, they might be dead already," said Nibbick Bunge. "What if there are more than just Bat Fangs out there? Could be snakes and wolves marching in from all sides."

Rudric shook his head. "It's too cold for the lizards. Besides, our scouts are vigilant. Our ships have been scouring the sea. The reason we were caught by surprise is because there was no attack elsewhere, no Fangs reported. We just forgot to look up. We didn't know they could fly."

"Then where did the Grey Fang come from?" asked Bunge.

Danniby glanced at the barred window. "Likely the wolf was flown here by one of those bats. Maybe a few of them could carry one that big."

"I only saw a few other wolves," Rudric said. "Let's hope that we mainly have the bats to battle. Hopefully the army at Finley is safe," said Rudric. "It's possible the Fangs have no idea they're out there."

"Oy! If that's true our army won't know about the Fangs, either," said Danniby. "I bet they're out there dancing reels and wonderin' what's keeping us."

"We need to get word to them," said Guildmaster Clout.

"How?" asked Bunge.

"The Durgans are more than capable of that kind of sneakery," Clout said. "Though it's true that none of our training has taken the sky into consideration. This new enemy changes things. Whoever goes will need to be fast. Fast and sly."

Suddenly, Kal knew whom Clout meant. And he knew that even though no one looked his way, everyone else was thinking the same.

Kalmar felt a thrill run through him. He was the fastest runner in Ban Rona, he could see farther, smell better, and sneak sneakier than Clout himself. And if he went, he could escape this dreaded strategy meeting. More than that, though, it meant he would escape the brain-numbing odor of the Nuzzard Fang.

"No," Nia said when she realized what Clout was suggesting. "My boy stays with me. He's part of the reason Gnag sent the creatures in the first place, and if he gets caught we lose more than a soldier. We lose the High King, and Gnag gets exactly what he wants."

Danniby spoke up. "Your Highness, we have no idea what's out there. If we storm the Great Hall and are met with ten thousand of those flying critters, we'll be overrun and the High King and the Song Maiden will be lost. If we can sneak but one Durgan out, and if he or she can get to the reinforcements, then it can only be for our good."

"Oy, and it will be for their good, too," Rudric said, still not looking at Nia. "They need to be warned. If they're caught unawares and out in the open, they'll be even worse off than we are. We're running out of time."

"I can do it." Kalmar didn't realize he had stood until everyone in the room looked up at him.

"Kalmar, no," Nia said with an edge of anger in her voice.

"Mama, I'm the fastest. I'm the sneakiest, too. And besides, I might be able to blend in."

"I said no."

Nibbick Bunge cleared his throat. "With all due respect, Your Highness, he's the High King, not you."

"Easy, Bunge," Rudric warned. But he addressed Kalmar, avoiding Nia's eyes. "Kal, if you really think you can do it, I believe it's our best option."

"Mama, I think this is up to me. I'll be all right. You've seen me run." He didn't mention that the odor of the Nuzzard Fang was like noise in his brain, and he was afraid he might lose himself he didn't get out soon.

Nia stood with her fists clenched at her sides. She and Kal stared at one another for what felt like a long time, and it was Nia who looked away first with a sharp intake of breath. All these years, she had been grooming him to be a leader. Now that he was leading, how could she stop him?

"How do I get out, Rudric?" Kalmar asked, turning away from his mother.

"I'll show you," Rudric said. "There's a cellar door that latches from the inside. It should be covered with snow, so the bats won't know it's there. It empties into the grove behind the hall. The trees are thick, so you should be able to make it away from the grounds undetected. After that, you'll be in the open, so it's a matter of speed until you get over the first hill. We'll provide a distraction at the dungeon door where we entered. If we're lucky, you'll have a few seconds before you're spotted."

"I understand." Kalmar's heart pounded. He was afraid, but the thrill of the quest was upon him so the fear was almost pleasant. Also, aiming his thoughts at something noble caused the Fang-fog in his head to clear. "Who do I talk to when I get there?"

"Ask for Gravin McKeeth, Chief of Ban Soran." Rudric put a hand on Kal's shoulder. "They're the best archers in the Hollows. He'll know what to do. Ready?"

Kal grinned, and for once he didn't mind that his fangs were showing. At last, here was something he could do—something he was *made* to do. To sneak, to run, to carry a simple message. This was so much better than meetings and processions and tributes.

"Let's go, lad," said Rudric as he ducked out of the cell. "Clout, give us a minute, then make some noise at the main door."

"I love you," Nia said, grabbing Kalmar's hand. "Please come back alive."

"I will," he said, his smile fading. He had a strange feeling that he wouldn't see her again for a long time. Nia slid to the floor and sat with her face in her hands, murmuring prayers. "Leeli, now might be a good time to play one of your songs," Kalmar said. "Mama needs it."

Rudric grabbed a lantern and led Kalmar through the corridors, past Hollowsfolk who watched him with respectful silence, as if word of his mission had already spread. Rudric turned left, into a narrow passage that led to a stair. The Keeper of the Hollows held his lantern high so that Kalmar could see at the top of the stone steps a square trapdoor set at an angle and secured with a lock. Rudric removed an iron key from his belt.

"Ready?" he said.

"Yes, sir."

In a swift motion, Rudric turned the key and heaved open the door. Snow and light fell into the passageway.

"Go, lad! Hurry!"

Kalmar leapt into the light. His wolf ears heard the stirring sound of Leeli's whistleharp dancing faintly out of the dungeon: a battle song, urging him onward to great deeds.

11

Smells and Sounds
and Squealings

Kalmar stood knee deep in a drift of snow, his back against the rugged stone of the Great Hall. In the summer the rear of the structure was a shady stand of fat redroot trees, which would have provided the perfect cover. But, now the only thing between Kalmar and the gray sky was a tangle of bare branches, and above those—a black, wheeling cloud of Bat Fangs. There were thousands. They screeched, they called to one another in shrieking voices, they waved swords, and they swooped earthward, out of sight below the trees and rooftops. Kalmar knew by the screaming that they were swooping at Hollowsfolk in the streets.

He had to hurry. The sooner he mustered reinforcements the sooner they could start saving lives. It was as easy as that. But what had sounded so simple while hidden in the dungeon seemed impossible now that he was outside and in plain sight—or was he? Bats were more or less blind. Everyone knew that. Maybe Bat Fangs were too, and maybe getting away was more a matter of silence than of concealment.

Rudric peeked out of the trap door. "Maker help you, lad."

Kalmar pointed at the sky. "He already has." Among the hundreds of wings, he saw a few dangling legs. The Bat Fangs were carrying Grey Fangs and dropping them into the city. Ground troops. "Now I won't be the only wolf."

"It's a bad day in the Hollows when Grey Fangs dropping from the sky is a good thing," Rudric said. "Now, go. Our people need you."

The door shut quietly and Kalmar heard the lock click into place. He scooped some snow onto the door to hide it, then crouched low and looked for the best route. There was a fence about an arrow shot away, beyond the grove. Past the fence and a short jog down the slope a small stone pump house stood like a sentry in the snow. He would make it that far and figure out what to do next. Janner would probably demand that he come up with a plan first, but planning had never been Kalmar's strongest trait.

"Who needs a plan?" he said under his breath. Then he bounded forward and ran with all his might. He hardly noticed that he was smiling with his tongue dangling out of the side of his mouth.

Kalmar leapt the fence, raced to the pump house, and slid to a stop. He held still, all his senses tingling. Through the squealing of Bat Fangs he could hear the clash of swords from lower Ban Rona, a dog growling, a woman—probably a mother—calling for someone named Fisher, and, faintly, a baby's cry. He heard more than that, and found that he could attend to the sounds one at a time as if he were looking at the details of a painting. He heard the bark of Grey Fangs shouting orders and laughing, and he could make out what the bats were saying high above him:

"—we need to get into that dungeon—"

"—there are archers in that house. Kill them—"

"—are the Wingfeathers in the keep? Did you hear the third one?"

So they suspected Janner wasn't with them. But they *didn't* know Kal had slipped out of the Keep. His nose twitched with the onslaught of bitter, rotten smells. The Grey Fangs stank, but these Bat Fangs smelled worse somehow; they had a sharper odor that made his snout curl. After a few moments, he found that he could distinguish between the Bat Fangs, and the same was true of the wolves, as if each odor was shaded, like many hues of the same color. He could smell individual Hollows-folk, too, some of whom he knew—and he could smell their fear.

Kalmar edged his way around to the far side of the pump house. At the bottom of the hill a brushy creek bed offered some cover. He waited for a rise of volume in the noise of battle, hoping it would draw the Fangs' attention, then he sped downhill. Near the bottom he slipped on an icy slab of stone and crashed into the brush, making more noise than he intended. He knew that the other Fangs could hear as well as he—the Bat Fangs even better, perhaps. So he lay in the brush as still as he could, listening, listening.

"What was that?" he heard from high above.

"Go," said another voice.

Kalmar peered up through the brush and saw one of the Bat Fangs break away and fly directly toward him. It would be upon him in moments, and even if it couldn't see well it could certainly hear.

Kalmar drew his sword and swaggered out of the brush, making his meanest, scowliest Grey Fang face. The bat landed a few feet away and folded its wings as it slunk toward him. The crea-  ture was lanky and appeared almost fragile, as if its bones were as thin as twigs. But what it lacked in strength of frame, it gained in hideousness. Its eyes rolled around in their sockets as if they had no purpose except to repulse. Its ears, though, were large and triangular, catching sounds the way sails catch wind. It was difficult to look at its face as it snorted and lurched closer.

"Nothing here, sir," Kalmar growled.

"What are you doing here, wolf?" the bat squeaked, eyes spinning as it leaned forward, seeming to look everywhere but directly ahead. Its ears were perfectly still and pointed at Kalmar.

"Thought I saw something. I was mistaken." Kal knew he could best the beast if it decided to attack, but the noise would only bring more of them swooping down. His grip tightened on his sword, but he told himself to stay calm, to think before acting. Now was the time to think like Janner, even if it didn't come naturally.

"You smell . . . different." The bat snorted and licked its teeth with a pointy little tongue. "Why do you smell different?"

"I was fighting some of the stinky humans. One of them, uh, threw some soup on me."

The creature's white eyes spun, its ears flitted up and down, and its nose twitched and sniffed quizzically. Then a mighty crash came from the other side of the Great Hall. The giant ears whipped backwards and the monster gurgled with pleasure. "At last. They're breaking down the dungeon door. They'll need your help, wolf."

"Excellent," Kalmar said, faking a cruel smile. He had to get to the field. *Now.*

The Bat Fang turned and unfolded its leathery wings, but its ears were still aimed back at Kalmar; it was waiting for him to follow. Kalmar took a few steps in its direction and the creature seemed satisfied. It flapped its wings and lurched into the air, squeaking with glee as its fellow Fangs battered the Great Hall. But as soon as Kalmar turned to run, the creature tipped its wings and swooped toward him, shrieking a warning to its fellow bats.

"The wolf king! He's here!"

12

The Center of the Storm

Kalmar put all his energy, all his attention, into running. He pushed through the snowdrift at the top of the hill beyond the brook and ran. But as he crested the hill he heard, too late, a whoosh of air and smelled the reek of the Bat Fang who had sounded the alarm. Claws scraped at his shoulders and caught hold of his cloak. He was lifted into the air, kicking and flailing.

"I've got you, *boy*," said the Bat Fang into his ear.

Kalmar struggled and twisted, engulfed by the stench of death and filth. He managed to grab the hilt of his sword and with great difficulty drew it from the scabbard. The Fang's flying wasn't graceful, as Uncle Artham's would have been—this was a lurching, heaving flight, which made it almost impossible to swing a sword. The Bat Fang screeched again, and Kalmar's wolf ears heard answering calls in the distance. The others knew. Every time the Fang's wing lifted, Kalmar saw more of the bats turning his way and flapping nearer.

He gave up swinging his sword and instead pointed it backwards, under his armpit. With both hands on the hilt, he thrust it behind him and heard the Bat Fang gurgle with pain. The claws slackened and Kalmar cried a triumphant, "Oy!" before looking down and realizing that he was about to fall a great distance.

The Fang crackled into dust, and Kalmar plummeted to the earth. When he hit the snow, his teeth clacked together and every bone in his body shuddered. But seconds later he realized he was sliding, then tumbling downhill. Without wasting a moment to collect his wits, Kalmar found his feet and raced toward the Field of Finley, thinking not of the gathering monsters behind him but of his family, his friends, and the Hollowsfolk who needed his help.

It wasn't until he crested the next hill that Kalmar realized he still had his sword—a good thing, too, because a moment later a shadow passed over him. Without turning or looking behind, he swung the sword, dimly aware that he had sent another Bat Fang's ashes into the snow. Kalmar raced with all his strength, slowing only to batter at all the claws and wings and teeth that encircled him. The screeching was so loud and constant that he scarcely heard it anymore. All he could think about was the fire in his legs, a strangely pleasurable sense of purpose, and the army that waited.

When at last Kalmar reached the hill that overlooked the encampment, his strength was spent. He stood on the hilltop, swinging his sword wildly at the cloud of beasts as they feinted and screamed and circled in the air.

It was Carnack Ban Soran who saw him first. He was standing with his clansmen around a fire, holding a skewered hen leg over the flames when he glanced to the west. As he would later tell it, he saw a cloud of darkness whirling about the hilltop. He thought it was smoke, but instead of rising, it spun downward like a bewitched storm wind. Then he spotted Kalmar Wingfeather at the center of the churn, covered in green Fang blood and dust, wielding his sword like a hero of old. Ear piercing shrieks broke over the Field of Finley, yet through the awful sound cut the clear, golden voice of the High King of Anniera: "Help!"

Arrows sprang from a hundred bows. The archers cleared the air of Bat Fangs in moments, then thousands of the fiercest fighters in Aerwiar poured over the hills to the aid of Ban Rona.

Kalmar fell to his knees as the warriors raced past him. "Arrows . . . archers . . . to the Keep," he panted. "Help them."

Then he collapsed into the snow.

Carnack would later boast that it took two men to pry Kalmar's fingers from the hilt of his sword.

13

Fighting for Bones

When Kalmar woke, he was on his knees in the snow, fighting with two dogs over a leg of roasted hogpig. He looked at his hands. They were moist with mud and meat. He didn't understand where he was or what he was doing.

The dogs snarled at each other and lunged at the bone again. Kalmar scrambled backward in shock. He tasted hogpig meat on his lips and in his whiskers. He must have been gnawing on the bone with the dogs—but he had no memory of it. All he remembered was arrows, the swirl of Bat Fangs, and the welcome sight of warriors rushing past.

Kalmar looked around to see if any Hollowsfolk had noticed him fighting the dogs. They were always watching him, it seemed, waiting for him to prove their worst suspicions. He petted the dogs, not just to show anyone looking that he was in control but to prove it to himself as well.

"Ho, King Kalmar."

Kalmar whipped around, hoping he had no meat dangling from his snout. An old woman approached with a basket of greasy bones, probably leftovers from lunch. Judging by the sun, it was late afternoon now, and his stomach was growling. He fought the urge to smack his lips like one of the dogs. The woman showed no indication that she had seen him on his knees in the mud. "Glad to see you're up and about."

Kalmar wiped his hands on his Durgan cloak. "I was just checking on the dogs."

The woman wore a dirty apron over her winter coat. Her long, gray hair was pulled back in a ponytail and wisps of it hung about her wrinkled face. She looked like she had been working hard. "Got word about an hour ago that the bats were driven back to the skies. Ban Rona is secure." She threw another bone to the dogs. "Thanks to you, Your Highness."

Kalmar smiled, reached over to the basket, and tossed the dogs a few more bones, resisting a mighty urge to shove one into his mouth. "Are my mother and sister all right? What about Rudric and Mister Reteep?"

"Danniby brought word a little while ago. Your mother and sister are fine, as are the Keeper and the fat fellow. As for your grandfather, it would take more than a few Fangs to put an end to him. You'll be wanting to get back to your family, I reckon."

"Yes, ma'am," he said, looking over the tops of the tents at the hill where he had collapsed. The snow there was brown with the dust of dead Fangs. He did want to get back and be sure his family was safe, but he couldn't shake the memory of the shriveled Gray Fang in the dungeon. He still had its scent in his nose, and it frightened him. And as much as he wanted to check on his mother and Leeli, he couldn't bear the thought of going anywhere near the madness down in that dark cell.

He was afraid that he was sinking deeper and deeper into the same animal mindlessness that had overcome the captive Fang. Was this why Fangs were never garrisoned in one place for longer than a few months? He remembered that in Glipwood the Green Fangs were regularly replaced, and the ones who stayed, like Commander Gnorm, left a few times a year and seemed to return stronger and meaner. But what did it mean?

Kalmar wished Janner could tell him what to do. He knew what he *wanted* to do. He wanted to run away. What if he woke one day with something worse than henmeat or hogpig in his teeth? His throat tightened and tears moistened his eyes. He looked away so the old woman couldn't see, but too late.

"Brave lad," she said, placing a weathered hand on his arm. "There's no shame in joyful tears. Hollish though I am, your courage today made me want to be Annieran. The Shining Isle is in good hands with you on the throne."

If only her words were true. She wouldn't have said that if she knew what was inside him. The tears that dampened his furry cheeks were those of sorrow, not joy. He knew what was in his heart. He remembered with a stab of shame the despair he had felt when he walked into the darkness of the Stone Keeper's chamber that day in the Phoob Islands. The Shining Isle wasn't in good hands. *No*, Kal thought, clenching his jaw, *as long as I'm the High King, Anniera is doomed*. Doomed to be ruled by a weak boy who was poisoned and dying, while the wolf grew and growled from the shadowy corners of his mind, waiting for the day when it would reign in his heart, a snarling beast crouched on a bright throne, ready to pounce on those who loved him. He was so sorry for who he was and afraid of who he was becoming.

Kalmar hung his head. There was no stopping the coming madness. He was sure of it. If his fate was to slowly lose his mind, then he had to do what he could before it was too late. He had to get to Castle Throg. He had to find Gnag and stop him, or die trying. And he would do it alone. Alone, so he couldn't hurt the people he loved.

"I'd better go," Kal said with a sniffle.

"Aye, Your Highness." The old woman threw the last of the bones to the dogs and turned to hobble back to the food tent. "Go and protect the ones you love. There's a battle to be fought."

Kalmar felt a great weariness as he climbed the long slope west of the Field of Finley. When he reached the top, he looked back over the empty encampment. He heard the dogs still fighting over scraps. He looked toward Ban Rona and saw smoke rising from the city.

As usual, he had no plan. So he ran.

He skirted the field, then turned southeast and ran straight for the Killridge Mountains—toward Gnag the Nameless, praying that the boy inside the wolf would live long enough to do what needed to be done.

Squoon was a student of history and language, handsome in his way but misunderstood by the burly warriors of the Hollows because of his bookishness and reserve. Bonifer never attended the games, and indeed he cared little for the world outside the library. It was the past that fascinated him. So when Madia appeared one morning in the library, he had no idea who she was. He and Madia were fast friends, and for weeks they read together, ate together, and walked the streets of Ban Rona. Being secretive and shy, Squoon told no one of his heart's capture by the young woman. He was as enchanted by her quick mind and poet's tongue as he was by her beauty, and he resolved to marry her. But he spoke of her to no one—until one day, just before the Finnick Durga, he confided in the nearest thing he had to a friend: Ortham Greensmith, a young man with whom he had nothing in common other than the street where they lived.

Ortham was kind of heart and spoke often with odd little Bonifer even as they grew up and apart—Bonifer into bookish solitude and Ortham into great strength and fame among the warrior folk.

'Ortham,' said Bonifer that day as he stood at the front door to the Greensmith house on Apple Berry Way. 'I need to speak with you.'

Ortham, recognizing the seriousness in Bonifer's manner, stepped outside. 'Yes?'

Bonifer fumbled with his words before blurting out the secret that would lead to his great wounding. 'I'm in love with a girl named Madia.'

Ortham burst into laughter. It was not laughter intended to belittle his friend, but belittle Bonifer it did. 'My friend, all of Ban Rona is in love with Madia Wingfeather!' And without realizing that his words cut to Bonifer's heart, he continued. 'In fact, Bonifer, I plan to marry her! Tomorrow, after I win the Finnick Durga, I shall declare my love. She's to be the queen, you know.'

Bonifer heard little else that Ortham said, so smitten was he with grief and shame. A queen! Bonifer had thought she was just a girl from Anniera. His cheeks flushed with embarrassment.

Just then, Madia and her family passed by and the two young men turned and waved, Bonifer aching with jealous desire, Ortham oblivious to his friend's torment. Madia smiled and waved in return, and both men believed her smile was aimed at him alone. Ortham bade farewell to Bonifer and shut the door, his heart full of affection; Bonifer stood alone on the stoop, his heart full of anger.

—From *The Annieriad*

14

Another Hollow, Another Monster

Janner's lungs felt shallow and hot. He had been running for hours, first uphill through snow as deep as his waist, then downhill into the next valley, sometimes tumbling head over heels until he reached the bottom, where Baxter would be waiting. All he could think about was getting back to Ban Rona, to Chimney Hill.

He was elated when at last he came upon a road, the first sign of civilization he had seen. But his heart quickly sank. The ruts were dusted with a couple of inches of fresh snow, and it hadn't snowed in days, which meant it had been a long time since anyone had passed that way. He looked to his left and right, but there was nothing to see, just hills and more hills.

"Should we take to the road, boy?" he asked Baxter as he bent over to catch his breath. "I think there's a town somewhere west of here. Molcullen, or something." His gut told him to keep following Baxter south, but the thought of leaving the first road he had come to worried him. Not only would he be thrust into the lonely wild again, he would have to keep trudging through all that snow. The snow on the road was only ankle deep. And the road would lead him to *something*, maybe a town, or even just a farmstead where he could borrow a horse or a houndrick.

Janner kicked the snow. He couldn't afford to waste any time, but he didn't want to make the wrong choice. After a gulp of water from his canteen he decided that the road might lead him too far out of the way and cost him precious minutes. And if minutes mattered, then he couldn't afford to rest any longer.

Janner patted Baxter's warm flank and left the road behind. He ran and ran, conscious of the falling light, his failing strength, and how cold the coming night would be.

After the next rise, he saw a stone cottage on the valley floor. It was surrounded by a few outbuildings and fenced pastures. Just beyond the cottage a creek, spanned by a narrow bridge, threaded its way through the valley. Baxter bolted ahead, aiming for a goat pen where Janner could see several animals nosing about. He saw no one, but the presence of animals and the well-trod look of the snow around the homestead told him that this was no abandoned house.

"Hello!" he called. This far from a village or city, the occupants would surely be wary of strangers. Baxter trotted along the fence line, barking happily at the goats. Janner headed down the hill, still calling and growing more disappointed with every step. There was no smoke rising from the chimney. No horses poked their heads out of the barn windows. Whoever lived here was gone, probably mustered to the Field of Finley with the rest of their clan. Well, at least he could refill his canteen in the creek, and one homestead likely meant there would be another, and maybe a town sooner rather than later.

As Janner neared the rear of the house, Baxter lost interest in the goats and padded around to the front porch. Then Janner smelled something—something foul. It wasn't a Fang, he was sure of that. But he had smelled it before, and it evoked a pang of fear in his chest. It brought to mind Glipwood Forest, the rockroach den, and their escape to Fingap Falls, though in the seconds before he turned the corner he couldn't sort out why. Baxter darted around the house and growled. The growl reminded him of Nugget.

Then Janner remembered. *Trolls.* The Fang hordes had marched through Glipwood Forest with trolls in their company, and the wind had carried the odor before them like an ocean wave. The Fangs smelled bad enough, but the trolls reeked of sour earth and flatulence.

"Baxter, no!" Baxter's growl was answered by a moan that shook the branches of the trees. Janner heard a meaty thud, then the dog flew through the air and crashed into the snow in the front yard.

Janner drew his sword. He fully expected to see the troll leaping from the front porch to tear him to pieces—but he saw nothing. The door swayed on its hinges. Janner heard the troll huffing inside the house, moaning from time to time—and as strange as it seemed, the moaning had a note of sadness in it. Was the troll crying?

"Want to go home," it mumbled in a deep voice, then it sniffled and banged around inside the house, breaking things and moaning louder.

Janner still couldn't see the troll, but he had the feeling that it might emerge at any moment. "Wake up, boy," he said, shaking Baxter. "We have to get out of here. Wake up!"

The dog's eyes fluttered open. He whined and struggled to his feet. Blood flowed from a wound in his shoulder, darkening the snow, and though no bone protruded from his fur, Janner could see that something was broken. When Janner tried to lift him, Baxter yelped with pain.

"Can you walk? Come on, boy." Janner patted his thighs. "Come with me." Baxter took a careful step forward without touching the bad foot to the ground. Whining with every step, Baxter followed Janner across the yard to the footbridge. Heart pounding, Janner led him over the bridge and hid behind a tree. He didn't know what to do. He couldn't leave Leeli's dog behind, but at this pace he would never reach Ban Rona in time to warn the others.

Then Janner heard voices, low and quiet, drifting toward him in the deep silence of the homestead. Several figures emerged from a bend in the creek upstream. Ridgerunners. Another company of them, at least thirty this time. They signaled to one another as they crept, quiet now that the house was in view. Their little spears and daggers were drawn as they inched along the creek bank. Janner felt some dark satisfaction that the sneaky little thieves were about to encounter more trouble than simple farmers defending their fruit. He lay quietly next to Baxter, waiting to see what would happen.

The little men and women sneaked toward the house as silent as the snow, then they divided into two groups. One group skittered like thwaps to the roof of the house and unfolded a large net while the others huddled against the side of the cottage. One of the Ridgerunners dangled from the eaves and nodded to one on the ground. It coughed conspicuously and then stomped noisily through the front door.

The silence was shattered by the troll's terrible roar and Janner nearly jumped out of his cloak. The ridgerunner dashed out of the house with a shriek, and the troll emerged and stooped on the porch. The troll was smaller than the others Janner had seen. This one had a little tuft of black hair and was only as tall as the roofline, though its bare chest and shoulders were so massive they barely fit through the doorway.

"Leave me ALONE," the troll said, shaking its fist and stepping down from the porch.

The moment it set foot in the front yard, the ridgerunners on the roof flung the net over it and leaped down. The troll struggled fiercely, but the net held. The ridgerunners jabbed it with spears and swords while one of them drew an arrow and dipped the tip in a small bottle. The little creature took aim, grinned, and shot the troll in the rump. As Janner watched, the troll staggered forward, dropped to one knee, moaned once more, and collapsed just a few feet from the bridge. The ridgerunners shouted with triumph and danced around the fallen beast.

Suddenly Janner felt sorry for the young troll. Why in Aerwiar would ridgerunners want to capture it, especially if all they ever cared about was fruit? And why was the troll alone this far out in the wilderness? And why was one of the ridgerunners now raising his sword, ready to plunge it into the base of the troll's skull? Janner had never known them to be this vicious and violent, especially to a helpless creature. Troll or not, he didn't want the thing to die.

Janner leapt to his feet, shouting for them to stop. And then he was trudging through the snow to confront a gang of enemies who had just proven themselves capable of killing something much more dangerous than Janner Wingfeather—even if he was thirteen years old.

15

Janner Gets Carried Away

Wait! Stop!" Janner waved his arms and ran towards the creek, coming to a halt before he crossed the bridge. It wasn't much, but he felt safer with the creek between them. "What are you doing?"

The ridgerunner standing on the troll's back cocked its head and narrowed its eyes. The others circled the troll and brandished their weapons as if they were protecting a treasure. They sneered, their little legs bent and ready to spring.

"That should be obvious, boy." The leader lowered its sword, but only by a little. "Isn't it obvious, my sneaks?"

"Quite," answered another. "The boy is a fool, Grouzab. Probably dislikes fruit, too."

The ridgerunners hissed at this suggestion as Janner stepped to the middle of the bridge and held up his hands. "No! I love apples. And sugarberries and plumyums." The ridgerunners relaxed a little.

"It should be clear that I'm about to execute this troll," said Grouzab.

"But why? Aren't you on the same side?"

"Side?" said Grouzab. "We are on no side but the fruity one. Gnag the Nameless has offered us fruit by the wagonload for the head of every troll who tries to escape his army."

"Fruit!" cried a ridgerunner, and the others shook their weapons.

"But you can't just kill him." Janner couldn't believe what he was saying. The thing stank, it was from a race of brutes, and it would happily squeeze them all to death if it were awake. Then it would roast them over a fire, if the stories were true. But it wasn't awake. It was helpless, and it just wanted to go home. Janner remembered the way Kalmar had cared for the cloven—the cloven which had turned out to be their father. Janner almost laughed at the thought of this young troll turning out to be a distant cousin. "Take him back to Gnag if you want. But don't kill it."

"Too much trouble. Much easier to carry a head than a whole troll."

Grouzab raised his sword again, and before Janner could stop himself he dashed the rest of the way across the bridge, meaning to shove the ridgerunner from the troll's back. The other ridgerunners leapt forward to protect their leader. Janner dodged them but tripped over the troll's arm and landed face-first in the snow.

When he looked up, spitting snow from his mouth, the ridgerunners had the point of every spear, sword, and arrow trained on his face. He glanced at the troll, which was only inches away, and saw its eyes barely open but looking directly at him. They were small and close together, hidden in the shadow of a heavy brow, and Janner was surprised to see the light of intelligence there. That glint of understanding told him the troll was aware of what Janner had done—which was a relief—and that the troll was no longer unconscious—which was terrifying.

The troll leapt to its feet, toppling Grouzab from its back. One of its arms pulled free of the net and swung around like a living hammer. Ridgerunners flew through the air, crashed into the cottage, sailed over the roof to land in the goat pen, splashed into the creek, and lay prone.

The troll, still groggy from the poison, panted and spun in the snow to be sure it had dispatched all of the ridgerunners. Then it turned its tiny eyes on Janner, and Janner waited for that hammer hand to smash him flat into the snow. He heard little groans of pain and saw the ridgerunners picking themselves up from the snowy ground, stunned and blinking. They were tougher than their size implied. One of them was already hefting a spear.

The troll growled at the ridgerunners. It took a step forward, but its foot was caught in the net and the troll slammed into the snow again. Janner drew his sword and scrambled over to the fallen troll. It looked at Janner with a question in its bright eyes.

"It's all right," Janner said, struck by how pitiful the beast seemed.

The troll's bony features softened and it nodded. Janner hewed at the net as the ridgerunners collected their wits and began to hiss. By the time the little creatures had them surrounded, the troll was free of the ropes and standing unhindered.

The leader drew an arrow with one hand and discreetly uncapped the bottle of poison with the other.

"That's a bad idea, Grouzab," Janner said. "I won't let you kill this troll."

"Have you any fruit?" Grouzab asked.

"Not for you, I don't."

"Then Gnag's offer is better than yours. Go, boy. Leave us to our mischief."

Grouzab dipped the arrowhead into the bottle. Janner felt panic rising in his chest. He should be running for Ban Rona. He should be busy making a shelter in the falling light, or tending to Baxter. Instead he was surrounded by ridgerunners, in defense of a troll. A troll! This was what he got for acting without thinking first—like Kal always did.

Then again, Kal, who always managed to get himself into trouble, also managed to get himself out of it. So what would Kalmar do next? One thing was sure. Kalmar wouldn't stop and consider all his options. He would simply *do*. Kalmar followed his instincts, and somehow it worked out.

But Janner didn't trust his instincts. As soon as he felt one, he questioned it. So what was his heart telling him to do? Not his fear, not his brain, but his heart.

No, that wasn't right either. It wasn't his heart he needed to listen to—it was the *love* in which his heart rested. That was what he needed—the love of Nia, Kal, Leeli, Podo, and the love of the Maker who had kept him safe thus far. He rested in that—and he acted.

Grouzab smiled and drew the arrow, and Janner muttered, "Kal, I hope this is right." Then he jumped forward and struck the bow with his sword, shoving Grouzab aside. But he was too late. The bow twanged and the arrow flew—not at the troll, but at Janner.

It only grazed his shoulder, but it stung, and Janner immediately felt drowsy. He blinked slowly, staggered, and fell to his knees. He had only been thirteen for a few days, and already he had been drugged twice.

Janner was dimly aware of the troll behind him, of ridgerunners soaring through the air again, then he felt himself lifted by a strong arm. He was nearly asleep, and he imagined it was Esben's great arm bearing him up, carrying him to safety. "Papa," he slurred, and forced his eyes open one last time before falling unconscious. He saw the strangely kind eyes of a smelly troll. Janner was too astonished to be afraid, then he was too sleepy to be astonished.

As he drifted toward sleep he thought of poor Baxter bleeding in the snow. Poor Leeli, too. She would be heartbroken to learn that her dog had been hurt, maybe even killed.

Janner's eyes were barely open, but he caught a glimpse of the dog, still lying beside a tree. With great effort he formed two words with a mouth that didn't want to move. "Find . . . Leeli."

Baxter heard. As the troll trudged out of the valley with Janner dangling over its shoulder like slab of meat, the dog staggered to his feet, sniffed at the air, and knew in a flash which direction would take him to Leeli and Ban Rona and the houndry.

As the sun set on the cottage, tracks led in three directions: one set was left by a gang of ridgerunners limping back to the Killridge Mountains, having decided that some things were simply too much trouble, even for fruit;

another set was left by a troll stomping through the hills, looking for a place to hide; and the last was the bloodstained trail of a dog running toward home.

16

The Wounded and the Woeful

Leeli and Nia stood in the dusty mess of the Great Hall beneath the mighty tree, tending to the wounded. The dead were wept for and laid in rows under their own cloaks until their families were found. The Fang armor and weapons were collected into a pile outside the keep, while a group of boys scoured the dust and clutter for undamaged arrows.

Leeli had seen terrible things in her short life, but never anything to match the carnage around her. So many familiar faces were either dead or dying or wincing with pain while healers stitched up wounds and wrapped them with bandages. Since she knew nothing of medicine, Leeli followed Nia around the hall, comforting the wounded or fetching supplies for the healers. She wondered about Thorn and the dogs at the houndry but she dreaded news of what had happened there, so she focused on the tasks at hand.

At first she had been unsettled by the sight of blood and the cries of pain, but she quickly grew numb to it out of necessity, like everyone else. This wasn't the time for tears, but for work—though as soon as she stopped moving, the horror of it threatened to overcome her.

Oskar bustled about with a ledger on which he wrote the names of the wounded and dead. Whenever a page was full he tore it from the book and sent it outside so that messengers could announce the names and send word to the bereaved families. When Leeli had last seen Rudric, he was surrounded by Durgans, shouting orders as he hurried from the Keep. She felt safer knowing he was in charge, but his urgency implied that more attacks were imminent.

Then, to Leeli's great relief, Podo and Freva (along with little Bonnie) arrived. Leeli was glad to see that some of her grandfather's old fire had been kindled.

"Praise the Maker, yer safe!" Podo roared as he limped through the wounded to his daughter and granddaughter. He hugged them both so long and so tight that Leeli had to ask him to let go so she could breathe.

Freva's face paled and she lifted Bonnie to shield her eyes from the gruesome sights in the hall. "I'm going to go back, ma'am," she said to Nia. "Bonnie shouldn't be here, and we'd only be in the way. I just wanted to be certain you were safe. Chimney Hill is untouched."

"Good." Nia pried Podo's arm from around her shoulder and pecked his grizzly cheek. "We'll need every empty bed to tend to the wounded, so please get the house ready for visitors. Thank you, Freva."

"Ma'am?" Freva asked, with some hesitation in her voice. "Is Master Janner coming back soon?"

Podo, Oskar, and Leeli were all silent, looking first at the floor, then at Nia.

"I don't know," Nia said. "Guildmaster Clout says he's due back any time now. These new Fangs were concentrated here, on the city, which means he should have been as safe as ever out in the hills."

"Which isn't very safe," Oskar said quietly, clearing his throat.

"He found us in the Ice Prairies," Leeli said, taking Nia's hand. "That was much farther away, and the Stony Mountains were crawling with Grey Fangs. Remember?"

Nia took a deep breath and looked around the room, as if remembering where she was. "Yes, I do. Janner's going to be fine."

"Where's Tink?" Podo asked with a pirate's growl. "I want to squeeze that lad like a pumpkin. The whole city is blubberin' about his flight to the Field of Finley. They say he dusted a thousand bats!"

"Carnack says he's recovering at the field, under the care of his own mother. He said she'd send him back here as soon as he wakes." Nia smoothed the front of her dress and knelt to change a woman's head bandage. "He did well, didn't he, Papa?"

"Aye. And I'm gonna squeeze him like a pumpkin." Podo lowered his bushy eyebrows and looked Leeli in the eye. "What about you, Lizardkicker? You all right?"

"Yes sir," Leeli said. She added some growl to her voice and swung her crutch in the air. "I ain't afraid of no bats."

"That's my girl."

"Grandpa, can you take me to the houndry?"

"Aye. If it's all right with your mother."

Nia didn't look up from changing the woman's bandage. "If you think it's safe. I'm sure the O'Sallys could use her help. We'll need the dogs ready for the next attack, and some of them will be grieving."

Leeli and Podo limped from the hall, speaking words of encouragement to the wounded and woeful as they weaved their way toward Podo's sled. The sun was setting, and its light caught both cloud and smoke and turned the sky buttery and bright.

"The sky is pretty even if the city isn't," Leeli said as Podo lifted her to the seat.

"Aye, lass. The sky may be the only beautiful thing left to us for a while." He grunted his way into the sled and shook the reins. "I wish I were younger. I'm as useless as a bad tooth out here. Look at Rudric." Podo's voice grew quieter as they moved away from the Great Hall, as if he were speaking to himself. "He's doing the work of ten men. And that's *after* the battle. He'll be doing the work of twenty when the fighting starts again. I need to do something, lass, but I don't know what. These fighters are all stronger than me. There's no use for an old pirate when there's a war boiling."

"You can help me at the houndry," Leeli said.

"Aye. I can do that, I reckon."

The streets of Ban Rona told the story of the battle. Many buildings were destroyed, and it was clear that if the clans at the Field of Finley had come a moment later the Fangs would have overrun the city. Everywhere Leeli looked she saw pain and destruction.

Several minutes later they found the Guildling Hall teeming with children and parents, dogs and guildmasters. During the battle, many of the Hollowsfolk had fled either to the Great Library or to the Guildling Hall, because the larger buildings afforded more space, more rooms, and more places to hide. But now, as in the Great Hall, there were wounded to care for.

Head Guildmistress Olumphia Groundwich stood at the base of the courtyard statue, one hand on the forearm of the stone horseman, and the other pointing in whatever direction she shouted her orders.

"Podo!" she bellowed, in a voice that made her whiskers curl. "Take over!"

"Eh?" He reined up the sled at the gate and climbed down. "I thought ye said fer me to take over."

"Oy! That's exactly what I said!" Olumphia's lanky body leapt down from the statue and landed on her tiptoes between two wounded women. She flung her arms about to keep her balance, then danced from spot to spot, over and around people, until she stood beside the sled, panting. "Hello, Leeli." She nodded at Leeli curtly, then hurled her attention back at Podo. "I need to get inside and make sure the Cookery Guild is supplied—and someone needs to oversee the Fletchery. Rudric says we need more arrows. Most of the adults are either busy or wounded or—"She glanced at a passing stretcher bearing someone who was worse than wounded. Olumphia clenched her jaw and narrowed her eyes. "The Fangs will be back. Maker knows when. And we need to be ready. I need you to make sense of this chaos. We can't have people lying about in the sun, and we're running out of room here." She glanced at the sky, dismayed by the fading light. "Take charge. Understand?"

It was odd to see someone give orders to Podo, but Groundwich's urgency seeped into the old man. His eyes narrowed like Olumphia's, and for a moment they looked like the same person—just as whiskery, just as fierce, and just as masculine. Whenever the next battle happened, Leeli was sure the safest place to be was right between the two of them.

"Aye. I can do that, ma'am." Podo smiled a terrible smile and clambered up the base of the statue. He held to the stone horse's neck like a ship captain at the mast and picked up exactly where Olumphia left off. "You!" he cried. "Count the wounded! You, lad. Figure out how many can walk, and send them to the Great Hall! They may be hurt, but they're in the way. Oy, the name's Gruk, ain't it? Grak. Sorry. Spread the word that the guilds are to gather in their own guildery. The night is coming, and the Bat Fangs may come with it!"

People nodded and obeyed. It was doubtful any of the Hollowsfolk in the courtyard could tell the difference between Podo and Olumphia, nor did they care. They needed someone in charge, some order to push back the disarray. They were adrift, and Podo gave them a port.

"You should get to the houndry, Your Highness," Olumphia told Leeli. "Biggin is distraught. Many dogs were lost today." Olumphia directed a horse and sled to the gate, shouting for someone to load it with wounded and transport them back to Ban Rona.

Leeli hurried to the houndry. Before she opened the door she could hear the whines of many dogs in pain and distress. Torches burned on the walls, illuminating more dogs than Leeli had ever seen in the barn. Not a single tail wagged. Biggin O'Sally sat on the floor, holding a brown and white dog in his arms. When he looked up at Leeli, she saw that he was crying.

"They got Sounder," he said. "But he put up a good fight, didn't he?" The dogs nearby rumbled with half-barks and licked the dead animal's fur. "He took down the Gray Fang before it could get to the pups. That's my boy." Biggin stroked its head and pointed at another heap of fur lying beside the bench. "That's Barala. She and her pack kept a whole flap of those bats out of the Dining Hall until help arrived. Saved many children."

"Where's Thorn?"

"Out at the Field of Finley with a houndrick, looking for the wounded."

"Then he wasn't hurt? He's safe?"

"Oy, thank the Maker." Biggin wiped his nose. "It's the hounds that took the bludge of it."

Leeli made her way through the dogs, touching their heads as she passed and thinking of Nugget. Brave Nugget who had leapt into a company of Fangs to protect her.

When she reached Biggin, she sat on the floor beside her Guildmaster. A resurgence of the day's horror washed over her as night fell on the Hollows, and her soul was dark with sorrow. She saw the same sorrow in the eyes of her dogs, and heard it also in Biggin's voice. There had been so much death, so much suffering—and yet, in the face of it, so much bright defiance. So many brave men and women whose stories would be in the hearts of the Hollowsfolk for the rest of time, because they had died for the sake of their friends. It did little to ease the present sadness, but she wept—for she knew her tears were medicine—and she realized that Gnag the Nameless's best efforts to blacken the world would only serve to scatter light like the stars in the heavens.

When Leeli closed her eyes and inhaled the pleasant musk of the many hounds and felt their noses nudging her shoulder and shins, she recalled the look on Nugget's face as he clawed at the Fangs on Miller's Bridge. His courage was as big as the world, and when he died a bit of the world died with him. And yet here she was, months later, on another terrible day, experiencing a miraculous lightening of her heart's burden at the memory of Nugget's selfless act. It was as if a strand connected that day with this one and the Maker's pleasure was coursing through it like blood in a vein. Then she thought of this one battle, in which there were countless acts of heroism, sacrifice, and honor, which were seen and would be remembered long after the heroes died and became points of light in a dark sky, connected by memories like constellations, each of which painted a picture that all the darkness of the universe could never quench. Light danced along the strands. Gnag couldn't stop it in a million epochs. Leeli grieved but knew, in a way she couldn't explain, that her grief would lead to something good.

Sometime before dawn, Thorn returned from the Field of Finley. "Leeli," he said.

She lifted her sleepy head from Biggin's shoulder and saw her friend standing in the doorway. The tremble in his voice told her something was wrong—something more wrong than the battle, and the deaths of his countrymen and his dogs.

Thorn stepped aside and Baxter limped into the light. His front paw barely touched the ground, and blood matted his fur from his shoulder down. Baxter's tongue drooped low and he whined once before collapsing to the houndry floor.

Leeli rushed to his side and flung her crutch away. "Baxter! Where's Janner? What happened?" The dog's eyes fluttered, then closed. He drifted into unconsciousness as Leeli sat and placed his head in her lap. She looked up at Thorn. "Where did you find him?"

"A scout spotted him a few hours beyond the field and brought him back. He's hurt real bad. I'm sorry Leeli." Thorn gently slid Baxter's legs out of the way so he could close the door. "Is he alive?"

"Yes, but not by much." Leeli listened to Baxter's breathing. "Did you see Kal?"

"No, I reckoned he was with you."

Leeli's head shot up. "I haven't seen him since the dungeon."

"An old woman said he came back to the city just after noon."

"That can't be right. We would have seen him." Leeli imagined Kal slinking around looking for food or trying to avoid whatever it was kings were supposed to do after a battle. She felt guilty and dismissed the thought. That was the old Tink. Maybe he was off doing some secret Durgan thing for Clout or Rudric. Still, she felt a tremor of worry, an intuition that Kal was in trouble.

She sat up straight. "Thorn, quick. Get me some paper and a quill. Dugger, come!" She clicked her tongue and a young herder dog padded to her side. Thorn returned with a roll of parchment, already uncapping an inkbottle. Leeli scribbled a note to her mother explaining that neither Kal nor Janner had returned. She slid it into a tube fastened to Dugger's collar, then held the dog's face in her hands. She clicked her tongue and whispered, "Find Nia. Hurry!"

With a bark that filled the other dogs in the room with excitement, Dugger bounded through the dog door and into the night. Leeli took a deep breath, stroked Baxter's fur, and pulled her whistleharp from her cloak. "Maker, please let this work."

"What are you doing, Highness?" Biggin asked from across the room as she tuned the strings and strummed.

"Looking for my brothers."

17

General Fithyhoop's Scout

Kalmar ran across the snow-swept hills, his cape flying out behind him. He ran by the light of the moon and, when the moon sank, by the light of the cold stars. Unlike Janner, he had no map in his mind, no real memory of the geography of the Green Hollows to guide him. He gave himself over to instinct, to smell and sound, to the peace of the wild, though he was careful to remain conscious of what he was doing. Kal was too afraid of the Fang inside him to allow it free rein. Instead, he imagined that he was riding the wolf, the way a man rides a horse—a dangerous and unpredictable horse.

After hours of scaling steep hills on all fours, then bounding down into valleys to leap over creeks or gullies, he realized he was tired. He stopped to rest, panting like a dog, and drank from a stream under the stars.

Where am I going? he asked himself. He had to keep his mind active in order to subdue the inner wolf. *To stop Gnag.*

As crazy as that sounded, it was better than being stuck in Ban Rona to languish in counsels, listening to wiser men discuss strategies he didn't understand. Back there they'd force him to give speeches or to order people around. He didn't want that. Most of all, he didn't want to wake up one day with something worse than hen blood on his hands. People already looked at him like he was a monster. They had been nice enough lately, but Kal could always tell that their eyes lingered on him a little too long, that they laughed a little too hard at his attempts to be funny, that they seemed anxious to escape the room when he was present. How would they behave if they knew what really lurked inside him? Their worst suspicions were true. He *was* a monster. At least, he was becoming one.

Kalmar wiped his mouth with his forearm and straightened. He hadn't even noticed that he had been crouched at the creekside, lapping up the water like a dog.

"What's my name?" he asked himself. "My name is Kalmar. My father was Esben Wingfeather, and I am his son, the High King of Anniera."

Those were the words he had spoken on the *Enramere* all those months ago as they sailed to the Hollows. Again and again, Nia, Janner, Leeli, and Artham had asked him his name—his true name. Janner had told him stories, and those stories had called him home. Now those stories were like lampposts along the pathway, guiding his course. Whenever he remembered his name he felt more like himself and less like the Fang. So he repeated it into the cold air of the valley floor, "I'm Kalmar. My father was Esben Wingfeather."

As he watched the fog of those words rise and vanish, remembering Esben's last breath on the boat that night, he caught the sound of voices somewhere to the north. He held still, then sniffed at the air and sensed a sweet, leathery odor. It divided itself into several shades. It was a group of—something. He couldn't tell what. The scent was familiar but he couldn't place it. They were at least three hills away and still talking, which meant they didn't know he was there.

Kal hopped over the creek, crept up the far side of the hollow and scanned the next hill. Even with his wolf eyes and the bright stars, he detected nothing. As quietly as a breeze, he trotted down the hill and up the next. The voices were louder. As soon as he made out a few words it was clear that they were ridgerunners.

"I think we should go back and get it."

"Well, I think that's a fruitless idea."

"We're already fruitless!"

"And we'll be headless if that troll has its way."

"What about the boy?"

"He's probably already in the troll's belly. And good riddance, for all the trouble he caused. Even if he liked plumyums."

It could have been any boy, Kal told himself. Surely not everyone in the Green Hollows had come to the Field of Finley. Surely there were those unable or unwilling to fight, families who stayed home to tend their flocks and farms. But Kalmar knew, in the same way he knew which direction to run, that it wasn't just *any* boy they were talking about.

Kal lay on his stomach and inched forward until he could see the huddle of ridgerunners a little way down the slope. They hunkered around a small fire in a stand of squat, bare clumpentine trees. He knew already, by the different shades of scent, that there were eighteen of the little creatures. Spears and swords leaned against tree trunks and several unstrung bows lay among the roots. Narrow ridgerunner faces glowed in the firelight. Kal waited to hear more but they said very little and sat puffing pipes and staring at the embers.

Kalmar stood up, took a deep breath, then strode down the hill to the ridgerunners. As he assumed they would, they scrambled for their weapons and hissed at him as he approached. Some of them scrambled into the trees.

"Put down your weapons, fools," he growled in his best Grey Fang voice.

"What do you want?" One of the ridgerunners stepped forward with a spear raised.

"I'm a scout. Scouting the land. For scouting purposes." Kal folded his arms and stood as tall as he could. "We got word of a troll. Something about a boy and a troll."

The ridgerunner narrowed his eyes. "We sent no such word. What did you hear?"

Kalmar should have come up with a good story first, but it was too late for that. "That's none of your business. I've been sent to scout for trolls. We need them in Ban Rona." That sounded better, Kal thought. "The battle went badly and General, uh, Fith—uh, Fithyhoop . . . sent me to find help."

"General who? I've never heard of a General Fithyhoop."

"He's new."

"New." The ridgerunner tilted his head a little.

Kal got ready to run. He wasn't concerned about losing a fight with ridgerunners, but he didn't want to hurt them.

"I've never heard of him," the ridgerunner said. "What breed is he?"

Breed? Kal had no idea how to answer that question, so he went on the offensive. "Silence, ridgerunner! I'm here to find out about trolls, not to answer questions from you lot. Now tell me where you last saw the troll and I'll be on my way."

"Fine," said the ridgerunner. "I'll tell you, but it won't do you any good. It's one of the runaways. Won't fight. We were sent to bring back its head."

"For fruit," said one of the others sadly.

"Yes, for fruit. But a rotten boy interrupted our execution. He wouldn't let us kill it."

Kalmar had to hide a smile. It was definitely Janner.

"And what happened?" Kal growled. "You didn't let it escape, did you?"

"The boy cut its bonds. The troll attacked us and took the boy, probably for food."

Kal's inner smile vanished. But again, something in his blood told him that Janner was alive. "Where is it? I'll have to kill it myself, I suppose."

"The last we saw of it, the beast was east of here, about half a day's walk. I'm sure you'll find its tracks and whatever's left of that blasted boy."

"You won't find any fruit, that's for sure," said another ridgerunner.

The leader sighed and sat down, which signaled the others to lower their weapons and join him. They looked so forlorn that Kalmar almost wished he had a basket of apples to give them. Then he had an idea.

"I have another message from General Fithyhoop. Gnag appreciates your willingness to help in his campaign, and he has bequeathed to you a secret storehouse of fruit."

"What? Where?" The ridgerunners jumped to their feet and circled Kalmar like schoolchildren about to get candy.

"We are Gnag's humble servants," said the leader with a bow.

"If you travel north and west, you'll come to a lake in the shape of a shoe." Kal knelt and traced a map in the snow. "Turn due east and travel into the forest for a day, until you come upon a snoak tree with a hole in the trunk big enough to fit a full-grown digtoad. You can't miss it. Travel north again for a half a day until you see a stone binhouse. It's filled with every kind of fruit you can imagine."*

The ridgerunners' eyes twinkled, and a few drops of drool spattered into the snow.

"Spread the word to any ridgerunners you see," Kal said. "Gnag is generous. He values your people!"

The ridgerunners were wild with glee. In seconds, the fire was stomped out, their camp was struck, and the little creatures dashed away to what Kalmar hoped was the middle of nowhere. He stood alone, pleased with himself and wishing Janner had been there to see it.

Kal sniffed the air to be sure the ridgerunners were indeed still moving away from him, then he dashed away too, hoping to find his brother before the troll had him for breakfast.

---

* Kalmar had no way of knowing this, but south of Grrk in the Troll Kingdom there is, in fact, a lake in the shape of a shoe, which was discovered in the by these very ridgerunners after a seventeen-year quest. This expedition was later known as the Fithyhoop Quandary, and the descendants of these ridgerunners remain scattered throughout the Jungles of Plontst to this day.

18

The Mystery of the Dream Window Thing

N ot long after Leeli began playing her whistleharp, Dugger returned to the houndry with a note from Nia.

> Leeli,
> Stay put. You're in Biggin O'Sally's care until morning. Chimney Hill is full of the wounded, so we needed your bedroom anyway. I have to believe that if Kalmar left, it was to find Janner and bring him home. If you find them in the song, send word immediately. Maker help us.
>
> Love,
> Mama

Leeli capped the tube on Dugger's collar and patted his head. "She says I'm to stay at the houndry."

"Good," said Thorn with a yawn. "It's better for the pups with you here anyway." At first, Thorn had sat with her and listened, but whenever he offered a helpful word of encouragement Leeli's concentration broke and she found it harder and harder to be kind to him. She had played through every song she could remember; Hollish reels, sailing songs, battle songs, sad songs, happy songs, Skreean dirges, soup songs, bacon songs, gravy songs, goat lullabies, songs about the Maker, to the Maker, and even some songs that were so old people claimed they were written *by* the Maker. But nothing happened. No visions. No mysterious connection with her brothers.

Thorn was siphoning fresh water from the cistern to fill the trough. He'd been looking at her with a puzzled expression all night. "How could they hear you if they're out in the hollows somewhere? I mean, your playing is loud, and pretty too. But not that loud."

"I don't understand it either," Leeli told him. "But sometimes, something weird happens when I play. The music opens up and makes it so we can all see each other."

"Like a window?"

"Sort of. More like a dream. Actually, it *is* like a window, but a window in a dream." Thorn nodded as if he understood, but Leeli knew he didn't. She smiled. "I know it sounds strange."

"Real strange. But at least you've got the dogs dozing. All but Frankle." Thorn aimed the water spout at the next trough and pointed at Leeli's feet. The little dog's paws and snout stuck out from beneath the bench, eyes twinkling in the lamplight. "He's been watching you the whole time."

Leeli bent over and scratched the little dog's chin. "I didn't realize he was there." She sighed. What *else* was she missing? The other times the magic had worked it had been an accident; she hadn't been thinking about much at all.

"The first time it happened I was singing an old Annieran song on the cliffs in Glipwood." Leeli paced the room, scattering hay with her crutch as she went. "The dragons stopped and listened. The second time was when Nugget died."

"Your giant dog?" Thorn asked. "I would like to have seen that one."

"Then I played on the way to the Ice Prairies. I was worried about the boys, and I played, and all of a sudden I could see them both. But later, when Janner got to Kimera we tried to find Tink and it didn't work. Nothing. Not until Gammon took us prisoner. Then I hummed, and Janner saw Tink again." Leeli closed her eyes and tried to imagine what had changed. She had been crying and afraid. She remembered that. She was trying not to show it, but she was afraid now, too.

"When was the last time your window-dream-thing worked?" Thorn asked over his shoulder as he topped off the final trough.

"On the deck of the *Enramere*, when the sea dragons came to kill Podo. I played this old song called 'Yurgen's Tune,' and suddenly we were all connected. I could hear the dragons, too."

"Creepy," Thorn said with a yawn.

"What?" Leeli said, with a yawn of her own.

"The dragons. You're probably used to them, as much as you've seen them, but I think they're creepy."

Leeli stopped walking.

"What is it?" Thorn asked.

"The dragons," she said.

"What about them?"

"Maybe the magic works best when they're around. It's happened almost every time I've seen them!"

"Great," Thorn said with a smile as he sat down on the bench where Frankle was hiding. "All you need is a sea dragon. Easy."

Leeli plopped down beside him and banged her crutch against the wall. Several dogs sat up. "If I could get close to the sea, maybe it would work."

"Maybe if you play that 'Yurgen' song he'll come swimming up."

"It doesn't work like that. The dragons come when they choose to. Besides, the last thing I want is for them to actually come out of the water."

"Why's that? I thought you said they weren't evil."

"Not all of them are. But the main one—Yurgen—is old and twisted. He wants to kill Podo, and I don't trust him. He scares me."

Thorn dangled a henleg bone over the edge of the bench and smiled as Frankle's nose edged out to sniff it. "Maybe you just need to bait them. Wave a henleg and they'll come close enough for your song to do its thing."

Leeli's head shot up. "Thorn, you're brilliant! I don't want them out of the water. I just need them to come closer. I need my grandpa."

"Pa told me he went back to Chimney Hill a while ago."

Leeli threw on her coat and clicked her tongue as she made her way to the houndry door. Six dogs awoke and padded out with her. "Thorn, can you help me get my sled ready?"

The sky hung low and the fog was thick as Leeli drove her sled down from the Guildling Hall to Ban Rona. Piles of Fang armor seemed to float out of the mist, along with Hollish sentries standing watch, smoldering houses, broken doors, and muddied piles of snow. Whining dogs wandered the streets, unable to find their masters. The air was dank with sadness and fear of the next attack. Leeli turned south and drove the dogs up the road to Chimney Hill.

"Hail, Song Maiden," a voice said as she dismounted the sled and limped to the front steps. Danniby, dressed in his black Durgan uniform, materialized from the shadows and bowed, then he raised a steaming mug in her direction. "Sippin' bibes to warm the bones. Is everything well? Your mother told me you were to spend the night at the houndry."

"I need to speak to Grandpa. Is he awake?"

"He tried to sleep, but he's been out to see me every few minutes, asking after your brothers. I'll see to your dogs." Danniby moved to unharness the team.

"Don't," Leeli said. "I'll be right back."

She pushed through the door and found Oskar and Podo beside the fire. There were makeshift cots spread around the room where the wounded slept or tried to sleep.

"Leeli girl!" Podo said quietly as he grunted his way out of his chair. "What are ye doing out in the night? Those bats could be circling!"

"Grandpa, I need you. Mister Reteep, where's the First Book?"

"In the words of Cletus John Jimmyjames, 'At this hour? It's in my room.' I've been studying the First Book—along with some old accounts of the Annieran kings and queens I found in the library. I think you'll find it all *very* interesting. Fascinating stuff. For example, did you know that Old Hollish was used in the courts of Anniera by scribes up until only eighty years ago? And the original character for *gleef* was *yimple* with the exception of *sumpo* in the tertian tense . . . " he trailed off when he realized no one was listening. "I'll get the book. And I'll be very quiet." Oskar stood and let out a little gasp. His eyes twinkled and he raised a finger. "It'll give me a chance to practice my Durgan sneakery! I've been reading all about it. Observe."

Grunting like a pen full of hogpiglets, Oskar dropped to all fours, then rolled to the foot of the stair and tiptoed up the steps, making enough noise to rattle the windows. Several irritated groans came from the cots.

"What's the trouble, lass?" Podo put an arm around her and sat her down beside him by the fire. "I thought you were Janner and Kal, come home at last."

"I've been trying to find them. But the song won't work."

"Blast. It's too bad, but it's no surprise," Podo said. "That sort of thing never works when you mean it to. It's the Maker's way of driving ye mad."

"But I think I might know how to get it to work." Leeli took Podo's hand. "It's the dragons."

Podo's eyebrows lowered and he pulled his hand away. "The dragons?"

"Whenever I've played the song and they were nearby, the magic worked."

Podo stood and limped over to his chair. "Magic," he said as he eased himself down and propped up his foot. "It never did anyone any good."

"But that's not true. I was able to see Kalmar and Uncle Artham when we were in Kimera. And I was able to stop the dragons on the *Enramere*. If I can get it to work, maybe we can find the boys."

Oskar peeked over the banister, and Podo and Leeli pretended not to notice as he made his way stealthily down the stairs, rattling the windows with every thump. He scooted on his back across the floor to the hearth, hid behind the nearest chair, and held out the First Book, waiting to surprise Leeli. "Thank you, Mister Reteep," Leeli said without turning. Oskar emerged from behind the chair, dabbing his forehead with a handkerchief. He sat down with the book in his lap, looking dejected.

"What's all the racket?" said Nia from the top of the steps. Her hair was a mess and she was dressed in a soiled apron. When she saw Leeli, she blinked away her sleepiness, hurried down the stairs, and hugged her. "Please tell me you found them."

"It won't work," Leeli said, holding up her whistleharp. Nia's face fell. "But I think I know why, Mama. We need to be near the dragons."

"Dragons," Podo spat. "You can't trust them."

"We don't *need* to trust them," Leeli said. "We just need them out there in the harbor for the song to work. I think. It's worth a try, isn't it? What's the worst that could happen?"

"The dragons could come out of the sea and eat us all," Podo snapped.

"They don't want to eat anyone but you." Leeli said firmly. "And they won't come out of the sea if you don't set foot in the water." She knew him well enough to know that his anger was just a mask for his fear. "Grandpa, please. If it doesn't work, then fine. But we have to try. And we have to do it before the Fangs come back. Don't you want to know if the boys are all right?"

Podo heaved a sigh, then clomped to the door and put on his coat. "I'll get the sled ready." Then he grabbed his legbone and a sword and stepped outside into the cold dawn.

By the time the sun rose, Leeli, Oskar, Nia, and Podo were riding west toward the harbor. The sunlight that pushed through the gray mist was weak and eerie. And though they didn't know it, above the clouds, a vast flock of Bat Fangs circled in the airy silence, awaiting the signal to attack.

19

What Kalmar Saw

Kalmar smelled the troll long before he found its tracks. Just before sunrise he spotted a set of footprints as big as flagstones in a budding apple orchard. Though the stench of troll flesh stung his nose, he could smell Janner too. He was alive.

Kalmar crept through the orchard slowly, recalling every Durgan principle of sneakery. He had to be quiet, because surprise might be his only advantage. He might be able to beat a Fang, but a troll? They were big, their skin was as thick as bark and they were strong enough to throw a boulder. Kal had seen them do it at Miller's Bridge.

At the edge of the orchard, the footprints veered to the left and wound into a brushy ravine. If it weren't for the footprints, the terrible smell, and all the broken branches, he would hardly know the troll was there at all, Kal thought with a grim smile. Trolls weren't exactly masters of stealth. As he crept down the hill and into the brush, he could hear the thing breathing, a huffing, snorting sound, like a giant hogpig gobbling slop. He hoped it wasn't gobbling his brother.

He dropped to all fours and crawled under the haythorn brambles, stopping now and again to tug his cape loose from a thorn or twig. The smell grew stronger and stronger until Kal's eyes watered and bile rose in his throat. He worried that his nose would be permanently damaged, like the nasal equivalent of staring too long into the sun and going blind.

Kalmar reached a muddy boulder and peeked around it, discovering at last the welcome sight of Janner sitting among the haythorn with his legs tucked up to his chest and his black cape wrapped around himself for warmth. But Kal still couldn't see the troll. It had to be on the other side of the boulder.

Kalmar wanted to whistle or snap, but it was too risky. He waved at Janner, but he wouldn't look up. Kal leaned against the boulder and scooted his way around to the other side, where he saw the troll's gray, lumpy foot, its toenails yellow and cracked. The foot was attached to an enormous leg, and the leg was attached to an enormous body, and at once he realized the boulder wasn't a boulder at all. It was the troll's back. And Kal was leaning against it.

He shrieked mostly with disgust that he'd actually touched the thing. Janner's head jerked up and the look of confusion on his face might have been funny if not for the danger. Kal fell backward into a tangle of brush, scrambling to draw his sword.

The troll grunted then stood and spun around. It saw Kal and narrowed its beady eyes. The fat lower lip curled downward and it sneered. Kalmar's cape was hopelessly tangled in the scrub, his sword was beneath him at an odd angle, and he was so frightened that even if he could move he wouldn't have been able to.

The troll raised its mighty arms over its head and curled its fingers into battering ram fists. Kal closed his eyes, regretting, among many other things, that the last thing he would smell would be troll sweat.

"Oood!" Janner cried.

Kal was aware, in what he thought was his last moment, that this was a strange thing for Janner to shout. When the blow didn't come, he opened one eye and saw Janner standing between him and the troll, waving his hands.

"Oood, no! He's not a Fang."

After a pause, the troll spoke in a deep rumble. "Fang. Bad Fang."

"No, Oood. This is my brother." Janner put a hand to his heart. "Brother."

"Brudder." The troll studied Kalmar and eventually lowered its arms. "Brudder?"

Janner extended a hand to Kalmar. "Kal, get up. Slowly."

Kal took his brother's hand and disentangled himself from the brush, willing his legs not to shake. He had no idea what was going on, but he knew better than to ask questions. He put his arm around Janner. The troll growled again.

"It's all right. He's not a Fang."

"Good Fang?" the troll asked, cocking his head a little.

Janner smiled. "Yes. Good Fang. Brother."

At once, the troll broke into a grin. Before Kalmar could say a word, the troll grabbed them both and lifted them to his chest in the stinkiest hug of Kalmar's life. He held his breath, though the embrace was so tight he couldn't have breathed anyway, and just when he thought he would lose consciousness, the troll released them both and patted them on their heads with surprising gentleness.

"Me Oood." The troll thumped his great chest and peered down at Kalmar. Its eyes were twinkling with intelligence. "You brudder."

"Oood," Kalmar said, pointing at the troll. Then he pointed to his own chest. "Kalmar."

"Kahmmer," the troll replied with another grin so hideous it was beautiful. Then it sat down with a crash and began cleaning between its toes.

Kal's knees gave way and he plopped to the ground. "I don't even know what to ask," he said, smiling weakly at Janner.

Janner smiled back. "How did you find me?"

"I got lucky, I think. I ran into a band of ridgerunners, and after that it was a matter of sniffing you out. What happened?"

After Janner explained how he had rescued the troll, he said, "When I woke up, the troll was sitting beside me eating a goat haunch. It offered me a hunk, which I forced myself to eat, and then I guess we were friends." The troll looked up from its toes with a smile and waved at the brothers.

Janner waved back, then grew serious. "But we can't stay here. Listen, Kal. I ran into another band of ridgerunners, and they said Gnag had already ordered an invasion. I was trying to get home to warn everyone when I bumped into Oood. The attack might come any day now."

Kal stared at the muddy ground. Janner had no idea how bad things really were, and he hated to be the one to tell him. "The Fangs attacked yesterday."

"What?" Janner jumped to his feet. "We have to go!"

"Listen," Kal said. "It's too late. They've invaded. We won the battle, but not by much. They have these Bat Fangs. They fly."

Janner glanced at the sky. "How bad was it?"

"Pretty bad. They caught us by surprise in the Great Hall. Mama's all right, and so is Leeli. Podo and Oskar made it, too."

"Rudric?" Janner asked.

"He's alive. They're getting ready for the next wave of bats, and I'm sure there will be Grey and Green Fangs to follow. If the clans hadn't been at the Fields of Finley, Ban Rona would have been lost."

"They sent you to find me?" Janner asked.

"Well, not exactly." Kalmar took a deep breath. He wasn't sure how much to tell Janner. Should he admit that he was afraid of becoming a Fang—or worse, a mad Fang? Or should he tell him the other part of his plan, about trying to sneak into Throg to defeat Gnag alone? Either way, he was sure Janner would make him feel like a fool. And why shouldn't he? He *was* a fool. That's what got him Fanged in the first place. "I came on my own."

"You did *what*?" Janner said with the irritated tone that Kalmar knew all too well.

"I'm going to Throg. To find Gnag." Janner said nothing, and Kalmar willed himself to look him in the eye. "I've thought about this, believe it or not. I'm useless in Ban Rona. We know Uncle Artham found a way out of the Deeps through the Blackwood, which means there's a way in. But an army could never do it."

"What about the Durgans? They can sneak better than us."

"Think about it. Rudric needs them all to defend the city. So I decided to do it myself. And I want you to help me." Kal lowered his eyes again. Janner's gaze was unreadable, and it was too heavy besides. He waited for the rebuke. Janner meant well, he knew that; he had been hammered with all that "take care of your brother" business since they were toddlers, so he couldn't help treating Kal like he was a baby.

After a pause, Janner nodded. "I'm with you."

Kal couldn't believe his ears. "Really?"

"You're the king. I'm with you. Besides, it's not a bad idea." Janner smiled. "We're already this far into the Hollows, and the Fangs are focused on Ban Rona. If someone wanted to sneak into Fang territory, you have the best disguise anyone could ask for. I'm with you. Brudder."

"Brudder!" Oood said.

Kalmar was so relieved he couldn't speak. He was about to tell Janner his other reason for running, but Janner whispered, "The question is, what do we do with our giant friend here?"

The troll had abandoned the cleaning of his toes and was now scraping at his upper tooth with a rock. When he noticed the boys looking his way he smiled again and said, "Go to Throg. Oood squash Gnag." Oood smashed a fist into the ground and growled while the boys laughed nervously.

"I guess that settles it, Your Highness," Janner said. "To the Blackwood we go."

Then Janner and Kal heard a melody that seemed to seep up through the earth and into their bones. Kal's head swam with misty images, and he and Janner looked at one another knowingly. Somewhere, Leeli was playing, calling to them with the Maker's magic. The ravine, the troll, the haythorn brush all faded away until they were lost in a stream of music and words and vision that stretched across Aerwiar like a braid connecting the Jewels of Anniera.

They sensed each others' presences. Kalmar thought he saw Artham too, but he was far away and faint. Leeli was at the harbor of Ban Rona, surrounded by Nia, Podo, and Oskar. Then, in a way that he couldn't explain later, Kalmar aimed his attention at another presence, another consciousness that lurked at the edge of the magic. It was swathed in shadow, hunched over like a broken thing. The song, which in Kalmar's mind usually shaped itself into vivid images, shied away from the figure, as if a dark wind was blowing out the melody's flame.

It was no dragon. It wasn't a cloven or a Fang. It was Gnag the Nameless—and Gnag *wanted* them to know it. Kal could see the enemy smiling.

20

What Leeli Felt

Podo reined up the horse at the west end of Priminy Avenue, just before the cobblestone road descended to the harbor. The city was coated with a fog that made the sun reluctant to break through, as if it too dreaded the coming battle. The grownups kept glancing at the sky, and Leeli wished they would stop pretending like they weren't worried. Whenever they looked at her they gave her a smile that said, *Everything's all right, little girl.* But she knew it wasn't. And she could handle it. It was the same with her limp—she didn't mind help now and then, but she didn't want to be treated like she was helpless or naïve.

"Seems like this might be close enough, don't ye think?" Podo reined up the horse and looked down at Leeli.

Leeli grabbed the reins from Podo and shook them. "A little closer."

"No need to get feisty," he said, glancing at the foggy sky again.

"I think there's plenty of need to get feisty," Leeli answered. The way her eyebrows worked when she spoke removed any doubt that she was Podo Helmer's granddaughter. "The bats up there could attack at any moment, and we can't sit here all day doing nothing." She noticed with some pleasure the way Podo and Nia exchanged surprised glances. Oskar began to whistle nervously.

As the sled horse clopped toward the water, Durgans in cowls and Hollowsfolk in armor emerged from the fog, nodding at them as they passed. Leeli's stomach fluttered at the thought of dragons swirling and swimming just below the surface of the water—dragons who had nearly killed them, and who wanted to swallow Podo whole. She was asking a lot, and she knew it. Leeli took Podo's gnarled, trembling hand in hers and felt terrible for forcing him into this.

"Don't be scared," Leeli said.

"Ah, Leeli. How young you are. It ain't the fear, lass." Podo's voice trembled. "It's memories that give an old man pause."

Leeli held tight to Podo's hand. By the time they reached the waterfront, the fog was so thick that their clothes were beaded with dew. The dock disappeared into the mist a few yards out from the shoreline, and Leeli could hear the slap of water on hulls and the creaking timbers of boats moored along the quay.

"Leeli, girl, I hope this is close enough," Podo whispered.

"Yes, sir." She asked Oskar to choose a song. "An old one. The oldest you can find. But nothing about a dragon. And something sad if you can find it."

"Of course, Highness," Oskar said, and Leeli heard the rustle of pages. "Ah!" Oskar clapped. "How about 'Gladys and the North Wind'? It tells of her sorrow when Omer died." Oskar passed the book to Podo, who held it open for Leeli while staring at the water with dread.

Leeli studied the notes, fingered them on her whistleharp, then raised it to her lips and began to play. At first there was nothing, then a tingling started in her toes and ran up to her ears. The sensation warmed her like sunlight emerging from behind a passing cloud. She heard a music that was deeper than the song she was playing and realized dimly that her eyes were closed. She was playing "Gladys and the North Wind" without looking at the page.

Images passed through her mind like waves, and soon she was aware of a woman with long, dark hair, dressed in a simple yet beautiful dress—the kind of thing a girl could play in and still feel pretty, Leeli thought. The woman was strolling the stony shore of a green island. It was Gladys, the first woman. The music was painting pictures of the events that inspired it.

The woman was weeping, then kneeling at the body of a young man, then playing a whistleharp (which looked a lot like Leeli's) beside a gravestone. Leeli felt the woman's sadness, and it seemed that if she played long enough she might tumble bodily into the song and speak to Gladys face-to-face—the magic was working.

But she was looking for her brothers, not playing for pleasure. Leeli shook her head and had the eerie sensation that Gladys bade her farewell before vanishing into a mist like the one hanging over the harbor.

Where are you? Janner! Can you hear me?

Still playing, still faintly aware of Podo's presence beside her, she willed the mist to part so she could see her brothers. They were together, standing in the snow as something huge and rock-like lurked at the periphery of her vision. Then they both looked directly at her.

Where are you? she asked.

Somewhere in the Hollows, Janner answered. His lips didn't move, but she heard his voice as if he were standing right in front of her. *Are you all right?*

We're all worried about you. Baxter came back, but he's hurt pretty bad.

Now it was Kalmar who spoke. *We have to go, Leeli.* His eyes looked troubled.

What do you mean?

We're going to Throg, Kal said.

Leeli's fingers slipped from the whistleharp holes for a moment. The vision flickered until she found the melody again. So Kal wasn't going to find Janner after all. It didn't come as a surprise, not when she thought about it. He had never wanted to be a proper king anyway. But that wasn't what troubled her. The vision showed her his heart, and she saw a dark cloud there. She felt his fear, and she could tell it was more than fear of Gnag or fear of the journey. He was hiding something.

Is something wrong? she asked.

Kalmar didn't answer. Then Leeli became aware of a fourth presence in the vision, a shadow like the one in Kal's heart, only a thousand times bigger and blacker, smoldering at the edges. She felt in that other heart a roiling anger, murderous and mean. It made her flesh go cold as death.

Leeli could tell the boys sensed it too, and she was about to ask them about it when suddenly Kal's eyes widened and a look of terror came over his face. Janner gasped, and she heard him screaming in her mind. At first she thought the boys were in trouble, but then she made out Janner's words: *Leeli, run! They're coming! RUN!*

She slowly became aware that there were other voices mingling with Janner's. They weren't coming from the vision or the music, but from right beside her. It was Podo's voice, then Nia's. Someone jerked the whistleharp from her hands and the vision vanished like a door slamming shut.

Leeli blinked, confused about where she was. The harbor. The sled. Then the world crashed into her senses.

"Bats!" Podo was bellowing as he waved his legbone in the air. "Bats! Oskar, Nia, draw your swords!"

Leeli looked up at the featureless gray above them and saw shapes wheeling about in the mist. Wings, legs dangling from the belly of the clouds, and Grey Fangs dropping from the sky like debris in a storm. There were thousands of them.

Then a final remnant of magic pulsed through her mind, another voice like the crashing of mighty waves.

Scale Raker will die if he sets foot in the sea, girl. It was Yurgen.

"Grandpa, get away from the water!" Leeli cried, praying that the churning sea wouldn't erupt with dragons as it had near the Ice Prairies.

"That's what I'm trying to do!" Podo fumbled with the reins as he waved his sword in the air.

None of the Bat Fangs had come close enough to attack, but more swooped down with every passing second. Leeli knew her family wouldn't last long in the open. The foggy harbor was at their backs, the lower city was before them, and Fangs were above. If they didn't get to the heart of the city they would be driven onto the docks, where the dragons lurked.

Nia and Oskar stood at the back of the wagon with their swords drawn. The horse whinnied as Podo tugged at the reins, trying to turn the wagon enough that they could charge back up the lane. At last he managed it and whipped the horse into a gallop.

Bat Fangs and Grey Fangs choked the streets. Hollowsfolk poured from every doorway to meet them. Leeli clutched the seat as Podo drove the horse into the fray. Swords clashed, wolves growled, and bats shrieked as they flew past. Leeli leaned against Podo, glad above all that they were far enough from the harbor to no longer worry about Yurgen. She never wanted his old, dark voice in her head again.

"Take *that*!" cried Oskar, "and that!" He bulged over the side of the wagon, whacking his sword at everything they passed. Nia, meanwhile, did the same on the opposite side with less bulging and more accuracy. Even Podo got in a swipe or two as he drove.

He piloted the wagon madly through the streets until they burst through a line of Hollish warriors, where Rudric dashed to and fro, shouting orders. The line had formed on the street outside the Great Library, and though the trees crawled with Bat Fangs, the archers stationed beneath the branches thinned them out in moments.

"Get inside, quick!" Podo yelled as he leaped from the seat.

Leeli would have loved to obey Podo's orders. She would have loved to have followed her mother and grandfather into the relative safety of the old building. But instead she was being lifted above the rooftops, above the morning haze, and into the bright, cold sky. Two long, misshapen hands had wrapped their bony fingers around her arms, and when she looked up she saw the heaving chest of a Bat Fang as its wings flapped her skyward. Below, the buildings of Ban Rona looked like tombstones rising out of the fog.

"And away to Gnag we go," said the Bat Fang with a wicked laugh.

21

What Janner Heard

Janner stood in the snow with Oood and Kalmar, heart pulsing with Leeli's song. The words were as clear as if spoken into his ear. He heard Yurgen the Dragon King, muttering about Podo's many sins. He even heard, as if from a great distance, Artham screaming something, though he couldn't make out the words. Maybe he was in a battle, or maybe he was too far away or too crazy to notice Leeli's song. Either way, hearing that voice made Janner ache to see his uncle again, to help him if he could.

But Janner heard something else, too. Something close and creepy, as if it was standing behind him and speaking into his ear.

Gnag the Nameless.

His dripping, dark voice crawled in Janner's brain like a maggot. *I'll find you, Wingfeathers.* Then the voice laughed a terrible laugh that made Janner feel nauseated. Now that he had heard the real Gnag speak, he felt silly for having ever confused him with sea dragons or a cloven. Gnag's voice was more menacing, more inhuman by far.

And *this* was the thing Kalmar wanted to fight? Suddenly their quest seemed like a terrible idea. Not only that, their family needed all the help they could get.

"We need to go back," Janner said breathlessly when the connection broke. "Those Bat Fangs are everywhere. Grey Fangs, too."

Oood looked around fearfully. "What you mean?" Oood said. His little eyes blinked in confusion. "Oood see nothing."

"It's hard to explain," Kalmar said. "It's a kind of magic, I guess. It just happens sometimes."

"Magic?" Oood asked. "What is . . . magic?"

"We don't have time for this." Janner was already climbing out of the ravine in the direction they had come. "Leeli and the others are in trouble."

"Janner, wait! You said you were with me. We're halfway to the Blackwood already."

"We have to help them," Janner said over his shoulder.

"The best way to help them is to get to Throg."

"Bat Fangs will overrun the city! Our whole family is there, and that vision was a sign that this quest of yours is a mistake. Now come on. Please."

"No." Kalmar's snout twitched and he let out a growl, his sharp teeth gleaming. "I'm not going back."

"Why not? What are you trying to avoid? A few ceremonies? Is it that you'll have to be in a council, or give a few speeches? Or is it that you're scared?"

"You don't understand." Kal's lips curled back. His eyes were flecked with yellow. The same yellow as when he had first been Fanged.

"Kal," Janner said, his voice breaking. He was suddenly afraid, as if he were no longer standing in front of his brother or even a Gray Fang, but a feral wolf about to pounce. Oood's chest rumbled.

From the corner of his eye, Janner saw movement near a stand of fatberry trees. Kalmar noticed too, because he suddenly sped off on all fours, growling like a wolf, in the direction of the movement. Oood and Janner looked at one another in surprise. Before they could follow, Kalmar emerged from the trees with a snowfox in his mouth. The little creature was lifeless.

"Kal?" Janner said.

Kalmar stood upright again. He blinked and looked at Janner and Oood in confusion. His eyes changed back to their normal blue.

"Mmff," he said. Then he realized there was something in his mouth and he spat it out. When he saw the snowfox at his feet, he jumped back with revulsion, wiping at his mouth. "What—what happened?"

"I was going to ask you the same thing," Janner said warily, edging back down into the ravine.

"Bad Fang," Oood said. The troll stepped between Janner and Kal.

Kalmar closed his eyes and nodded his head. "Bad Fang."

Janner hated the pause that followed. He wanted to fill it with encouraging words, but he couldn't think of anything to say. He knew that Kal had lapsed into . . . Fangishness . . . when he'd fed Esben in the cave, and when he fought Grigory Bunge, and when Janner had found him at the chicken coop. And he knew that Uncle Artham still went a little crazy from time to time. But this seemed something deeper and more dangerous. "How long has this been happening?"

"Ever since I changed—ever since I sang that song like a coward, it's been getting worse." Kal clenched his fists. "I screwed everything up, Janner. I'm supposed to be a king, but I'm a monster." Kal scraped at the fur on his arms, as if it were a costume he could remove. "And I can't stop it. No matter how I try to be good. No matter how I try to be what everybody wants me to be. I want to—I really do—but in the end I'm still a monster. And Janner," Kal said with tears in his eyes. "I think it's getting worse. I'm afraid I'll hurt someone. That's why I have to try and stop Gnag while I still can. Because I'm running out of time."

Janner wanted to hug his brother and tell him it would be all right, but he didn't want to lie. He didn't know if it would be all right. He had seen the yellow eyes, the bared teeth—Kalmar was still Kalmar, but there was something else in him too, something that ran deep and dark, and Janner didn't know how to rid him of it.

He imagined what might happen if they went back to Ban Rona and Kal hurt Leeli or Nia, and he understood why Kal didn't want to go back. He also wondered what would happen if Kalmar attacked *him*. It had happened once, on the *Enramere*, and Janner had the scars to prove it. But he was the Throne Warden, and though he was afraid, he knew what he had to do. He knew what Artham and Nia and Esben would want him to do.

"I guess we'd better find Gnag." Janner put his hand on Kal's furry shoulder. "We'll keep to the plan. Get into Throg. Find Gnag. And then we'll figure out how to heal you."

"Do you really think—?" Kal said, looking hopefully into Janner's eyes.

"Ships and Sharks. There's always a way out." Janner looked away before Kal could see how unsure he really was. "Oood?"

The troll grunted.

"Kalmar is *not* a bad Fang. He wants to be good. Right?"

"He forget to be good sometimes?" Oood asked.

Kalmar chuckled and wiped his nose. "Yeah, that's it. I forget."

"Me too," said Oood with a smile.

"Then I'll help you remember," Janner said to Kalmar. "What's your name?"

Kal winced and bowed his head, as if the words caused him pain. "My name is Kalmar Wingfeather, son of Esben Wingfeather."

"High King of Anniera," Janner said.

"High King of Anniera."

"Now let's get to the Blackwood."

22

Leeli's Secret Weapon

Leeli struggled, but the Bat Fang's grip was strong. Then she stopped squirming, having realized that if she broke free it would mean a quick plummet to her death. But she couldn't let the Fang carry her off to Throg without doing *something*.

She forced herself to breathe slowly and tried not to think about all the empty space between her and the ground. She saw Ban Rona's rooftops rising from a field of white. Arrows shot out of the mist, some of them so close that the Bat Fang lurched to dodge them. Leeli didn't want to be hit by her own people, so she decided to let them know where she was.

She held the whistleharp to her lips and played the first notes of the worst, shakiest rendition of "Fellyn the Fair" she had ever played. The Bat Fang screeched at her and tumbled earthward briefly before regaining its height. Leeli closed her eyes, pushed back at her fear, and played again, this time making it through the first verse without faltering.

"Quiet, girl!" the Fang squealed. It shook its hideous head and flew in an erratic course that drifted downward, downward, toward an enormous tree that reached out of the fog as if it wanted to catch Leeli. She played louder, gaining courage with every note. The more beautiful the melody, the angrier the Bat Fang became, and the lighter its grip, until at last, as they lurched over the tree, Leeli twisted her shoulders and fell free of the claws.

The Bat Fang shrieked and dove for her. Its mouth was open so wide that its face seemed to be all teeth and tongue—and it was the last thing Leeli saw before she slammed into a fat limb and lost all her breath. She gasped for air and clung to whatever she could. Branches snapped off in her hands and scratched her palms as she tumbled through the boughs of the tree. She doubled over a strong limb and came to a stop. Tears rolled down her cheeks as her lungs slowly opened enough for her to gasp.

Panting, Leeli flexed her fingers and kicked her legs to be sure nothing was broken, then looked around in terror at the foggy white mist that enveloped her. From below her came sounds of fighting: screams, steel on steel, growls from Grey Fangs, and cries of defiance from Hollish warriors. Above her there was an airy silence broken only by the flapping of wings and occasional screeches. She was far from safe, but she was invisible for the moment, and except for a few scratches and bruises, she was uninjured.

"Where is the girl?" said one of the bats overhead.

"I lost her, commander," answered another. "The brat still has the noisy thing."

"The whistleharp?" sneered the first voice.

"Yes, commander. It hurt."

"Yes, I heard it too. Find her. And this time, rid her of the weapon."

Weapon? Leeli looked at her whistleharp. She had never thought of it that way, but her little instrument was the only reason she wasn't halfway to Throg. She clutched it to her chest.

"Yes, sir," answered the bat. A gust of wind churned the fog, and Leeli saw, among the Fangs wheeling overhead, the flapping silhouette of the one who spoke. "I'll crush it to pieces. She can't be far."

Then the fog thickened again and she began a mad scramble toward the ground.

As Leeli reached the lower branches, the street below materialized out of the mist, and she saw figures running to and fro. Hollowsfolk. Leeli breathed a sigh of relief.

"Excuse me," she said as a detail of warriors tromped by. No one heard her. Four more men trotted past—weapons drawn, grim-faced. "Help!" she called out.

One of the men looked up and recognized her. "Come down, Your Highneth! Quickly!"

Leeli dangled from the branch and dropped into his arms.

He smiled at her with a dirty, bearded face. He was missing one of his front teeth. "Thorry. Got punthed by a Grey Fang, and lotht my pretty thmile. Word came that you had been taken. Praithe the Maker, I'm glad you're thafe." He turned to the other men. "Go on, brotherth. I'll get her back to the library. For the Hillth and the Hollowth!"

"Oy!" they grunted, and they pushed on toward the battle.

"My name'th Ladnar G'noll," the man said as he shifted Leeli onto his back. "Hold on tight, now." He hunched over, drew his sword, and dashed back the way he had come, shouting, "I have the printheth! Make way!"

As Ladnar raced through the foggy streets, Hollowsfolk cheered. Leeli had always imagined battles were long, drawn-out affairs, but this one had seemed to last only an instant—more of a passing thunderstorm than a steady rain. She knew from the shouting that somewhere the battle still raged, but here it had passed through like a storm wind, and the shattered windows and broken doors mirrored the broken and wounded warriors that littered the way. The only visible evidence of Fangs was the brown dust and armor littering the streets. But before long, the fog thinned and the sun shone through, illuminating the full measure of the day's destruction.

At last, Ladnar reached the Great Library and burst through the front door. He tried to catch his breath as he eased Leeli to the floor and spoke to a Durgan on guard. "Thpread the word. I have the Maiden."

Leeli nearly wept at the sound of jubilation that echoed through the library at the news. Nia and Podo rushed down the main stairs with arms outstretched and lifted Leeli into an embrace.

Nia looked her in the eye. "You're all right?"

"Yes, ma'am. Are we winning?"

"No, lass," Podo said.

Nia sighed. "I fear Ban Rona may be lost. We're making plans to retreat. The Gray Fangs were driven back to the north side of the city, but the Bat Fangs are still on the roof. Too many of them. We're running out of arrows, and they just keep coming. Gnag has been busy. I was certain you were lost. How did you escape?"

"With my weapon," Leeli answered, holding up the whistleharp. "Mama, I think we can beat the Bat Fangs."

"In the words of Badly Bunsome, 'How?'" said Oskar as he arrived with the First Book under one arm.

"Take me to the roof."

"That's my girl," Podo said, giving Leeli her crutch. "Make way for Batwhacker!"

They raced up the winding library stairs, past books and wounded Hollowsfolk, past the librarian who drifted in and out of the shadows offering help to whomever needed it, and to the door that led to the roof. Several guards, including Danniby and Rudric, held it shut against the pounding of Bat Fangs outside.

"Leeli! I'm glad you're safe," Rudric said with a weary smile as she approached the door. "What are you doing?"

"Fighting back," Leeli said. Something in her voice kept them from asking further questions, and the big men parted so she could stand in front of the door. She took a deep breath and played "Bog of the Bark Owl" with all the emotion she could muster. The pounding on the door ceased, and after a pause the Bat Fangs outside loosed a chilling screech.

Rudric smiled grimly. "Thank the Maker for the Jewels of Anniera," he said, drawing his warhammer from his belt. "Play on, girl."

Rudric threw open the door and rushed into the sunlight. Danniby and a stream of Hollish warriors followed. Leeli and Podo stepped onto the roof and beheld the blue sky and bright sun, and Leeli's music poured into the air over Ban Rona.

The mist burned away and the Bat Fangs scattered before the song as if a terrible wind drove them.

23

The Batwhacker of Ban Rona

Leeli was surrounded by armed men and women, all with their backs to her. The air was fraught with the smells of sweat and fire, the sounds of war and striving. She leaned on her crutch and played, dreading the end of every tune because whenever the music stopped the Bat Fangs fought harder.

Thorn O'Sally later said that from the Guildling Hall it appeared as if the roof of the Great Library had vanished in a cloud of wings. He said that the music seemed to draw the Fangs—"like how you grab yer leg when it's bit by a dog"—as if the enemy knew the battle was lost if they couldn't stop the Song Maiden.

Leeli played for hours. She stood in the center of that bladed, bellowing ring of Hollish protection and played every song she knew. Nia knelt beside her, one arm around her waist, speaking words of encouragement all the while. Leeli's lips and fingers grew numb, and when her legs gave out after an hour, Nia eased her to the ground and yelled for water. Leeli was desperately thirsty but she didn't want to stop playing long enough to drink.

She heard Rudric above all the others, shouting defiance at the winged army and rousing his people to fight on. Elsewhere in the city, Grey Fangs broke away and rushed toward the song. The Hollowsfolk pursued until the fighting on the ground as well as in the air was centered on the Great Library.

"Play on, Leeli!" Rudric shouted, and on she played, until tears rolled down her cheeks and her lips were chapped to bleeding. She fell into a trance, her fingers plucking strings and drumming the whistleharp's holes for so long that she hardly knew what she was playing anymore. "Topper's Reel," Nia would say, and even if she had played it five times Leeli played it again, though with each repetition the song lost some of its effectiveness.

More than once throughout the day the song connected Leeli with her brothers, and each time she became more aware that it wasn't just Janner and Kalmar in her head, but also that other, brooding presence, the face she couldn't quite see, but which she knew saw her. She shut her eyes and tried to shake the darkness from her mind to no avail. The thing watched her as she played. Her brothers seemed to sense it too, and she came to dread the magic when it came. It exposed her to that other spirit, whom she believed was Gnag the Nameless. The last time it happened, his dark eyes floated from corner of her mind to the center and grew as big as the world—leering, hungering, sinister.

Leeli's hands slipped from the whistleharp, and she felt her insides quiver with exhaustion. *No!* her heart cried, and with the last dregs of her will she held to consciousness and renewed her melody. She forced herself to look back at those eyes, to defy them, and she gained a trickle of joyous strength when they shrank back. She heard Podo's raspy growl nearby: "Take that, ye bug eater! And that!"

Then she heard cries of triumph—Rudric's voice roared with an exuberance born of hard won victory. The warriors surrounding her moved away and she felt the welcome flush of sunlight just before she crumpled into her mother's arms. When she found the strength to open her eyes, she saw, as if in a dream, the exhausted yet happy faces of Hollish men and women cheering.

"Is it over?" Leeli murmured.

"Yes, my brave girl. It's over." Nia kissed Leeli on the forehead and held her tightly. "They've taken to the skies and the sea. Ban Rona stands."

Leeli felt Podo's strong old arms lift her. She felt the familiar bristle of his whiskers against her forehead and the warm musk of his pipe as he carried her from the roof into the warm dimness of the library. The glad shouts faded, and in the halls of the library she saw many Hollowsfolk, both wounded and hale, watching her as she passed. Their eyes were wide with wonder, and they whispered to one another.

By the time Podo bore her down the stairs and out the front doors, the shouts had died away. Throngs of Durgans, clansmen, sword maidens, and chiefs gathered on the war-torn street and watched as Podo lifted her into the first wagon he saw. A boy handed the old man the reins as Nia and Oskar climbed on.

"Hail Leeli!" someone shouted, and as the wagon rolled up the street and away from the Great Library, every soul in the city took up the cry, "For the Hills and the Hollows and the Shining Isle!"

Leeli smiled with the last of her strength, then fell into a deep sleep.

When she woke, she was in her bedroom at Chimney Hill. A single candle burned on the nightstand. She smelled cheesy chowder and bacon, and saw Nia asleep in the chair beside her.

"Mama?" she whispered. Her lips hurt when she spoke. Nia stirred and smiled. Leeli wanted to smile back, but she couldn't. Fresh tears sprang from her eyes and she began to tremble.

She had been dreaming of Gnag the Nameless.

24

Visitors at Chimney Hill

W hat did you see?" Nia asked.

Leeli wasn't sure where to begin. She was still so tired, and her lips were so cracked and swollen that speaking at all was a great effort. She adjusted her pillow and sat up straighter, then winced as she sipped henmeat broth from a wooden spoon.

"I saw Janner and Kal."

"Where are they? Are they safe?"

"Yes—and no. I think. They were with someone else. Or something else." Leeli shook her head, frustrated that she couldn't be more specific. "They were near the Blackwood, but they didn't seem hurt."

Nia was silent as she spooned more broth into Leeli's mouth. "Are they coming home?"

"No. They're going into the forest."

"What? Why?" Nia straightened, as she always did when she was afraid.

"They're going to Throg." Leeli fussed with the covers and averted her eyes. "To find Gnag." When Nia said nothing, she went on, "I think Kal is changing."

"What do you mean, 'changing'?"

"His eyes. They had yellow spots in them. He's afraid he'll go crazy again, like Uncle Artham, so he's going to Throg to find Gnag."

"Fools," Nia said under her breath. "They can't just defeat Gnag. If it was that easy, someone would have done it already. They don't even know what he is."

"We know he's human. Bonifer said so, remember?"

"But what if he's changed too? What if he's melded himself with something? What if he's just another kind of Fang? He's been trying to get you three to Throg all this time, and now they think they can just show up and fight him? They can't do this."

"It's too late. They're going, and Janner asked me to tell you to trust him. He said he had to protect Kal and this was the best way to do it. Kal was going, with or without him, and Janner's the Throne Warden. What else could he do?"

Nia sighed and leaned back in her chair, showing her weariness at last. She stared at the ceiling, thinking hard, perhaps pleading silently with the Maker.

"Mama?"

Nia looked at Leeli, her eyes heavy with grief. "My girl, you were magnificent today. Ban Rona would have fallen without you. But my sons!" Nia's voice broke, and she paused to regain her composure. "Why must the Maker try a mother's heart? I lost my land, my people, my husband— I lost him *twice*. I cannot bear to lose my sons. Do you understand?"

Leeli nodded. "What will you do?"

"I should never have let them out of my sight. All this striving, all this death. A storm swirls around us. For years we've been at its center, and I don't know how much longer I can bear it."

Nia scooted Leeli over to make room on the bed, then pulled the quilt over their legs. Leeli put the bowl on the night stand and settled beside her mother, and the two of them rested in silence until Nia breathed the breath of sleep.

Leeli turned her thoughts to the heavens, and took up her pleading where Nia's left off, praying a blessing of safety on her brothers, who even now walked deeper into darkness with each step.

Strangely, she felt no anger toward Gnag, who had wrought such evil on the world—only pity. And that pity aimed her prayers toward her brothers and their safety.

What could she do? Her leg was twisted by Fangs, and she was only nine years old. She was as weak as a flower. She stroked Nia's hair, as Nia had often stroked hers whenever she was afraid. Then her hand drifted to the whistleharp. If she couldn't go with her brothers into the heart of darkness, she would defend the Hollows. She would play. Her song was all she had, and she would send it skyward as long as she had breath to do so.

Long into the night, the Song Maiden of Anniera practiced fingerings in silence, recalling song after song and arranging them as a warrior might lay out weapons and sharpen blades. If, when the sun rose, the Fangs returned, she would be ready. A slight knock came from the bedroom door, and Podo poked in his head and smiled.

"Trade me places, lass. You have visitors."

Leeli eased out of the bed as Podo slid in beside his daughter. Nia stirred but remained asleep, resting on her father's great chest as she must have as a young girl. Leeli had never seen her mother so weakened, and she had never loved her so much.

"Yer crutch is by the door. Good as new." Podo winked at her. The crutch was carved with her new nickname: Batwhacker. It wasn't a pretty name, but since Podo had come up with it, she approved.

Leeli made her way downstairs in the quiet of the house. She knew there were wounded Hollowsfolk in most of the rooms and didn't want to disturb them. When she reached the bottom floor she heard the murmur of voices and the clink of dishes being cleaned in the kitchen. Oskar stood at the door and smiled when he saw Leeli.

"Leeli! I'm glad you got your rest. It was a day to write about, I say!" He bowed, which made his swoop of white hair flop from his bald head. When he straightened, the white strands stood up like a plume of feathers until he palmed them down again. "Someone is here to see you."

He opened the door and Leeli stepped out into the cold night. First she saw Thorn O'Sally standing beside Kelvey and their father, Biggin. They smiled proudly at her, then stepped aside so she could see beyond them.

Dogs had congregated in the front yard of Chimney Hill—it seemed that every dog in the Hollows had come. They sat at attention, tails wagging furiously, though their faces were grave. Baxter limped forward and barked once. Hundreds of dogs answered with a single *woof.*

Leeli smiled so wide her lips cracked and she grunted with pain. Baxter cocked his head and whined at her in answer. She stepped down from the entrance and moved through the dogs, patting heads and scratching behind ears. There were so many that they made a pool of warmth in the cold night.

"I don't know dogspeak half as well as you, but it was pretty clear they wanted to see you real bad," said Biggin. "They wouldn't leave us be until we marched straight here from the houndry."

"They're waiting for orders," Thorn said.

"And they'll only take them from you, Miss Wingfeather," Kelvey added.

"I don't know what to say." Leeli stood in the sea of dogs and looked to Biggin for help.

"Tell them what they're supposed to do next," he said.

Leeli felt one of the dogs licking her ankle. She knelt down and found Frankle, the rowdy pup. Leeli clapped her hands and he jumped into her arms. She stood up with Frankle as still as a sleeping babe in her arms and looked around at the Houndry Corps, feeling a pleasure that made her proud and humble all at once.

"We fight back," she said. Then she whistle-clicked the same words in dogspeak.

Frankle raised his head and howled with all his might—which wasn't much. The rest of the dogs joined him. Their howls rose into the night and the Hollowsfolk who were awake to hear them were glad.

Beyond the Watercraw and in the crags along the Dark Sea of Darkness, where Bat Fangs and Grey Fangs lurked, the dogs' howls spread through the shadows and planted, for perhaps the first time since they had been Fanged, the seeds of doubt in the Fangs' minds. Doubt that victory was certain. Doubt that the battle was nearly over. Doubt that they would ever be able to topple the defenders of the Green Hollows.

Part Two:

SKREE

Bonifer sped to the library and slumped at the table where he and Madia had spent many long hours together, waiting for her to join him as she usually did. But she never came. The sun set, and he was alone with his books and an empty heart. Full of anger, Bonifer stole to the homes of each of the contenders for the Durga and conspired to make Ortham the target of each warrior's strength. The warriors, thinking it nothing more than sport at Ortham's expense, agreed in hopes that a concerted effort to outwit the young warrior would increase their chance at victory.

On the day of the games, Bonifer watched with secret glee for the humiliation of his friend and anticipated the surety of his union with Madia Wingfeather. The boot was hidden in the hills, the horn blew, and the young men of the Hollows dashed away to find the boot and return it to the field. When after several hours the Hollish men appeared on the horizon in pursuit of the boot holder, it was no surprise that Ortham possessed it. Bonifer was unconcerned, because he could see that his plan was working. From his vantage point it was clear that Ortham was limping and badly wounded. There was no way he could win, especially now, at the finish, when a hundred unwounded men pursued him.

Bonifer saw Madia stand and put a hand to her mouth in fear for Ortham's safety—and then Bonifer understood his folly. For Madia was no ordinary woman, impressed only with victory and strength of limb. She had eyes to see strength of heart and courage, too. And it was courage that drove Ortham, wounded and weary, to the Field of Finley at the last.

Bonifer's minions set upon Ortham with ferocious intent, but they could not wrest the boot from his grasp, for it was love that drove him more than victory. Beneath a heap of strong men, Ortham lay motionless, clinging to the boot that he believed would win Madia's heart. And it did. She raced to the field and kissed his forehead though he had passed from consciousness, and Bonifer knew that he himself had passed from hers. Ortham had won, despite Bonifer's treachery. The warriors who had dealt unfairly with Ortham were silent in their shame and told no one of Bonifer's conspiracy.

So it was that when Ortham was returned to health, he knew not that his friend had betrayed him. Instead, he kept Bonifer close. He included him in his wedding plans. And on the day the princess of Anniera and Ortham Greensmith were wed, Bonifer stood by as Ortham's friend and compatriot.

—from *The Annieriad*

25

The Flabbit's Paw

Three days earlier (while Janner was eating the thirteenth muffin at Chimney Hill) Sara Cobbler and Maraly Weaver stood outside an inn and tavern called The Flabbit's Paw, which was nestled deep in the grimy heart of Dugtown.

An unseasonably warm spring morning had risen upon the land of Skree, and the sun had stirred up swarms of flies, gnats, and snidges, all of which celebrated the new season by biting or stinging every square inch of flesh they could find. They buzzed around horse-drawn carriages and wagons as they rolled past, and descended in droves on the droppings left behind.

The two girls outside the tavern swatted at insects as they talked. Sara Cobbler stood straight and poised; Maraly Weaver slouched, kicking listlessly at the mud. Sara wore a bright blue dress and a cloak with the hood pulled back; Maraly wore dirty leggings and a tattered overshirt. Sara's hair was pulled back in a ponytail; Maraly's hair was stringy and damp. Sara wrinkled her nose at the ever-increasing stench of the warming city; Maraly spat and swallowed a burp. A passing stranger might have thought that proper Sara was buying something from poor Maraly, or that perhaps fierce Maraly was in the process of robbing innocent Sara. But in truth, the two girls were close friends, drawn together by their mutual concern for the occupant of room twelve of The Flabbit's Paw.

"How is he today?" Sara asked.

"The same. Still won't eat much."

"Is he awake?"

"Hard to tell. You know how he is." Maraly picked at her teeth with a twig. "We better get him up. They'll stop serving breakfast soon enough."

Sara followed Maraly into the tavern, ignoring the sullen looks of the patrons who slumped wearily over their tankards or plates of food. The girls climbed the stairs to room twelve and entered without knocking. Artham P. Wingfeather lay on the cot, thrashing in the throes of a nightmare.

"Esben, no," he mumbled. "I'll come back. I'll—"

"Artham," Sara whispered as she sat at the edge of his bed. "Artham, wake up."

"Don't sing the song!" he shrieked as he sat up and looked around wildly. He spread his wings wide and trembled. Then he blinked, saw the girls looking at him with concern, and covered his face with his reddish hands. "I was dreaming."

"It's over. We're here now," Sara said.

"Have a drink," Maraly said. She poured him a mug of water from a pitcher by the bed and handed it to him. "Then we're taking you downstairs for breakfast."

"Thank you, girls. But I'm not hungry." Artham lay back down and stared at the wall. "Not hungry, hot nungry, got notty bungle bee."

At first, Artham's babbling had disturbed Sara, but now she was used to it. He was feeble and harmless when he was like this, but when she looked into his sad eyes she saw that there was someone else in there—someone with a strong voice and no hint of insanity. That was the voice he used when he was sleeping. But ever since the Fork Factory—when he had collapsed to the ground shrieking about a song and someone named Esben—Artham had done little more than babble and dream terrible dreams. All winter long he had lain in bed or paced the room, staring at his reddish claws and weeping.

Maraly said Artham was a Throne Warden of Anniera, and she even seemed sincere when she said it. But Sara had never been sure whether the Shining Isle of Anniera was a real place or just a fairytale people told little children. It sounded too good to be true. Maraly (and Gammon, her adoptive father) claimed that Artham had been captured by Fangs and had been transformed, but instead of turning into a monster he had turned into this strange, majestic bird-like man.

Most astonishing of all, though, was the fact that if their stories were true—if indeed Artham Wingfeather was one of the Wingfeathers from the Shining Isle—then Janner Igiby, whom she had known since the Dragon Day Festival in Glipwood, was also a member of the royal family. He had certainly behaved like a prince, braving the coffin in the Fork Factory in order to enact his plan of escape. There was something in his eyes that had seemed different from the other children, but Sara wasn't sure if it was real or if it was only her imagination.

And yet, at the very mention of the Isle of Anniera, she felt warmth in her bones. As a girl, she had heard Armulyn the Bard sing of it; she had heard her mother and father tell stories of it, and those stories were seeds planted deep inside of her that had grown shoots and green leaves around her heart. Part of the reason she always came here was that Artham reminded her of Janner. And though she hardly dared admit it to herself, she also came because she yearned for the stories about Anniera to be true. Being near Artham Wingfeather helped her to believe.

Yet there he lay in a feathery heap on the bed, blabbing at the wall.

"Come on, then," Maraly said, yanking the pillow from under his head. "I waited on breakfast so I could eat it with you, birdman. They'll stop serving any minute. And I happen to know it's eggs and hogpig steamers today."

"All right, all right," Artham said as he swung his feet to the floor and stretched. When he did, his feathers shook. "Stoggy."

"What?" Maraly asked.

"Eggypigheamers and stog."

Sara and Maraly rolled their eyes at one another as they helped him up. They led him downstairs, trying to ignore the glares of the grungy Dugtowners. Once they were seated at a small table in the corner, the proprietor arrived at the table with his arms folded and resting on his paunch.

"We'll have three breakfast plates, please," Sara said.

"Aye. I bet you will. And who's paying for this?" he growled.

Maraly narrowed her eyes and scowled back. "You know who."

"Well, he'd better. I ain't seen him in two days."

"He's busy defending your city from Fangs, in case you forgot," Maraly said, sneering. "And he won't be too keen if he finds out you've been skimping on the arrangement."

The proprietor and Maraly engaged in a staring match, which Maraly won. Then he shook his head and bumbled off to the kitchen, muttering about freaks and Stranders. Artham ignored the whole business and sat quietly, drumming his fingers on the table and bobbing his head.

"How are the orphans?" Maraly asked.

"Everyone's on edge with the change in the weather," Sara said. "They're worried the Fangs will attack any day."

"Me too." Maraly leaned back in her chair and drew one of her throwing knives, then began cleaning her fingernails with it. "I'll be glad when they do, to be honest. I hate all this waiting around."

"Well, *something's* going to happen. There's no way the Fangs will just let us keep to ourselves for the rest of our lives."

The proprietor arrived and flung their plates down, then marched away without a word. The Flabbit's Paw was as filthy as any other tavern in Dugtown, but Sara had to admit the food was delicious.

Artham poked at his breakfast but didn't eat. Sara filled his fork with food, shivering at the thought that she had probably helped to make that fork in the factory. "Open up," she said, and Artham's jaw fell open. She fed him like a baby, then put the fork in his hand and encouraged him to eat on his own. Maraly tapped him on the shoulder and offered him some water to drink when she wasn't shoveling eggs into her own mouth. For all her gruffness, Maraly was tender when it came to Artham.

Suddenly, a dark figure burst into the tavern. All conversation ceased. Patrons peered at the caped man silhouetted in the light streaming through the door.

With a flourish of his cape, the man leaped into the center of the room, struck a pose, and said, "Aha! Avast! 'Tis I, the Florid Sword, and I seek Maraly Weaver with mine own eyes and noble intent!"

26

Snoot's Livery and Cupcakes

The Dugtowners in the tavern glared at the Florid Sword as Maraly, Sara, and Artham excused themselves. Considering that Artham and Gammon had led the charge against the Fangs and freed Dugtown the previous winter, the residents should have feigned some kindness. But even before the Great War, Dugtown was a villainous hive of scum and wretchery, and nine years of Fang oppression had only made the Dugtowners more hostile.

Sara wished she could handle them the way Maraly did. Maraly seemed right at home, sneering back at anyone who gave her an ill look, her hands drifting to the knives hanging at her belt. Sara only nodded and smiled nervously as she led Artham by the hand. He stared at the floor and shuffled along like an old man, which was good, Sara thought, because at least he was oblivious to all the leering eyes.

"We fly! Aha! Away!" cried the Florid Sword. He swished his blade through the air thrice, then removed his wide-brimmed hat and bowed low. "Resume the consumption of thy eggish scrumption!" He smiled. "I believe I made that word up. And it rhymed! Gleeful are the delights a new day bringeth!"

When Artham and the girls had exited the room, the Florid Sword spun around and marched outside.

"What's wrong?" Maraly asked as they bustled up the street.

"It's Claxton," Gammon said darkly.

Maraly stopped on the front steps. "I ain't going back."

"Don't worry. I won't let him take you. But he *is* your father, and I think it's fair that he at least gets to lay eyes on you before—"

"Before what?" Maraly asked.

"Before I kick him out of Dugtown. I don't trust him. There are Dugtowners who think the Fangs are going to win this war, and they're trying to come out on the right side."

"Spies?" Sara asked.

"Lots of them," Gammon muttered. "It's hard to know who to trust."

"You can trust us," Maraly said, taking Gammon's hand.

He smiled at her, eyes twinkling in the black cloth of his mask as he led her to the left and down Veemin Court. "You can trust me, too."

"You can must treeee!" Artham said with a flap of his wings. He scratched his head. "Trust me. Trust me. Trust *me.*"

Sara took his bird-like hand as Maraly had taken Gammon's, and the four of them turned another corner.

They scooted past Dugtowners leading goats or carrying baskets of root vegetables, all of whom grunted and grumbled as they passed. Gammon led them uphill for several blocks, past terraced buildings where people lounged out of the upper windows and gabbed with one another, occasionally hurling a shoe or a handful of food out of anger or plain mischief.

Outside a place called Snoot's Livery and Cupcakes, a small crowd had gathered and was harassing two Kimeran warriors who stood stoically at the doorway with their hands folded over their sword hilts. The crowd was made up of Stranders. Sara could tell by the smell—and by the matted hair, the harshness of their voices, the knives, and the clouds of flies.

"Maketh space!" Gammon said, resuming his Florid Sword voice. "Widen now the area betwixt the doorish entry and thy boorish haunch! Passeth we must!"

The Stranders turned their straggly, warty, lumpy, sickly faces to the man in black and sneered.

The Florid Sword gripped the edge of his cape, raised his chin defiantly, then flung aside the cape and drew his sword. "Fight me," he said, waving them forward with his other hand. "I beg thee. It would happify my morning."

"Is that Maraly Weaver?" one of the Stranders asked.

"It is!" shrieked one of the women—at least, Sara *thought* it was a woman. The beetles in her whiskers made it hard to tell. "Don't ye recognize me, Maraly? It's yer sweet fourth-aunt-cousin on the Weaver side! Cousin Poggy!"

"Aye, I know you." Maraly folded her arms. "And you may be my fourth-aunt-cousin, but I ain't no relation to you anymore. I belong to Gammon now."

"Who's *Gammon?*" Poggy sneered.

Gammon cleared his throat before Maraly could answer. He waggled his sword in the Stranders' faces, and they hissed in answer. "Claxton Weaver's in charge of the lot of you, is he not? He asked to parlay with the Florid Sword, and the Florid Sword am I. Behold, my volage."* He thrust out his chest so they could examine the "F" and "S" stitched in scarlet thread.* "It behooves you to let us pass, and to leave my men alone. Avast!"

"Thank you, my lord," said one of the guards with a nod as the Stranders backed away. "Weaver is inside."

Gammon eyed the Stranders as he held the door for Sara, Maraly, and Artham. Inside the livery and cupcakery were several more guards whose attention was fixed on the back door. Sara followed Gammon through the store, the floor of which was covered with hay, manure, and baking flour. She made a mental note not to try any of the cupcakes.

*volage: n. from the Old Gullish "vullidge," which means "symbol on a hero's chest, for use of identification, propaganda, and marketing."

The back of the building looked more like a barnyard than a store, out of place in the middle of town. There was a hayloft, where several Stranders sat with their legs dangling over the edge. On the left was a stall containing a few goats and on the right was a stone oven where a short, fat woman was removing a tray of piping hot cupcakes. The Kimeran guards moaned with pleasure at the aroma.

But everyone's attention was aimed toward a table in the center of a small, cobbled courtyard where horses or cows were normally kept. A group of men and women sat around the table, some of whom looked almost as dirty as the Stranders, and others of whom looked like the displaced wealthy class from Torrboro. Slouching in a chair at the head of the table was a large, hairy man whose odor spread throughout the room and made the occupants ill.

"Stay close," Gammon whispered.

Maraly squeezed his hand. Artham followed in silence without paying much attention to anything but his feet.

When Claxton Weaver heard them approach, he leapt to his feet. His beard spilled out over his chest in a series of matted locks that wriggled with the occasional insect or worm. His eyes were fierce and flat, as if he were always angry and hadn't the brains to know why nor the heart to care. He was dressed in rags and his boots were muddy, but he was no beggar. His frame was fearsome and his chest broad. He looked like he could break the table in two, and the men and women seated there seemed to know it.

"Maraly!" he roared. Sara saw a flash of hot rage flicker in his eyes before his face contorted with what was supposed to be joy. Since Claxton Weaver had no idea what joy was, however, he mainly looked sick. His voice was as dark and grating as a ship's keel scraping the stony bottom of the River Blapp. "I never thought I'd see ye again!"

"Aye," Maraly said, peeking out from behind Gammon. "And I never *wanted* to see you again."

"It's time ye came home, lass." Claxton tilted his head and smiled a rotten smile. "We've missed ye so."

"I *am* home. And you stopped being my father the minute you locked me in that cage."

"Perhaps," said Gammon in his Florid Sword voice, "We should sit and affect a discourse with our mouths before our fists commenceth toward bashery."

Claxton dragged his gaze from Maraly and set it on the Florid Sword. "I don't know what ye said, but I think ye mean we should talk."

Claxton sat down and the chair creaked under his weight. Gammon moved to the opposite side of the table. He sat, and Maraly stood behind him, staring warily at Claxton, her head just higher than Gammon's shoulder.

"I want to know who this Gammon fellow is, and why he thinks he can steal my daughter," said Claxton. "Me sweet daughter, whom I love like a bucket of glipperfish." It was clear that he meant it as the highest compliment.

"All you need to know is that Gammon cares very much for Maraly," said the Florid Sword evenly. "He would die for her."

Claxton narrowed his eyes at Gammon. "I've heard of you, you know. 'The Florid Sword,' who fights the Fangs in the dead of dark. You caused a fair piece of trouble. The lizards would love to see you flayed."

"The feeling is felt with mutualness, I assureth thee!" Gammon said. "You asked us to meet you here, and we agreed because we in the war council," he indicated the men and women on either side, "want to know whether or not thou shalst pledge your Stranders to our glorious cause. A battle brews, and will soon boil over the pot. The Skreeans— of whom you are one, Strander though you be—welcome any allies they can muster."

"The Stranders will do as I say—the whole lot of 'em, since I'm king of the East Bend as well as the Middle and West, now." Claxton grinned and pulled his pone from his pocket (a gold medallion) along with two others (a silver ball and a baby's shoe). "Got their pones just before the battle." He leaned forward and stared at Maraly while he spoke. "And I'll order them to fight the Fangs. But only on one condition. You tell that Gammon fella that my girl don't belong to him. She's *mine*."

"I thought Maraly didst already maketh that clear," the Florid Sword said. "Thou hast forfeited thy right to fatherhood. Some might say you forfeited your right to freedom." Gammon stood and put a hand on his sword hilt. The more he spoke, the less he sounded like the Florid Sword. "We have jails, you know. And the members of this council have agreed to act as a court. Should we proceed in that manner, or will you leave the business with Maraly alone?"

Claxton stood. The members of the council, who looked strong and capable enough, exchanged nervous glances. Claxton balled one of his fists and held it in Gammon's face. "I swear on the Strand and Growlfist's mammy that I'll have my daughter back, Florid Sword. I'll get her either way. The question for you is this. Do you want my Standers to fight for Dugtown or not? If so, you've got this one chance to give me that girl. Otherwise, we'll make ourselves scarce."

"You would really fight alongside the Fangs of Dang?" Gammon asked with a shake of his head.

"We'll fight for whoever's winning."

"I brought Maraly here because I deemed it fair for you to have a chance to say goodbye. I hoped you would see that she is well loved and cared for, that you would be grateful at least that she has a home."

"I ain't going back," Maraly said. Her voice trembled. "I don't want to be a Strander no more."

Claxton's face was set like stone. A bug skittered across his beard and burrowed between the whiskers again. From where Sara stood, she could see Claxton's dark eyes. She studied them, looking for some glimmer of compassion, but it was like staring into the muddy river.

Gammon backed away from the table and moved Maraly behind him. The council members stood and drew their swords, forming a protective ring around Gammon and the girl. The guards in the livery drew their weapons and advanced on Claxton. Artham, to Sara's relief, looked sane. He watched the proceedings with a steady gaze.

"You won't fight for Dugtown, then?" Gammon asked.

"Not without my daughter."

"Then I should put you under arrest, Claxton Weaver, for treachery and sedition. I ought to put you under arrest for being a terrible father, too, but I suppose that falls under the treachery category." Gammon removed his mask and tossed it on the table. "My name is Gammon, and if you want this girl you'll have to kill me to get her. Stand back, Maraly." She backed against the wall and Gammon drew his sword.

Claxton surprised them all by rearing back and shaking with laughter. When his laughter faded, he turned around and suddenly had a long, jagged knife in each hand. The Stranders in the loft hissed and flashed their knives. Artham yanked a dagger of his own from one of the guard's scabbards. The council members, Gammon, and all the rest edged closer to Claxton, whose laughter had subsided into a menacing chuckle. Sara backed away, wishing she could grab Maraly's hand and escape before the fight began.

But there was no fight. Claxton bared his yellow teeth and laughed again, then turned his back on Gammon. At once, Claxton relaxed and snapped his daggers back into his belt as the Stranders in the loft rolled out of sight.

"This was easier than I thought it would be. I'll be going now," Claxton said. "Try and arrest me if you like."

"I don't ever want to see you in Dugtown again." Gammon nodded and the confused guards parted so Claxton could pass.

As he stomped toward the door Claxton scowled at Artham and muttered, "Freak."

When the livery door slammed shut, everyone breathed a sigh of relief and turned back to Gammon.

"What was that all about?" one of the councilmen asked.

"I don't know," said Gammon. "Maraly, are you all right?"

But no one answered.

Maraly was gone.

27

Villainous Wretchery

"Maraly!" Gammon cried. "Maraly!" He frantically searched the area, banging on walls and kicking at every crack in the floor. "Sara, did you see anything?"

"No sir," Sara said, her voice thick with fear.

"Is there a Strander burrow here?" Gammon shouted.

"Not that I know of," answered Snoot, the proprietor. He was a paunchy, bald man with large sideburns hanging from his jowls like saddlebags. "I've only lived here a few years, but I never heard of one, I swear it!"

"If you're lying I'll have you in the dungeon," Gammon snapped. Snoot held his hands up and trembled. Gammon tipped the table over and kicked at the boards beneath it, looking for a seam in the floor. "Everyone, look for an entrance—a trigger they might use to open the door. *Something.*" Gammon threw a chair aside and poked his sword at the dirty floor. "Blast! That's why Claxton insisted on meeting here. I should have known."

"They're gone, sir," said one of the guards, bursting in from outside. "As soon as Weaver left the building, they all split up and vanished."

"Come on, Sara. I'll need two sets of eyes," Artham said. Sara looked up at him, surprised to hear him speaking in such a steady voice.

He took her by the hand and led her out to the street, then lifted her into his arms and leapt into the air. Sara gasped as Artham beat his wings and they rose over the gray rooftops of Dugtown.

He circled the neighborhood and the two of them scanned the crowds for any sign of Claxton or his Stranders. The problem was that the average Dugtowner was almost as grungy as a Strander; it was impossible to tell them apart from above. No one in the streets seemed to be in much of a hurry, and the only time Sara could see anyone's face was when they happened to glance up at the strange birdman flying above them.

Artham flew to one of the torch towers and set Sara down. "Do you see anything?" he asked as he leaned out over the edge and scanned the streets.

"Nothing," Sara said. She had heard of Strander burrows but was astonished that Claxton had been able to snatch Maraly from right under their noses. "Where would they take her?"

"I don't know. Back to the East Bend?" Artham said.

"But there's nothing out there," Sara said. "And he knows Gammon will send more troops to get her back. Unless . . . "

Sara and Artham had the same thought. Their gaze drifted away from Dugtown and across the River Blapp to the city of Torrboro. Even from this distance, they could see Fangs teeming along the riverfront.

"He's going to join the Fangs," Artham said.

"He won't hurt her, will he?" Sara asked, tears filling her eyes.

Artham didn't answer.

"What do we do?"

Artham lifted Sara into his arms again. "We get her back."

He stepped off the edge of the tower and they glided back down to the livery, where Gammon was still shouting. The guards outside shifted around uneasily, unsure of what to do and fearful of the wrath of their leader. Artham and Sara entered and found Gammon in the courtyard, beating on the oven with his sword.

"Someone had to see something!" he bellowed. "Bring me the owner." The guards dragged Snoot over. Gammon leaned in close and stared him down. "Where's the entrance?" he asked.

"I don't know, I swear it," blubbered Snoot.

"What's your name?" Gammon asked.

"My name's Lazron Snoot, like the sign says, and I don't know a thing, sir."

Gammon punched him in the stomach. "Where's Maraly?"

The man doubled over and gasped for breath, pleading for Gammon to stop. It was obvious to Sara that the poor fellow knew nothing.

"Gammon, don't," said Artham. "Hardly anyone knows where the Strander burrows are."

Gammon ignored Artham and jerked the man upright again. He grabbed the scruff of his shirt and pulled him close. "Tell me!"

Seeing Gammon so angry frightened Sara, and tears sprang to her eyes. She had seen him behave nobly in battle, and she had seen his tenderness towards Maraly. She knew he was better than this. "Please," Sara said. The guards and councilmen watched in silence as Gammon shoved the livery owner against the wall. "Gammon, don't!" Sara shouted. "He doesn't know anything. It's Claxton you should be angry at!"

Gammon ignored her. He pinned Lazron to the wall with one hand and with the other drew his sword. Sara ran forward and grabbed Gammon's arm.

"Get back, Sara," Gammon said. He pried his arm out of her grip. "This is between me and Lazron Snoot."

"Artham, do something!" Sara cried.

Snoot blubbered like a toddler. Artham took a step forward as Gammon hefted his sword and narrowed his eyes at Snoot. Sara hid her face.

"Gammon," Artham said.

Gammon raised his blade. "This is your last chance, Snoot," he said through gritted teeth.

Snoot's face went pale, and he pointed at the goatpen. "The trigger's there," he said. "At the base of the gate."

Sara looked up in shock.

"Thank you," Gammon said. He shoved the man into the arms of the guards. "Have him thrown in the jail to await trial by the council."*

Gammon inspected the goat pen's gate and toed aside a little pile of dirt, exposing a tiny wooden lever and the mechanism that concealed the hole with fresh sand. He stepped on it, and dirt drained through a rectangular seam in the dusty floor. The trapdoor swung open, revealing a ladder that descended into darkness.

Gammon pulled Sara gently to her feet. "I'm sorry you had to see that, Sara. But this is Dugtown. You can't trust anybody. I have to go. Artham, I could use your help."

"Of course," Artham said.

Sara watched Gammon climb down the ladder, then Artham gave her a quick smile, folded his arms and wings, and dropped into the hole. Sara prayed that they would bring Maraly home before Claxton could hurt her; she also prayed that Artham would stay sane long enough to help.

What else could she do?

She righted a chair that Gammon had kicked over and sat near the trapdoor. She couldn't stop thinking of Maraly being dragged through those dark tunnels—probably to Torrboro and the Fangs. She didn't know which was worse, the Fangs or the Stranders. It didn't take her long to decide that Claxton Weaver was worse than a hundred Fangs, at least to Maraly. It was one thing to hate humans and want to enslave them because Gnag the Nameless told you to. It was another to want to cage your own daughter.

Poor Maraly, Sara thought. The man who should have loved her most had betrayed her. What would that do to one's heart? Her own parents were long gone, probably killed by the Fangs soon after the Black Carriage had taken her. It would be better to lose your father to death, knowing he loved you to the end, than to have your father hate you while he lived.

---

* In the years following the war, Lazron Snoot reformed his ways and expanded his livery and cupcakery business to include free dancing lessons for the less fortunate. Whenever a child in Dugtown was seen dancing, it was not uncommon to overhear the remark, "But for Snoot, that boy would just be picking his nose." Snoot's Livery, Cupcakery, and Jiggery expanded to include locations in Torrboro and Bylome as well.

But Gammon loved Maraly; Sara knew that. And Maraly knew it too. Maybe in that black tunnel, the light of Gammon's love would keep Maraly company.

"Queen Sara?" Sara looked up to discover Borley, her little ally from the Fork Factory, standing with a tray of food and a cup of something warm. "I looked for you at the inn, but they said you were here. Are you hungry?"

"Borley," Sara said. "I *am* hungry, thank you."

She took the tray and realized with the first whiff of the butterberry roll that it was past lunchtime. Borley sat cross-legged at her feet, looking first at her then at the opening in the floor. "What's that?"

"The entrance to a Strander burrow," she said after a sip of hot cider. "The Stranders kidnapped Maraly."

Borley stared at the hole as if a Fang might pop out at any moment. "How are the orphans?" she asked.

"Good," Borley said, still staring at the hole. "Sort of. That's why I came to find you."

"What's wrong?" she asked.

"We're out of room."

"There was plenty of space just yesterday."

"I know, Your Highness." Sara had tried to keep the orphans from referring to her as their queen, but they had politely ignored her requests so long that she had grown weary of resisting. "But a man showed up with more. A lot more. I don't know what to do, Queen Sara."

Sara sighed. She wasn't doing Maraly any good just sitting around, and it would be nice to have something to do. Gammon's guards were stationed in the livery and cupcakery, and they were better equipped to help if help was needed. Besides, if Artham and the Florid Sword couldn't find Maraly, no one could.

"All right. Do you know the man who brought all these children?"

"Of course I know him," Borley said with a smile. "He's Armulyn the Bard."

28

Groaches in the Sewer

ome on, girl," the Strander growled. "Stop kicking or I'll teach you what boots are for."

Maraly had been in the livery, watching Gammon from behind, proud that he was her guardian—then a hand had clamped over her mouth and dragged her into darkness.

It happened so fast and so silently that she was too shocked to scream or struggle. Then this Strander, a man she didn't know, had thrust his shadowy face into hers and whispered, "Make a sound and you'll rue it." Maraly knew that Stranders didn't make empty threats.

He had jerked her to her feet, put an arm around her neck, and dragged her through the tunnel for ten minutes before he let go. As soon as he did she had sprung. She punched him in the neck, then ran back the way they had come.

But the Strander was quick. He was vicious, too. He tackled her to the ground, produced a rope, and moments later she was bound like a ratbadger and gagged. He took her knives, too. Well, he took all but the ones hidden in her boots and the folds of her clothing. Still, those would do her no good if her hands were tied.

The Strander had thrown her over his shoulder and was now trotting through the burrow, grunting with effort and whacking Maraly from time to time to keep her from squirming. Her ankles were tied, too—but she could kick.

"I said stop kicking!" the Strander shouted. He heaved her off his shoulder and she slammed onto the cold, wet ground. It knocked the wind out of her and tears leaked from her eyes. She bit down on the gag and curled into a ball, waiting for the boot he had promised. The ropes around her wrists were so tight she had little hope of getting to one of her knives.

"Easy, Wonkin," said a voice Maraly knew well. "You wouldn't want to be guilty of hurting the Strander King's daughter, would you?"

"Eh? No, my lord," said Wonkin. "But she's feisty, she is."

"Of course she is. She's me daughter."

Maraly opened her eyes and saw her father by the light of a lantern. He stepped forward, as big as a troll, and shoved Wonkin against the wall. Then Claxton leaned over and pushed Maraly onto her back. He pinned her to the ground with one of his massive hands and looked at her. She saw his muddy eyes glistening in his muddy face, his matted beard dangling over her like moss.

"Maraly. How I've missed you." He stared at her for a sickening moment, then pried the gag out of her mouth. "There. Now you can tell me how much you've missed me too."

"I hate you," Maraly said. She didn't care what he did to her. Her time with Gammon and the Wingfeathers had taught her what family was supposed to look like, and this wasn't it. She didn't want to be a Strander any more than she wanted to be a toothy cow.

Claxton smiled at her words, his rotten teeth made all the more hideous by the shadows. "I hated my father too," he said. "You're upholding the finest of Strander traditions. Well done. Wouldn't you say, my friends?"

From nooks and clefts in the tunnel more Stranders slinked forth, hissing and chuckling. Poggy, the one who had been outside Snoot's Livery and Cupcakery, cackled and clapped her hands.

"What do you want with me?" Maraly scooted back against the wall and sat up. "I'll never fight for you."

"I know that, my sweet girl," said Claxton. "I came to protect you."

"Protect me from what? I was fine with Gammon."

"Is that what you think?" Claxton sneered. "Could Gammon protect you from the Fangs of Dang?"

"He's not afraid of them. Or of you."

"Well he should be. They're coming." Claxton folded his arms. "Tonight, in fact."

"What do you mean?" Maraly said.

"They're crossing the Blapp. We've got troops of them already smuggled into the city. And when they crush Dugtown, they've promised to make me the king. Not just the king of the Strand, mind you." Claxton raised a fist into the air. "The king of Dugtown!"

The Stranders cheered and Claxton growled like a wild animal. He punched Wonkin in the gut, seemingly for the fun of it. Wonkin fell to the ground, gasping for breath, and to Maraly's disgust lay there cheering for Claxton all the louder, along with all the other Stranders.

Tears burned in her eyes as she thought of her months in Gammon's care, her friend Sara, and the few moments of peace she had experienced in her short life. She wanted to go home—and the word "home" conjured up not a place but the smiling faces of the Wingfeathers, of Gammon, and of Sara Cobbler and Artham.

There were times in Kimera and Dugtown when Maraly had pined for the freedom and wildness of the Strand, when the clothes they made her wear chafed and the thrill of thievery called to her. But she had slowly come to cherish the safety of Gammon's fatherly affections. She had never really understood until now how wicked her life among the Stranders had been, and the thought of going back made her ill. She wished she could peel off her skin, rid her blood and bones of any relation she had to Claxton, and clothe herself forever with Gammon's name and nobility.

Maybe Claxton was telling the truth. Maybe the Fangs would invade and kill every Skreean in Dugtown. Maybe Claxton would be the king. But she would rather die fighting with her friends than sit in victory with the Stranders.

Before the tears reached her eyes she pushed them back down. They would do her no good if she spent them here.

"Gammon will come for me," Maraly said.

"I hope he does," Claxton replied with a shrug. "Not only will I get to kill him, but he'll leave Dugtown without a leader. That will make it even easier for the Fangs."

"Claxton," Poggy said, "we should make feet for Torrboro while there's time."

"I know that," Claxton snapped. He towered over Maraly with his fists on his hips. "Keep her tied. She thinks she ain't one of us, but she'll learn. Get her, Wonkin."

Wonkin picked himself up from the floor, then heaved Maraly over his shoulder again. This time she didn't struggle. With this many Stranders about, she knew there was no hope of escape. She had to wait. She had to keep still until the right moment. Then she'd find a way to warn Gammon that the Fangs were coming.

The Stranders followed Claxton, creeping through the twists and turns of the burrow like groaches in a sewer.

29

A Moon in the Dark

Sara hurried through Dugtown with Borley at her side, feeling less safe than she had in months. It was as if everyone she saw was a Strander in disguise, as if every wall or trashbox or alleyway was in fact the entrance to a burrow into which anyone could be abducted at any moment. As if the Fangs on the other side of the Blapp weren't dangerous enough, now Gammon said there were spies and treachers right here in Dugtown.

Sara and Borley passed the Flabbit'sPaw, then made their way up Grimppity Avenue to the barracks where Sara's orphans stayed.

The building had once been a linen factory called Thimble Thumb's Threads. Fangs had made a wreck of the place in the years after the invasion, but the orphans had made quick work of cleaning it out and cutting sheets and blankets from the piles of discarded linen in the basement. The children were well used to hard work in the Fork Factory, and had been so desperate for a place to call their own that in a week's time Thimble Thumb's had been transformed into the coziest spot in Dugtown.

As Sara climbed the front steps she heard singing inside—this wasn't unusual, except that the children's voices were now accompanied by the soaring melody of a whistleharp skillfully played. Borley smiled at Sara and opened the door.

There were dirty faced children everywhere, sitting on the floor, lying in their bunks, perched in the rafters like thwaps, all entranced by a scruffy looking character with long dark hair and bare feet. He stood in the center of the crowd with his back to Sara, swaying with the song and bobbing his head.

Sara's orphans, scattered among the others, exclaimed, "Queen Sara!" They rushed forward, all of them talking at once. She hushed them, smiling at their joy, and turned her attention to the man now bowing to her.

"So this is your queen," he said with a smile. "It's an honor to meet you, Your Highness."

"Armulyn the Bard. It's really you," she said with a curtsy. "I heard you sing at the Dragon Day festival in Glipwood. When I was little."

"Ah, Glipwood," he said. His voice was a bit raspy, but kind and quick. "The people there were more blessed than they knew. Not everyone in Skree gets to hear the dragons sing, you know. It could wake the Annieran in all of us, couldn't it?"

"I suppose so." Sara realized she was only agreeing because she was nervous. "Actually I don't really know what you mean."

"Tell me, Queen Sara," Armulyn said, "what do you remember about the Dragon Day festival?"

The orphans pressed in closer and sat on the floor as quiet as a field of totatoes.

Sara forced her mind back to the Dragon Day festival when she had first heard Armulyn sing of the Shining Isle. "I remember *you*," she said with a nervous laugh. "I remember the Fangs slinking around like they always did. I remember the summer moon coming up as the sun went down." Sara shrugged, suddenly feeling foolish. "I don't know."

"What do you remember *feeling*?" he asked. "How did the Fangs make you feel?"

"Frightened." Sara closed her eyes. "Very frightened. I was little."

"And what about my songs?"

"Well, they made me feel sad. But a good kind of sad—the kind you feel when you're happiest. They made my heart . . . hungry."

"And the sea dragons?" Armulyn asked. "What about their songs?"

"I don't know how to put it," Sara said. "But they made me feel like I could see better—farther, for a thousand miles. And closer, too, like I could count the veins in a butterfly's wing."

"Did the music make you brave?"

"Yes sir," Sara said. "Brave and—homesick."

"Exactly," said Armulyn, smiling at the children. "That's just how an Annieran would feel if she were in exile, on the wrong side of the Dark Sea of Darkness. *That's* what I mean when I say the dragons could make anyone feel like an Annieran."

Sara held up her hand, as if she were in school and the bard was the teacher. "But does that mean *you're* Annieran? Everybody used to wonder about it."

"Maybe." Armulyn winked.

Sara looked around at all the new faces. "Where did all these children come from?"

"All over," Armulyn answered.

Why did his answers all have to be so vague? "All over *where*?"

"All over everywhere. I've been traveling, you see. Last summer I saw something—someone—and I've spent the last year out beyond the edges of the maps, spreading the news."

"What news?"

Armulyn the Bard's face beamed. "That the Jewels of Anniera are alive. That Gnag, hard as he tried, could not quench the light. The news that the dawn is coming."

"Are you talking about Janner?" Sara asked, unable to conceal a smile. Artham had told her that Janner was the Throne Warden of Anniera. She even believed him, though all this talk about the Shining Isle still struck her as wishful thinking.

"Janner Wingfeather, yes," said Armulyn with surprise. "The first-born. Then you've heard? The Skreeans know about the rising hope?"

"I don't know about all that," Sara said. "The Skreeans don't care much about Annieran legends—except when *you* sing about them, I guess. They're more worried about the Fangs than anything. And to be honest, I feel the same. The Stranders took my friend Maraly this morning, the Fangs will attack someday, and there aren't enough weapons in Dugtown to go around. I'm sorry, but the Shining Isle is a long way from here." Sara looked down. "So is Janner."

"That doesn't mean it isn't true. The Shining Isle exists as surely as the floor you're standing on. It may be hard to believe, but it's *real*, I tell you. Sometimes in the middle of the night, the sun can seem like it was only ever a dream. We need something to remind us that it still exists, even if we can't see it. We need something beautiful hanging in the dark sky to remind us there is such a thing as daylight. Sometimes, Queen Sara"—Armulyn strummed his whistleharp—"music is the moon."

Something in his voice, some light behind his weary eyes, worked a kind of magic on Sara's heart. "You never told me where the children came from," she said.

"You wouldn't believe how beautiful the country is, out beyond the maps." Armulyn's eyes gleamed with wonder. "Plains and mountains and lakes and deserts—everything. And the animals! So many creatures!"

"Do people live there, too?" Sara asked.

Armulyn lowered his voice so the orphans wouldn't hear. "Not anymore. The Fangs had ravaged every settlement I found. These are the ones who escaped. I drew them out of hiding with my music and had no choice but to take care of them. As we wandered the land we found more and more. From Farrowmark to Dunwarg the poor souls had been scrounging for food since their families had been taken. Blast those Fangs."

Sara noticed a few of Armulyn's orphans had tears in their eyes. "Children," she said loudly so all could hear. "Welcome to our little kingdom in Thimble Thumb's Threads! My name is Sara."

"Queen Sara!" one of her orphans cried, pumping a fist in the air.

"Our home is your home, and your home is here. We have food, beds, and friendship to offer. Borley, will you and Chug show our new friends around and help them find bunks?" Once the children were busy, Sara turned to Armulyn. "Let's talk outside."

They stood near the front steps of the threadery, watching the Dugtowners on the street bustle by. More than once, one of them recognized Armulyn and shouted a greeting.

"Do you know where the Fangs come from?" she asked.

"I have my suspicions."

"They come from people. That's why the Fangs have always kidnapped Skreeans—they're turning us into Fangs. There's this lady the Fangs call the Stone Keeper, and she uses some creepy old rock to change you. I don't understand it all, but Artham said they torture you until you *want* it, or it won't work."

Armulyn stared at Sara with his mouth hanging open.

Sara giggled. "What?"

"Did you say Artham? As in, Artham *Wingfeather*?"

Sara laughed again. "Yes. He's in the burrows under the city looking for Maraly now."

"First Janner, now Artham Wingfeather, the Throne Warden of Anniera! A legend running around under Dugtown." The bard seemed like a little boy. "You're a moon in the dark, Sara Cobbler."

30

Into the Burrows

Gammon and Artham sped through the tunnel. Gammon had heard about Strander burrows, but he had never before been in one. He was shocked by how expansive they were, how many dead ends, how many forks—and not just forks to the left and right, but also tunnels that went either up or down. He had imagined such tunnels formed a grid that followed the streets, more or less, but now he realized they were more like an ant's nest, an intricate maze.

It was dark, too, but luckily, they had come upon a stash of lanterns, matches, and oil near the foot of a ladder. While Gammon lit a lantern, Artham climbed the ladder and felt the trapdoor at the top for a latch.

Gammon was amazed at the change that had come over Artham. Gone was the stuttering, blubbering talk, the childlike look on his face. Now his eyes were steady and his aspect fierce. "What are you doing?" Gammon asked.

"I want to see where we are. It'll help to get our bearings." There was a quiet click, then the trapdoor fell open. Artham poked his head through and Gammon heard a scream. "Sorry," Artham said. "Sorry to interrupt." He flinched as a frying pan flew over his head and crashed into something.

Gammon heard a woman shouting, "Out! Out with you! How did you get into my floor? Get away!"

Artham slammed the trapdoor shut and hurried down the ladder. "They were having lunch," he said.

"Well, at least we know they didn't go up that way," Gammon said.

They hurried through the tunnels, Gammon swinging the lantern at the floor to inspect every possible sign of Maraly's passing. They followed a set of tracks for a while before several sets footprints split and led in three different directions. "This is no good," Gammon said, banging a fist into the wall. "We'll never find her in here."

Artham dropped to a crouch and looked down each tunnel in turn. "Hold on. Let me listen." He shut his eyes and held still. His ears seemed to move at every drip of water, every slight sound that echoed in the burrow. His nostrils flared, and his head twitched like a hawk's surveying the ground for its prey. The tips of his wings draped lightly across the ground behind him. Artham Wingfeather might be crazy, thought Gammon, but he was a magnificent creature.

Artham's eyes snapped open. "This way." He said, and darted down the tunnel on the left.

"Is it them?" Gammon said from behind.

"Maybe," Artham said. "It's someone, at least."

Gammon raced after Artham, turning left and right, up inclines, down ramps, through tunnels large as a house or so small they had to crawl in the mud, until finally Artham drew up short and stopped so abruptly that Gammon bumped into him. Gammon tried his best to control his breathing so he could detect whatever it was Artham heard.

There was no fork, only the tunnel stretching on into darkness before them. Artham took a step backwards, then another. Then his arm shot into a recess in the wall that Gammon hadn't noticed, and he yanked a filthy woman into the lantern light. She was covered in dirt from head to toe and blended perfectly into the walls of the burrow.

She hissed and struggled, and Gammon caught sight of the glint of steel in one of her hands. Artham slammed her into the opposite wall and the dagger fell to the floor. The woman bared her yellow teeth and snapped at Artham like a wild animal. Gammon set the lantern on the floor and helped pin her to the wall, wondering how many other Stranders they had passed without knowing it.

"Let me go!" she shrieked.

"We'll let you go when you tell us where Claxton Weaver is," Artham said.

She smiled wickedly. "Never."

"No?" Artham said. He flexed his claws, spread his wings to their full width and loosed his most terrifying hawkish scream. The woman's eyes shot open so wide that Gammon almost laughed.

"He went that way." The woman pointed a trembling hand down the tunnel. "Bear to the right at the first fork, then down at the next three. Turn left and climb the ladder. That's where they're meeting, or so I heard. I hope you catch him. Us in the West Bend never liked him besides." She grinned. "See if you can get his pone!"

Artham released her and she dropped to the floor like a pile of rags. He nodded at Gammon and off they ran.

The woman's rattling voice echoed after them: "I'd be quick! There ain't much time!"

"What does that mean?" Gammon asked. Artham didn't answer, but the two men ran faster. Gammon had a difficult time keeping up. All he saw was those fluttering wings in the yellow lamplight ahead of him and occasional glimpses of Artham's white hair.

"Duck!" Artham shouted, and Gammon just had time to slide beneath a dip in the tunnel ceiling before the two of them tumbled down a steep, muddy slope. They came to a jarring halt at the bottom. Gammon stood and brushed himself off.

"I guess that's the first downward fork," Artham said, peering ahead. "Two more, then a right."

"After you," Gammon said.

They hurried on and soon came to the fork the woman had told them about. They veered right down another tunnel, took the next left turn, and after a stone's throw stood panting at a dead end, craning their necks up at the top of a ladder.

"The question is," Gammon said, "can that woman be trusted?"

"She can't," Artham said with a shake of his head. "But at least we're not wandering aimlessly. If this is a trap, we'll just have to spring it, eh?" He smiled at Gammon as he drew his sword. "Ready?"

"The Florid Sword doth be ready at all moments of timeth," Gammon said wryly. Artham started up the ladder, but Gammon stopped him. "Let me go first. If it's a trap then you can—you know—do your bird thing and fly out. That'll give them a pleasant shock, eh?"

"I like it," Artham said as he stepped aside and flexed his wings.

Gammon handed Artham the lantern and inched his way up the ladder, the top of which disappeared into a narrow shaft well over both their heads. Gammon's shoulders touched both sides, and he had to retreat back down into the open so he could arrange his sword with the point facing upward. He noticed as he climbed that the rungs were soiled with fresh mud. Someone had come this way not long ago.

"Hold on, Maraly," Gammon whispered.

He couldn't see much, but he fumbled around at the edge of the trapdoor until he found the hidden trigger, then paused. He heard footsteps, the creak of floorboards, and muffled speech, but it all seemed to come from another room, so he pulled the little lever and heard a muted click. Gammon held his breath and pushed up the trapdoor.

Light shone through the crack and blinded him momentarily as his eyes adjusted. The room was empty—of feet, at least. He saw the legs of a few chairs, a chest of drawers, and the edge of a blanket hanging a few feet away. He lifted the door enough to get his head out. It was a cozy bedroom. Sunlight beamed through a window and dust motes danced lazily in the glow. Gammon climbed through the trapdoor and snuck into the nearest corner, barely breathing, listening to the voices in the other room. The bed was made, a few reading books rested on the nightstand, and a pair of slippers were tucked under the edge of the bed. Whoever slept in this room was no Strander. Claxton Weaver had never worn a pair of slippers in his life.

When Gammon was certain his entrance was undetected, he knelt by the trapdoor and whispered for Artham. Artham shouldered his way through the opening, losing a few feathers in the process. They floated briefly in the sunlight before settling on the floor, and Gammon smiled as he thought of the mystery those reddish feathers would pose to the owner of the house.

The two men snuck across the room, wincing at every creak of the floorboards. Gammon placed his hand gingerly on the doorknob then raised his eyebrows at Artham, who nodded and readied his sword. Gammon took a deep breath and turned the knob.

The voices in the house fell silent. Gammon and Artham looked at one another in panic, then Gammon flung open the door. The two of them jumped into the room and brandished their swords.

More than twenty Green Fangs looked at them in surprise, then bared their terrible teeth and hissed.

31

Fangs in the Streets

It's him!" one of the Fangs shouted, pointing at Artham. "The one with wingssss! Kill him!"

Gammon stopped in the doorway as the familiar reek of Fang flesh wafted over him. Artham grabbed Gammon's arm and pulled him back into the bedroom just as the Fangs rushed toward them. He slammed the door shut, but it didn't latch, and the onrush of lizards crashed into it so hard the house shook. Artham was thrown to the floor by the impact. Gammon, finding his wits again, jumped forward and held the door until Artham got to his feet.

"How in the Deep did Fangs get into Dugtown?" Gammon shouted. "There are too many of them to fight!"

Artham glanced at the trapdoor, then at the window. The Fangs slammed into the door again. "If we can get outside I might be able to lift you!"

"Go! I'll hold the door!"

With a mad flap of his wings, Artham leaped for the window and crashed through.

The Fangs banged on the door and inched it open, their scaly claws reaching through the crack like a mass of wriggling worms. First a sword then an axe stabbed through the door only inches from Gammon's face. He couldn't hold it much longer. The window seemed impossibly far away, on the other side of the bed. The Fangs shoved the door open another few more inches and Gammon's boots slid across the floor. He pressed his back against the door with all his might, glad to hear shouts of pain as the Fangs' fingers were crushed.

Another blade smashed through the wood, and with a mindless yell Gammon released the door and bounded onto the bed, diving headfirst for the window as the Fangs poured into the room. He soared through the opening and felt Artham's hands on the back of his belt and the collar of his coat as he was lifted into the air. Gammon heard hissing, the splintering of wood, and the furious rush of Artham's beating wings.

Artham strained and flapped and rose slowly over the eaves and then let go, sending Gammon crashing face-first into the roof.

Gammon blinked and shook his head. Where was his sword? Where was Maraly? Where was *he*? He staggered to his feet and climbed to the apex of the roof as the Fangs poured into the street. This shouldn't be so difficult, he thought. The Florid Sword had escaped worse situations than this—but that was always at night, and he always had the advantage of surprise.

Artham alighted next to him and handed him his sword. "You dropped this," he said. "Also, you're heavier than you look."

"It's all brains and muscle," Gammon said.

He tried to ignore the Fangs clambering through the window and into the little back garden as he scanned the rooftops to get his bearings. He knew Dugtown well, and thanks to his night prowling as the Florid Sword, he knew the rooftops of Dugtown better than anyone.

He saw the spires of Castle Torr in the distance, the kitten's tail and ears lifting over the misty river in the south. He spotted several torch towers, the hulk of the Fork Factory to the west, and knew that they had emerged on the eastern end of the city. The bulk of his army was centered near the marketplace at the waterfront, but there were sentries stationed at either end of the city.

So how did so many Fangs make it into Dugtown without being seen? The answer was obvious: Strander burrows. Claxton had been smuggling Fangs into the city for a surprise attack. That was why he had come for Maraly. That was why the woman in the burrow had said there wasn't much time.

One of the Fangs scrambled over the edge of the roof and crouched, blade drawn and fangs bared. Venom dribbled down its chin and steamed on the shingles. Artham waited until the Fang leaped, then spun and easily dispatched the creature with his sword. It tumbled from the roof and landed among its fellow Fangs, its scaly skin already shriveling and crumbling to dust. More Fangs burst from the house and congregated in the back garden as well as the front. Gammon heard shouts and cries of alarm and saw Dugtowners in the streets, shocked at the sight of Fangs in the city again after so many months.

"I suppose it goes without saying," Artham said as he wrinkled his nose at the green Fang blood on his blade, "that you need to get out of here."

"Why's that?" Gammon said with a grin.

"I'd carry you, but all those brains of yours makes it impossible."

Another Fang leapt to the roof and attacked. Gammon parried a blow, planted his boot on the Fang's chest, and sent it flying into its comrades below.

"Wings would be nice about now." Gammon dragged a forearm across his brow and glanced over his shoulder at the line of rooftops stretching back along the north side of the city. He pointed to a two-story house across the street. "Can you get me to that building?"

"I think so," Artham said.

"If you can get me over there, I can manage. Then I need you to fly to the market on the waterfront. Find Errol. Tell him the battle is begun. We need to muster at the market and set up barricades. There's no telling how many Fangs are in the city."

"What about Maraly?" Artham said.

Gammon shook his head. He had no idea how to find her now. Claxton could have taken her anywhere. "I'll find her. But finding her will make no difference if we lose the city. Ready?"

Just as two more Fangs scrambled onto the roof, Gammon saw something that made his heart lurch. Across the street a door flew open and another company of Fangs streamed out. The frightened Dugtowners in the streets doubled their panic. Then, further down the lane, more Green and Grey Fangs leaped forth, breaking windows and joining the poor Dugtowners in battle. Claxton had been busy.

"Hurry!" Gammon shouted. "Get me to that rooftop!"

Artham wrapped his arms around Gammon's chest from behind. "Jump on three," Artham said. "I'll need all the help you can give me."

They charged the Fangs in front of them, counting as they ran. On three, Gammon jumped with all his might. Artham flapped as hard as he could and the two men sailed over the heads of the angry Fangs—but they dropped immediately. Gammon's boots bumped the heads of several Fangs and they clawed at his legs.

"Higher!" Gammon screamed.

But Artham's strength gave out, and the two of them landed in the middle of the Fang-choked street. The lizards hissed and advanced.

"Three!" Artham shouted again, and Gammon jumped.

This time they rose over the Fang's heads and lurched upwards, closer and closer to the rooftop. Gammon reached out and closed his fingers on the gutter. Artham let go and left Gammon dangling there. The birdman soared a circle over the Fangs' heads, then alighted on the roof and pulled Gammon up.

The two men collapsed and lay on their backs, catching their breath as chaos erupted below them. They looked at one another and nodded, then without another word Artham took to the sky and sped to find Errol.

Gammon looked out on the battle unfolding in the street. He saw Skreeans fall with every passing second, but also saw with pride that many Fangs crumbled to dust, too. He struck his best Florid Sword pose and raised his voice. "Skreeans! This is your city! Fear not the Fangs of Dang, for they are soulless and heartless, and fight for nothing but war itself! You fight for your comrades and families. You fight for your home and freedom! 'Tis I, the Florid Sword, and I fight for thee! Help is at hand! Aha!"

The Dugtowners and Fangs stopped fighting long enough to shout an answer. The Fangs screamed for Gammon's death. The Skreeans bellowed their battle cries. Then the Dugtowners pushed back at the Fangs who were streaming from their hideouts in greater and greater numbers.

Gammon dashed from rooftop to rooftop, black cape flying, a shadow that swept across the city as he roused his people to war. All the while, he scanned the streets below for one wretched face, Claxton Weaver, and one lovely soul, Maraly Weaver, for whom he planned to lay down his life when the time came.

32

The Weaver Family Reunion

Maraly huddled in the corner of a house she didn't know. The windows were shuttered and candles were lit, though some sunlight crept through the cracks. It appeared to have been a well-kept home at some point, but the Stranders had taken care of that. Not only had they made a wreck of the place, it stank now from floor to ceiling. Maraly had spent enough time with Sara and Gammon that for the first time in her life she wished the people around her would bathe.

Stranders of the East, Middle, and West Bends were crammed into the house, rifling through cupboards for food to eat, pocketing whatever they could find that had the least bit of shine. Two of them—an old man and a younger woman, who were each so filthy they were hard to tell apart—had already come to blows over a small looking glass. They had argued over it for a few minutes, then they had fallen to the floor wrestling over it, then they had started kicking and punching while the others goaded them on. In the end, they were both bloodied and unconscious with the looking glass (now broken) lying on the floor between them. Maraly's fourth-aunt-cousin Poggy had promptly snatched it up, pointing her knife at everyone in the room. "I need it most, anyhow," she sneered, peering at her reflection. She licked her dirty thumb and stroked her eyebrows.

Maraly had once enjoyed these people's company. She shook her head shamefully and pressed herself against the wall, hugging her knees. Only a year ago *she* might have been the one scrabbling on the floor over the mirror.

Claxton sat near the fireplace with his legs sprawled out. He picked little things out of his beard and chewed on them like candy.

"Mammy!" Claxton grunted. "I need some spunkel soup. Be quick about it."

Nurgabog? Maraly had assumed her grandmother long dead. Janner had told her of how Nurgabog had helped him to escape the Fangs in the river burrow. According to Janner, Nurgabog even told him where Kalmar had gone. But she had been badly wounded when he left her. Surely she had died.

Then again, Nurgabog was a Strander. One didn't live long in the East Bend without being tough as an udder, and Nurgabog had lived longer than any person Maraly knew. She could be as rotten as the rest of them, but she had always been kind to Maraly—kinder than Claxton had ever been, anyway.

Maraly tried to catch a glimpse of her granny, discreetly peeking past the men and women standing about and belching (among other things).

And there she was. It had only been a few months, but Nurgabog seemed to have aged ten years. She could barely walk, and she was filthier than ever, her eyes downcast, her hair hanging ragged around her muddy face.

Maraly wanted to call out to her, mainly to give the old woman something to smile about. She would be glad to see her granddaughter alive and well, wouldn't she? But Maraly decided not to draw any attention. Her hands and feet were bound but she still had a few knives hidden away, which meant that she might be able to escape if the right opportunity arose—and escaping was far easier if one didn't draw attention.

Nurgabog hobbled over to Claxton with a bowl in her trembling hands. He took it from her roughly, then shouted at her when some of it spilled. Nurgabog stood there as bent as a tree branch, nodding contritely to her wicked son. When she turned, Maraly noticed that Nurgabog kept one hand on her side, where Janner said she had been stabbed. Maraly's reasons to despise her father were mounting by the minute.

A man Maraly didn't recognize entered the house, flooding the main room with light and rousing a chorus of curses. He was as tall as Claxton but skinny as a paddle—he was as wet as a paddle, too. Water dribbled from the braids in his beard. He shut the door and bowed, then said, "Permission to come near, Strander King?"

The room fell silent. Claxton wiped his chin, put down his bowl of spunkel soup, and shrugged. "Aye. Come near, Jimbob. What news from our Fang comrades?"

"The battle is on, sir. The Fangs are fighting not three streets away, all along River Road."

The Stranders' silence deepened. Maraly thought she saw a flash of worry cross her father's face, but it was hard to see much beyond the beard. "That's sooner than they told me. It was supposed to happen after sundown," Claxton said.

"Aye. They say the birdman started it."

Claxton stood and threw his soup bowl against the hearth. Nurgabog bent to pick up the shards.

"Leave it be, Mammy," Claxton spat.

Either Nurgabog didn't hear him or she ignored him, and Claxton pushed her to the floor with his boot. Nurgabog hissed with pain and her hand went to her side again. Even for a Strander, his actions were offensive. Everyone in the room must have known that he'd administered the wound in his mother's side, because their attention—perhaps even some impossibly small amount of actual pity—was on Nurgabog.

Claxton didn't seem to notice. "Where's the birdman now?"

"I don't know, Strander King."

"What about the other fellow? Gammon?"

Maraly's heart kicked at the mention of that name. She also noticed that Claxton's dark eyes were on her when he said it, and though she tried to conceal her hope, she knew Claxton saw it in her face.

"I don't know where he is, either," said Jimbob.

"So why did you come?" Claxton asked Jimbob, though his eyes were still fixed on Maraly.

"The Fangs say they need our help." Jimbob's voice trembled. "They say that if you don't come and fight, they'll treat us like all the other Dugtowners."

"Is that what they said," Claxton muttered, turning his attention back to Jimbob.

"But you told us we didn't have to fight nobody!" one of the Stranders said. "We don't fight for nobody but ourselves! You told us that!"

"Aye, you said we just had to hide here until the fightin' was over! We ain't nobody's soldiers."

"And you said we'd get some cupcakes!"

"Quiet, all of you!" Claxton roared. "First of all, the cupcakes were fer the ones who came with me to Snoot's. I said I'd *try* to bring ye back a few. I'd *try*. Ain't that what I said, Poggy?"

"Exactly," Poggy said. "And even us that went didn't get none." Maraly noticed her face was smeared with bright yellow icing.

Others noticed it too. "What's on yer cheeks?" one of them shouted.

"It ain't icing. It's—it's water."

"Sticky yellow water?" said the second man. "Poggy, that makes no brains!"

"Quiet, I said!" Claxton bellowed. "Forget the cupcakes! If ye want some, we can get 'em tomorrow after the Fangs have run of the place again. Second of all, no, we don't have to fight. Jimbob here's going to send word back to the Fangs that he found us fighting the Dugtowners out in the mudfields to the north. It's all part of me plan. He's gonna tell 'em how brave we are, aren't you, Jimbob?"

"If it means I can get one of those cupcakes tomorrow, then yeah," Jimbob said, rubbing his hands together. "I'll tell 'em anything."

"Can I have a dip of some of that yellow water on your cheeks, Poggy?" the first Strander asked.

"Nobody's eatin' cheek water!" Claxton shouted, banging his fist on the wall. "I don't care what color it is! Now listen," he continued in a conspiratorial tone, "we just have to hide here and keep quiet. The Fangs will do their battling, my mammy will keep bringing me soup, and in the morning"—Claxton thrust out his chest and beamed—"I'm the King of Dugtown. Actually, I would like a nibble of that goop on yer cheek, Poggy."

"But what if the Fangs come to this house?" the second man asked.

"We duck into the burrow."

"What if they come into the burrow?"

"They don't know about the burrows, you dafter! Burrows are for Stranders!"

Claxton pumped his fist and the Stranders, on cue, shouted, "Aye!"

"But ain't the burrows how you snuck all the Fangs into the city?" the man asked.

"Aye!" the crowd shouted uncertainly.

Claxton paused and scratched his beard. They all stared at him in silence.

Then Maraly heard a strange sound—a high-pitched, wheezing sound coming from the floor behind Claxton. It was Nurgabog. She was curled up in a ball like a little girl, one hand on her wounded side and the other covering her mouth while she cackled.

"What's so funny?" Claxton snapped. He leaned over Nurgabog menacingly, and Maraly felt herself tense. If he hurt the poor old woman again Maraly wouldn't be able to keep quiet.

"Claxton . . . Claxton the Strander King!" Nurgabog said between breaths. "Too dumb to realize he dug his own pit!"

Claxton reared back as if he were about to punch her when a knock came at the door. It was more than a knock. Someone was pounding on the door as if they meant to break it down.

Jimbob opened it and a Green Fang filled the doorway. "Out!" it ordered.

"I'll take care of this," Claxton said, turning from Nurgabog. "I'm Claxton the Strander King. What do ye want?"

"Greetingsss, Claxton. I was sent to summon you. Commander Varaggo says, 'The time hassss come to prove your loyalty.' What shall I tell him?"

"Tell him—" Claxton looked around at the Stranders. "Tell him I'll be there when I'm good and ready. Nobody tells a Strander what to do."

He pumped his fist again, and the Stranders said, "Aye!" with even less enthusiasm than before.

"And Stranders fight for none but our own," Claxton continued. "You tell him that."

"Are you sssseriousss?" the Fang said with surprise.

Claxton answered by marching across the room and slamming the door in the Fang's face.

Maraly was only a young girl, but it was obvious that Claxton had no idea what he was doing. First he was allied with the Fangs, now he was slamming the door in their faces? She was surprised the Fang didn't smash the door to pieces.

The very second she had that thought, the Fang smashed the door to pieces.

33

Maraly's Name

The Stranders may not have wanted to fight in the Fang war, but they had no qualms with fighting for their own lives. The first Fangs through the door met a grisly end that involved knives and a few stubby Strander teeth.

But Maraly could tell from the snarls outside that there were plenty more Fangs where those came from, not to mention the fact that for some reason, Stranders from the West Bend were fighting those from the Middle, and both East and Middle Benders were fighting those from the West.

Maraly decided it was time to go. She worked her way awkwardly to her knees, looking for a hiding place where she might be able to remove one of her knives and cut the rope around her ankles. On the other side of the room there was a table that she might be able to scoot under.

Just before she started to crawl forward, she realized with a terrible shock that Claxton's eyes were fixed on her from across the room. They regarded one another for a terrible moment, then he was shoving his way through Fangs and Stranders alike, trying to get to her.

Maraly scrambled toward the nearest door, dodging men and women and snakes and knives, praying she would make it through before her father laid his enormous hands on her.

She shouldered the door open and tumbled inside to discover a cluster of Stranders jammed up to the waist through a high kitchen window. All of them were scraping and screaming at one another in their madness to escape. Out of the corner of her eye Maraly saw a closet door swing shut and heard movement on the other side. It had to be the entrance to a burrow.

She hopped to the door, too afraid of Claxton to stop and try to cut her bonds, and turned the doorknob with both hands. Sure enough, there was a trapdoor below the scattered bags of flour and jars of food. She hopped inside and pulled the door shut behind her, trying to ignore Claxton's bellowing in the main room, and sat, dropping her feet into the dark hole.

She knew Claxton would be close behind, but there was a chance she might have time to cut her bonds and vanish into the maze of tunnels. She had to try.

"Ow!" someone said. Maraly couldn't see much, but a sliver of lantern light speared out of the tunnel below, illuminating the head she had just stepped on. Several Stranders were shimmying down the ladder and into the burrow. Maraly followed, hopping down one rung at a time, struggling to keep a grip on the ladder with her wrists bound.

When she reached the bottom she heard Claxton shouting her name from above: "MARALY! YOU'LL HAVE NO FATHER BUT ME!"

As the other Stranders sped away with their lantern, Maraly hopped over to the wall beside the ladder and fumbled with her pantleg, searching for her knife, dreading the moment when Claxton would darken the entrance above.

"MARALY!" he boomed. Maraly jumped, her trembling fingers straining to reach the knife at her ankle, but the bonds around her legs held it fast. Light fell through the shaft from above. Claxton's silhouette appeared, and he sniffed. "Are you down there, girl? I can smell the clean on you."

Maraly held her breath. She squinted her eyes shut and worked the handle of the knife back and forth, edging it out with agonizing slowness. There was no way she would be able to remove it before her crazy father found her.

She wanted to hide, but there was nowhere to go, so she pressed herself against the earthen wall and held still. The sound of Claxton's boots thudding on the ladder mixed with the booms, crashes, and shouts in the house above and with the violent pounding of Maraly's heart until she was no longer able to tell them apart.

Where was Gammon? He had promised to protect her, but where was he? She felt a strange thickness in her chest and realized it was a sob trying to make its way out. How long had it been since Maraly Weaver had cried? She didn't remember ever feeling this afraid or this sad.

She saw the outline of Claxton's body as he reached the bottom of the ladder and turned around, sniffing the air. The faint light from the kitchen fell on his forehead, on the bridge of his nose, and now as he smiled, on his round cheeks above the ratty beard.

The sadness she was only beginning to recognize swelled inside her until it dwarfed her fear. This man, this monster, was supposed to love her. She had belonged to him at some point, and fathers were meant to care for their daughters, even on the Strand. Was she so unlovable? Was she as worthless as a bad dog, something to be caged and hunted, as he had done—to be put down, as he might have tried to do?

As Claxton stood over her with his big arms folded and his ratty beard trembling with a sinister chuckle, Maraly gave way to her tears. She sobbed and was shocked by the inhuman sound she made. Maybe she *was* just an animal. Her father certainly was.

Someone poked his head into the trapdoor.

"Don't come this way," Claxton barked. "There are Fangs everywhere! Run!"

The Strander shrieked and disappeared, slamming the trapdoor and plunging Maraly and Claxton into total darkness.

"There," he said in his muddy voice. "Now we're alone." Claxton struck a match and lit a lantern stashed behind the ladder.

Maraly put her head down and cried like she had never cried before. She didn't think he would kill her. He had, after all, gone to a lot of trouble to get her back from Gammon. But she knew his fists. She knew his anger. He had caged her before.

"Why don't you love me?" she said.

Claxton placed the lantern on the floor between them and cracked his knuckles. He squatted in front of her and stroked his beard. "Why should I?"

Maraly's eyes were closed, but she could feel him smiling. Then she felt his hand on the collar of her shirt. She screamed as he jerked her to her feet and pinned her against the wall, his hand around her throat.

"Because—you're—my—father," Maraly sputtered, kicking him and scratching at his face as he smiled on unfazed.

"I thought *Gammon* was your father." Claxton's smile turned to a hateful sneer.

Maraly was out of words. She stopped fighting. She could still breathe, but barely. She closed her eyes and waited for whatever punishment Claxton had to give, thinking of Gammon and Sara Cobbler and the good days she had spent among them.

"Your friends have made you weak. Did they teach you how to cry like a babe at her mammy's side? Stranders don't cry, Maraly."

"I'm not a Strander," she said, looking him in the eye.

"Then I'll have to *make* you one," Claxton barked. "You've got my blood in yer veins, girl, and nothin' can change that. You've got *my* name written in yer bones. Maraly Weaver. You can go take yer bath and eat yer fancy food and giggle with yer friend, but you'll always know deep down that you were born in the mud of the Strand, along the mud of the Blapp, and once that mud gets on you, *nothin'* ever gets it off."

Claxton seemed to know Maraly's deepest fear and was speaking it aloud. She had lain awake at night, fighting to believe that Gammon's fatherly love was real, that the change she had been feeling—the lightening of heart and the almost painful flashes of joy—was more than a silly girlish notion. She thought back to the day of the Battle of Kimera, when Gammon had looked her in the eye and held out his hand and asked if she would let him care for her. Even then something had bubbled up in the dry well of her soul, and over these last months she had felt that spring slowly, slowly fill her. With the coming of the warmer sun she had finally allowed herself to believe that the water was pure enough to drink—but every word Claxton spewed poisoned the water, darkened it, muddied it like the Mighty Blapp, and now she felt herself drowning in it.

"I'm going to give you one last chance, girl. Either Claxton is yer father or Gammon is. Only one of those names is true to your nature. Answer carefully now. Who's your father?"

Maraly shook her head and wept. She wished the Fangs would appear, or more Stranders—she had given up on wishing for Gammon. That sort of thing only happened in storybooks.

"*Who's your father?*" Claxton bellowed. He struck her in the face. Stars spun in Maraly's head and she tasted blood in her mouth. "You're a Strander down to the bone, girl! Who's your father? What do you think runs thicker than the blood in your veins?"

Maraly mumbled.

"What?" Claxton shouted, clenching her throat tighter.

She blinked through her tears and took a trembling breath then looked him in the eye as fiercely as she could manage. "Love."

"Love," Claxton sputtered. He snorted with laughter.

Maraly sniffled and said, "Love runs stronger than blood. Deeper than any name you could give me."

"You worthless dog," Claxton spat. He balled his fingers into a fist and reared back to strike.

Maraly smiled through her tears. She knew she had chosen well, because she had *been* chosen. She believed in her heart that Gammon was even now fighting to find her, that his affection was more real than the hand that gripped her throat and the fist that was about to pound her. She closed her eyes and waited for the pain.

But Claxton's blow never fell. He gasped and made a choking sound, and his grip on her neck loosened. Maraly crumpled to the ground, looking up at Claxton in confusion. He staggered backwards and spun around, and she saw a knife in his back, buried to the hilt.

"Maker help you, boy," said a woman's thin, quavering voice. "Maker help me, too."

Nurgabog stood with one hand on the ladder and the other clutching her wounded side. She was bent over, but her face was lifted to the lamplight and wore a look of tortured triumph.

"There's only one soul in Aerwiar I love more than you," Nurgabog rasped, "and it's her."

"But—but—I'm the Strander King!" Claxton said between gasps. He dropped to his knees in front of his mother and held out his hands. "You can't hurt me."

"And you can't hurt her," Nurgabog said with a weary smile. "Not anymore."

She hobbled forward and hugged Claxton, and the two of them collapsed to the ground in one another's arms. Claxton buried his face in his mother's shoulder and coughed.

"Run, girl," Nurgabog said. Her breathing was watery and weak. "The Fangs are coming. Go, find him."

Maraly pried her knife free and sawed at her bonds. She struggled to her feet and staggered down the tunnel blindly.

"Gammon!" she cried, turning the knife around to cut at the ropes on her wrists as she ran. "Gammon, I'm coming!"

34

Artham's Shame

Artham flew with all his strength for Riverside Road to find Errol. For months he had been dimly aware that the Skreeans were readying for an impending battle. Gammon had sent emissaries far and wide to proclaim their victory in Dugtown and to summon more Skreeans to war—Maraly and Sara had told him as much. But in Artham's madness, during which he was aware of his babbling but was unable to stop it, he knew little but the general facts. He couldn't explain why his mind had been clear since Maraly disappeared, but he was thankful for it. He was the only person in Skree with wings, and right now, wings were one of their only advantages.

"To arms!" he shouted, skimming over the heads of Skreeans as he flew deeper into the city. "The Fangs are in Dugtown! War is upon us!"

Artham didn't look back to see whether or not they believed him. They would believe him soon enough, whether they wanted to or not.

Artham passed over Crempshaw Way, then zoomed over Riverside Road, screeching, "The Fangs are in the city! The Fangs are in the city!"

His eagle eyes narrowed and he scanned the Dugtowners and Kimeran soldiers thronged among the tents and merchant stands that spread along the riverside. He recognized a few of the men and women, then his gaze locked on a man leaning against a wall with his arms folded: Errol. Gammon's second-in-command.

As soon as Errol heard Artham's shrieking voice, he stood at attention and drew his sword. Artham tipped his wings and dove straight for him. He landed in a rush of feathers and grabbed Errol's shoulders.

"It's Claxton and the Stranders. They've been smuggling Fangs into the city through the burrows."

"How many?" Errol asked.

"I don't know. Hundreds. They started at the eastern edge, out near the mudfarms, but I think they've infiltrated the whole city."

"Where's Gammon?"

"Last I saw him, he was riding the rooftops like the Florid Sword."

A crash came from the eastern end of the market, followed by cries of alarm. But Artham's warning had done some good. Instead of fleeing, the Dugtowners in the market surged angrily toward the commotion to meet the Fangs in battle.

"Elmer! Olsin!" Errol shouted at two of his comrades as they ran past. The two warriors approached with their swords drawn, itching to fight. "Send word to the western edges. Tell them to muster, and muster quickly."

"But the battle is here," Olsin said, pointing his sword at the skirmish.

"No, lads," Artham said. "The Fangs are in the city. The battle is everywhere."

Elmer and Olsin looked confused, but then a crash echoed through the building to their right. The window exploded as Green and Grey Fangs burst forth in snarling fury.

Errol screamed and swung his sword wildly. Artham leapt into the air and attacked the cluster of Fangs from above as one of the snakes bit Elmer on the forearm. Elmer screamed and fell while his comrades held the ground around him; he shuddered and writhed and then lay still. Artham and Errol fought on, dusting Fang after Fang until at last it seemed the Fangs in the house were finished. Olsin knelt at Elmer's side and shouted his name, but his friend was dead.

"Olsin," Errol said. "You have to warn the others. Go."

Olsin nodded, placed a hand on Elmer's head, and ran.

"Artham, go north. We need to summon everyone. Soldiers, citizens, anyone you can find. We're spread out all over the city and if we don't mount a defense, the Fangs will pick us apart like warm bread. Call everyone to the market. With our backs to the water, Riverside Road will leave the Fangs only one clear avenue of attack. If we can hold anywhere, we can hold here. But we must have help, and have it quickly. Fly, Artham, or the city is lost."

Artham took to the air as Errol shouted orders to form barricades at every street leading into the market. North he flew, low over the heads of frightened Dugtowners, ordering them to make haste to the riverfront. He weaved his way down every street, around every turn, screaming till his voice was spent, stopping only long enough to aid any Skreeans under attack from the Fangs emerging from house after house, storefront after storefront.

Outside a tavern called the Roundish Widow he saw a thin fellow with a wide moustache hurling tankards at an onrush of Fangs. Artham skidded to the ground and fought beside him long enough to fend off the Fangs. The man croaked a hearty thanks.

"Get to the market at the riverfront," Artham told him. "Bring as many with you as you can."

Artham angled his way ever northward, glad to see that word was spreading. Dugtowners streamed through the streets with weapons drawn, heading toward the river with Fangs on their heels.

He landed outside the Flabbit's Paw and ducked inside, looking for Sara. The tables were overturned and ashes from the fire were strewn across the floor, but there was no one inside. "Sara!" he called. He ran upstairs to his room and saw no one. "Sara?"

Artham looked at the bed, the covers strewn on the floor, the tray on the nightstand where the girls had served him tea, and remembered the terrible dreams he had dreamt. They hovered at the back of his mind and assaulted him with familiar taunts: *Coward. Failure.*

He shook his head and clamped his eyes shut. "No," he said. The voices grew louder. He felt himself tremble, felt a sluggishness in his mind, disorientation and fear pulsing like dark music.

"NO," he repeated, trying to hold onto his wits. He had to find Sara. He had to sind fara. The enemy was attacking. The attacking was enemy—find Cara Sobbler—she was in danger—Janner had told him to find her—to thank—thoo tank her—*I left him!*—I'm a Throne Warden—*but you left him*—the Fangs are coming—*and now he's dead, dead, dead, dead*—

"NO!" Artham screamed. He dropped to his knees and tottered, and suddenly sleep seemed like a very good thing. He fell to his side, wings splayed out on the floor, and pressed his knuckles against his forehead. Some terrible feathery beast in his soul screeched triumphantly and chased away every thought, every word, before it could be formed.

He saw Esben chained to the wall in the Deeps of Throg, his lumpy, bearish face pleading—*Don't leave me, Artham.* He saw the slick walls of the Deeps as he wriggled his way through the—*You were supposed to protect me*—dark heart of the mountain and soon to the Blackwood where—*Come back for me, brother*—his shame was doubled by his relief at having escaped Gnag's prison.

Artham heard himself babbling like a baby even as Skreeans shouted and hurried through the street below his window.

35

General Borley's Plan

Sara saw a figure run past the front window of Thimble Thumb's Threads, but when nothing else happened she turned her attention back to Armulyn. He was telling her about the places beyond the maps, the strange creatures he had seen, exotic cities and towns, the shape of the land, and above all, his gratitude to the Maker for having thought up such a world.

Another figure rushed past the window. *Probably nothing*, Sara thought, then looked over her shoulder at the orphans in the factory. Armulyn the Bard's orphans were still timid, still adjusting to the strange city after having so recently lost their parents to Fangs. She didn't want to alarm them. But suddenly more people ran past, this time with weapons and tools in their hands.

Sara interrupted Armulyn and stepped outside. "What's wrong?" she shouted to anyone who would listen. "Someone, please! Why are you running?"

A young man with a hoe hollered over his shoulder, "Fangs in the city! Grab a hoe and get to the market! Gammon's orders!"

Sara stared after him blankly. Fangs? In the city? She knew a battle was coming, but she had assumed there would be some warning—some, well, *formality* to it. Gammon had watchmen stationed around the perimeter of the city and on the torch towers, ready to raise the alarm in time for the battle. How could the Fangs have invaded so suddenly?

"What's wrong, Queen Sara?" said Borley from behind her. A girl named Grettalyn stood at his side.

Sara forced a smile. She didn't want to frighten them, but she also owed them the truth. Borley was a smart boy and had already shown great courage in the face of great danger. Still, she found it difficult to speak. Their last few months in the orphanage had been sweet and peaceful, and it brought her great sorrow that it was over.

"Ma'am?" Grettalyn asked. "Why are you sad? And where's everybody off to?"

Armulyn approached and stood beside Borley and Grettalyn. "It's happening, isn't it?"

"Yes," Sara said, swallowing her tears. "We have to get to the river. Borley, you know what to do."

"Yes, Queen Sara," he said, puffing out his chest as they hurried back inside. "Come on, Grettalyn."

Sara shut and locked the door as Borley and Grettalyn marched over to a table and climbed atop it.

"Attention!" Grettalyn said, since her voice was much louder than Borley's. "Attention! General Borley has an announcement!"

Sara's orphans shushed Armulyn's and pointed their attention to Borley.

"What's he doing?" Armulyn asked.

Sara lowered her voice and folded her arms. "He's got it in his head that I'm his queen, and a queen needs a general. He makes for a good one, don't you think?"

Borley clapped twice and put his hands on his hips. "Queen Sara has informed me that the time has come." Sara's orphans whispered among themselves until he held up his hands for silence. "Company commanders, stand at the perimeter with your soldiers! If you've recently arrived with Armulyn, divide yourselves evenly among the commanders. When we've organized into companies, weapons will be distributed and further instructions given." No one said a word, so Borley clapped again. "By Queen Sara's orders, get to it!"

At once, twenty of the older children chose spots along the walls of the main floor. Some stood on benches or chairs and raised their hands, calling out their company names.

"Sea Dragons here!" said a girl named Quinn from a chair near the kitchen door.

"Horned Hounds!" cried Wallis, the former Maintenance Manager, who stood on a chair near the opposite wall.

Sara watched with pride as her orphans dutifully made their way to each of their leaders, bringing groups of Armulyn's children with them. In a matter of minutes, all the children in the hall stood awaiting orders in twenty companies of ten or fifteen children each. Another group emerged from a storage room carrying a wooden chest for each company. The boxes were opened and the group leaders passed out forks.

Armulyn shook his head, impressed. "Did you organize all this?"

"It was Borley's idea," Sara told him, trying to keep calm in spite of the mounting chaos in the streets. "He drills them a few times a week."

There weren't quite enough forks to go around, so each group divided them among their oldest and strongest. They encouraged the smaller children and told them to keep close once the fighting started.

Once the weapons were divided, the room fell silent and Borley extended a hand to Sara. "Your troops are ready," he said gravely. If he hadn't been so serious, and if there hadn't been real danger outside, it would have been humorous.

"Thank you, Borley," Sara said as she mounted the table and stood beside her noble general. She proudly surveyed the children in silence, partly because of the lump in her throat and partly in defiance of the fear in her gut. They looked to her for courage, and she was determined to give it to them—what little she had, anyway. "The Fangs are in the city. Gammon has summoned us all to the market at Riverside Road to make our defense." She waited for the whispers to die down. "If we hurry, we can be there in minutes. But the streets are crowded with Dugtowners, and there are likely to be Fangs out there, too. We have to hurry, but we can't lose our heads. Commanders, keep your companies together at all times. Children, obey your commanders. Follow them. Stay close until you reach the river. I don't want to lose even one of you. Do you understand?"

"Yes, Queen Sara," they answered.

Sara turned to Armulyn. "Sir, will you play for us as we go?"

"Yes, Queen Sara," he said with a bow.

"Children, if you get lost or separated from your company, listen for the bard's whistleharp and follow the song."

There was little time to say anything else, but Sara dreaded issuing the command to go. The orphans were in her keeping, and she felt the weight of each of their young lives resting on her shoulders. She didn't want any of them to suffer more than they already had.

Outside, Dugtowners hurried past. The clash of battle grew nearer, filling the streets. Just as she was about to give the order, the door crashed open, and there stood a Grey Fang, panting like an angry dog. It saw the mass of children, smiled, then arched its back and howled.

Armulyn stepped between the children and the Fang and strummed his whistleharp. He blew on the whistle and played a fast jig, tapping his feet on the floor and working his elbows like a duck. But the melody was shaky and out of tune; there were so many wrong notes that Sara cringed.

The Fang's howl was cut short and it cocked its head at Armulyn, wondering what in the world the strange man was doing. Then it began to laugh. Two more Fangs appeared in the doorway in answer to the first one's call, and the three of them pointed and laughed at the bard, mocking his dance and howling all the louder. A bead of sweat trickled down Armulyn's cheek.

He finished his shaky song and struck a pose with one hand out, as if he were waiting for applause. The Fangs doubled over with laughter. "Do it again!" the first one barked between breaths.

Armulyn raised his whistleharp once more, and Sara saw that his hands were trembling. This time, however, the notes were clear and beautiful, and the Fangs covered their ears, doubled over, and whined.

Suddenly Borley leapt from the table. "For Queen Sara!" he screamed, and the orphans surged forward. Sara stood on the table in shock as her army streamed past her, past Armulyn, and overcame the three Grey Fangs before they knew what was happening.

The children filed out by company, trampling Fang dust and armor underfoot. Sara hopped down, took Armulyn's hand, and joined their mad rush to Riverside Road.

The streets were jammed with Dugtowners. Armulyn struggled to play his whistleharp while he ran, but the music was more pleasing than before. He wiped sweat from his brow and said, "Sorry, Sara. It's hard to play when you're scared."

"It doesn't matter how pretty it is," Sara huffed. "It lets the children know you're still alive. Keep playing!"

The street was a river of people, and Sara and her army were swept along in its current. Whenever they passed a side street or alleyway, some of the Dugtowners darted to the left or right, seeking a quicker way to the Blapp, like streams in a rainstorm. She saw Wallis and his company bolt off to the left, and two more companies followed. Just ahead she spotted the green scales of several Fangs as they battled the onrush of Dugtowners. The traffic slowed, and more of her army sped away down an alley to the right. They were splitting up, which she hoped was a good thing. If Fangs blocked the main roads, then at least some of the orphans might make it to safety.

The more Armulyn played, the better his music became, until at last he sounded the way Sara remembered him at the Dragon Day festival. The Dugtowners took heart from his playing, and some even recognized him.

"Armulyn the Bard!" they shouted and clapped him on the back as they ran. "I like your songs!" they said, laughing absurdly as more Fangs appeared in the streets.

He began an old song, something that sounded Annieran to Sara, and it made her heart ache for its beauty as they rushed past the Flabbit's Paw.

36

Too Good Not To Be True

Artham P. Wingfeather was lost in an agony of remembrance. He tossed and turned on the floor of his room in the Flabbit's Paw like a child in a fever dream. He mumbled and wept, drooled and whimpered. In his mind he lay on the floor of a dark chamber as specters and ghouls lurked in the shadows around him, beating leathery wings, taunting, sneering, laughing.

He clapped his hands over his ears and tried to silence their words. *Traitor. Coward. Freak.* But the harder he tried to ignore them the louder their voices became. Hideous, wicked faces darted out of the shadows and scowled at him every time he opened his eyes. He had the sense that his soul was shrinking, or the version of himself in the dark chamber was shrinking, as the monsters grew and grew in their flapping madness.

With all that was left of his diminishing voice he pleaded with the Maker to help him, to quiet the voices, to speak light into his darkness. But the ghouls only laughed louder, grew more violent in their gyrations, closed in on him like the teeth of a giant mouth about to chew him up and swallow him.

Then, as if from a great distance, the faint strains of a luminous melody floated into his mind. The evil voices in his head changed subtly, as if they too heard the song. They snarled and redoubled their efforts, but the angrier the voices became the brighter the music seemed. Artham's breathing slowed. He listened. He yearned for the song he heard, reached for it desperately like a drowning man for a rope.

Then he saw her.

Leeli Wingfeather in the dark, on the roof of the Great Library of Ban Rona with Nia at her side. She was surrounded by wings—dark, leathery wings like the ones in his nightmare—but on she played. Her courage burned like a sun. Her songs woke his heart and called to him: *Artham. Protect. Protect those in your keeping. Fight for them.*

He sat up as if he had been poked with a hot iron. He blinked, looked at his surroundings in confusion, and staggered to his feet. Where was he? The room was familiar. Room twelve. There was his bed. He saw a teacup on the nightstand, and remembered a girl sipping from it while she watched over him.

Sara. Sara Cobbler. He closed his eyes again, listening for the melody that had awakened him—Leeli was playing somewhere, sending the song of her beautiful heart out over the rooftops of Ban Rona.

But now, though Artham was awake, he still heard the melody—something vaguely Annieran—and he realized the song wasn't only in his mind, but in his ears as well. The melody, nearly drowned by the clamor of voices and the clash of battle, drifted through his window and filled his heart like pure water poured onto the soil of a thirsty garden.

"Sara!" he cried. He ran to the window and flung it open.

Multitudes ran through the street below, and in the distance, Fangs roared and fought them. Then he saw her: Sara Cobbler running beside a scrabbly looking fellow with dark hair and bare feet.

"Sara!" he shouted, and she stopped and stared at him as the rushing crowd jostled her.

From across the street, a Green Fang leapt from the door of Blarn's Grocery and swung his sword at the Dugtowners running by. The Fang inched closer to Sara with every swipe.

Artham dove from the window, spread his wings, and descended upon the Fang. He wrenched its sword away, dispatched the beast to its dusty fate, and turned just as Sara Cobbler wrapped her arms around his waist and held him tight.

"Hello," said the man with the whistleharp, wonderstruck as a little boy. "Are you—are you *him*?"

"Artham Wingfeather at your service."

Armulyn smiled and stared at Artham as if he had come face to face with the stuff of his dreams. After all, he had. "Then it's real?" he said. "I mean—*really* real?"

"What's real?" Artham said with a smile.

"Anniera," Armulyn whispered.

Artham laughed. "Of course it's real. Where do you suppose the songs come from?"

"I was never certain," Armulyn said. "I hoped. I dreamed. But it all seemed too good to be true."

"Too good *not* to be true, you mean."

Armulyn the Bard wiped a tear from the corner of his eye.

"Well don't stop playing *now*," Artham said with a smile and a shake of his wings. "We need those songs. Now more than ever. Go on."

The bard played again, without a trace of fear, weaving a melody that roused the Dugtowners to greater courage as they ran. The Fangs of Dang within earshot cringed and buckled in the face of the Skreean onrush. Artham strode beside Sara like a king in a parade, his sword aloft for the Dugtowners to see, and Armulyn the Bard led them.

37

Dugtowners at the River Front

As soon as Artham, Sara Cobbler, and Armulyn the Bard were safe behind the barricade, Borley pushed his way through the crowd and hugged his queen.

"We made it, Sara! Every one of us!" he cried. "Your subjects are gathered near Johanicle's Bootery awaiting your instructions." He bowed, smiled at her with gleaming eyes, and stood at attention, ignoring the amused looks from the grownups around them.

"Well done, Borley." Sara kissed him on the forehead. "I couldn't ask for a better general."

Borley's jaw fell open and his cheeks turned red as apples. He fell briefly into a sort of glassy-eyed trance until Artham patted him on the back and snapped him out of it.

"Good work, lad," Artham said with a smile. "Why don't you check on your soldiers?"

"Soldiers," Borley said dreamily.

"I'll go too," Armulyn said. "I need to check on my orphans."

"Orphans," Borley murmured as they left.

Artham turned to Sara. "Where's Gammon?"

"I was going to ask you the same thing. I haven't seen him since you left." Sara was afraid to ask him if they'd found Maraly, so she didn't. If they had, Artham would have said so. But surely it wasn't too late to find her, even with the city overrun. Sara scanned the multitudes of people crammed into the market, foolishly wishing she might see Maraly spitting and laughing with the rougher characters.

"Artham!" someone shouted over the din.

"Errol," Artham said. "Any word from Gammon?"

"No. The worst of the fighting is still in the east. I suspect that's where the Stranders were sneaking the Fangs into the city. A few Fang companies made their way to the north and west, but they were easily overtaken." Errol, ragged from fighting, looked over the heads of the milling Dugtowners behind the barricade. Men with bows crouched near the top and shot arrows at Fangs on the other side. "He's out there somewhere."

"If anyone can make it back, it's Gammon," Artham said.

"Well, I hope he gets here soon. It's getting dark and the Fangs in the streets are only part of the problem."

"What do you mean?" Artham asked.

"I'll show you."

Errol led Artham and Sara through the crowd to the riverfront. The Blapp was muddy as ever, slogging between Torrboro and Dugtown, indifferent to the battle on its banks. It had flowed for epochs, and would continue to flow long after this war was a distant memory.

Errol pointed across the span at a cluster of boats and barges stretched as far as Sara could see to the east and west. They teemed with Fangs, and the hulking shapes of trolls rose among the Fangs like mountains over foothills.

"What are they waiting for?" Sara asked.

Artham took a deep breath. "Night."

As if it had been waiting for the mention of the word, the sun slid behind a wall of clouds in the west, casting the land in dull gray light.

"My guess is that the Fangs in the burrows weren't supposed to attack until nightfall," Errol said, "which would have drawn our attention away from the river."

"Then the larger force would surprise us at the waterfront," Artham said.

"Right. Something must have triggered the attack in the city." Errol looked at Artham. "I bet that something was you and Gammon."

Artham nodded. "If we hadn't been looking for Maraly, we wouldn't have run into the Fangs. They would have caught us by surprise at nightfall."

"Aye. And it would have worked, too," Errol said. "Even so, we're in trouble. Our leader is missing. There are Maker knows how many Fangs in the east city. And once the sun goes down, we're going to have *them* to deal with." He pointed across the river. "Do you suppose you could find a few more guys with wings?"

"Other than chorkneys, you mean?" Artham pointed his thumb at a corral of chorkneys in the west end of the market. They honked and shuffled as they were being saddled and fitted for battle.

Errol grunted. "If only they could fly."

"Can they swim?" Sara asked.

Errol and Artham started to answer, then looked at one another questioningly. Both said, "I don't know."

"I bet their webby feet could do as well in water as on the snow."

"If we can upset their vessels we can upset their whole attack," Artham said. "How many boats do we have?"

"Not nearly enough. Five? Ten? The Fangs had control of the river when we took Dugtown back. They ended up with most of the boats."

"How many chorkneys?"

"That's the whole cavalry there. Forty-three."

"Well, until Gammon gets back," Artham said, putting his hand on Errol's shoulder, "it looks like you're in charge. If I may advise you, it's time to see how those birds do in the water. Do you think you can find forty-three fighters to brave the Blapp on the back of a chorkney?"

"Aye. And the bigger ones can carry two."

"Good."

"What are you going to do?" asked Sara.

"I'm going to find Gammon."

"And Maraly."

"Yes, of course. And Maraly." Artham took a running start and flew over the heads of the startled Dugtowners. He circled the nearest torch tower, then disappeared beyond the rooftops.

"I'm sure she'll be fine," Errol said, clearing his throat. He looked out at the mass of Fangs and trolls mustered on the far shore, then added in a quiet voice, "I'm sure we'll all be fine." He marched off in the direction of the chorkneys to inform his soldiers of the plan.

The flame of Sara's hope, which had managed to stay lit even in the Fork Factory, was beginning to wane. There was no one left to help them. Gammon's Kimerans were already here. Almost every Skreean north of the Blapp was gathered in Dugtown, and the rest had already been captured by the Fangs or were scattered across the continent, unorganized, weaponless, and leaderless. Fangs hemmed in the Dugtowners and only the barricades held them back. More Fangs stood ready to cross the Blapp.

"Queen Sara?" Borley said.

Sara hadn't seen him approach, and she jumped a little.

"Ma'am, the orphans are hungry. And they want to see you. Everyone wants to know what's going to happen."

Sara put her arm around Borley's little shoulders. She could tell he was afraid but didn't want to show it. "The Fangs are going to attack us," she said. "And we're going to fight. That's all I know, Borley."

"I miss my parents," Borley said quietly.

"Tell me about them."

Sara led her little general back to the others. He told her all he could remember—his father had been a tailor, his mother a "really big lady," as Borley put it—but Sara was only half-listening. She was thinking about her own mother and father, probably taken years ago. Even if Sara survived the battle, the war, she and the others would still be just as orphaned and just as homeless as they had been before.

Sara imagined taking all the children to some beautiful, unspoiled place after the fighting—Glipwood, maybe. Then they could all watch the sea dragons from the cliffs every summer at the half moon. They could grow up together. Maybe she would even find a young man to marry and have children. Not Janner—he was long gone. She had nursed the hope that she might see him again, but he was a world away.

She had to be realistic. She had to think about Skree. Her orphans. She had to find a home for them. It was difficult to imagine a world without Fangs, but it was worth the effort. She had never experienced it, really, but there *had* been a time before Gnag the Nameless. Maybe peace would come again, and maybe she would live to see it.

She didn't allow herself to look back over her shoulder at Torrboro and the monsters that were coming with nightfall. If she did, the wind might snuff out what was left of her light.

38

The Roof of Flombode's Seedery

Maraly had grown up hearing about the Strander burrows but had only ever seen them once, years ago, so she had no idea where she was going. Not only that, the tunnels were crawling with Stranders and Fangs, so she often had to snuff out her lantern and duck into a muddy cleft or pretend to be dead or unconscious like the other Stranders she had come upon. She climbed several ladders, poked her head through the trapdoors, and listened, hoping to find a safe house where she could hide, but every time she had seen or heard Fangs and ducked back into the burrow.

Surely there were Dugtowners some-where. There had to be, or the Fangs wouldn't have anyone to fight. And if there was even one person left to resist the Fangs, it would be Gammon. She knew it.

The tunnel took a sharp left and forked. Lamplight glowed from the right and she heard approaching Fang voices, so she scrambled into the darkness of the other shaft. She felt a cavity behind a ladder and backed into it. The lamplight grew along with the voices until she could make out what they were saying.

"Isssssthere no way in?" said a Green Fang.

"Not that we can find," answered a deeper voice—a Grey Fang. "They've barred all the trapdoors at the market. We'll have to breach the barricades."

"It won't matter," said the first one. "The Stone Keeper will launch the attack sssoon enough. Having them all in one place will only make it easier."

"Shh! I smell one of them."

The Grey Fang sniffed. The shadows cast by the lantern on the opposite wall shifted. Maraly's heart pounded. She looked up at the ladder, wondering if she could make it through before the Fangs caught her— and what would happen if she emerged into a house full of more Fangs?

"I don't sssmell nothing," said the Fang.

"That's because you're a lizard, you fool."

"I'd rather be a lizard than a puppy."

"I'm no puppy," the Grey Fang snarled and hit the other one. "Puppies can't punch."

"But lizards can!"

The Green Fang hit back, and Maraly listened to the hissing and snarling of a fight unfolding around the corner. If she could hurry up the ladder, maybe they wouldn't notice. The lantern fell to the floor and cast the shadow of the two Fangs on the wall where she could see. The Grey Fang jumped on the snake's back and assailed it with punches, snapping its teeth furiously, but the Green Fang's neck was long enough that it was able to whip its head around and bite the wolf on the neck. The Grey Fang fell back with a whimper. Maraly covered her mouth as the snake kicked the prone Grey Fang and a cloud of dust rose. Some of the dust drifted down her tunnel and floated in the lantern's beam.

"Ouch," said the Green Fang, inspecting its wounds. "Puppies bite." It grabbed the lantern and slunk away, leaving Maraly panting in the darkness.

She climbed the ladder and poked her head into a dimly lit storage room. There was fighting outside, but there didn't seem to be anyone in the house. She eased her way out of the burrow and gently closed the trapdoor. The kitchen was empty, and the hallway that led to the front door was, too. She tiptoed down the hall and peeked out the narrow window beside the door. There were Fangs in the street, standing over a group of fallen Dugtowners. The Fangs sheathed their weapons and congratulated themselves, then marched off, leaving the dusky street empty.

"I just have to make it to the market," Maraly whispered to herself. "Maker let Gammon be there."

She edged out to the front stoop, thankful that with Claxton gone she only had Fangs to worry about. After listening for a breathless moment, she struck out, keeping close to the buildings in case she needed to hide. A block away, at the intersection of Ewang Avenue and Yuplo Street she encountered several heaps of dust and piles of Fang armor outside of Flombode's Seedery and retrieved a rugged dagger.

Maraly looked to the left and right, frustrated that she couldn't tell where she was. She didn't remember either of the street names, and had never heard of Flombode's. The light was fading fast and she didn't want to waste a minute going the wrong way.

She craned her neck and looked up at the eaves above her, then slipped into the seedery. She crept through baskets labeled TOTATOES, YIMPLES, SUGARBERRY STARTERS, and RUTYPAMS, looking for a stair that would lead her to the roof. At the rear of the store she found it and climbed the steps, wincing at every creak until she reached the top floor and ascended a steep set of stairs to the roof. A veil of high clouds crept in from the west, and in the east the first stars were beginning to twinkle. She knelt at the edge and waited for a troop of Fangs to pass, then peeked out over the city.

Several streets away she saw the river, and to her right, in the distance, lay the waterfront market. Between two rows of buildings she saw the dark mass of the barricade the Fangs had mentioned. Figures hunkered at the top shooting arrows into the shadowy streets where she knew the Fangs were concentrated. It was a long way. She had no idea how to get there, or how to get past the barricade and into the safety of the Dugtown army. If the Fangs had no way in, then she didn't either.

Maraly spat and sat down, leaning her back against the rooftop rail. She felt terribly alone. Everyone she knew was in the marketplace, and she was stuck in the dark where she could do nothing but wait for the battle to be over.

"*Maraly!*" someone shouted.

"Now I'm hearing things," she muttered.

"*Maraly, where are you!*"

That wasn't her imagination. She spun around and looked over the city again. In the distance to the left, she thought she saw a shadow flying through the night, bounding from rooftop to rooftop. Just behind it, a howling mass of Fangs pursued.

"Gammon!" she cried, before she could stop herself.

The shadow didn't pause, and she heard the voice again: "*Maraly!*"

The Fangs were gaining on him. Maraly's heart leapt into her throat. She stood up and waved her arms, but she knew it was too dark. From such a distance, Gammon would never see her.

Another group of Fangs appeared in front of Gammon. The shadow stopped at the peak of a roof and spun, slinging his dark cape as the hunching Fangs scrambled toward him from the front and rear.

"No," she said with a scowl as she backed away from the edge. "This ain't how my Gammon is going to die."

The distance to the next building wasn't great—no different than some of the trees she had jumped between in Glipwood Forest. If she could make it, she would have an unbroken strand of rooftops to dash across. She might be able to get close enough to distract the Fangs and give Gammon a chance. There was no way in Aerwiar she was going to sit there and watch him fight to the death.

Maraly took a deep breath, ran with all her might, and jumped from the roof of Flombode's Seedery.

As soon as she was in the air, she knew she had underestimated the distance. Her arms flailed, the cobbled street rushed up at her, and a scream escaped her throat. She didn't make it.

39

Strander, Birdman, Florid Sword

I've got you," said Artham as he lifted Maraly up over the rooftop. She was shocked, then relieved, then shouting orders at Artham all in the space of three seconds.

When she had realized she was going to miss the roof, she was irritated more than anything else; irritated at herself for not being able to jump far enough, and also that it was a silly way to die. She had time to feel a stab of sorrow that Gammon would have no one to help him. But then two strong arms had come from nowhere and scooped her up. Now that she wasn't dead she was left with nothing but the irritation.

"We need to help Gammon!" she shouted, wriggling out of Artham's grip and running along the roof again.

"Maraly, wait! I need to get you to safety!"

"I don't want safety!" she yelled over her shoulder. "I want Gammon!"

If the birdman wanted to help, then good, but she wasn't waiting around for him.

As she ran she felt his arms under hers and her feet lifted from the roof. "*Put—me—down*," she snapped, kicking the air like a child throwing a fit—which, in fact, she was.

"Easy!" Artham said with a laugh. "You'd better have that dagger ready."

Maraly stopped squirming and realized that Artham was flying straight at Gammon, who, though he had managed to keep the Fangs at bay, was running out of tricks. She pulled the dagger from her belt and grinned.

"Gammon!" she shouted.

Gammon thrust his sword at a Grey Fang that was scrabbling up the roof and glanced over his shoulder. The light was nearly gone, so she couldn't see his face, but she heard the tremble of wonder in his voice just before Artham released her.

"Maraly?"

She landed in a crouch, one hand gripping the roofline and the other waving her dagger at the Fangs. They hissed at her and she hissed back. "You look like you could use some help," she said. "We can hug later."

"Aha!" Gammon bellowed, but not like the Florid Sword. He bellowed it like a man whose child was dead but had come back to life.

He and Maraly stood back-to-back, one on each slope of the roof, swinging their blades at the Green and Grey Fangs that surrounded them. They faced death with full hearts. And they probably would have died, too, because more and more Fangs rallied to their position, scaling the buildings and thronging the streets below—but Maraly and Gammon weren't alone.

Artham flapped over the Fangs' heads, swinging his blade, at times landing lightly to aid either Maraly or Gammon, then taking to the air again. Fangs struggled to keep their clawed feet from slipping on the steep roof as they fought, and more than once when one fell he took several others over the edge with him. When night fell, the Fangs regrouped.

"We can't keep this up," Gammon said. "Artham, can you light that torch tower? If we could see I think we could make it to the barricade."

"If I leave you, you'll never make it."

"If we stay here, we'll never make it."

"If you two keep arguing, we'll never make it," Maraly said. "We can hold them off long enough for him to light a match. I can, anyway." She elbowed Gammon, then hissed at the Fangs that scampered around the edges of the building.

"Well, the boss has spoken," Gammon said. "Hurry back, Artham. There are matches on every tower. And the wood is oiled and ready to burn."

Maraly couldn't see the men's faces and was glad they couldn't see hers. She was much more afraid than she sounded. She was tired and knew it was sheer luck that a Fang sword hadn't nicked her. Still, she was glad she had come. She loved Gammon, and fighting was one of the only things she really knew how to do—that and tackleball, which was basically the same thing.

In the darkness, she hadn't noticed that Artham had already flown. The Grey Fangs, however, knew it at once and advanced. Their shadows crept up the incline of the roof like daggerfish skimming the river.

A faint orange glow sputtered overhead and quickly blossomed into a towering blaze. It was then that Maraly and Gammon saw how desperate their situation really was. The torch tower illuminated hundreds of Fangs milling about in the streets below, climbing the sides of the building, edging their way toward them like smoke. Yellow eyes gleamed. Teeth and tongues gleamed. Scales and dark fur glistened. The beasts didn't speak a word; it was as if they had given themselves wholly to a mindless animal hunger.

"Loose!" someone shouted.

Arrows thunked into the nearest Fangs. Maraly spun around.

Errol and a company of archers crouched on top of a building on the opposite street. The nearest Fangs howled and hissed, then slid back down the roof and knocked more of their comrades to the street below. Errol waved his hand and another volley of arrows decimated the Fangs to Maraly's right.

"Maker bless Errol," Gammon said with a laugh. "Come on, Maraly."

He took her hand and ran for the opening Errol had made. They made their way over flat rooftops, leaping narrow alleys, drawing nearer and nearer to the marketplace. Soon Maraly saw Artham gliding overhead, his red wings aglow in the torchlight.

Gammon lowered Maraly down to the waiting Dugtowners beyond the barricade. Upon seeing their leader, the multitude raised a cheer that even the Fangs across the River Blapp must have heard.

Gammon hopped down after Maraly, dropped to his knees, and the two of them hugged. Maraly rested her head on his shoulder and closed her eyes, giving thanks to the Maker with the best words she could think of. She thought about Claxton's arms and fists, how he had used them to abuse her—and then rested in Gammon's protective embrace, the feel of his hands gently patting her back. She was home at last.

They were still hugging in the middle of the crowd when Errol and his archers returned.

"Sir," Errol said. "It's good to have you back."

Gammon released Maraly. He stood and wiped his eyes. "Errol, my friend, you saved our lives. As did you, Artham. Thank you."

"It's her you have to thank," Artham said with a laugh.

"Aye," said Gammon, bowing his head to Maraly. "Thank *you*."

She spat, wiped her mouth, and shrugged. "Don't get all mushy on me. That hug was like an hour long."

"I guess I should keep my hug short, then," Sara Cobbler said. Maraly grinned and ran to her friend, squeezed her tight. "You made it," Sara said. "Is Claxton . . . ?"

Maraly looked at the ground and nodded. "He won't trouble me no more."

Errol tossed the Florid Sword mask to Gammon. "You left this back at Snoot's."

"Left it behind I did, though 'twas not my purpose to so do. Verily, with gratitude I thank thee," Gammon said as he tied on the mask. "'Tis a goodly mask for fighting foul Fangs. Fiends! Fie!"

"Hey, when do I get one of those?" Maraly asked.

"If we survive this night," Artham said, "I'll sew you one myself."

"Sir," said Errol. "We need to talk."

Gammon took Maraly's hand and followed Errol through the crowd, nodding sagely at the men and women looking to him for their courage. As they walked, Errol explained how he had rationed the weapons among the people, counted arrows and food stores, and given jobs to those unable to fight. They reached the riverfront and walked out to the end of the dock, where a single torch burned.

Gammon looked over his shoulder at the mass of Skreeans who had fallen silent as they watched. Their little barricaded stronghold looked small and helpless, trapped between the heavy night, the dark river, and the Fangs that surrounded them.

"They're out there," said Errol pointing at the other shore. "Thousands of them. Trolls, too."

All Gammon saw beyond the torchlight was blackness. The river was a brooding mass that reeked of garp and daggerfish. Somewhere out there, an army waited to attack—an army that hopelessly outnumbered the Skreeans and was better armed. Gammon saw Dugtowners staring fearfully into the dark, equipped only with shovels and hoes. Numbered among them were Sara's orphans, armed with forks.

Gammon had little doubt that when the Fangs attacked they would crush his little army. And he had no idea what to do.

It was then that a figure in a black robe floated toward them out of the darkness. Gammon knew at once that it was the woman who melded the Fangs.

The Stone Keeper.

40

Parley

The boat emerged from the inky blackness with four snakish Fangs rowing. The robed figure seemed to hover in the prow like a ghost. The hood of her black robe hung low over her face, the fingers of her thin, white hands interlocked at her waist. The swish and plunk of the oars carried across the water and echoed off the riverfront buildings. When she was a stone's throw away from the end of the dock, Gammon stepped forward and raised his sword.

"That's far enough!" he shouted.

The Stone Keeper raised one hand and the Fangs pointed the nose of the boat upstream and worked to keep it in one place. The hooded woman surveyed the Skreeans in silence. Then she slowly reached up and pulled back her cowl. In the orange glow of the torch, her face, framed by her raven hair, shone as white as a moon floating just over the water. She smiled.

"Gammon," she said in a voice that floated across the surface of the river like a tendril of smoke. "I have come to ask for your surrender. You know you cannot win. Why doom your people to their deaths?"

Gammon drew his sword and pointed it at the sky. "We would rather fight you to the death than live another day under Gnag's dominion." A flock of crows cawed in the distance, as if in mockery of his words.

The woman smiled again. "Is your mind made up, then?"

"It is," he answered. Maraly felt Gammon's hand tighten around hers and she didn't think he knew he was squeezing it.

"And what of your people?" she asked, raising her voice and waving a pale hand at the Dugtowners behind him. "Are they as foolish as you? Do you all wish to die? Here? Now? On this night? It is not too late. We can give you all new names—and new power. Gnag extends his hand to you in mercy. Join us, and you too can sing the song of the ancient stone. You will know great power, as do all my children! Is this rotten land worth dying for?"

The men and women in the marketplace murmured and shifted their feet. Maraly knew that Claxton had sent prisoners to the Fangs to be changed, and she had heard of this woman with a magic rock and a soothing voice. She noticed that Artham Wingfeather was trembling and looking everywhere but at the woman.

Something splashed into the water to Maraly's right. She looked back and saw a little boy standing beside Sara Cobbler. "Go away, lady!" he shouted. He grabbed a fork from a girl beside him and threw it as far as he could. "We fight for Queen Sara, not you."

"Dear boy," the Stone Keeper said in a soothing voice. "Surely the queen you speak of would rather you saw the sunrise than die under the blade of a Grey Fang."

"Quiet your tongue!" Gammon shouted. "I'll not suffer your charms and neither will these brave Skreeans. The power you speak of belongs to the Maker alone. We would rather face your wrath than his. Now be gone, or Errol's arrow will deliver you to the Mighty Blapp."

Errol nocked an arrow and aimed it.

The Stone Keeper's smile faded. She replaced her hood, gestured to the Fangs in her boat, and said, "As you wish."

The boat veered away and faded into the darkness. The crows in the distance cawed again, and Maraly—along with many of the Dugtowners—couldn't help but imagine the birds feasting on carcasses.

Gammon sheathed his sword and strode back to the shore with a fierce smile that all his army could see. He jumped onto a barrel near the water's edge. "We shall live to see the sunrise, Skreeans! And if we do not, then we go to our graves with the Maker's good pleasure and the blood of freedom staining the ground! Our descendants will sing of this night!"

The people answered with a half-hearted cheer. Armulyn the Bard played a soulful Annieran tune called "Hill and Valley, Horse and Hand," and when it was over he shouted, "Fangs are ugly!" Nervous laughter rippled through the crowd.

Gammon gave a good speech, Maraly thought, and Armulyn's song was nice, but they did little to remove the fear from the faces she saw. "What do we do now?" she asked.

Gammon tied on his Florid Sword mask. "First, we light every torch tower we can get to. The better we see, the better off we'll be." He nodded at Maraly. "Then we sharpen our blades and wait."

41

Storytime with Artham

Sara sat on the cobbles with Artham and Armulyn the Bard. The orphans, most of whom were asleep, were gathered around as if it were storytime. And storytime it was. Armulyn the Bard seemed to have grown ten years younger in Artham P. Wingfeather's presence, and was sitting cross-legged in front of him, asking every question he could think of about the Shining Isle. Artham indulged him, laughing at the bard's delight over the tiniest details.

Sara widened her eyes at Maraly and pointed secretly at Artham as if to say, "Can you believe it?"

After all this time, *this* was the Artham Sara had been looking for. When he had arrived at the Fork Factory, he spoke with a strong, clear voice and his eyes were brave and kind. Even with his wings and reddish skin, he was somehow handsome. But ever since that day, Artham had lost himself. Sara was glad he was back.

She scooted over to make room for Maraly. They sat under the steady glow of the torch towers and listened.

"Yes, yes," Artham said. "There are mountains—but mostly in the center of the island. As the land slopes down to the sea, the hills roll out like a floor of green pillows."

"Are the mountains snowy in the winter, like it says in *The Legend of Eremund the Brave?*"

"Snowy, yes. And when they catch the light at sunrise, they blush like maidens."

"Tell me about the towns. Are there many? Most of the stories are about Rysen."

"The towns are perfect."

"What do you mean?"

"Let me put it like this. Imagine you're walking one of the footpaths that cut through the countryside. You have a staff and rucksack, and after a brisk few hours you think to yourself, 'I could use a hearty bowl of limpiny stew right about now.' The villages in Anniera are so perfectly spaced that as soon as you have that thought you crest a hill and see a village in the valley below, with smoke in the chimneys and the smell of hay on the wind. You stroll into town, and after some bibes from the village fount—every village has a fount for travelers—you turn around and see a little inn or tavern, likely next to an apparelry or a bookstore."

"There are bookstores?"

"In every town. It's a requirement, you see."

Armulyn sighed.

"You stride into that inn and lean your walking stick by the door, and no sooner than you've sat down and sipped a pint of something warm, the proprietor brings you a bowl of limpiny stew."

"But how does he know?"

"They always have what you want in Anniera." Armulyn looked skeptical, but Artham continued. "It's not that the cooks are magic. It's the *land*, you see? When you're walking through that part of the island, the shape of the hills, the color of the leaves, the way the light hits the tree trunks, the cool of the morning, and the smell of crops— probably limpiny sprouts—all contrive to make you want exactly the right thing at the right time."

"I've never heard of limpiny stew," said Armulyn, "but I want some. And the same is true of the cooks, I suppose? I mean, they would wake up that morning with limpiny stew on the brain?"

"Yes. Of course, they make a variety of things. Not every traveler wants the same thing at the same time, but when they walk through the door the proprietor can usually tell by the look of them what they'll need. The people of the Shining Isle are attentive to the way the Maker shaped the world—but it's not just that. They're also attentive to the way the Maker made the heart. And they're just trying to be good subjects—trying to give each other what they were made to give."

"So in Anniera, what you want and what you need," Armulyn said, "are one and the same."

"Exactly. That's what the Maker intended from the beginning," Artham said. "It's not always so, but on the best days that's how it feels. If the kingdom hadn't fallen apart in the First Epoch, thanks to Ouster Will, I think it would still be that way the world over. As they say, 'If the weather is bad, it's Ouster Will.'"

"Ouster Will, Ouster Will, he breathes on your ankles beneath your bed," Armulyn chanted. "Waits till you're sleeping and sneaks in your head."

Borley shivered and scooted closer to Sara.

"I haven't heard that in a while," Artham said.

"So, Ouster Will—he was real, too," Armulyn said with a shake of his head. "The world is more terrible and more wonderful than I imagined. I've had that song stuck in my head since I first learned it at the whistleharp academy. *Darkens your dreams till you wish you were dead, under the ground on the graveyard hill with Ouster Will, Ouster Will.*" Borley shivered again, and this time the bard shivered too.

"I'm surprised that you know it," Artham said.

"Oh, I know everything about Anniera." Armulyn's eyes twinkled and he suddenly looked like a little boy. "Well, everything you can know without actually *going* there. I've dreamed of it since I was young. My parents told me about it, fed me a steady supply of books, and once I learned about the Annieran songs I dedicated my life to keeping them alive here in Skree. Especially after the Great War, the songs seemed to wake up something hopeful in the Skreeans. And the Fangs absolutely hate them." Armulyn thought for a moment, then asked, "After my limpiny stew at the village tavern, would I stay the night?"

"No! It's only midday, remember? You'd pay the owner and strike out over green fields of totato and fotraw in bloom. You wouldn't need a map, for there are signposts exactly when you need them, and as soon as you were hungry for supper you'd come upon another village, another fount, another bookstore, and another tavern. You might even be invited in to stay with a farmer for the night."

"I want to go there, Queen Sara," Borley said with a yawn. "Can we?"

Sara squeezed Borley. "Anniera is on the other side of the ocean, dear. Our home is here in Skree."

"We don't really have a home anywhere." Borley pointed at the orphans spread across the cobbles of the marketplace like a garden of sleeping children.

"Don't worry," Sara said. "When this is over, we'll make a home here."

"Anniera does sound nice," said another voice. Grettalyn was awake, a few feet away. "My ma used to tell me stories about it when I was a baby."

"What kind of stories?" said another voice, as small as a mouse. A girl Sara didn't know sat up and propped herself on her elbows.

"The same as I told you on our way here, Lola," Armulyn said gently. "Remember?"

"Yes, I remember. But I still like to hear them."

"Me too," Artham said. He stared up at the flames roiling on the torch tower and sighed. "It's a lovely place for a traveler, for the whole land feels like home. Why, if you brought your whistleharp, Armulyn, you'd never want for a meal or a bed. Annierans treasure music like no one else."

"And what of the castle?" Armulyn asked.

Sara and Maraly glanced at one another, then at Artham, who was still staring at the fire.

"The castle?" Artham closed his eyes. "It's beautiful. It looks like it grew straight out of the stone itself. Spires, flags flapping in the east wind, smoke rising from chimneys, and children laughing in the courts. It's a peautiful blace. How I song to lee it again."

Armulyn gave Sara a confused look.

"Maybe we should change the subject," Sara suggested.

Artham bobbed his head to and fro and clapped his reddish hands. The claws clacked together oddly.

"The king-king-king would dimply be selighted to have you, patoo-too-too!" He grinned and wiped a tear from his cheek. "He's my brother, you know. The Shing of the Kining Isle. Shing, shing, SHING!"

"What's happening?" Armulyn said. A few of the children sat up and looked afraid.

"Shh," said Maraly, scooting over to Artham and stroking his arm. "It's all right, sir."

"But I left him," Artham whimpered. He laid his head in Maraly's lap. "And now he's dead. I was the Throne Warden, you know."

Sara tilted his head back and gave him a drink of water. "You're still a Throne Warden."

At those words, Artham squinted his eyes and grimaced, weeping silently. The water dribbled out of his mouth and glided across the bright feathers of one wing till it dripped to the ground and disappeared between the cracks of two cobblestones. That was what always happened to her words of comfort, she thought. They passed right over Artham without sinking in and then vanished.

Borley crawled over and put his hand on Artham's arm. Then Grettalyn placed a soothing hand on his forehead. The little one named Lola bobbled over and laid her head on Artham's shoulder. At the sound of his crying, the other orphans awoke and surrounded poor

Artham, hundreds of innocent hands patting his arms and legs and stroking his wings, saying, "Don't cry, Mister Artham." "It's all right, sir." "Don't be scared."

Artham's eyes remained closed, but his weeping subsided.

Then the wind carried a sound out of the darkness, from the direction of Torrboro. It was the sound of oars splashing, of boats thumping against one another, of trolls grunting and growl-moaning, of Fangs hissing and snarling. Above it all they heard the sound of crows squawking overhead, messengers of the coming doom.

Maraly stood and drew her knives as the orphans around her drew their forks and held them out in trembling hands. Armulyn the Bard stepped over Artham and moved forward with his whistleharp in one hand.

"AWAKE BROTHERS AND SISTERS OF SKREE!" Gammon screamed from the end of the dock. He stood with his sword in the air. He turned his back to the river so all could see his black hat and mask. The F and S glowed blood red on his chest. "NOW IS THE TIME FOR COURAGE. WE MEET THE ENEMY WITH STEADY HEARTS, FOR DAWN HAS CONQUERED DARK SINCE THE MAKER SPOKE THE WORLD. THE NIGHT IS DEEP, BUT LIGHT RUNS DEEPER. LET OUR BLADES AND BLOOD PROCLAIM IT!"

Every man, every woman, every child in the market that night raised their weapons and bellowed their defiance of the Fang army and Gnag the Nameless and every wicked thing that ever soured the sweet world. Their shouts tore across the River Blapp and echoed off the walls of the Castle Torr, returning to them like a gust of wind and doubling the din.

As the shouting died away, thousands of eyes peered into the darkness, Gammon's first among them, straining to see the first of the Fang boats. The splashing continued, the snarls grew quieter, and Gammon shouted over his shoulder, "MAKE READY!"

42

Beholding the Dawn

Gammon and the Skreeans waited, and waited, and waited, but the Fangs didn't come. The pale of dawn glowed in the east so that the shape of the Castle Torr and the outline of the buildings on the waterfront were faintly visible, but they saw no Fangs. No trolls. The Skreeans murmured in confusion, weary after keeping watch all night. Then someone announced that the Fangs beyond the barricades were gone as well.

"The streets are clear?" Gammon asked Errol.

"Yes sir. I can't explain it. We didn't hear them leave. We thought it was part of a ruse, but I sent Olmin out to check the buildings and he found nothing. It's like the earth swallowed them up."

Gammon looked from his people to the barricades to the river, and a smile of relief came to his face. His shoulders slumped and he bowed his head in a prayer of thanksgiving.

"Are they gone?" Maraly asked as she trotted out onto the dock. "Is it really over?"

"For now at least. We'll know more as the day unfolds."

"Speaking of day," Errol said, pointing east along the Blapp. The sun hadn't peeked above the horizon yet, but it had lit the sky with fiery clouds whose glory was reflected in the still of the river.

"Behold the dawn!" Gammon shouted. He thrust the point of his sword into the dock and left it shuddering there as he and Maraly, arm in arm, walked back to the waterfront. A mighty cheer arose, louder even than the battle cry in the night.

As the Skreeans discovered later that day, there were no Fangs there to hear it. Errol and a group of his men bravely took a boat across the river to Torrboro and returned jubilant.

"It's true, sir," Errol said. He shook his head as if he struggled to believe his own words.

As the barricades were dismantled and the Dugtowners streamed through the city again to inspect the damage to their homes and businesses, Gammon and Maraly sat over cups of berry cider in a tavern called Klert's Pipe and Pint.

Errol sat down beside them and thanked the proprietor for his steaming mug. "There's not a Fang in the city, sir. No dust, either, so they weren't killed. We saw fresh mud on the road east to Fort Lamendron."

"Then we take the battle there," Gammon said.

Errol's face fell. "Sir?"

"The Fangs must be gathering their strength at the old fort. If we can attack quickly, perhaps we can catch them off guard. Surprise them. It would give us an advantage. There are thousands of Skreeans, but many thousands of Fangs. We need all the advantages we can find." Gammon rubbed his chin. "Maybe you and I should do some scouting. This could be a trap. We'll sneak out past Glipwood to Lamendron and see what they're up to."

"I want to go," Maraly said.

"No, lass. This is dangerous work."

Maraly folded her arms and narrowed her eyes at Gammon. "Dangerous? Who was it that fought beside you on the roof? And who was it that survived a life among the Stranders of the East Bend? And who is it that has felled six toothy cows and she ain't yet thirteen?"

"All right, all right." Gammon laughed. "You can come. Clearly, I'd be a fool not to bring you. Errol, if indeed the Fangs are at Lamendron, we'll need to strike hard and fast. Stay here, and have all those empty Fang boats dragged to our shore so we can be ready to move when the time comes."

"Where are you going?" asked Sara from the doorway. Artham stood beside her with his head down. His wings drooped, the tips dragging on the dirty floor.

"Artham," Gammon said. "Just the man I wanted to see. Maraly and I are striking out into Fang territory. I could use another set of eyes—and a set of wings, come to think of it. Would you come?"

Artham tilted his head and smiled pitifully at Gammon, then nodded. His eyes were bloodshot from crying, and his hands were clenched at his chest. "Only if Queen Sara can come," he said. "I can't leave her. Someone has to seep her kafe-kafe. Keep her safe. Yes. I need to seep her kafe."

Sara forced his claws apart so she could hold his hand. "He needs someone to protect," she said.

"It could be dangerous," Gammon said.

"If there's danger, there's no safer place than Artham Wingfeather's side." Sara squeezed his hand and Artham bobbed his head.

"What about the children?" Maraly asked.

"They're back at Thimble Thumb's, and Armulyn is doing a fine job of entertaining them. He says he has enough stories and songs about Anniera to keep them happy for days."

And so, Sara Cobbler, Artham Wingfeather, Gammon Felda, and Maraly Weaver mounted a ferry with four horses and crossed the Mighty Blapp under a warm spring sun. They arrived at the opposite dock in silence, unsettled by the emptiness of the streets. Errol bade them farewell and took one of the Fang ships back to Dugtown while the rest led their horses down from the ferry and up into the city.

Other than the occasional dog or thwap scampering across the littered streets, they were alone. It was Maraly's first time in the city, so she marveled at the finely cut stone walls of the buildings, the archways and verandas. Though Fangs had abused Torrboro for nearly a decade, it was easy to see the city's former glory. After an hour during which the only sound was the clop of horse's hooves on the streets, they passed through the city gate and followed the road to the east. They passed a sign that indicated that the Glipwood Township and Fort Lamendron lay straight ahead, and the Plains of Palen Jabh-j were to their right.*

"To Glipwood we go," said Gammon. He didn't notice the way Artham shuddered.

They rode hard all day, Gammon and Maraly at the front with their eyes roving the forest to the left and the grass to the right. They saw no Fangs or trolls, though it was clear from the churned mud that they had marched that way the night before. More than one toothy cow mooed from deep inside the forest, and as night fell a chorus of horned hounds howled. They rode south, away from the forest, until Gammon declared that it was time to rest. None of them had slept the night before, and the tall grass looked as soft and welcoming as a feather bed. They made no fire, but huddled together for warmth and fell fast asleep under the glittering sky.

At dawn a mist lay on the plains and obscured all but the tops of the glipwood oaks. They passed around some berrybuns and hogpig strips for breakfast then mounted their horses and pushed on.

"We'll be there in a few hours," Artham said, surprising them all with the clarity of his speech. It was the first he had spoken since the tavern the day before. "Glipwood by the Sea." He smiled to himself. "Such a nice little village. I doubt there's anything left."

"You know it?" Gammon asked.

"He lived there, back when he watched over the Igibys." Sara smiled. "The *Wingfeathers*, I mean. I still can't get used to calling them that."

---

* The sign also pointed to the north, northeast, northwest, and southwest, informing the traveler that there was "The Blapp, Eventually," "Some Grass, then the Blapp," "Some Grass, then Some Rocks, then the Blapp," and "Some Grassy Hills, then Another Sign," respectively.

"In the forest. In my castle," Artham said.

"You had a castle?" Maraly asked.

"Yes," Artham said, scratching his head with one of his clawed hands. "I think so. Up in the treeeeeeees." Gammon and Maraly looked at Sara with concern. She shrugged as Artham continued. "I didn't have wings yet. Just socks."

"Socks," Maraly said.

"Yes! On my hands. It was a disguise."

"This is very strange," Sara said. "Are you all right?"

"I think so," Artham said with a wave of his hand. "It all started because of a dog, you know."

"What do you mean?" Gammon said.

"Everything. The end of the war. The Iggyfeathers in the carriage. Kimera. The Heen Grollows—Green Hollows. Everything."

They rode in silence. Somewhere in the forest a cow mooed.

"It was Nugget. He bit a Fang. Leeli fought it, and the boys came to help. But the Fangs were going to hurt them, so Zouzab the ridgerunner threw a rock. Then Nia used some Annieran jewelry to get them out of the Glipwood jail, and that's how they realized they were the Jewels of Anniera—the children, I mean. Next thing you know, the Fangs are chasing them all across Skree. That's how they ended up in Kimera, then Ban Rona. All because of Nugget. Brave little Nugget."Artham reined up his horse, startling the others. "Ah! There it is. The Glipwood Township."

43

The Glipwood Township

The noon sun shone on the rooftops of the Glipwood Township as Artham, Sara, Maraly, and Gammon rode their horses down Main Street. Sara remembered the town from when she was little; years before, she had met Janner and his family there on Dragon Day. They rode past Dunn's Green, where people used to play everything from zibzy to handyball. But now the streets were as deserted as Torrboro, and some of the buildings on Vibbly Way were in ruins. Of those still standing were Books and Crannies, Shaggy's Tavern, and the Only Inn, where Sara's family had once stayed when she was younger. Now the inn was forlorn and empty, with spring weeds growing up over the stoop and entwining the porch rail. Even the cobwebs were old and abandoned.

From the corner of her eye Sara saw Artham twitching. If the little town held memories for her, it had to be much worse for Artham.

A muffled sound came from the outbuilding behind Books and Crannies, and Gammon signaled for everyone to stop. He slipped off his horse, handed the reins to Artham, and tiptoed through the dusty alley beside the bookstore.

They heard a crash, then Gammon's voice: "I've got you both! Stop struggling or I'll give you something to grounce about!"

He reappeared dragging a ridgerunner in each hand. They wiggled and kicked like children.

"He stole it!" one of them said.

"I did not! You stole it first. We found them together. I stole nothing! They're not stolen if you stole them first." A bright yellow ermentine dropped out of one of their pockets and the two little creatures struggled to grab it. "That's mine!"

"No it isn't! You stole it!"

"From a thief, which cancels out the crime!"

The two ridgerunners scrapped with one another until Gammon shook them by their collars and ordered them to be quiet.

"Didn't you used to help the bookstore man?" Sara asked. "Your name starts with a Z."

"His name is Zouzab," said the first ridgerunner.

"Quiet, *Mobrik*," said the other. "Why don't you go ahead and blab about everything in the world while you're at it?"

"Maybe I will!" Mobrik shouted. "The Fangs—"

"Quiet!"

"The Fangs are gone, you know." Mobrik folded his arms and stuck his nose in the air. "And I am *not* an ermentine thief. I merely stole it to keep it safe."

At this, Zouzab renewed his struggle, swiping at Mobrik and hitting Gammon in the process.

"It's nice to see you again, Zouzab," said Artham.

Zouzab stopped fighting and squinted up at Artham. His eyes widened. "The Sock Man."

Sara, Gammon, and Maraly looked at one another with surprise. He really *had* worn socks, apparently.

"If you're looking for the Jewels of Anniera," Zouzab said with a sneer, "I haven't seen them."

"I know just where they are." Artham leapt from his horse and floated down with a flap of his wings. Zouzab and Mobrik cowered. "Far enough away that they will never again be troubled by your treachery." He stepped over to the little ridgerunner, grabbed his shoulder, and looked him in the eye. "Now what's this your friend is saying about the Fangs?"

Zouzab sneered, but he finally said, "They're gone."

"Gone where?"

"To Ban Rona."

"Why?" Artham said, straightening and giving his wings a shudder.

"I don't know. I heard them say that Gnag has no more interest in Skree. He needed them to sail for the Green Hollows straightaway."

"Is that everything, Mobrik?" Artham waved the fruit in the air. "I'll give this ermentine to whomever tells me the most."

"Yes! That's all we know!" Mobrik and Zouzab strained against Gammon's grip, stretching for the little yellow fruit that Artham held enticingly before them. "We tried to get on the ship but they wouldn't let us. The Green Hollows is home to much fruit, you know."

"Fruit," Zouzab said under his breath.

"When did they leave?" Gammon asked, giving the ridgerunners a good shake.

"This morning at low tide!" Zouzab shouted. "Now give me that fruit!"

Artham nodded at Gammon and he released them. Then Artham hurled the ermentine as far as he could, over the back of Books and Crannies. The ridgerunners dashed after it, fighting each other the whole way.

A voice called from further down the street. "Hello?"

Gammon drew his sword and Artham took to the air. Sara and Maraly tensed, ready to steer their horses to safety. But it was only a man and woman—the man was bald, with a white moustache; the woman was thin, with grey hair and a beautiful face. They were dressed in tattered clothing and walked hand in hand, staggering now and then as if they were terribly weary. They saw Artham flapping in the air over the town and fell to their knees. They cowered and folded their hands as if they were praying.

Artham landed in front of them and lifted their chins. Sara heard him say, "Joe? Addie? It's all right."

They looked at Artham with wonder. "Peet?" asked Joe.

Addie took one of his hands in her own. "Where are your socks?"

"I outgrew them, I suppose." Artham smiled. "Where did you come from?"

"Fort Lamendron," Joe said. "The Fangs, this morning they—they just disappeared. One of the other prisoners managed to open his cage and he freed the rest of us."

"The rest of you?" Gammon asked.

Joe and Addie looked over their shoulders and Gammon's jaw fell open. In the distance, a parade of men, women, and children marched wearily up the hill toward Glipwood. They held to each other and looked hopefully at Gammon and Artham as they approached.

"It's true!" Addie cried waving to them. "The Fangs are gone!"

"Addie," Joe said. "We need to prepare the rooms. We'll have company soon, I'll wager!"

Joe and Addie Shooster hurried up the steps of the Only Inn (Glipwood's only inn) and began swiping at cobwebs and tugging at weeds. Minutes later the place looked alive again—and just in time, too, because the first of the Skreeans freed from Lamendron were marching into town, and some were climbing the porch stairs of the inn to ask for food. One of the upstairs windows flew open and Addie shook out a white sheet, griping about the dust and bugs.

Artham waved Sara and Maraly over, and they steered their horses through the crowd, answering questions as they went.

"Yes, I think they're really gone."

"Gammon, from Kimera—he freed Dugtown this winter."

"We don't know. They seem to have simply vanished."

To Sara's relief, Artham seemed at peace; his voice and eyes were steady. "I want to show you something," he said. He mounted his horse and led Gammon and the girls past a guttered building whose roof hung limply from the upper story. "That used to be the cobblery. A grumpy fellow named Rawstyme ran the place. Hated the fell of smeet."

"*The smell of feet*," Maraly mouthed to Sara.

"Where are you taking us?" Gammon asked.

"To the Igiby Cottage. Or what's left of it. I thought you might like to see where Janner, Tink, and Leeli grew up."

Sara felt a pleasant tingle in her stomach. She had thought so often of Janner Igiby, that brave boy who had left behind some of his light in the Fork Factory, just for Sara. That boy who, Artham claimed, had sent him to find her. An ocean separated them now—but it made her happy to know that he had thought of her. And maybe, just maybe, someday he would sail back to Skree, and maybe he would find her and—

Sara shook her head, thankful that everyone was too busy ducking under the overgrowth of spring briars and low branches to notice her rosy cheeks. They rode past a broken fence and came upon a humble cottage beside the charred remains of a barn. Black timbers rose from the weeds like gravestones. The cottage windows were all broken, the door hung limply from its hinges, and many shingles were missing from the roof. A dragonfly zipped by, shot into one of the windows, then back out through the door. Gulpswallows sang in the sweeping branches of one of the biggest glipwood oaks Sara had ever seen.

Even in its dilapidated state the homestead was a beautiful spot. Sara had the secret thought that she would like to live there someday if she ever got married, but she blushed again when she realized that Janner Igiby was the husband who popped into her head.

Artham dismounted and walked up to the porch. "This is where they lived."

"It ain't a bad spot," Maraly said, spitting and wiping her chin with her forearm. She pointed beyond the house at a trail that led into a little stand of trees. "What's through there?"

"That's the Glipper Trail," Artham said. "I'll show you."

They dismounted and traipsed through spring weeds so green and wild they seemed to have erupted from the ground that morning. They slipped in among the trees and wound down a short slope of rocky switchbacks. All at once, the trees parted and the Dark Sea of Darkness spread out below them like a gray sheet.

Maraly clutched the nearest tree, dizzied by the height.

"That's something you don't see every day," Gammon said. "Beautiful."

"And scary," Sara said.

"It's not scary at all," said Artham with a laugh. He ran to the edge of the cliff and jumped. The others gasped and then fell into nervous laughter as he spread his wings and soared out over the water.

Sara inhaled the salty air, felt the cool wind whispering up over the cliff, and closed her eyes with a sigh. Could it be that the Fangs were truly gone? Gone forever? She didn't understand why they had left, but the air around her and the ground beneath her feet tingled with a long-withheld joyfulness. Was it possible that the land itself knew that the shadow of Gnag the Nameless had passed from Skree?

When Sara opened her eyes she glimpsed tiny shapes on the horizon, far to the east. She squinted one eye and pointed. "What's that?"

Gammon studied the horizon. His face broke into a smile, and his eyes glimmered with tears. "It's the Fang fleet. They're leaving!" Artham tipped his wings and rode a gust of wind back to the cliff, alighting gracefully beside Gammon. "Your bird eyes can see better than mine. Is that what I think it is?"

Artham launched himself out again and flew so far that he might as well have been the Lone Fendril in the distance. Gammon put his arm around Maraly. Sara saw her stiffen and then relax as she leaned her head on his shoulder.

The sight made Sara's heart ache like it hadn't in years. She missed her sweet father and mother and wondered what had become of them.

They had been either killed or tortured into submission by the Fangs. They might have even become Fangs themselves—something that Sara didn't hold against them. Artham was proof to her that even the noblest soul could be broken. If her parents *were* Fangs, maybe even among those on the ships in the distance, she prayed the Maker would be merciful. She shuddered, then she hugged the tree at the cliff's edge, wishing she had someone to love her the way Gammon loved Maraly. At least she had her orphans. They needed her, and that was just as good, wasn't it?

Artham flew back with a smile spread across his face.

"It's true! The Sangs are failing away. Dack to Bang—back to Dang!"

Sara laughed, wiping tears from her eyes. Maraly whooped and hollered her best Strander victory cry, and Gammon sat down like a weary farmer after tilling a hundred miles of land. The four of them sat looking over the Dark Sea of Darkness, giving silent thanks for their deliverance.

"What do we do now?" Maraly asked.

Gammon pulled the Florid Sword mask from his coat and turned it over in his hands. "We go home."

"Where's that?" Maraly asked.

Gammon shrugged. "Anywhere we want, I suppose. There are some beautiful little villages down in the Linnard Woodlands. I could go back to farming."

Maraly looked at him like he was crazy. "You said you were a terrible farmer."

"It's true," he said with a chuckle.

"There are always gonna be Stranders causing trouble in Dugtown, you know," Maraly said, "and someone needs to uphold the law—ride the rooftops and all that. And besides, Artham, you said you'd make me a mask of my own if we survived the night." She stood and drew one of her knives, striking a fearsome pose. "Who will protect the citizens of Dugtown from the thieves and Stranders of the night? The Florid Sword and his trusty companion, Shadowblade!"

"I like it," Sara said.

The men laughed, and Gammon said, "I like it too."

The four of them walked back through the trees to the Igiby cottage to fetch the horses. When they got back to town they found a small crowd milling about, laughing together and singing as if it were the Dragon Day festival. Joe and Addie Shooster waved at Artham and the others from their front porch. They had already filled buckets of water from their well and were serving it to the crowd. Smoke rose from their chimney and Sara smelled something delicious wafting out of the kitchen.

"We're going back," Gammon announced as he and Maraly mounted their horses. "Errol needs to know what's going on. We have good news, and that's been a rare thing in this land for too long."

Sara looked at Artham, who was pacing in front of Books and Crannies with his head down. She knew she needed to get back to the orphans, but Glipwood was such a haven of pleasant memories that she hated to leave. "Can we stay a while?"

"I want to see my castle, Cara Sobbler." Artham blinked several times and shook his head as if to clear it. "But I don't want to go by myself-self-self."

Gammon looked her in the eyes. "You'll be all right?"

"Yes, sir. Tell Borley and the orphans that I'll be back soon. Bye, Maraly."

"That's Shadowblade to you." Maraly lowered her voice. "But don't tell nobody. They can't know my true identity."

Sara waved as Gammon and Maraly trotted back to Dugtown to herald the peace that had come at last—and, of course, to roam the rooftops of Dugtown by night, keeping her citizens safe.

"Ready?" Artham said.

Sara nodded and began to mount her horse, but Artham stopped her. Before she knew it, Sara was resting in his arms, rising over the smiling faces of the people on Main Street. She clung to Artham's neck as they soared over the fields behind the houses, up the grassy slope of the land toward the line of Glipwood Forest.

They flew over the charred remains of a large estate where Sara spotted several strange statues, then they glided along the forest's edge, passing farms and meadows and fenced pastures before turning north into the forest proper, over treetops that seemed like soft green clouds. The new leaves were so bright and beautiful that it was difficult for Sara to imagine how dangerous the forest really was.

"This should do it," Artham said, and they swooped below the canopy into a small clearing. He placed Sara gently on the ground and listened to be sure there were no animals on the prowl. "Here we are," he said, putting his hands on his hips proudly. "My castle."

44

Peet's Castle

Sara didn't see anything resembling a castle. Then Artham lifted her chin. Nestled high in the branches was an impressive treehouse covered in brown leaves. Rope bridges spanned between limbs, leading from one room to another, then out into other trees.

"You lived here?" Sara said breathlessly.

"Aye. And so did the Iggyfeathers for a while."

Artham dropped to all fours and rooted around in the mulch like a dog after a mole, scattering leaves everywhere. "Aha!" he said.

"What is it?"

"My journals. Looky."

Artham brushed aside a pile of twigs and old leaves, revealing a bundle wrapped in weathered canvas. He unwrapped the covering and held up a leatherbound book. He handed it to Sara and did a backwards somersault, sitting back up with leaves stuck in his hair.

"You want me to read it?" she asked.

Artham didn't answer. He hopped to his feet, climbed the tree, and banged around in the different rooms of his castle. Sara opened the book and read.

The writing was in a beautiful, precise script. She read poems about Anniera's white shores and fair green hills, poems about sailing, about the Castle Rysen at sunset and sunrise, about Esben and Nia, poems about the children. She skimmed forward until she found one about

Janner. It described his thoughtful eyes and strong back, the good work he did in the fields and the way he always watched over his brother and sister. It said he looked like Esben, the king, and then the handwriting grew jittery and wild.

As Sara reached for another journal she heard a rustle in the leaves behind her. Then she heard the most frightening sound one can hear in Glipwood Forest: "Mooo."

She turned to face the beast. It snorted and pawed the ground, then opened its terrible maw and mooed again, drool dribbling from the ends of its yellow teeth. Before she could scream, Artham lifted her over the treetops.

"Sorry about that, Queen Sara," said Artham as they soared.

He flew her back to Glipwood and asked the Shoosters if Sara could stay with them for the night. He planned to stay in his castle.

"Maybe forever," he told them.

Sara lay in a soft but musty bed after a delicious meal of steamed wild vegetables. All the rooms of the Only Inn were occupied, and she heard the pleasant murmur of conversation through the walls, conversation untroubled by the fear of the Fangs of Dang for the first time in nine years.

But Sara was troubled. She couldn't stop thinking about Janner, and the danger he was in. Nor could she stop thinking about her beloved orphans, who had to build new lives now that the Fangs were gone.

If the war was really over, everything would slowly return to normal, and sorrow over the loss of their parents would come crashing over them like a wave—she knew it because she could feel it crashing over her. She had never felt so alone as she did that night in the soft bed, surrounded by strangers in Glipwood, where it seemed the ghosts of her parents haunted the streets. She longed for her home like never before.

The other occupants of the Only Inn laid awake that night, long after their talking ceased, and they wondered who was crying.

When Sara woke, Joe and Addie Shooster treated her like a queen. They served her breakfast in bed, Addie brought Sara her coat (freshly washed and dried beside the fireplace), and all three of them had their tea on the porch. While they sat, they bade farewell to the parade of Skreeans still trudging up from Fort Lamendron, departing for their old homes and villages.

"Excuse me, ma'am?" asked a ragged man as he approached. A woman with hollow eyes limped beside him. "Have you seen any children?"

"Our daughter Grettalyn was lost to us two years ago," said the woman.

Sara's teacup clattered to the floor and she leapt to her feet. "Grettalyn with the curly red hair?"

The couple looked at Sara with shock and nodded dumbly.

"Yes!" Sara rushed down from the porch and took their hands. "She was with me at the Fork Factory. She's in Dugtown, and she's fine!"

The man dropped to his knees and looked up into Sara's eyes. "Take us to her. Please."

Sara didn't realize she had forgotten to thank the Shoosters for their kindness until she was halfway to Dugtown. As she walked with Grettalyn's parents, rumor spread among the Skreeans on the road that a girl named Sara Cobbler knew every orphan in the city. Men and women surrounded her, pleading, sometimes going away sadly but often rejoicing upon learning that their children had survived. By the time Sara took the ferry across the Blapp the next day she had located the parents of dozens of her children.

She didn't allow herself to hope that she might see her own parents again, but as the ferry bumped into the dock she mustered the courage to privately ask a man named Portis (Trilliane's father) if he had heard her parents' names during his imprisonment. He hadn't, and he was so distracted by the hope of seeing his own daughter again that he didn't notice the way Sara's face fell. She decided not to ask anyone else.

It was late afternoon when Sara led the weary men and women to Thimble Thumb's Threads and witnessed many happy reunions. By nightfall she and Borley and twenty-six other orphans were all that were left. No one said much, and it took great effort to express their gladness that so many of their friends had been reunited with parents or relatives.

The factory was sad and silent that night. Sara lay in her cot thinking about her mother and father. In her soul a spark of hope that they might still be alive glowed stubbornly, but she did her best to snuff it out. They were gone. She was alone. Better to get used to the idea. She scolded herself whenever she thought of Janner Igiby, because he was gone too. Maraly had Gammon. Joe Shooster had Addie. Even Janner, wherever he was, had his family.

"I'm still here, Queen Sara," Borley whispered from his bunk, as if he knew her thoughts.

"I'm glad," she answered.

She dreamed of her parents, and when she woke their absence was more painful for it. Sara feigned cheerfulness as she and Armulyn prepared breakfast for the orphans, but she sensed that Borley, who never left her side, knew better. His quiet, steady presence was a great comfort, and by the time the meal was served and eaten, and the kitchen was cleaned, Sara's heart was lighter.

She wasn't alone—not as long as she had Borley and the others to care for. Gammon would help them whenever they needed it, and Armulyn, too, at least until his wanderlust carried him off. They had managed in the Fork Factory, and in the war against the Fangs, and they would manage now.

Sara was sweeping the floor that afternoon when the door to Thimble Thumb's Threads opened and light poured in. She couldn't see the silhouetted woman's face.

45

Found and Lost

Sara's skin tingled. Her broom clattered to the floor. The woman gasped and opened her arms, and Sara took a hesitant step forward.

"It's you!" the woman cried.

Sara's heart leapt and her joy was so great that she was unable to speak.

"It's you!" the woman exclaimed. "My Borley!"

"Mama?" Borley said uncertainly from beside Sara.

The woman rushed in and swept him up. Little Borley was too stunned to cry, and his eyes were on Sara even as his mother held him.

That was the moment the last spark of Sara's hope was vanquished. Stiffly, she picked up her broom and continued to sweep, unable to cry, unable to think, unable to feel.

Before he left, Borley begged Sara to come with him.

"I would be glad to have you as a daughter, dear," said Borley's mother. "We'll need help putting the farm back together."

"I can't. I have the others to care for." Sara kissed Borley on the head and looked him in the eye. "It's all right, General Borley. I'll come visit you sometime."

"We'll expect you," said Borley's mother. "We're just a few miles south, toward the Linnard Woodlands. A lovely little village called Stellen, near Warren Downs. Come and see us."

When Borley left, the sun left with him. Armulyn lit a lantern and sang the children their goodnight song while Sara busied herself cleaning the factory floor, pretending not to notice the way the last twenty-five orphans watched her. She didn't feel any better in the morning, but she willed her sorrow away and found that at times she managed to feel nothing at all.

As the days passed, Armulyn grew anxious, often looking out the window, eager to escape the orphanage to fetch supplies from the market or run some other errand, and Sara knew he would soon be leaving them too.

"You can go, you know," she told him one morning at breakfast. "It's all right."

Armulyn stared at his cup of bean brew. "No, it's not."

"We'll miss you, but we'll manage."

"It's not that. I know you can take care of yourself and the orphans too." Armulyn took a sip and looked out the window. "I've spent my whole life traveling, Sara, always looking to the next town, the next city, the next adventure—and I never knew what I was looking for until now. I used to think it was the thrill of new places, new people, the satisfaction of singing a story they've never heard. There's a powerful magic in songs, you know. They can aim the heart, point it at what matters. My own heart has been aimed ever at the far horizon, and my feet have followed. But now I'm as tired as an old bed. I thought that with the Fangs gone I might settle down here and help you with the children. It seemed like a good home. But my feet are still restless, Sara. I'm tired of moving and yet I can't wait to leave. I'm homesick—I've always been so. I can't rest until I finally learn what that means." Armulyn took Sara's hand. "I'm sorry."

"When will you leave?"

Armulyn answered by pointing a thumb at his backpack, which was resting near the front door and stuffed with supplies. When he told the orphans, they begged him not to leave—especially those who had come with him from beyond the maps. He put on a cheery face and promised to come back and visit soon.

Sara and the others stood on the street outside Thimble Thumb's Threads and watched him go. Armulyn's steps were lighter than Sara had seen them in days, but his leaving felt terribly wrong. She was homesick too, but she couldn't just pack a bag and strike out for the countryside. She had to make do.

If she couldn't go looking for a home, she would stay and make one. That's what the Shoosters were doing. That's what Artham Wingfeather was doing in his treehouse. Nothing in their stories had happened the way they wanted—Artham's mind was broken and his family was on the other side of the sea; the Shoosters were childless. Countless Skreeans would rebuild their lives atop the rubble of what was lost, and Sara would stay and care for her family of fellow orphans. The only home Sara would ever know would be the one she made for herself and for the children in her care. There was no home out there somewhere, no mystical land where all your restlessness was stilled and all your hopes fulfilled.

From a distance, Armulyn waved at the orphans clustered in the street. He bowed to them then rounded the corner as he played the first notes of an Annieran tune.

Sara's heart broke. She looked around at the rubbish in the streets of Dugtown, the broken glass still littering the ground from the battle, the smudged faces of all her parentless children. She thought of Artham Wingfeather alone in the forest. The melody tugged at her heart and suggested a great beauty that lay beyond her ability to imagine.

"I want to go home," said a boy named Cliffin.

"Me too," answered a few other children.

"This is our home now," Sara said firmly. She put her hands on her hips and looked at the sign over the door. *Really?* she thought. *Thimble Thumb's Threads is our home?* Armulyn's song faded among the sounds of the city, and Sara sighed.

"What do we do now, Queen Sara?" asked a little girl named Layna.

"We make the best of it." Sara bustled the children back inside. The truth was, she didn't know what else to do. All she knew was that everything felt wrong. It felt wrong that Armulyn was leaving, that she was staying, that Borley was gone, that Artham was alone in his treehouse—that Sara's parents had never come.

The only thing that felt right was Maraly and Gammon in masks, fighting the bad guys in Dugtown by moonlight.

Part Three:
THROG

As was the custom in the long alliance between the Green Hollows and Anniera, Ortham bade farewell to Ban Rona and lived with his wife in the Castle Rysen on the Shining Isle, bringing with him a trusted friend and advisor. He chose, of course, Bonifer Squoon. And so, in time, Bonifer became the chief advisor to the High King of Anniera, and his soul was riven by his love for the queen and his hidden hatred for the king. He knew, with what was left of his conscience, that the cost of his nearness to the queen was the destruction of whatever goodness was left in him, yet he remained, watching for the moment when he might have revenge on Ortham Wingfeather.

Bonifer Squoon was bequeathed a small house near the Castle Rysen and he filled it with books. He spent whatever time he could spare reading histories and accounts of battles and strategies of great kings, and indeed he was a valuable advisor to the king whenever enemies from the Woes of Shreve or the Jungles of Plontst made trouble for the free peoples of Dang. When the Pirates of Symia traded in dragonflesh and visited terror on sailors of the Symian Straits, it was Bonifer's advice, according to many, that ended the strife.

So Bonifer was well known in the lands and traveled often in search of books and knowledge. But when he returned home to his small house near the vast castle he felt again and again the knife in his heart of Madia's love for Ortham. He sought to grow wealthy, to show her that he could be great as Ortham was great. He sought to show her his strength, and though he knew it would change nothing, his corrupt mind could not resist the urge to make himself visible and of great value in Madia's eyes.

During Bonifer's travels he gathered word that a wise man living high atop the Killridge Mountains paid good money for animals of many sorts, and he seized the opportunity. Bonifer began quietly shipping cattle and dangerous beasts (lizards, snakes, bears, and wolves) from Anniera and Dang to the mysterious sage in the peaks. He thought little of what the man wanted with the animals and much of the gold he acquired in their sale. He planned to build a great house in Anniera, greater than the Castle Rysen, all for Madia. All for love.

—From *The Annieriad*

46

A Poet of Plontst

Day broke bright and clear, and a windless warmth melted the snow along the Outer Vales where Janner, Kalmar, and Oood camped. Several times during their long walk south and eastward toward the Blackwood and the foothills of the Killridge Mountains, the brothers' minds sang with Leeli's music and they had to stop until the vision passed.

In the visions, Janner heard her weary thoughts and the words to the songs she played but saw only hints of the many shadows whirling about her. Kalmar, however, quaked at the vivid sight of the Bat Fangs, describing to Janner their upturned noses, their needled teeth, their veiny brown wings, and their milky eyes. He saw Leeli's cracked lips, her wavy hair swaying as her head bobbed with the music, and he saw Nia beside her, then Podo swinging his legbone beside Rudric. But always, Gnag the Nameless lurked at the edges, taunting them, and Janner heard his gurgling old voice in his head: *I'll find you, Wingfeathers.*

When the visions vanished, the boys had no choice but shake off their fears and journey on. Late in the afternoon, when it happened for the last time, the boys saw that the Fangs had been driven back and their family was safe. They whooped and hugged one another while Oood looked on in confusion. Janner tried to explain the magic to the young troll but couldn't make him understand.

On the first day of their journey, they encountered no ridgerunners and no creatures more dangerous than a guggler. They camped in a

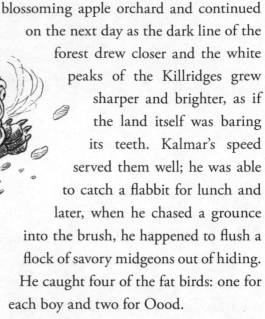

blossoming apple orchard and continued on the next day as the dark line of the forest drew closer and the white peaks of the Killridges grew sharper and brighter, as if the land itself was baring its teeth. Kalmar's speed served them well; he was able to catch a flabbit for lunch and later, when he chased a grounce into the brush, he happened to flush a flock of savory midgeons out of hiding. He caught four of the fat birds: one for each boy and two for Oood.

On the third day they made camp near the first gangly trees of the Blackwood and decided that, with both a Fang and a troll in their company, a fire was safe enough. Besides, toothy cows were still hibernating and posed little threat so early in the spring.

Janner, the first to wake, squatted beside the embers and nudged them to life. He heard Kalmar stir and turned to see his brother's legs twitching with a dream. Janner tried not to think about how much it reminded him of Nugget, chasing thwaps as he slept. Kal had had no further lapses; Janner had seen no traces of yellow in his eyes, and even when Kal hunted he was himself when he came back, carrying his kill in his hands and not his mouth.

But Janner couldn't deny that something was happening to his brother, something he didn't understand and couldn't stop. He had told him again and again on their walk, "You're the High King of Anniera. Your name is Kalmar Wingfeather." He had made Kal repeat it back to him until it turned into a kind of chant: "I'm the son of Esben, King of the Shining Isle. I'm the son of Esben, King of the Shining Isle. I'm the son of Esben, King of the Shining Isle." Janner heard Kal whispering it to himself as they walked. Even Oood, who must have thought it was a marching song of some kind, grinned at them and said, "I'maguhsunnub Esben, kinga da shiny eye!"

But now, as he slept, Kal looked like a wolf. He looked like a *Fang*. Only when Janner could see his brother's eyes was he certain that it was the same old Tink. As Janner turned his attention back to the fire, he was startled by Oood's voice.

"Good Fang still?" the troll asked. He was lying on his side, a living, lumpy flesh pile at the edge of the camp. He had one fat finger deep in his ear, scratching away as if a family of mice had made a nest there in the night. Janner shuddered to think what might really be in there, and then he needed no more imagination because Oood removed his finger, caked with wax, and flicked it into the snow behind them. He laughed when Janner gagged. "Boy think Oood is yucky?"

"No!" Janner gulped. "Well, yes, but I don't mind. Janner *like* Oood."

"Oood bring Janner to his home someday."

"To the Jungles of Plontst?" Janner couldn't imagine wanting to go there—if Oood smelled as bad as this, what would a whole city of trolls do to his nostrils? To his brain? Even a honeymuffin would be better than that. "What is it like there?"

"Treeeees," Oood said with a sigh as he rolled onto his back and aimed his tiny eyes at the sky. "So many trees Oood can't see blue. Big trees. Oood climb trees, trees no bend. Not dumb little trees like this," he said, gesturing at the edge of the Blackwood, where some of the trees were as big as any Janner had ever seen.

"Do you live in the trees?" Janner asked.

"No, silly boy!" Oood laughed. He absentmindedly scratched his bellybutton with a stick. "Oood live in castle. Not toy castle like Throg, *real* castle."

"A castle?" Janner could hardly believe his ears. He had assumed trolls all lived in caves or swamps. "Are you a prince?"

Oood laughed again, enough to finally wake up Kalmar. "No, not prince. Oood have big family. Family friends with king, but not king. Oood family make words." The troll's heavy brow furrowed as he struggled to convey his meaning. He held his giant hand out with the stick between his fingers as if he were holding a quill.

"Write? You write?" Janner asked with surprise.

"Write! Yes. Oood write. Oood's papa write, his mama write."

"What do you write?" Janner asked.

"Is breaffrst ready?" Kalmar mumbled as he sat up and yawned.

Janner ignored him. "Do you write . . . stories?"

"No stories. Oood write . . . pretty words. Words about this." He pointed at his own chest.

"Words about your heart?" Janner asked. "Poems?"

"Ha! Yes. Oood write *poems*."

Janner was speechless. Not only did trolls live in castles, they wrote *poetry*?

"Poems?" Kal said with disinterest. "That's great. Get him to recite one tonight so I can get to sleep faster. What about breakfast?"

"Do you know any poems?" Janner asked, ignoring Kalmar.

"Poems? Ho ho!" Oood laughed again. His smile was so hideous that Janner couldn't help but smile back. "Oood know poems! Poems and poems and POEMS." Oood sat up and looked at Janner distrustfully. "Janner want Oood to say poem? Janner not make joke?"

"No, I'm not joking," Janner laughed. "I like poetry."

Oood's mouth widened into a smile so big his eyes disappeared between his cheeks and his brow. It was a face that hadn't had much reason to smile for a long time. Little bits of dirt that had been caked onto his skin dropped to the ground. Oood clapped. Even Kalmar stopped rooting around in the midgeon bones and listened.

"Oood not supposed to say poem to humans. But papa and mama not here. Boys not tell. Right?"

"Right," Janner said. "It's our secret."

Oood cleared his throat and took a deep breath. "Oood say poem called—called—in boys' words it called 'Rain and Fire.' Right?"

"Right," Janner repeated.

After a moment of silence, during which the sun broke the horizon and a chorus of birds sang, Oood closed his eyes and spoke in a voice that was at once soft and booming:

Grrk. Glog-glogackwoggy!
Grrk. Glog-glogacksnock-jibbit,
Ooog, wacklesnodspadgenoggy,
Nacketbrigglesweeeeeem! Grrk. Squibbit?

When it was over, the birds had fallen silent.* Janner found that, even though the sounds had been strange and, to his ears, unpleasant, Oood's rich voice and passionate recital had stirred his heart. Kalmar looked at Janner and raised his eyebrows as if to say, "That was a pleasant surprise."

Oood blinked and came back to himself, then looked at the ground bashfully.

"Thank you, Oood," Janner said. "That was beautiful."

Oood's head whipped up and his cheeks flushed, if not red, at least a less sallow shade of warty flesh. "Boys like poem?" he asked with wonder.

"Yes," Kal said, stepping over and patting Oood on the shoulder. "It was great. Who's hungry?"

Oood shrugged shyly and poked his stick at the ground, so pleased with himself that he couldn't meet Janner's eyes. "Oood's papa wrote poem. His papa GREAT poem maker." Then his great shoulders slumped. "Oood's papa gone. Bad trolls take papa to Gnag." Oood's

---

* Troll poetry hadn't been uttered in the Green Hollows since the Second Epoch, when the troll king Goot the Wise blessed the Keeper of the Hollows (a woman named Berinelle) with a recitation of the now obscure "Varkyvar Gickle Snop," or, in Hollish, "Be Thou Ever Hale and Let Thy Heart Be Glad."

chest rumbled in a way that would have terrified Janner in any other situation. The troll threw the stick into the fire and smashed his fist into the ground so hard that sparks flew.

"Gnag took our papa too," Janner said.

"Gnag—is—BAD," Oood boomed.

"So let's go get him," Kalmar said quietly. "After breakfast."

Oood nodded. Janner nodded too. Kalmar sniffed at the air and spun around.

"What is it?" Janner asked, reaching for his sword. Kalmar pointed a little way south, at the edge of the Blackwood, and Janner spotted movement but couldn't tell what he was looking at.

"Toothy cows. They must have smelled the fire." Kalmar looked at Janner with worry. "A herd of them, coming fast."

"I guess that means they're out of hibernation," Janner said. "Which means they're hungry."

47

A Toothy Stampede

Cow?" Oood stood and peered into the distance. "Oood kill cow. Eat cow, too."

"Not one cow, Oood! Many cows!" Janner shouted as he shoved supplies into his pack and buckled his scabbard to his belt.

"Many cows?" Oood patted his belly and smiled. "Oood eat MANY cows!"

"No!" Kalmar yelled. "Many cows eat Oood! Eat boys, too!"

At last, the sound of the stampede reached them—horrible moos, the rumble of hooves, the gnashing of yellow teeth. Finally Oood seemed to understand their peril. "*Too* many cows!"

"We have to go!" Janner said.

Oood scooped the boys into his arms like babies and ran straight for the forest. He carried them deeper into the trees with every stride, crashing into branches that Janner would have preferred to duck under. The Blackwood enveloped them while the stampede thundered toward the fire—but Janner knew the toothy cows would catch their scent soon enough.

Janner had no time to think about Oood's stench or the branches scraping his face because there were more toothy cows in the forest, many of them emerging groggily from burrows or stretching as if they had just awoken. It seemed all the toothy cows in the Green Hollows had chosen this particular day to wake up hungry.*

* As is widely known, not all breeds of toothy cows hibernate. Some are evil all winter long.

The cows were slowed by the trees, but so was Oood. With every glance behind them Janner saw that the beasts were getting closer, and the racket was waking more of them by the minute.

"Oood, get up into the trees!" Kalmar shouted. "Cows can't climb!"

Oood grunted as he leaped for the nearest branch. Janner and Kalmar braced for what was sure to be a jolting climb, but the branch broke and they all crashed to the ground. The boys tumbled through the leaves, then wobbled to their feet.

Janner wanted to grab Kalmar and scramble up one of the trees. But what about Oood? They couldn't just sit in the branches and watch as their friend was gobbled up. Besides, the trees were so thin that with so many cows, it wouldn't take long for the beasts to gnaw the trunk down.

The forest around them mooed with fury as cows of all sizes and colors charged them from every direction. Oood snapped the boys up again with a growl-moan, knocked a cow aside with one arm, and pushed on through the forest.

Suddenly, Oood howled with pain and lurched. Janner looked over his shoulder and saw a young, skinny cow snapping at the troll's leg. Janner drew his sword, but Kalmar had already swung around, holding Oood's belt with one hand and swinging his sword at the cow with the other. Oood managed to reach back and punch the cow in the jaw. It tumbled to the earth and tripped several cows that were just behind it.

More and more cows were coming, Oood was running but wounded, and there seemed to be no end to the skinny, twisted, useless trees.

Then Janner saw Esben.

Well, not exactly Esben, but it looked so much like his father's cloven form that Janner's skin went cold. He only saw the creature for a moment, something lumpy and gray, hunched against a tree. It hadn't appeared concerned about the toothy cow stampede, which was odd, but even odder was the fact that the cloven had been holding a sword.

"HELP!" Oood shouted. "HELP!" It was a word trolls seldom used.

Janner turned, wondering who in the world Oood was speaking to, and saw a mossy stone wall looming over them. At the top of the wall stood an array of monsters—hairy ones, scaly ones, skinny and girthy ones, many of whom held torches, and all of whom held weapons.

A wide, timbered gate swung open as Oood approached, then slammed shut behind him. The cows roared and crashed into the gate, but it held. Oood staggered and fell to the ground, which hurled Janner and Kal through the air.

Janner landed ten paces away and shook his head to clear the stars out of his eyes. He looked around at a silent multitude of cloven.

Janner was too astonished to be afraid.

The creatures were so varied in shape and color that Janner had a hard time distinguishing them from one another. They were like a mass of breathing body parts with eyes.

Janner stared, dumbfounded, until one emerged from the crowd. It had the body of a horse, the torso and arms of a man, but its face was lumpy and cat-like. It wore a sword slung over its shoulder. It bowed its head at the boys and said in a rich, raspy voice, "Welcome to Clovenfast."

48

Elder Cadwick

Janner, Kalmar, and Oood were bustled away by a womanish creature with fish scales along her arms and neck, but with the ears of several animals—dog, sheep, flabbit, and more—sprouting from her face, hands, and every exposed bit of her body. Yet she moved with grace and spoke with a voice that was, Janner supposed, woman-like. Her eyes rested too low on the sides of her face, and her lips were blue and turned downward in a pout like a glipperfish.

She led them past the congregation of cloven and into a simple but sturdy log building where she told them they would be interrogated by the cloven leader, whom she called Elder Cadwick.

Janner was shocked that they hadn't been eaten yet. By all accounts, the cloven were deadly monsters that the Hollowsfolk of the Outer Vales had kept at bay for years, and yet these seemed civilized and almost hospitable.

The earish, womanish cloven brought a platter of earthen cups and a jug of water, smiled, and left them alone. Oood sat on the floor since there were no troll-sized chairs, while the boys sat at the table sipping water and exchanging befuddled looks.

"Well. This is a surprise," Kalmar said.

"Oood surprised too," the troll said without looking up from his wounded leg. He winced as he poked at it, and Janner realized for the first time how deep the gash was.

The door banged open and in walked two more cloven: one with the head of a Grey Fang but the body of a large thwap (which was still rather small—his head barely cleared the table), the other a bear with its head on backwards and knobby bones protruding from its shoulders, like wings that had failed to sprout. They carried between them the widest rocking chair Janner had ever seen, placed it behind Oood, and then helped him into it. They bowed when they left, and the backwards-headed bear said, "The medician is on her way. She will mend yourrrrr*AAAAAWR*—I'm sorry. Your foot."

It turned around and backed out of the room—or didn't, depending on how one looked at it. The thwap Fang bobbed its head like a baby and smiled in a way that showed its teeth were, in fact, not fangs but square. Like a horse's teeth, Janner thought.

"This is the weirdest thing ever," he said to no one in particular.

"There was the gargan rockroach. That was pretty weird," Kal said—then he paused and nodded his head. "You're right, this is weirder."

The door opened again and a short, stocky woman entered the room, along with the backwards bear. Her movements were quick and sure, like she was used to being in charge. Her black hair was cut short and framed a pleasant face. She carried a satchel bulging with supplies: scissors, knives, rolls of cloth, bottles of ointment.

"Wounded troll, I hear?" She put her hands on her hips and looked from Janner to Kal, and finally at the troll. When none of them said anything, she put her hands on her hips and shook her head with annoyance. "Well? Which one of you is it?"

Janner and Kalmar pointed at Oood, who raised his hand.

"Right, then. As I suspected. You have the look of a troll." The woman waved a hand at the backwards bear. "Wizzle, let Elder Cadwick know the refugees aren't sure which of them is the troll. They're more damaged than we thought." She marched across the room and took Oood's wounded leg in her hands, turning the foot this way and that. "Looks fine to me. Is it broken?" Oood grunted and pointed a giant troll finger at the gaping wound on the back of his giant troll calf. "Yes, yes. But is your foot broken?"

Oood looked at Janner and back at the woman before saying, "No?"

"Good! Then we'd better have a look at this cowbite. It's too late to save the foot, but we should be able to stitch that wound up in no time. My name is Mother Mungry. I'm sure you three have questions. Elder Cadwick will be here soon. He's assuaging the cows you so foolishly boogled."

"Boogled?" Janner asked.

Mother Mungry retrieved a wad of leaves from her satchel and applied them to Oood's leg, murmuring soothing words when he hissed with pain. "Easy, big fellow. What's your name?"

"Oood."

"And you're a troll?"

"Yes." His answer sounded sleepy.

"That's all? Only a troll?"

Oood didn't answer because he was fast asleep. Mother Mungry stowed the wad of leaves in her satchel and removed something that looked like a fishhook. She squinted one eye as she threaded the hole and set to stitching up the wound. "Yes, *boogled*. They don't usually come this close to Clovenfast. We hear them at night when they're hunting, but it's been a long time since we've had a boogle of them at our gates. We're lucky they didn't breach."

She tied a knot in the string and appraised her work. She nodded, gathered her things, and turned toward the door. Janner and Kalmar gasped when they saw that she had a long, furry tail, at the end of which was a perfectly formed human hand. Its fingers were spread open like a spider's legs, and as she walked it followed her like a pet on a leash.

She smiled when she saw the look of shock on the boys' faces. "Are either of you hurt?"

"No, ma'am." Kalmar forced a smile.

"Good. Elder Cadwick will be here shortly."

There came a knock at the door, and Mother Mungry opened it to reveal the horse-like creature who had spoken to them outside.

"All is well?" he asked as he ducked through the door.

"Yes sir. The troll—he's the big one there. His foot is fine, but I repaired the cowbite and he should be awake in a few minutes."

Elder Cadwick closed the door behind him and studied the boys and the troll. Janner didn't want to stare, but he couldn't help it. Cadwick was a fascinating mixture of animals, a frightening thing to look at, but the way he stood, the way he crossed his arms and looked at them without fear or malice, struck Janner as noble. Soon Janner realized that the creature was staring at *him*. Not at Kal, and not at Oood.

Elder Cadwick's gaze was steady. He—or it—took a step forward. "You're a boy," he said. Janner tensed, unsure if maybe the four-legged creature was about to strike. "An actual boy?"

"Yes sir," Janner answered, hating the way his voice squeaked.

"Tell me," Cadwick said to Kalmar, "how did a cloven like yourself fall into the company of a boy?"

"Cloven?" Kalmar said with a nervous chuckle. "I'm not a cloven. I'm Kalmar. And this is my brother."

Now Cadwick laughed. "Not a cloven, eh? Mother Mungry was right—you're more damaged than you realize."

"I don't understand," Janner said.

Cadwick returned his gaze to Janner and tilted his head. His face was so strange that Janner couldn't tell what the look meant, but once again he had the sense that the creature meant them no harm.

"Let me try to explain . . . *boy*." Cadwick said it as if it was a new word he was getting used to. He stepped closer and his knobby horse legs knelt at the end of the table so that he seemed to be sitting in a chair. Lamplight caused his bluish skin to shine and his large, dark eyes to glimmer. He folded his hands and thought before speaking. "You are in the Blackwood. You know this?"

Janner and Kal nodded. Why did everyone seem to think their brains didn't work?

"You have come here without invitation, without warning, and you have brought with you a herd of toothy cows. I was eating breakfast with my wife this morning at dawn when I received warning that cows were coming. And, I thought, if cows are coming, then something has caused this to happen. But surely there would be no Hollowsfolk in the Blackwood. They would never be so foolish. And yet, here you are." He was looking at Janner again. "A boy."

"We didn't mean to come, sir," Kalmar said. "The cows chased us."

"And what, brother cloven, were you doing in the Outer Vales in this strange company?"

"I'm not a cloven," Kal said.

"Indeed," answered Cadwick with a grunt.

"No sir."

"You're not a Fang, though. It is plain that you are not fully melded."

"No sir, I'm not a Fang either."

Elder Cadwick leaned forward and studied Kal's face. "Then what do you suppose you are, brother?"

"I'm the son of Esben, King of the Shining Isle."

"Speak not that name in jest. What do you mean?"

"I only meant what I said. My name is Kalmar Wingfeather. My father was the king, but now he's dead. That makes me the king—I guess."

"And I'm the Throne Warden," Janner said.

Elder Cadwick leaned back and folded his arms. "So it's true," he said to himself.

"What's true?" Janner asked.

"Esben's story."

49

Cave Paintings

Janner and Kalmar stared at Elder Cadwick in shock.

"You knew our father?" Janner asked.

"If your father was a cloven bear named Esben, yes."

"What story are you talking about?" Kalmar asked.

"I could tell you everything, but I think it would be better to show you. Come with me." Cadwick stood and looked down at Kalmar and Janner with wonder before leading them to the door.

"What about Oood?" Janner asked.

At the sound of his name, Oood sat up and smiled. "Oood awake now." He poked at his stitched wound and said, "Where we go?"

"Oood, you may stay here if you like. Your companions will come to no harm. My people have sacked one of the toothy cows and even now are butchering it for the spit. If you'd like to stay and eat, you're welcome to. Besides," Cadwick said with a smile, "Mother Mungry thinks you need to stay off that foot. She has a thing about broken feet. I think you'll find that many of us at Clovenfast have . . . *quirks*. Mother Mungry is one of the sanest of us. Shimrad is crazy about fenceposts. He admires them for hours." He nodded at Oood. "What do you say, friend?"

Oood looked at the boys with uncertainty, then he patted his stomach. "Oood *is* hungry."

"Don't worry. We'll be back," Janner said, then he turned to Cadwick. "Where are you taking us?"

"To Esben's den."

Janner's skin tingled as they followed Elder Cadwick out of the room. He led them into a courtyard crowded with cloven, who paused whatever they were doing to watch the Wingfeathers. Sunlight fell through the treetops and warmed the ground in bright patches, illuminating the roofs of wooden huts, which lined the walls of the village. The huts were simple but well made, and the areas around them were neat and swept clean of leaves.

"Hello, Shimrad," Cadwick said to a man-like creature with rumpled wings and a pig's snout. The thing nodded as they passed, then turned back to its business (staring lovingly at a row of fenceposts).

Another group of cloven stood around a fire where chunks of toothy cow cooked on a spit; it smelled delicious and reminded Janner that they hadn't eaten any breakfast. Kalmar veered away and would have joined the group at the fire if Cadwick hadn't called him back.

"Careful, brother cloven," he said with a chuckle. "Those are some of the wilder of us. It's too early in the morning for a fight."

The cloven around the fire watched them pass with indecipherable expressions; they might have been angry, or curious, or welcoming, or disinterested, but each face was so different, each feature so misplaced or twisted that Janner could interpret no meaning from their monstrous shapes and instead averted his eyes.

As they walked deeper into the forest settlement, Janner saw that it was lined with many paths and was home to hundreds of cloven, maybe more. Soon they approached a lane which was crowded with dwellings—not quite houses, but an assemblage of lean-tos and sheds with doors of varying shapes and sizes made to accommodate the corresponding oddities of the cloven who lived there.

As he looked around, Janner realized that the cloven who stopped to watch them pass were fascinated by *him*—they hardly glanced at Kalmar. Janner felt self-conscious, almost wishing he were a cloven and not just a regular boy. This must be what Kalmar felt every time he walked through Ban Rona; no wonder he hated appearing in public.

"Clovenfast has been here for many years," Elder Cadwick said.

"I thought cloven was a nickname the Hollowsfolk gave you," Janner said.

"They named us?" asked Cadwick with surprise. "I wasn't aware the Hollowsfolk had seen enough of us to bother."

"They've known for years that the forest was full of—monsters." Janner gulped. He waited for some reaction from Cadwick, but none came.

"I knew there was restlessness in the Blackwood, cloven ranging farther into the vales, but I did not think they were enough to cause trouble. I shall have to increase my pleaders at the forest borders."

Pleaders? Janner wondered. Everything Cadwick said opened up whole libraries of questions. They turned a corner and came at last to the rear wall of the fort.

Cadwick paused at the gate. "This might bother you, boy. These are not the tame ones." Elder Cadwick heaved open the gate, revealing a path that led through darker and thicker trees before it disappeared around a bend. Gulpswallows flitted about in the sunbeams. Cadwick ducked through the doorway and stepped into the forest. "Stay close."

Immediately there was noise in the brush beside the path. Janner and Kalmar pressed against Cadwick's flanks as they walked, ready either to run or to climb onto his back—though Janner wasn't sure Cadwick would allow it.

"Look!" Kalmar said, pointing at something large and scaly as it slithered out of sight. Another rustle came from the other side of the path, and Janner spotted a creature skittering up a tree with spidery legs—it was no bigger than a dog, and he thought he saw human hands grabbing twigs as it climbed. As they walked they saw more and more creatures, some so hideous that they defied description. One lumped across the path, legless and gurgling. Another, visible deep in the trees, had limbs as long and thin as poles and strode through the boughs tearing leaves and munching them with long black teeth. In each misshapen face Janner saw the shadow of a deep sadness, as if the eyes were windows into a dungeon where a prisoner wept.

These were the broken, the "untame" as Elder Cadwick called them, and their sorrow filled the forest so that even the birdsong was lonesome.

"Careful," Cadwick said, pulling Janner from the edge of the path—he had almost stepped on the front foot of a thwappish digtoad with a woman's face and long, blond hair pooled around it on the ground. "That one is a pouncer."

"Sorry," Janner said to the digtoad-thing, and to his shock, she answered, "No matter," in a voice that sounded like a burp.

On they walked, until they halted at a pile of mossy boulders. A footpath led between the massive stones, and Cadwick pointed. "Here we are. See for yourself."

The boys stepped cautiously toward the entrance. It wasn't a cave, but the trees overhead were so thick that it felt like one. The place held a troubling aura of pain and memory, and seemed to be waiting just for Janner. He didn't want to look inside. Kalmar stepped past him and out of sight behind a slab of stone. With a deep breath and a last look at Cadwick, Janner followed Kalmar into their father's home.

He found his brother on his knees, crying.

The place was no bigger than a shed, the dirt on the floor packed with years of habitation. There was a ratty blanket piled in one corner, and rodent bones piled in another. It reminded Janner of the cave where Kalmar had tended to Esben. A flood of emotions rose in Janner's chest and tears leaked down his cheeks.

Kalmar was kneeling in front of the far wall with one arm out-stretched before him, his hand on the cold grey stone. The rock was covered with images, drawings in charcoal that had been tinted with some kind of dye. Janner knelt beside his brother and wiped his eyes.

The name ESBEN was scrawled at the center, and around it were written four names: Janner, Kalmar, Leeli, and Nia.

Chills tickled Janner's shoulder blades. The letters were sloppy, but the images were not: One was of an island surrounded by crashing waves. A many-spired castle rose high above the green island, and little sailboats floated near the shore. In another picture, dark lines were dotted with bursts of green—furrowed fields with crops rising out of the earth, Janner realized—men, women, and children stood among the rows with baskets on their shoulders and glad expressions on their faces.

"Janner, look. It's us." Kal pointed to the wall in the deepest part of the den.

There was Nia's face—in fact, there were many drawings of her face. Some were smiling, some were sad, some were serious, and all were nearly as beautiful as the woman herself.

Next to the collage of Nia was a likeness of Uncle Artham. It was Artham before he had changed into a birdman, before his hair had changed to white and his eyes had filled with regret. It was an image of a sure young man, an Artham that Janner had never seen before.

Below Artham were three children standing together on the deck of a ship—Leeli in a dress with a crutch under one arm, Janner with bandages on his legs and his arm in a sling, and Kalmar—who looked like a boy. It was the children as Esben had seen them in Leeli's song, when they arrived at the Green Hollows—but the drawing of Kalmar showed no sign of wolf ears or fur. A sooty hand had wiped across the stone and smudged his face. Kal hung his head.

A little farther to the right, Janner discovered a large and carefully drawn Fang, the blue eyes so vivid that they seemed to be staring straight at him. Beneath it was written, "My boy."

Janner took Kal's shoulders and turned him gently toward the painting. When Kal saw it his tears flowed all the harder. The brothers rested in the memory of their father's love so long that Cadwick stepped to the doorway to be sure they were all right.

"You knew him?" Janner asked.

"Yes," answered Cadwick. "And no."

"What do you mean?" Kal wiped his nose and stood.

"Perhaps we should tell this tale over a hot meal. Can your questions wait that long? There's someone I'd like you to meet."

"Do we have to walk back through the 'untamed,' or whatever you called them?" Kalmar asked.

"No, brother cloven."

"I'm not a cloven."

Cadwick narrowed his eyes. "I will take you to the heart of Clovenfast. There you will see that it is not such a bad thing to be broken."

50

Arundelle

Clovenfast was much larger than Janner first thought. The fort where they had escaped the toothy cows was one of several outposts scattered along the edge of the Blackwood, and from the rear of each walled fort, a road led to the city proper.

And a city it was, though not built by cloven; it was an ancient ruin of stone structures. Ornate archways and columns towered among the trees. The cobbled road was bordered by tumbledown stone walls that were green with winter moss and budding vines. The nearer they drew to the center of the city, the more structures stood unbroken in the shade of mighty trees. Roots pressed between flagstones and wrapped around foundations, as if they were engaged in a thousand-year dance with the ruins.

But *ruins* was the wrong word, Janner decided. The city was far from ruined, and the way it melded with the forest made Janner think it must be more lovely than it had been when it was new.

Once they moved out of the wild and into the city, they saw more cloven who could walk upright and speak. Janner even saw children: young cloven playing, riding on the shoulders of their elders, sitting on steps and laughing with one another. Many were deformed Green and Grey Fangs, and a few had milky eyes like the bats Kalmar had described to Janner.

"Do you have children?" Janner asked. Elder Cadwick waved, greeting a cloven who carried a basket of pomply pears in two of its five arms.

"None of us have children, lad," said Cadwick. "Not anymore."

"But what about all the young ones?" Kalmar asked.

"We find them in the forest. We bring them here. Someone has to care for them, just as someone cared for me when I was abandoned in the Blackwood many years ago."

"So did you all come from Throg?" Janner asked.

"Yes. And before we were thrust from the Deeps of Throg, we were human."

"Do you remember anything? From before?" Janner asked.

Cadwick lowered his eyes and his voice grew quiet. "I remember a few things. I was a blacksmith. I lived in a cottage. I remember fields of white flowers, and a scent on the wind that stirs my heart. Now and then I remember faces—faces full of joy, but I know not who they were . . . nor who I was." He sighed as he ducked under a low branch. "We have learned that it is best not to remember too much. This," he waved a hand around him, "is what we have now. This is who we are."

"But our father—Esben—remembered, didn't he?" Kalmar asked.

"Yes, and it nearly drove him mad. Like many of us, he wandered the forest for years until he found a home in Clovenfast. Once he settled in the den, he hardly spoke to anyone. He spent his time making the pictures on the walls. Then one night he emerged from the den with a terrible roar and left the Blackwood. The pleaders could not stop him."

"Who are the pleaders?" Janner asked.

"Cloven at the borders, stationed there to keep the our people out of the Green Hollows. It does little good to try and stop them with force, so they plead. They try to help the roving cloven find their way home, back to Clovenfast. It usually works."

"Why do you try to keep them out of the Hollows?"

"Because we know that if too many leave the forest, they may harm the humans who live beyond it, and soon humans would enter the Blackwood and do harm to the cloven. We have found peace here, and we would like to keep it that way. Gnag has caused us enough pain.

We have no desire for the humans to add to it. The queen is trying to protect us."

"Queen?" Janner and Kalmar said at the same time, just as the road led around the corner of a stout stone building with another horse-like cloven peering down from the rooftop.

Before them stood a magnificent old building covered in floral ivy, at the center of which was an archway that led into a courtyard. The trees had been cleared away, and the area lay in the bright sun like a stone island draped in purple flowers.

"Yes, the queen. I sent word as soon as you arrived, and she has agreed to grant you an audience. Greetings, Halibart." Cadwick nodded at one of two guards on either side of the entrance. "Jaffann," he said to the other. The two sentries were as tall as Cadwick. Like his, their faces were catlike, and each of them held a sword.

"Elder Cadwick," Halibart purred. "Her Highness is expecting you."

Janner felt the guards' eyes on him as he passed into the courtyard. As soon as they were within the walls of the palace, the fragrance of the flowers washed over them and Janner was dizzy with delight. The ground burst with blooms and plants of many kinds, some of which already bore fruits and vegetables despite the winter cold. Little stone paths wound through the foliage, under arbors draped with clusters of flowers that hung like grapes.

"My queen," said Cadwick with reverence. "I present Janner and Kalmar, sons of the cloven Esben."

Janner saw no one at first. Then at the far corner of the garden he saw movement in the boughs of a tree with white flowers. He braced himself to encounter someone huge, someone tall enough to brush the upper branches of the tree. The branches seemed to rotate, then they moved closer. Janner and Kal watched with awe as the budded boughs rustled toward them with a hiss of leaves that stirred the air and heightened the fragrance.

The tree itself was the Cloven Queen. Her skin was smooth grey bark, her trunk was sloped and graceful, and her large, green eyes were set in the tree like jewels. Her mouth was a smiling seam in the bark, and she had no arms other than the many swooping branches held over her head as if she were praising the sunlight. Her feet were roots that snaked gently across the ground, caressing plant and earth and stone as she approached. When she stopped several feet away, the root-feet settled across the ground like the sweep of a gown and blended with the grass as if she had been planted there for a century. Her flowering boughs shaded the boys and she looked down at them with such kindness that Janner had to resist the urge to embrace her.

"Bow, lads," said Cadwick, who knelt between them.

Janner and Kal dropped to their knees so quickly that the queen laughed—a sound like running water over river stone—and her branches shivered. Out of the corner of his eye Janner saw other flowers and plants tremble with her, and the garden seemed to lean her way as if a breeze blew toward her from every direction at once.

"Welcome," she said in a voice so lovely that Janner's heart skipped a beat. "I am Arundelle, Queen of Clovenfast. Is it true that you are the sons of Esben?"

"Yes, ma'am," Janner said in a trembling voice.

"Did he find you?"

"Yes," Janner answered.

"And how is he?" Arundelle asked.

Janner's voice caught in his throat.

"He died, Your Highness," Kalmar said.

A silence fell on the garden. Every leaf held still as if listening.

"That is a terrible loss," she said quietly. "Such is the price of remembrance. I'm sorry, children. Some of us awaken to our true selves, and it leads us out of the forest and into pain. But it is a better pain than oblivion."

Janner didn't understand, but didn't say so.

"Kalmar, do you remember?"

"Remember what, Your Highness?"

"Your true self. Do you remember who you are?"

Kalmar glanced at Janner, then forced himself to look at Arundelle's face. "Yes ma'am. Most of the time. But it's getting harder."

The leaves rustled again, and Arundelle said, "Rise, sons of Esben. I see that you are hungry. Come and eat."

They followed the queen to a stone table deeper in the garden. Janner saw other cloven, small ones resembling foxes and cave blats, bustling from plant to plant, gathering vegetables which they piled on the table as the queen bowed over it, murmuring a prayer of thanksgiving. She smiled at the brothers and, with one of her branches, gestured for them to sit. One of the cave blat-like cloven filled two stone cups from a cistern by the wall and placed them before the boys.

"Go ahead," the queen said. "My food is the sun, my drink is the earth."

Janner bit into a long green vegetable and a sweet flavor burst into his mouth. Kalmar sniffed at a round blue fruit, took one nibble, then gobbled it up as the juice ran down his chin.

"You have questions. You may ask whatever you like."

Janner had so many questions that he didn't know where to begin.

"What happens if you get an itch?" Kalmar asked as he wiped his chin and peeled a speckled yellow vegetable.

"Kal!" Janner whispered.

"She said we could ask anything!" Kal said with a mouthful of berries.

But Queen Arundelle laughed again, sending motes of pollen drifting about in the sunlight. "I have plenty of birds to tend me, and bugs too."

Janner tried to ignore Kal's munching. "What do you know about our father?"

Arundelle gazed at Janner kindly. "I know that he loved you. He spoke little when he first arrived. I tried to help him remember, but that is a healing that causes much pain. The untame are those who refuse to remember. Many of them hide in the wild and never speak again. But some allow me to lead them into the forests of memory, and some, like Cadwick, come to know their true names again and find some measure of peace. Esben was the same. I helped him to find his name, and he told us of you—his children—and he told us of his wife. But he remembered only a little at a time, as do I. His name was familiar to me, but it was only much later that I remembered that he was my king." She smiled at the look of shock on Janner's face. "Yes, child. I am Annieran. I know who you are. Perhaps I should be the one bowing."

"No! Please don't." Kalmar waved a hand and poked around his plate for more fruit. "I don't like all the bowing." Arundelle bowed anyway, casting a leafy shade over the stone table, until Kalmar answered with a bashful nod.

"So once someone remembers their true name, they're cured?" Janner asked.

"I wish it were so. We all forget from time to time, and so we need each other to tell us our stories. Sometimes a story is the only way back from the darkness."

"You forget, too?" Kalmar asked, interested for the first time in something other than lunch.

"Yes. Even Elder Cadwick forgets. When he does we send pleaders to find him in the reaches of the Blackwood."

"And what about you?" Kalmar asked. "Who helped you to remember?"

The queen smiled again and stared into her own memory. "Few have asked me that, Kalmar. But I shall tell you, because you need to know. I was cast out of the Deeps, thrown to the forest floor like a dead log. I knew nothing but a terrible thirst until at last my roots found earth, and in time I was able to stand. For many months I stood in the forest as the seasons changed, knowing little but sorrow and fear. I saw many cloven cast from the dungeon, but none spoke and none seemed able to see me. But then," she paused, and a faraway look came into her eyes, "I saw my true love. He crept from the cave like a frightened child, and I could see that his sorrow was as heavy as mine. In those days, I knew neither how to speak, nor even to move. So I watched him pass me by unaware, and I could not even cry out his name nor reach for his hand as he passed. When he was gone, my broken heart at last gave me a voice for weeping. I remembered his name, and I wailed it into the Blackwood over and over and over, remembering with each cry who I was and what I had become."

"What was his name?" Janner asked, already knowing the answer somehow.

"Artham Wingfeather."

51

The Cloven Queen's Counsel

Arundelle the Cloven Queen swayed in the warm breeze. Her downcast eyes glimmered, then a tear trickled down the smooth gray bark of her trunk like sap. Her branches drooped so low that her leaves tickled the ground. "Did you know your uncle?"

"Yes, ma'am," Janner said, not knowing how much to say.

"I fear I shall never see him again. And for that, at least in part, I am grateful." Arundelle's trunk bent and her leaves rustled again. "He would recoil at what I have become."

"No, he wouldn't," Janner said, squinting up at the sunlight beaming through her branches. "He would find you as beautiful as I do. And yes, he's alive."

Arundelle's eyes widened and she leaned forward. "You have seen him? Where?"

Janner smiled. It was news he was happy to give. "He made his way to Skree, where we lived."

"Skree?" Arundelle whispered with wonder. "So far!"

"He was looking for us. He was—crazy. He could hardly speak. He lived in a treehouse in Glipwood Forest, watching over us for years, and then when the Fangs came, he fought for us."

"And he saved me," Kalmar said. "From the Stone Keeper. Now he's back in Skree, and I think he's fighting the Fangs again."

Arundelle's leaves shivered with joy. She raised her eyes to the heavens and murmured something Janner couldn't make out. Buds on her upper branches bloomed white and purple in an instant, and she grew more beautiful by the moment. "My Artham," she said, and the boys glanced at each other as they waited for her to recover.

"And now you have come, nephews of the Throne Warden, sons of the king, to Clovenfast. A thousand miracles a day, and yet I am still surprised by the Maker's good pleasure." She bent herself low and studied Janner's face carefully. "Could it be, Cadwick?"

"I don't know, my queen," he said from the edge of the garden. "It was not my dream."

"Could what be?" Janner asked.

Arundelle and Cadwick exchanged a glance. "I was told in a dream," she said, "that a boy would come to Clovenfast, and he would be the seed of a new garden."

"What's that supposed to mean?" Kalmar asked with a chuckle.

Janner didn't know anything about prophecies or dreams. But he knew he wasn't a seed, and he certainly didn't want to be planted. At least now he knew why Cadwick kept calling him "boy" with that awestruck tone.

"The Maker does not often speak to me thus, though I always sense him deep in the earth," Arundelle continued. Janner watched a few of her smaller roots stroke the earth and burrow into it. "The dream came to me years ago. I doubted a human boy would ever set foot in Clovenfast, but Cadwick and I spread the word to all the cloven to keep watch. As the seasons passed we thought little of it. But here you are. A boy in the Blackwood. Tell me, children, why have you come?"

"We're going to Throg," Kalmar said. "To stop Gnag from doing this anymore. Before it's too late."

"And how do you plan to do this?" she asked.

Kalmar opened his mouth to speak, then closed it again. "I don't know exactly. But Uncle Artham told us he found a way out of Throg and into the Blackwood. That means there's a way in."

"Sons of Esben, you cannot do this."

"Why not?" asked Kalmar.

"Throg is a place of madness. It is a black world of untame cloven and Fangs and wretched things. It is no place for the Jewels of Anniera."

"But we have to go," Janner said. "What else can we do?"

"Go back. Back to the Green Hollows. You can find a life, as we have, in the wake of Gnag's evil." Arundelle's roots snaked across the ground and she turned to face the garden wall.

"But there's no home to go back to."

Her trunk twisted around and she looked at them intently. "What do you mean?"

"The Fangs have already invaded," Kalmar said. "They're attacking Ban Rona right now. If we don't do this, he'll overrun the Hollows. He'll kill everyone we know. He's already destroyed Anniera."

"No, child. Clovenfast *is* Anniera. These are your people, this is what is left of your kingdom. Gnag sought to wipe it from Aerwiar, but it has found a home here. It has survived in the shadows of the Blackwood. Stay and rule us, Kalmar, where even Gnag cannot find you. Throne Warden, stay and fulfill the prophecy. Be the seed of a new garden for us."

Janner looked at all the cloven lurking at the edges of the courtyard, peeking their misshapen heads over the wall and snuffling in the brush. These were Annierans? He knew the Fangs were once people, but knowing they were from Anniera, from his father's kingdom, lit a fire of anger in his gut and he wanted more than ever to push back at Gnag and all he had wrought.

"I don't want to rule you," Kalmar said.

"Janner, please," Arundelle said. "Tell your brother this is foolishness. You'll both die in the Deeps of Throg."

"I'm sorry, Your Highness." Janner stood from the stone table. "I'm the Throne Warden, not a seed. I'm with the king, and the king is going to Throg."

Kalmar sat and stared at a crack that ran through the stone table. Arundelle turned her back to them again and silence fell on the garden. Even the spring birds stopped singing.

After an uncomfortable silence, the Cloven Queen spoke. "Elder Cadwick will take you as far as he can. I cannot promise your safety. I wish Esben were here to stop you."

"Thanks, Your Highness," Kalmar said.

She stood near the stone wall, sap trickling from her eyes and down her trunk to the dark earth. Kal and Janner retreated to the entrance of the garden where Cadwick waited.

"Will you not be swayed from this?" Cadwick asked.

"No, sir," Kalmar said.

"Then follow me."

52

Into the Blackwood

When they made it back to the fort, Oood was seated beside a bonfire, reciting poetry to a gathering of cloven who were pretending to enjoy it. He smiled when he saw the boys and limped over to greet them with a roasted toothy cow haunch in one hand.

"Cloven like Oood's words," he said happily. He waved at the cloven, who waved back, visibly relieved that the recital was over. "Go get Gnag now?"

"Yes, Oood," Kalmar said as he marched straight to the main gate. "Go get Gnag."

Janner jogged to keep up, waving apologetically at the cloven watching them pass.

When Kalmar got to the gate he tugged at it and found it locked. He turned to Cadwick. "Are you coming?"

"Yes, brother cloven," he said. "I would prefer to let you go alone, but Queen Arundelle has asked me to lead you into darkness. First I must bid farewell to my family. I may never see them again."

Cadwick fixed them both with a heavy look, then turned to the building where Mother Mungry had tended to Oood. When he reached the door, a feminine cloven with sleek black fur and the head of a quill diggle flung it open and embraced him. Two young cloven clambered around his four legs, and one of them shimmied onto his back.

"Remember, love. You are Cadwick, blacksmith of Pennybridge. You are in my heart, and my heart will wait for your return." The young ones cooed and gurgled as Elder Cadwick embraced them and kissed their malformed faces. "Farewell, children," said Cadwick tenderly. "Cling to Kinnan, for she loves you well."

Mother Mungry bustled through the door and handed Cadwick a satchel. "You'll find balms in here, as well as some cracklings. Is your foot well?"

"My foot?" Cadwick asked.

"Someone's foot was broken, was it not?" She poked at one of his hooves.

"It was the troll," Cadwick said with a chuckle.

"Ah!" She looked at Janner. "Is your foot well, then?"

Janner nodded, flexing first one foot and then the other so she could see. Cadwick placed the young ones on the ground, kissed his wife on the forehead, and joined the boys at the gate.

Elder Cadwick looked up at a sentry at the top of the wall. "Are the cows gone?"

"Yes, sir. For now. Be careful out there, sir."

Cadwick nodded, then the gate swung open and they stepped into the tangle of trees. The forest was silent and foreboding, and Janner suddenly wanted to stay. What did they think they were doing? Striking out into a forest of monsters, only to sneak into a dungeon of monsters, only to infiltrate the stronghold of a monster so powerful he had basically destroyed the world? It seemed like the height of foolishness, even for a seasoned warrior—more so for two boys who didn't know what they were doing.

The walls of Clovenfast were strong and sure. If Gnag had been dumping his failed meldings into the wilds all these years, then it seemed he didn't care about the Blackwood or consider it a threat. Maybe the best thing would be to bring Leeli and the rest of the family to Clovenfast where they could finally get some peace. But moving and running and hiding was all they had done since they escaped Glip-wood—first to Peet's Castle, then to the Ice Prairies, then to the Green Hollows. No matter where they went, Gnag the Nameless found them, attacked them, and in the process hurt everyone around them. Cloven-fast would be no different.

As they walked, Janner glanced behind him for a last glimpse of Clovenfast, but the gate was shut, already hidden by branches and bud-ding leaves. They may as well have been alone in the middle of the Blackwood. It was no wonder the Hollowsfolk knew nothing about Clovenfast. Maybe Gnag didn't know about it either, nor would he.

After walking in silence for an hour, the trees grew fatter and the branches fewer. They were following a faint path, probably made by wild animals or cloven, and Janner could tell by the slant of the late afternoon sun that they were heading south. "How far is it?" he asked.

"I don't know." Elder Cadwick didn't look at either of the boys as he spoke, but stared straight ahead as if he were walking in his sleep. "It could be hours, or it could be days. I have tried to avoid the southern forest since I remembered my name and hoped I would never have to go back. A foolish hope, it turns out."

There was an edge of anger in his voice, and Janner decided not to ask any more questions.

"You don't have to do this, you know," Kalmar said. "We were on our way to Throg before we even knew you existed. We can push on alone. Go back to your family."

Cadwick looked over his shoulder in the direction of Clovenfast. He curled his lip and shook his head. "The queen has ordered me. I will obey."

"Well I'm the king, and I'm ordering you to go back." Kalmar stepped in front of Cadwick and stopped in the middle of the path. "We know the entrance to the Deeps is south of here. We know it's somewhere at the base of the Killridge Mountains. We're trained Durgans. You may think we can't care of ourselves, but we made it this far. Go back to your family. Gnag has taken enough from you already."

Cadwick's tail twitched as he considered Kalmar's words. "If indeed your brother is the boy Queen Arundelle prophesied, then he must be kept safe."

Janner started to speak up for himself, but Kalmar interrupted. "We also have a troll on our side. Not many boys can say that."

"Oood smash," the troll said helpfully.

Elder Cadwick's front hoof pawed the ground and he adjusted his scabbard. "Very well. I'm going back."

"Really?" Kalmar said.

"I have young ones to care for and a city to protect. I wish you a safe journey." Cadwick turned and clopped back the way they had come.

"Wait!" Janner called. "I don't know if this is such a good idea! We might need you."

"Courage, boy. You have a troll on your side, remember?" Cadwick said over his shoulder.

"Kalmar, stop him! We don't know our way around this forest."

"Neither does he. He just told us so. Besides, he didn't want to be here, and I don't blame him."

"But—but—" Janner was so flummoxed he couldn't think of what to say. He looked from Kalmar to Cadwick, who was rapidly disappearing into the forest. Then he was gone. "And now we're alone," Janner said. "Why would you send back the one person in our little band who knows the forest best?"

"Because he scared me," Kalmar said.

That wasn't what Janner expected. "What do you mean?"

"I know what it feels like to . . . lose myself. It's awful. And the worst of it is, I don't know it's happening until it's over. Can you imagine what he would be like if he snapped and turned wild? He's almost as tall as Oood."

"Oood not afraid of horse-man," the troll said.

"I know you're not," Kalmar said. "But if Cadwick got weird on us and you had to stop him, those little cloven back there would lose the only father they're ever going to have. We only left a few minutes ago and he was already different. Meaner, or something. I was afraid of him."

Janner had to admit that he sensed the change, too. But now that Cadwick was gone, the forest seemed like the more frightening enemy. They had a long way to go. And the sun was beginning to set.

"Fine. Let's go," Janner said.

Kalmar sniffed the air and pointed. "This way, I think. Try to be as quiet as you can." He marched on.

"Why?" Janner asked.

"Because I can smell five toothy cows nearby. A bunch of cloven, too."

53

The Angry Ones Attack

They spent the night in the boughs of a tree so tall that Janner never saw the top. Though the new leaves were tiny, the tangled branches overhead were dense enough to hide the stars. All through the night, creatures, whether cloven or ordinary wild animals, snuffled and grunted and traipsed about on the ground below them, and more than once something sizeable skittered up or down the trunk opposite from where they slept.

When morning came, Kalmar gave the air a careful sniffing and warned them to wait as a flock of huppitousgleezes grazed. Once they were gone, he sniffed again and indicated that it was safe to climb down.

Neither Janner, Kalmar, nor Oood had any idea where they were going, but it was obvious that they were nearing the foothills of the Killridge Mountains. Every valley was deeper than the last, and they were confronted with increasingly steeper gullies mounted by boulders the size of buildings. Janner's mind raced with entries from Pembrick's *Creaturepedia*, attentive to any signs that might indicate a gargan rockroach den or something worse.

They ate berries collected along the way, and Kal and Janner used their bows to bag enough flabbits, thwaps, and snapping diggles to keep their bellies full. Kalmar's heightened sense of smell served them well; he was able to guide them to the east or west to circumvent gobbles of cows and other unidentifiable beasts in their path.

Even Oood was quiet when he needed to be—but his poetry recitals posed a greater threat. The dam had broken with "Rain and Fire," and Oood had flooded them with troll poems ever since. The boys feigned appreciation, but upon hearing the first syllables of troll-rhyme, birds and wild animals chattered and brayed and cawed with irritation until the poem mercifully ended. Janner even began to suspect that Kalmar smelled danger only as a pretense to silence Oood's poetry.

On the afternoon of their second day in the Blackwood, they encountered the first of the untame cloven—untame and angry. It leapt upon them from a boulder as they climbed out of a ravine. Its legs were long and scaly, but its body and head were one circular blob with hands sticking out of the sides like ears. Its lippy mouth opened wide to bite them, but before its jaws snapped shut, Oood dealt it a blow that sent it tumbling in a spray of leaves. It kicked in the air while the fingers of its head-hands wriggled about. It seemed to be throwing a fit.

As the brothers recovered, the creature calmed down, found its feet, and glared at them from several feet away. "*Meanies,*" it said indignantly, then it loped away.

"It's good to have a troll," Kalmar said with a smile at Oood.

"If he's your friend," Janner added.

"Friend," Oood said, and he thumped his chest.

"You didn't smell that thing coming?" Janner asked as they continued their hike.

"I smelled it," said Kalmar. "But I didn't think it would attack."

"Why not?"

Kal hesitated. "Because I've been smelling them all morning, and none have attacked yet. Cloven are everywhere. Maybe they're holding back because of Oood."

Janner felt chills as he peered through the forest—chills, because he couldn't see any cloven at all. That they were surrounded, being watched, almost made him wish the cloven would attack and be done with it. "How many are there?"

Kalmar sniffed the air and flattened his ears. "About thirty, I think. Maybe more. The farther we walk, the more of them I smell."

"Getting close?" Oood asked as he broke a large dead limb from a tree and swung it like a club.

"Maybe," Janner said. "There could be more cloven near the mouth of the Deeps, and if what Cadwick said is true, they'll be wilder."

Kalmar stopped in his tracks. "Janner, draw your sword. There's one just ahead. Do you see it?"

Janner slipped his sword from the scabbard and scanned the trees ahead. He saw nothing but forest and more forest. "Where?" he whispered.

"To your left."

From behind an old log, two stems rose, each of which was topped with a greenish orb that blinked. Eyeballs. Padded frog-like fingers draped themselves over the log, so that they looked like vines or caterpillars resting on the rotten wood. Janner had the troubling realization that the thing was about to jump.

Then something crashed in the underbrush behind him. Janner spun. Two hogpig cloven charged toward him, squealing. Their tusks were black with mold and as long as daggers. Janner swung his sword. His first blow missed, but his second made contact with one of the cloven's front legs—a front leg that ended not in a hogpig hoof but a human foot. Oood roared as he leaped forward and swung his fists, first at Janner's hogpig then at the other, which was attacking Kalmar.

The eyeball thing behind the log loosed a rumbling *gribbit* and leaped over the fallen tree. Its body was like a digtoad's but with spikes sprouting from a coat of luxurious white fur. Janner didn't want to kill it. He knew it had once been human. He knew it probably suffered from the same forgetful madness that haunted Kalmar.

Before it landed on him he hunkered down and raised his sword. The hairy digtoad slammed into him and rolled away with a groan.

Janner climbed to his feet and realized his sword was no longer in his hand. It was embedded to the hilt in the digtoad's belly.

The cloven's eye-stalks twitched on the ground as it gasped for air. The hogpigs were several feet away, one of them crackling to dust and the other wounded and struggling to breathe. Oood slowly turned in a circle, braced for any further attack, but none came.

Kalmar sheathed his sword and knelt at the digtoad's side. "Janner, it's trying to speak."

Janner averted his eyes from the wound he had dealt and knelt beside Kalmar. He wanted to speak but the lump in his throat silenced him.

"Are . . . you . . . a child? A *boy*?" the thing said between breaths. Its voice was gribbity, but there was enough human in it that Janner's sadness grew. The digtoad took a deep breath and said, "I remember. I was a boy once."

"I know you were," Kalmar said. He placed his hand on the thing's white fur. "I was, too."

"I'm sorry," Janner said. He wanted to say more, but had no words.

"Are you the one . . . who will seed the new garden?"

"I don't know," Janner said.

"I remember now," said the digtoad. "Anniera. My home." With something like a smile, it stilled and turned to dust.

Janner sniffed and shook the dust from his sword before sheathing it. He said, "I'm sorry," again, uselessly.

The other hogpig's breath rattled, then it died. Other shapes peeked from behind trees and boulders, eyes and lumpy faces, all watching him with what he felt was anger and accusation.

"I don't want to hurt you!" Janner said. It was a plea, not a threat.

Several cloven whispered and muttered.

"It's a boy."

"What's a boy?"

"A young one. Like we used to be."

"I remember!"

"I want to be a boy again."

"We should kill it. My thoughts hurt."

"We can't. He might be the seed."

Kalmar spoke to the watching eyes in the forest. "My name is Kalmar Wingfeather. King of the Shining Isle of Anniera."

"Anniera?" they whispered.

"I remember! It hurts! STOP IT."

"The Shining Isle. My mother's name was Norra."

"STOP IT."

The voices grew angry, hissing and snapping at the air, monsters visible only as shadows and shapes behind the trees. Others, though, stepped forward, cautious and blinking at Janner as if he were an apparition or a king. One of the angry ones bit the leg of a small, goatish cloven as it approached.

"Let it go!" Janner cried.

He ran to the squealing goat thing and pulled it from the jaws of its attacker, which was the most hideous cloven he had seen. It was lumpy and legless, like a giant slug, but its manlike face was stretched wide across a black, slimy mass, and every time its mouth flopped open Janner saw crooked yellow teeth.

"Get back! All of you, get back!"

The sluggish thing slimed its way behind a boulder as several others shrank back to their hiding places.

The little goat thing in Janner's arms stilled once it was free and turned its face to his. Its eyes were bright blue, like Kal's, and it was impossible to deny the soul that lived inside it. "I think my name was . . . Elin. That sounds right. Elin. But I'm afraid to remember more than that."

Elin the goat cloven trembled, then brayed and wriggled out of Janner's arms. It—she—landed on the ground and ran in mad circles as the slug-thing laughed nearby. The other cloven joined in with crazed laughter and animal calls—it was like feeding time in a barn, but with human sounds mixed in with the racket.

"Listen!" Kalmar called. "Quiet!" The cloven calmed down and whispered among themselves again as Kalmar stepped forward. "My father was Esben, King of Anniera. Do you remember Anniera?"

A few answered, "Yes." But some howled and scampered away.

"Whatever you've done, I need your help. We need to get to the Deeps of Throg. Do you understand? We need to find Gnag."

At that name, the forest grew deathly still.

"Will you take us to the Deeps?"

After a pause some of the cloven lurched into view and beckoned for them to follow. Kalmar and Janner looked at one another with apprehension then joined the odd procession through the Blackwood.

54

The Pain of Remembrance

Hours passed. Janner, Kalmar, and Oood trudged up and up, deeper into the forest and higher into the foothills. Sometime before the sun set, the trees opened into a little clearing.

"Look," Janner said, pointing at the snowy teeth of the Killridge Mountains towering overhead. They were terrifying—razor sharp and impossibly tall.

"So that's where we're going," Kalmar said.

"Throg," Oood rumbled.

The cloven moved on without a glance at the mountains. As they walked, more and more of the wild creatures joined them until the forest teemed with twisted limbs and lumpy faces. At first they were noisy, snarling and threatening so that the boys drew their swords and pressed against Oood. But when they saw Janner, the cloven either ran away or fell in line, seeming to understand somehow where they were going. Those who stayed limped and lurched through the trees, whispering to one another. All Janner heard were the words, "Boy" and "Anniera." Many of the cloven wept as they walked.

It got colder and more difficult to breathe, reminding Janner of his journey through the Stony Mountains with Maraly Weaver. The wind stirred the treetops, causing the icy stars to flicker overhead.

Their path led at last to the crest of a bald hill under a dome of stars. Janner would have called it a mountain had it not been dwarfed by snowy peaks towering ever higher above it. The brothers and Oood found themselves at the center of a great multitude of monsters, all of whom seemed to be waiting for—something.

"I've never seen anything like this," said a rich, familiar voice from among the animals. A tall figure stepped from the circle of cloven.

"Elder Cadwick?" Janner asked, peering into the darkness. "I thought you went back."

"And disobey my queen?" he said kindly.

"You disobeyed your king instead," Kalmar said. "And I'm glad you did. I don't know what's about to happen, but we might need your help." Kalmar looked around at the monsters in the starlight, snorting shadows with gleaming eyes and teeth.

"I was certain you would have needed it before now," Cadwick said. "I am surprised, this close to the Deeps, that I am . . . myself. But it's you," he said, turning to Janner.

"Me? What do you mean?" Janner knew he was being watched, but he didn't understand why.

"You're a boy," Cadwick replied, as if that explained everything.

"Why does everyone keep saying that?" Janner asked.

Cadwick placed one of his bluish hands on Janner's shoulder. "You remind us not just of what was lost, but of what may be found. For some, it is too much, but for these, you have kindled remembrance, and remembrance kindles hope. Queen Arundelle believed this might happen someday."

"I don't understand," Janner said. "What do they want me to do?"

"I don't know." Cadwick raised his voice and addressed the cloven. "Brethren and sistren! A boy has come into the Blackwood. He seeks the Deeps of Throg. What do you want of him?"

"We want him to heal us," one of them answered. "The queen said it might be so."

"I don't know what you're talking about!" Janner said, afraid of what they would do when they realized he couldn't help them. "Kal, tell them. I can't heal anybody."

"But you have already begun to," Cadwick said. "Only days ago I was afraid to come this close to the Deeps. In truth, I loathed the queen's command to accompany you. But the presence of a boy—an *Annieran* boy, the son of Esben, untainted by Gnag—quiets the madness of memory. It awakens the hope that our story is not over."

The cloven chattered and cooed eagerly. It was the eagerness that worried Janner most, because it was like hunger. But what could he do?

"We need to get to Gnag," Kalmar called. "He has the ancient stones. If we can stop him, maybe we can find a way to help you."

"Sing the song of the ancient stones," the creatures chanted, "and the blood of the beast imbues your bones."

Immediately the air changed, and the cloven snapped and pawed at the ground. Whatever tameness had prevailed only a moment ago was fading. Cadwick's hooves scraped at the ground, too, and Janner sensed a change come over him. He paced and shook his head as if trying to wake from a nightmare.

"Um," Kalmar said. "This doesn't look good."

Oood growled and assumed a battle stance as the cloven chanted. "SING THE SONG OF THE ANCIENT STONES, AND THE BLOOD OF THE BEAST IMBUES YOUR BONES."

The rhyme thundered on the bald mountaintop, and with each repetition the cloven grew wilder and edged closer to the boys, a clacking, snarling, snuffling mob. The mention of the stones had broken the peace, and Janner was the object of their anger. He was no "brother cloven" as Kalmar was. He was no formidable troll. He was an outsider, a threat perhaps, and a stirrer of bitter memories.

"*Go,*" Elder Cadwick said between gritted teeth.

"Go where?" Janner asked.

"Go," Cadwick repeated with a snarl. "You . . . must . . . hurry. The door to the Deeps lies in that valley. GO."

But they were surrounded.

"Oood, now would be a good time to lead the way," Kalmar said with a whine.

The troll needed no encouraging. He growl-moaned and ran for the valley, lowering his shoulder at the wall of snarling cloven. Janner and Kalmar raced after him, praying that he would clear a path through their present danger, even if it only led to a greater one.

Their dash into the valley was worse than a nightmare. Janner had never been so afraid, not even in the coffin at the Fork Factory. He huffed down the hill in the dark, aware of Oood's swinging fists and the cries of pain when the cloven were struck and sent sailing backwards. Janner drew his sword but he was running too fast and too blindly to use it. He heard Kalmar growling and knew the growl was that of a yellow-eyed Grey Fang. Whatever had caused the cloven to change had changed his brother too. Janner could only hope that when they reached the entrance to the Deeps he could call his brother back.

Suddenly they were in the trees again, speeding downhill with the cloven in pursuit. The darkness deepened, and Janner half-ran, half-tumbled down the slope, following Oood's odor as much as his bellow.

"Your name is Kalmar, son of Esben, King of the Shining Isle!" Janner screamed into the darkness. He repeated it again and again. The forest around them took on an eerie stillness, and Janner realized they were alone. The cloven had turned back. Their howls filled the Blackwood and drifted through the forest from every direction like ghosts. Oood stopped running.

"Are you hurt?" Janner asked in between ragged breaths.

"Hurt," Oood said softly.

"Kalmar," Janner called into the shadows. He could see Oood's hulking form in the darkness, but wasn't certain where his brother was. "Are you here? Do you know who you are?" Janner closed his eyes and listened for his brother.

Kal's voice came from somewhere to the right. "Yes. I think so." He sounded frightened. "Janner, it's getting harder to come back."

Oood's legs buckled and he crashed to the ground.

"Oood, how bad is it?" Janner asked, running over to where the troll sat.

"Not bad," he said. Then after a pause, "Bad."

Janner placed his hand on Oood's shoulder. "Where are you hurt?"

"All over," Oood said.

Janner rummaged in his pack and retrieved his matches, then struck one, afraid of what he would find. Oood was bleeding—everywhere. Cuts and scrapes covered him from his head to his feet. Some were puncture wounds from bites, others were slashes as if he had been attacked by a sword. The cloven had loosed their full fury on the troll.

"Friends safe?" Sweat and blood trickled down his face and dripped from his enormous chin.

"Yes," Janner said, unable to hold back his tears. Kalmar approached with a whine and rested a hand on Oood's forehead as Janner's match burned out.

"Thirsty," Oood said. Janner struck another match. Oood's eyes drooped and he lay back in the cold leaves and closed his eyes.

"Kal, get him some water."

Kalmar checked the canteens. "We're out." He sniffed. "But I smell some not far away. I'll get it."

"Kal, no. The cloven—"

"I don't care. I'm getting him water."

The second match burned out as Kal slipped away in his Durgan cloak, silent as a shadow. Janner listened to the distant howls of cloven and Oood's shallow breathing. Helplessly, he waited in the dark for what seemed like a long time, before he heard the slightest rustle of leaves nearby.

Janner struggled to lift Oood's head as Kal poured the water into his sagging mouth. The boys sat in the dark without speaking. Oood's breaths grew shorter and feebler, and the slow rhythm of his dying heart lulled the boys to sleep.

When rumors floated to Anniera that strange, dangerous beasts were seen lurching about in the Blackwood, Bonifer suspected that there was a connection between the monsters and the animals he smuggled. He often wondered what dark purpose the Lord of Throg had for the animals, but his greed compelled him. And so his stores of gold increased even as the cloven, as they came to be called, increased.

One night in the deep winter, a messenger arrived at Bonifer's door. The man was dressed in black and though a cloth masked his face, Bonifer saw the red flecks of bloodrock paint around his eyes—a Wanderer of the Woes, fierce folk who would as soon murder you as offer you wine. Bonifer accepted the message warily. He knew the animals he sold went by way of the Woes, but he never dreamed a Wanderer would appear at his doorstep.

The note was written in a shaky hand and was difficult to read, but he knew it came directly from the strange man in the Castle Throg. It thanked him for his help acquiring the animals, and offered an unbelievable sum for—what?—a human child.

A human child! Bonifer recoiled. It was one thing to sell animals in secret. It was another to kidnap a baby for some unforeseen and wretched purpose.

Bonifer slammed the door in the messenger's face and cowered in his quarters. That night as he lay in bed, his thoughts returned again and again to the wealth that could be his. But in the morning, he was ashamed to have even considered the offer.

Soon, Madia gave birth to a daughter, Illia. She was raised a fair warrior, to be the Throne Warden. She was three when word spread through the fields, vales, and villages of Anniera that the High Queen was expecting another child—the future king or queen of the land.

Bonifer loved Illia, for in his twisted mind he liked to imagine that Madia's children were his own. The joy with which Ortham raised his daughter and loved Madia was poison to Bonifer Squoon, and so he endeared himself to young Illia, as he knew he would also do to Madia's second child when it was born.

One night late in Madia's pregnancy, Ortham invited Bonifer, his old friend, to feast at the castle. Bonifer usually refused, so painful was it to see the king and queen together, but the king insisted. Bonifer arrived and discovered he was the object of a playful ruse. A maiden from the village of Bernhold, a few miles away, sat at the table in a fine dress, looking at Bonifer bashfully.

After an uncomfortable dinner during which time Bonifer's anger at Ortham increased tenfold, the king said privately to Bonifer, "Old friend, are you grown cold to love? The queen and I wish happiness for you."

With great effort, Bonifer held back the flood of bitter and biting remarks he might have made, for he was convinced that his only hope of happiness was for Ortham to die and Madia to accept his love. "I am happiest, King, at the service of Illia, Madia, and yourself, and would die alone before dividing that allegiance with a woman for whom I hold no affection."

So near did he come to losing control of his tongue, expressing his hatred of Ortham and thereby damning himself from Madia's presence, that Bonifer fled, and Ortham was left greatly vexed.

—From *The Annieriad*

55

Oskar Suggests a Song

As spring came to the Green Hollows and white blossoms shone on the trees, red blood stained the ground of Ban Rona.

For days, the Hollowsfolk had fought the Fangs—Bat Fangs swooping in from the cliffs beyond the Watercraw, Grey Fangs creeping into the city under cover of night. Rudric brought word that ships had been spotted in the distance, an armada of Gnag's forces mustered on the horizon, creeping closer by the hour, and it was to these ships that the Fangs retreated after each assault was beaten back.

At night the Hollish warriors slept in shifts while the air above them screamed with swooping Bat Fangs. The beasts were nocturnal so they increased their attacks at dusk and lagged at dawn. The Hollowsfolk suffered through their nights and looked to morning as their only hope of rest.

But as soon as day was upon them there was work to be done—the dead and wounded had to be tended, supplies inventoried, strategies discussed, redoubts repaired. It was a war unlike any before it, and Rudric and his commanders struggled to adapt.

Leeli collapsed onto a bed in one of the study rooms of the Great Library. It had been placed there after Nia decided it was time to abandon Chimney Hill. The outlying homes of Ban Rona had been perilously vulnerable, no matter how many forces stood guard. Even with dogs and Durgans patrolling the hills around the city, the possibility that the Fangs might cut them off from Ban Rona had been an ever-present concern.

Three days earlier, Nia, Oskar, Podo, Freva, Bonnie, and Leeli loaded their most precious and necessary belongings onto the wagon and bade farewell to their home. They had arrived at the Great Library amid a throng of hounds escorting them to safety.

Now, lying in her makeshift bedroom, surrounded by shelves of old books, Leeli heard her army of dogs barking outside.

She licked her sore lips, then reached for a little jar on a shelf beside the bed. Nia had acquired it from the apothecary and insisted that Leeli apply it as often as she could. It helped with the pain—but it smelled like a donkey's legpit. She held her breath while she uncapped the jar, then dipped in her finger and scooped out a dab of yellowish goo. She had asked Nia what it was made of, but she only said, "You don't want to know."

When Leeli dabbed the salve on her lips, the stench leapt into her nose and made her gag.

There was a knock at the door.

"Hello, Leeli girl!" said Oskar as he peeked in, wrinkling his nose at the odor. "You were splendid last night." Oskar sat at the edge of her bed, which made the boards creak and the mattress pitch like a ship in heavy wind. Leeli had to pretend she wasn't about to roll onto the floor. "The warriors are tired. We're all tired. But when you play," Oskar closed his eyes and smiled, "they seem to remember all the beauty in the world and they fight the harder. And it gives us such great pleasure to see how much the Fangs hate it." He tilted his head and eyed her through his spectacles. "But you need more songs, dear."

"I know," she said with a sigh. "Did you bring more?"

Oskar pulled a small book from his satchel and adjusted his spectacles. "It's called *Cousin Joe Bob's Slappy Swine and Other Tunes Equally Desirable*." He flipped through the first few pages. "Alas, there's no author's name, so I shan't be able to properly quote from it." He turned his twinkling eyes to Leeli again. "But the songs are Hollish and Anni-eran, and I recognize very few of the titles."

"That's good." Leeli pushed herself up and pulled out her whistle-harp. "We need ammunition."

"Aye, lass. That we do," Oskar said with a sad smile. "Shall I help you or leave you to it?"

"I'll be fine. I think I can follow it."

Leeli turned her attention to the book, intending to memorize at least a few of the melodies before she dozed. If the Fangs attacked before dusk, and they probably would, it would be best if she had a fresh song to sing—for her own sanity as well as its power against the Fangs.

Oskar, however, stood in the doorway, staring at the floor.

"What is it?" Leeli asked.

"Your Highness," he said, "there *is* one song you haven't played yet."

Leeli looked away.

"And you know the older the songs are, the more the Fangs seem to hate them."

Have I not done enough? she wondered. Her lips were blistered, she was exhausted, and she had put herself in danger on the roof every night, but Oskar wanted more. Everyone wanted more.

"And this song, Highness, is *very* old. And you know it by heart."

"No."

Oskar continued to stare at the floor, one hand on the doorknob and the other nervously scratching his belly. He sighed. "May I ask why?"

"Because I don't trust them. Especially Yurgen."

"But the dragons once aided Anniera. They might do so again if only you'll—"

"I need to practice. Please let me be." Leeli hated to speak to her old friend that way, but her heart was steaming with emotion and she didn't know where to put it. "I'm sorry, Mister Reteep, but I'm very tired."

Oskar nodded and shut the door.

Leeli held her whistleharp to her lips but didn't blow. She pretended to pluck strings with one hand and fingered the whistle with the other, imagining the melody without playing it. That was how she had always practiced in the bedroom at the Igiby cottage when she didn't want to bother the boys. Just thinking of the song, however, turned the hot emotion in her chest from anger into what it really was all along, from the moment Oskar had mentioned it: fear. Her fingers trembled at the thought of "Yurgen's Tune."

She remembered the great old dragon thundering out of the icy sea, its huge, glistening head swooping over the deck of the *Enramere* like a demon on the hunt. Yurgen the Dragon King, sniffing out Podo, wanting to kill them all to avenge the death of his young dragons. Leeli's heart broke to think of Podo, that sweet bear of a man who had loved her and her family so well, trembling with shame and terror before the dragon. Even now, the sight of the sea brought such pain to Podo that he could scarcely look to the west without a shadow passing over his face.

No, Leeli would not play that tune again. She didn't want to remember that day in the Ice Prairies, or the sea dragons, or her grandfather's many sins against them—and playing "Yurgen's Tune" would bring the bitter slap of those memories like nothing else.

But there was something worse—something more troubling than that memory.

Leeli knew that there was something stronger than Fangs haunting the Dark Sea of Darkness. The sea dragons, at least some of them, were still there in the harbor, watching and watching and watching for the moment when Podo Helmer might set foot on a ship again. She had felt Yurgen's great anger that day, and though he had given Podo one last passage across the sea, she had glimpsed in the dragon's ancient soul a troubling darkness.

Oskar had learned from the First Book that there had been an alliance between Anniera and the dragons, but she had no wish to restore that alliance—not with Yurgen. There was evil in him. She didn't trust the old dragon any more than she trusted the Fangs of Dang.

That was the real reason she didn't want to play the melody. She was afraid it would do more than madden the Fangs and rouse the Hollowsfolk.

It might summon the Dragon King—and if it did, something terrible would happen.

56

Kicking Despair in the Rump

Leeli woke at dusk to the familiar sound of battle.

"Sweetie," Nia said.

"They need me," Leeli murmured with her eyes still closed.

"Yes. I'm sorry to wake you, but the sun is setting."

Leeli stretched and sat up. She sighed, grabbed her crutch, and pushed herself to her foot. Her lips felt better, but they tasted even worse than her breath. She grabbed *Cousin Joe Bob's Slappy Swine* from the shelf by the bed but left the lip salve.

"Don't forget your medicine," Nia said.

"I'd rather bleed," Leeli muttered.

"But your people would rather survive." Nia's voice was still quiet but it had taken on a tone that Leeli knew well. "You're the Song Maiden, and whether you like it or not, your music has done more to win these battles than all the swords in the city. Apply the balm."

By the time they arrived at the fourth floor of the library, in the room labeled BOOKS ABOUT TREE ROOTS AND JEWEL THIEVERY, Leeli was wide-awake and hungry. Rudric and several Hollish chiefs and chieftesses rose when she entered and waited for her to sit before continuing their meeting. Podo clomped into the room with a tray of redberry porridge and a spinnamon roll. He set it on the table before Leeli and gave her a whiskery kiss on the cheek.

"Maybe two days," Danniby was saying. "Maybe less."

"Where did all those blasted ships come from?" Guildmaster Clout said, banging his fist on the table.

Madame Sidler, the head librarian, peeked her head around the corner. "May I help you?" she asked.

"For the fiftieth time, Sidler, no!" one of the men shouted.

Madame Sidler bustled away, looking deeply offended, as the council resumed.

"Sorry, all. I'm getting here late," said one of the chieftesses. "Why can't we open Watercraw long enough to get our ships out?"

Leeli dipped her spinnamon roll in the porridge. She liked to listen. She also liked the chieftess who had just spoken. Some of them were all gruff and no grin—especially the women who, whether beautiful or as rough as their husbands, could be so unruly that fights occasionally broke out among them. But Hemmica the Hairy (as Podo called her) was as sweet as she was sour. She was huge—so tall and bulky that she hunched over the table like a troll—and her skin was saggy and speckled with moles where there were no wispy whiskers. But her eyes were bright as candles and when she smiled her wrinkles smiled with her.

"Because, Hemmica," said a chieftain named Kayden Evergreen, "we can't spare the warriors. If we send out a fleet to stop the Fang ships, the city will be weakened. Our defenses will crumble."

"Not only that," added Rudric, "the Fangs have yet to turn their attention to the gatehouses at the Watercraw. They're locked up tight. But I fear that as soon as we send soldiers to open the gate they'll be under fierce attack, and if we lose the gates we'll only regain them at the cost of many lives."

"But sooner or later we have to open the craw." Hemmica cleared her throat and adjusted the battleaxe slung over her shoulder. "We'll have to risk them getting in in order for us to get out."

"And once we're out, what then?" asked Nibbick.

"Fight the Fangs," Hemmica said, as if it were obvious.

"Oy," said Nibbick, "but there are—how many ships did you say, Rudric?"

"Sixty, at least."

"Sixty ships!" Nibbick leaned back and put a hand to his forehead. "We've half that many. And it's been so long since most of our boys have sailed they hardly know a poop deck from a chamber pot!"

Hemmica frowned and scratched her warty chin. Everyone sat in silence while Leeli finished her porridge.

"So even with our fleet of thirty ships," Rudric said, "we can do nothing but wait for Gnag's new fleet to arrive. We might be able to fend off the Bat Fangs and the rest—they die by the hundreds every day. But the fleet is another matter. Maker knows what beasts prowl those decks, or where they came from."

"If I were them," said Hemmica, "I'd make it my first business to take the gatehouses and lower the chain at the craw. Then the ships could sail in and Ban Rona would be sacked like a spadge of totatoes."

"Well, why don't ye all just give up now and make it easy for 'em!" Podo growled from the corner where he'd been whittling angrily at his legbone.

"What do you propose, old man?" said Nibbick Bunge.

"A hundred things besides sitting here waiting for the end to come," Podo said. He got up from his chair and stomped to the table. Leeli noticed that Hemmica was smiling at him, her eyes twinkling like diamonds in dirty linen. "This is just like Ships and Sharks," he grouched. "If ye can't meet the fleet on the open sea, then pile every ship in Ban Rona around the Watercraw. Lash 'em together and drop anchor on the whole lot. That way they can lower the craw chain if they like, but they still won't get through. In fact, once they see the snaggle of ships they'll likely leave the gatehouses alone."

Nibbick's face changed from scrunched to thoughtful. "Not a bad idea," he said. "But we're still in the same boat, so to speak. The only difference is, once they take the gatehouses, they're burning our ships."

"But it gives us a little more time. It's something isn't it?" Leeli said.

"Oy, that's something," Rudric said.

The conversation continued, and Podo plopped back into his chair and lit his pipe. Leeli excused herself and joined him.

"Sometimes," he whispered with a wink, "somebody needs to kick despair in the rump. There's always a way out, eh lass?"

"Aye," Leeli growled like a pirate.

"Ye know," Podo said after a moment, "I've been talking with Oskar, and he thinks—"

"He thinks I should play 'Yurgen's Tune.'"

"Aye," Podo said quietly.

"Well, I won't."

Podo drew on his pipe and considered her. "And why not? There may come a time when we're outnumbered and those dragons might be our only hope. They fought for Anniera a long time ago."

"I don't trust them. And *they* don't trust you."

"Aye, that's true." Podo scratched his whiskery chin. "But I don't aim to be anywhere near the water. Should you choose to call them, that is."

"But Grandpa, even if I called them, even if it worked and I played the song and they came—who's to say they'll help us at all?"

"Who's to say they won't? You?"

Leeli fussed with the hem of her dress. "You didn't hear his voice like I did," she said. "There's something dark in that old dragon. There must be another way. Like Ships and Sharks, right?"

"Aye. I don't like those dragons any more than you do." He blew a puff of smoke. "Let's hope it don't come to that."

Leeli relaxed, and realized she had been clenching her jaw. She would never call Yurgen. Not for anything. The only thing worse than facing Gnag the Nameless himself would be seeing that wretched old beast again.

A Hollish warrior entered the room and called for Rudric. It was Ladnar, who had lost his tooth. "Keeper, the nighth's battle ith begun.

The batth are on the wing and a new wave of Grey Fangth ith creeping over the cliffths. We need the printheth."

Rudric cast his weary eyes on Leeli. She smiled, though it hurt her lips to do so. She pulled her whistleharp from the folds of her coat as if she were a knight drawing a sword, then followed Ladnar from the room.

57

Songs to Play,
Battles to Fight

Leeli climbed the steps to the roof of the library, flanked by a company of soldiers, men and women armed to the fingertips and looking warily at the air. Leeli couldn't see much over their shoulders, but she saw enough. Out beyond the harbor and the cliffs of the Watercraw, backlit by the purple dusk, a shadow moved slowly toward them.

"Thank you for coming, Your Highness," said one of the women. Her reddish hair was braided and hung over leather armor plated with rusty metal. She bowed her head. "I know you're tired."

"You're tired, too," said Leeli. "Where are the O'Sallys?"

"Right behind you," answered Thorn, who stood in the company with a dog on either side.

Leeli turned and accidentally let a smile spread over her face. "Ow," she said, touching her lips. She was embarrassed to be so happy to see her friend. She didn't want him to think she liked him. Or maybe she did. Suddenly her cheeks were rosy as the morning sky. She took a deep breath and straightened, just like Nia, then said as seriously as she could, "I'm glad to see you. What's the plan?"

"I was going to ask you the same." Thorn tore off a piece of hogpig jerk, chewed on it for a few seconds, then spat. "The dogs are worn out, but they'll do whatever you ask."

"How many did we lose yesterday?"

"Forty three." Thorn shook his head. "Hard to say how many are left. A few hundred, maybe. It's real bad."

"Really bad."

"Oy. Like I said."

It was a terrible thing, sending the dogs into battle. It weighed on Leeli every time she gave the order, knowing that many of them wouldn't return. But they were as eager to fight as any of the Hollows-folk, and in their simple way they seemed to understand what was at stake.

Many of the Houndry Corps spent every waking hour scouring and sniffing the city for spent arrows, returning them to the makeshift fletchery at the Orchard Inn. Another company of dogs dispatched messages from Green Hill Press on Cherry Lane to different parts of the city. Since the enemy wasn't gathered in a clear line on an open field, but rather came from above and could drop Grey Fangs in different parts of the city, communication was crucial.

Days earlier, Leeli had asked Rudric what the dogs could do to help, short of accompanying the warriors in battle. He had just entered the war room of the Great Library, fresh from a battle. He was sweaty, dirty, and exhausted as he answered questions from every direction at once. Leeli knew there were a thousand more important things demanding his attention so she stood near the wall and listened.

"We need soldiers at the south of the craw. Wolves are coming in over the cliffs," panted one of the men. Rudric gave him his new orders just as someone else burst into the room asking for more arrows at the Guildling Hall. Rudric gave another order, and another, and Leeli noticed that the men he dispatched were exhausted. That was when she had come up with the idea for the messenger dogs.

Dogs were faster, more agile, lower to the ground and therefore harder to see. She hobbled over to one of the men and asked him to write the message down and go find water and rest. She would see that the message was delivered. It would have been better if Rudric had approved it, but Leeli was correct in her belief that the less Rudric had to think about, the better a leader he would be.

She had asked Thorn O'Sally to call for Leaper. She dogspoke to Leaper, telling him that he was to bring back any reply, secured the note to his collar and sent him off into the night. Only minutes later the dog had returned, unharmed, having delivered the message and brought back a reply.

Rudric hardly noticed—until the next day when he realized that most of the battle's correspondence was being handled by brave Leaper, aided by Leeli's gift of communication. He had winked at Leeli and flashed a smile. That was the final approval she had been waiting for.

In the few spare moments when Leeli wasn't needed with her whistleharp on the rooftops, she and Thorn had gathered a passel of the smartest dogs: Leaper, Flag, Baxter (who had already recovered enough to help), and feisty little Frankle among them. Leeli knelt before them in Gully's Saloon and conveyed the plan to them in dogspeak. It was difficult, even for Leeli, to communicate it all to the dogs in such a short time, but the whole pack had sat at attention and locked their eyes on the Song Maiden as if they understood every word, and Leaper filled in the blanks for her with whines and little barks.

Thorn and Biggin fashioned tubes to the dogs' collars for the purpose of holding written orders. Leeli taught Thorn and Biggin how to dogspeak each of the commanders' names and positions, and it was up to the dogs to find them in the various sections of the city whenever they were sent with an urgent message.

It had worked brilliantly, but after the second day Leeli realized that half her messenger dogs were dead or wounded. Not only did that mean her soul was heavy with sorrow, it meant she had to train more dogs every day even as she grieved the ones who had fallen.

At Leeli's urging, the rest of the Houndry Corps bounded into the battle alongside the Hollowsfolk. They fought with a will and purpose that none of the Hollish warriors had ever seen. Dogs leapt from stone walls to snag Bat Fangs' legs; they circled Grey Fangs and either attacked or held them until Hollish warriors arrived.

There were no prisoners taken—not because the Hollowsfolk were unmerciful, but because the Fangs never, ever stopped fighting. Each morning, a film of brown and gray dust coated the city. And as the warriors bound their wounds and rested, the conversation in Ban Rona always drifted to the courage of the Houndry Corps and how indispensable the dogs were to the night's striving.

In years past, though dogs had always been central to the culture and community of the Green Hollows, the dogs had been trained to fight with their masters, and their masters taught their dogs individual skills as they saw fit. That meant that one dog wouldn't necessarily understand the command of another dog's master. Not only that, there were often fights between dogs, each seeking dominance or the establishment of territory.

But Leeli had changed everything on that moonlit night at Chimney Hill. Every single dog had raised its head and howled its allegiance to the Song Maiden, and from that moment, to Leeli's embarrassment, many of the dogs had begun ignoring their masters altogether. They had, in the face of battle, transferred their allegiance to the little girl with the twisted foot, the one whose music sang in their blood, the one who spoke their own language.

At first they had congregated on the lawn at Chimney Hill and were reluctant to leave if Leeli was there. When she did ride into town, the dogs followed her in parade. But she had dogspoken to them outside the Great Library and encouraged them to rejoin their masters, who no doubt needed them. The dogs dispersed, but not before each approached Leeli and nosed her open hand. It was a relief, because she heard angry mutterings from Hollowsfolk whose dogs had suddenly gone odd and only listened half the time.

Then she began to receive word from Biggin or Rudric's men that this front line or that was under heavy attack and there were no avail-

able warriors in reserve. So Leeli whistled a call to the dogs across
the city and sent pack after pack to the battlefront. Biggin and Thorn
O'Sally were the best dogspeakers in the Hollows, but they couldn't
have done as much. And so poor Leeli was not only needed on the
rooftops to play her music and confound the Bat Fangs; she was also
needed throughout the night again and again to command the dogs.

All who saw Leeli Wingfeather looked on her with wonder and
whispered among themselves with awe, for she never complained, never
flagged, and never showed any sign of fear. She played song after song,
beating back the enemy with all the passion in her soul, then knelt
and stroked the wounded heads of her loyal dogs as she whispered and
clicked to them her encouragement and commands.

When the dogs were off, she drank or ate enough to sustain her, then
she mounted the rooftop, tucked her crutch under her arm, and shot her
song into the bat-winged sky like a volley of arrows. Her guards, which
shifted throughout the day, fought not only for Ban Rona, or even for
their very lives—they fought for the Song Maiden of Anniera, who emptied her strength each night the way a cloud empties itself of rain.

Frankle never left her side. Leeli had ordered him away time and
again, tucked messages in his collar tube and pointed, but the little
whip happily disobeyed her every word. Irritated, she gave up and
turned her attention to her music. But soon Frankle's steady presence
became a comfort, a quiet companion in the heat of battle. He yipped
and snapped at the air whenever Bat Fangs swooped low, as if he were
as big as a bomnubble. Leeli's guards came to value his presence, too,
and if he trotted off to relieve himself or eat, they seemed uneasy until
he returned to plop his wagging tail on the ground at Leeli feet.

Now, Frankle was tumbling about on the ground and leaping at
Leeli's crutch, snapping at it playfully with his sharp puppy teeth.
Thorn tossed him a piece of hogpig jerk.

"I reckon it's the same as yesterday. Pa told me there was a breach in
the barricade over on Apple Way and they likely won't have it repaired

before the night wave crashes. Be ready to send a pack or two that way, first thing. I've done my best to teach the replacements the messenger posts, but I ain't sure all of them got it. If it gets confusing I may have to bring them to you."

"That's fine. Just don't bring them until there's a break in the battle. Things will get bad if I have to stop playing in the thick of an attack."

"Oy. Want some hogpig?"

Leeli crinkled her nose. "No, thanks. Just ate."

Thorn shrugged as he took another bite and chewed on it, looking out over the rooftops. "I like you, Leeli. Pa says if we make it out of this, we should marry. I think that would be real good."

Leeli had no idea what to think or say or do. She wasn't even sure he had actually said what she thought he had said. Thorn chewed his hogpig jerk, bent over, and scratched Frankle behind the ears. A few of the warriors tried to hide smiles, which made Leeli's cheeks turn from red to pale white. She gripped her crutch because she felt a wave of dizziness. An onslaught of Bat Fangs would have been preferable to the strange, delightful, and terrifying feeling that crackled all over her skin.

"Frankle's cute!" she blurted.

"Anyway," Thorn said, "I'll see you later." He strolled away, seemingly unaware that Leeli was gasping for air and most of the soldiers were grinning after him.

"Come on, Frankle," she said with a shake of her head, and she mounted a stout table that had been put there just for her.

She looked out over Ban Rona, at the broken windows, the smoldering buildings, the ramparts of debris and rubble. Torches were being lit all over the city. The cloud of Bat Fangs was but minutes way. A howl rang out across the rooftops from somewhere to the south, and it was answered by another in the north. Hollowsfolk shouted defiance. The city was rousing itself for another long night, another battle, and Leeli prayed to the Maker for the strength to play her song as long as she drew breath. She longed to see the dawn, to see these brave people push back at the wickedness again, and, somewhere deep in her heart, she longed for the day when she would be old enough to marry. But first, she thought, she would have to teach Thorn some grammar.

"Here they come," said the woman with the braid.

A Bat Fang shrieked overhead and a snarling Grey Fang dropped to the roof. Leeli's guards swung sword, hammer, and axe, and a bitter cloud of dust swirled in the air. Leeli strummed her whistleharp, then played a melody she had just learned from Oskar's new book. "Fetch the Pony, Tony." It was a rousing reel of a tune, and she immediately pictured herself adorned in white, dancing at her wedding. It sent such a thrill through her that, before she knew it, the magic shimmered the air and she saw Janner and Kalmar creeping through a damp darkness. The connection only lasted a moment, but it was enough to tell them she loved them before a swoop of bats cut her concentration and she forgot about weddings altogether.

There were songs to play and battles to fight.

"Come home," she whispered between verses. "Please come home, brothers."

58

Leeli's War

The battle raged all through the night. Leeli's lips bled, and she endured the smelly balm. The Fangs knew that she was their only true obstacle, but it was easy to see that they weren't allowed to kill her, either. Whenever a cluster of Bat Fangs swooped down to seize her, she played all the louder and her guards drew closer. And because her whistleharp's song carried far, its effects were felt throughout the city.

Several times each night, though, word came by way of her dogs that a fresh attack was centered on another part of the city and it was necessary that she be bustled off in secret. The guards would remain, and one of the smaller women, garbed in a similar dress and coat to Leeli's, stood on the table while Leeli slipped away. She would hurry under escort to a wagon, which would then speed through the streets to where she was needed. Leeli played, reinforcements pounded the enemy, and in this way the line was held. Then as quick as a clap she was escorted back to the Great Library to resume her station in the city center.

It confounded the Fangs every time, confirming the Hollish suspicion that though Gnag's army was strong in number, it was disorganized and easily duped. "But," Podo had reminded Leeli, "a swarm of bees can fell a toothy cow." And enough Fangs, fools though they might be, could fell Ban Rona.

For long hours Leeli played, improvising when she had exhausted every song she knew. One of her guards held open the new book so she could follow the notes of new songs. They did some good, but it was only when she had internalized a piece of music that she saw the biggest effect on the Fangs.

Nia remained at the periphery of the rooftop, watching her daughter and praying for her strength. She seemed to know exactly what Leeli needed and when, arriving with a canteen of cool water just when Leeli realized she was thirsty, or applying more of the balm, or ducking through the guards to bring motherly words of encouragement.

Leeli was hardly able to stand by the time the first hint of dawn backlit the hills in the east. The Fangs retreated at first light, and as the weary soldiers changed shifts, Podo appeared and lifted Leeli onto his back. Nia took her crutch and they walked to her room again.

How long could this go on? Would they fight every night until the Fangs were all dead? No. The new fleet of ships was coming, and Leeli knew that with it would come the end of the war.

Leeli lay on the bed with her eyes closed. Nia sat beside her, cleaning her face with a cool, damp cloth. She hummed a Hollish lullaby. It was sweet of Nia to sing, but Leeli needed no encouragement to find her way to sleep. Just as she closed her eyes, Leeli felt the pleasant thump of Frankle hopping into her bed and curling up at her feet.

"How is she?" Rudric said from the doorway.

"She's wearing thin," Nia said. "And you?"

"The same." There was a long pause. "They've taken the Guildling Hall. A sneak of ridgerunners crept through the defenses and distracted our fighters long enough to allow the Fangs inside. We lost—too many." Rudric sighed. "That's not all. The snow is nearly gone. The days are warm. Someone spotted a company of Green Fangs near the Watercraw just as the sun broke."

"Green Fangs."

"Yes."

"Which means legions are to follow." Nia's voice trembled. "This will end soon, won't it?"

"One way or another."

Somehow Leeli knew that Nia and Rudric were looking at one another. She risked opening her eyes a squint and saw them staring hard into one another's eyes. Rudric looked like he was going to speak, and Nia looked like she wanted him to. But a cloud of terrible sadness passed between them and he turned away. Nia stared long at the empty doorway, listening to Rudric's fading footsteps.

Leeli closed her eyes again and held still as Nia neatened the room, drew the makeshift curtains, and shut the door quietly behind her.

Weary as she was, Leeli sat up. She petted Frankle, who watched her happily as she gingerly brought the whistleharp to her lips. Her heart was full, and she needed a place to empty it. She closed her eyes again and gave voice to all her feelings—all her dashed hopes that Nia would find joy with Rudric, all her gladness that she had met her father that night on the boat, all the grief over his death, all her longing for her brothers' return, all her ache for the war to end.

She knew there was a dark presence in her music's magic, but today she didn't care. She needed to play; she needed the comfort of her brothers' love. And in the silence of her room she saw them again in the darkness, only now they were separated. Janner was afraid with a new kind of fear, and Kal was close to despair. Some blackness was in him that she didn't understand.

Kal.

She knew that he heard her. Janner heard her too.

We're still here. Still fighting. You have to keep fighting, too.

They didn't answer with words, only with a swirl of emotions and memories. The Jewels' hearts entwined invisibly for a little while, then instead of holding to the connection she bade them safe journey in her heart's language and ended her song.

A swell of weariness engulfed her and she collapsed to her pillow. But before sleep could take her, a voice rattled her mind and shook her so that she nearly tumbled from the bed.

I SEE YOU. I'LL GET YOU, GIRL.

"Mama!" Leeli screamed, and Nia burst into the room.

"What is it?"

"It was . . . it was *him*."

"Who?" Nia hugged Leeli tightly. "Was it a dream?"

"No," Leeli cried. "It was Gnag. He knows the boys are coming. He said he could see us!"

"Shh," Nia whispered. "You just had a bad dream."

Nia's voice was so soothing after Gnag's awful words that Leeli half believed her. "No, I saw the boys. They're in trouble. They're in the Deeps. After I stopped playing I heard his voice and he knows! We have to do something!"

Leeli sobbed into Nia's shoulder, so shaken she lost all her words. She wanted to get up, to rouse the Hollowsfolk, but her eyes were heavy with tears and weariness.

Frankle whined and nuzzled Leeli's leg. She was only nine years old, and her poor little body was out of strength. Nia's embrace, the warm bed, and her tears overcame the urgency of her fear and the world blurred. Sleep took her against her will as surely as Gnag had promised to take her, and she could do nothing to stop it.

59

Swallowed by the Deeps

When the boys woke in the Blackwood, Oood was gone—literally.

Janner and Kal sat up in the forest, shivering and alone. There was no sign of the troll's body. Blood stained the leaves where he had lain the night before, and bright green shoots sprouted where his head had been. The boys called for him, hoping against hope that he was alive and merely off gathering food or firewood.

"Do you smell him?" Janner asked.

"Nothing fresh. Everything here smells old—but not *dead*-old. Ancient old. And alive. It's hard to explain. I smell Oood's blood, and his usual stink, but only here where he was lying. This gives me the weirds."

"What do we do?" Janner asked, scanning the forest.

"We keep going."

"Is there any water left?" Janner was painfully thirsty, and hungry too.

"I gave it all to Oood last night." Kalmar shook the empty canteen. "I can go back to the spring, but it's a few miles that way." He pointed north. "In the wrong direction."

The boys turned south and looked in silence at the slope below them. They no longer needed a guide to show them the way to the Deeps of Throg. The deepest part of the valley below them seemed to breathe, as if their way led into a dragon's lair in one of the stories Janner loved.

Kalmar said, "I smell more water down there."

With a last look at the ground where Oood had died, Janner and Kalmar climbed down, wishing with every step that they could turn around and run home. The trees thickened, the land steepened, and soon they were hopping from stone to stone, grabbing old roots and low-hanging limbs for balance.

After a while, Janner heard dripping water. They followed the sound to a trickle running into the ravine between two boulders like blood from a wound. They refilled their canteens, guzzled it down, then refilled them again.

After hours of climbing down and down, deeper than Janner thought possible, they reached the bottom. They stood in a dank, earthen corridor, with walls of root and stone and a floor of soggy leaves. Weak sunlight sifted through the trees overhead.

Again, they didn't have to wonder which way to go. They were drawn to the Deeps like the trickle of water between the stones. They stepped over the rotten remains of trees, swatting at biter bugs as they slogged on for hours without speaking. Janner thought of Esben and Artham all those years ago, dragging themselves along this same path in the opposite direction, from darkness to light.

Then he saw a mildewed ribcage half covered in old leaves. Kalmar pointed further ahead at the skeleton of a many-legged beast, intact except for the missing skull. The farther they walked, the more bones they saw, until it became impossible to keep from stepping on them. Janner was glad they had filled their canteens at the last trickle, because now the only water was stagnant, gathered in little pools littered with tiny white bones and green sludge.

The boys rounded a tumble of fallen boulders and beheld the mouth of the cave. Above it rose a flat slab of rock, like an enormous gravestone, so tall that it disappeared into the trees overhead. Below it was the yawning black mouth of a cavern, swallowing the water that dribbled into it. At first they saw no way down, but Kalmar detected a path that led to and fro over rock and shale and slick root, into the Deeps of Throg.

"Let's eat," Kal said. He sat with his legs dangling over the edge and opened his pack. Janner was thankful, this once, for Kal's appetite, because it delayed them at least a few minutes. He sat beside his brother and ate a few crumbles of bread and a strip of dried diggle.

"I guess we have to go down in order to go up," Janner said as he capped his canteen and shouldered his pack. "I don't know about you, but this whole thing strikes me as a bad idea."

"The worst," Kalmar said with a smile. "You ready?"

They prayed to the Maker for aid, then hopped to the first ledge. Janner pretended his legs weren't trembling. He willed himself to go on, reminding himself that he was the Throne Warden, that he was older than Kal, that there was nothing to do but go on. Kalmar moved in quick hops along the path, stopping every few minutes to wait for Janner. The light faded, but Janner's eyes adjusted enough that when they reached the bottom he could still see a little, though there was little to see other than fallen rocks, bones, and spider webs.

He looked up the way they had come and was amazed by how welcoming the Blackwood now seemed. It was green with new leaves, and the sunlight that had seemed so dim before now looked as bright as a summer day. When he pulled his gaze away, back to the pathway descending into the Deeps, he saw only blackness.

"We need a torch," he said, embarrassed by how feeble he sounded. "I have some strips, and we can use one of these bones."

"I can see fine," Kal said.

"Well, good for you. I can't see anything."

"How much oil do you have?"

"Just the one flask."

"Keep the bone. We should save the oil for when it's too dark for me to see."

"I don't like this."

"I'll help you."

Janner felt Kal's hand on his shoulder. He swallowed his pride and took his brother's furry paw. "Just don't walk me off of a cliff, all right?"

Hand in hand, the Wingfeather boys made their way deeper into the cave, the light behind them fading to nothing the way Oood's breath had faded the night before. At first, Kalmar had to help Janner around big stones and across cracks wide enough to fall into, but after a little while he assured Janner that the floor was smooth and safe.

"What can you see?"

"The ceiling is lower. The walls are closer. It looks more like a tunnel now."

"Is there only one way to go?"

"I think so. And it looks like we're going up again."

That was a small encouragement. Janner didn't want to go any deeper, not if the Castle Throg was on top of the mountain.

Kalmar led them on for what felt like an eternity before he stopped. "I can't see. I just realized it."

"What do you mean you just realized it?"

"I've been smelling my way, and I can kind of hear where the tunnel goes. I just closed my eyes and realized that everything's totally dark now."

Knowing that neither of them could see almost unhinged Janner. He had begun to feel like the mountain was pressing down on him, crushing the part of his mind that knew light and shape until he was forever blind. He needed to light the lantern before he went mad. When he let go of Kalmar's hand he realized he had been squeezing it for a while now. But with nothing to hold onto he lost all sense of place and felt like he was falling. He staggered and caught himself against the wall. It was cold and damp, like the wall of the tunnel under Anklejelly Manor.

Janner chuckled.

"What is it? Why are you laughing?"

"I was just thinking about Anklejelly Manor. The ghost of Brimney Stupe. *Aaaaaaaaaaah.*" Janner snorted with laughter. "We were so scared that day!"

"The hungry ghost of Brimney Stupe awaits your BONES to swallow," Kalmar said, and now he was laughing too. "Remember how fast we ran home?"

"You were screaming like a little girl!" Janner wheezed and doubled over. It felt good to laugh, no matter how insane it seemed in their situation. As he leaned against the wall and slid to the floor, he wiped his eyes and saw a million colors. It was a comforting illusion. "That was the most afraid I'd ever been. And now we're in the Deeps of Throg, and neither of us can see a thing. If the ghost of Brimney Stupe showed up, I'd give him a hug."

It was, perhaps, the first time laughter had sounded in the Deeps of Throg, and when it had passed the brothers were braver for it. They rested a little while, each of them lost in their thoughts and thankful for the other's presence. That was when Janner heard the music. At first it was only a hint of a sound, enough that Janner held his breath and shushed Kalmar. He strained to hear it again, and soon the sound strung itself together into a melody so faint that even breathing made it hard to hear.

"Do you hear that?" Janner asked.

"Yes." Kalmar's reply was slow and soft. And wolfish.

Janner's skin crawled. "Kal?"

When he didn't answer, Janner dug blindly through his pack until he found his matches. He dropped them because his fingers were trembling and had to feel around on the floor until he found them. Kalmar was growling.

Janner's heart pounded as he struck the match and saw what he most dreaded to see: his brother, crouching only a few feet away, his teeth bared, staring at him with eyes so yellow they seemed to glow. The match fizzled and died, and the darkness fell over Janner like a curtain.

Then Kalmar pounced.

60

The Fang Attacks

Kalmar, no!" Janner screamed.

He felt Kal's claws digging into his forearms, heard his jaws snapping just inches from his face. Janner raised his feet to Kal's chest and kicked him away. He heard his brother slam into the cavern wall, growl, and spring again. Janner lunged aside and heard Kal crash into the stone behind him.

Only now did Janner understand how foolish it was to infiltrate the Deeps with Kalmar at his side. It was probably the most dangerous place for him, so close to where the melding happened.

"Kal!" Janner cried as he scooted along the wall. "Your name is Kalmar, son of Esben, King of the Shining Isle." The words came so fast they sounded like gibberish. He was answered by another growl. He heard Kal picking himself up from the ground.

Janner wanted to draw his sword, but he couldn't bring himself to do it. He couldn't hurt his brother, even if he was a Fang. It would be better to let Kal kill him. He heard Artham's voice in his head: *Protect! Protect! Protect!* But how? What was he supposed to do? If Janner fought, he might kill his brother. If Janner didn't fight, he might be killed—and when Kalmar came to his senses, he would realize what he had done. That would cast his brother into a shame even deeper than Artham's.

"Kal, please. Please come back. Your name is Kalmar, son of Esben . . ."

Janner couldn't go on. His voice broke and he couldn't speak without sobbing. He was afraid for his life, for Kal's soul, and he couldn't stop thinking about all the people who loved them both, people who would never know how deep Gnag's evil ran, how wretchedly the warden and the wolf king would die in the Deeps of Throg.

Janner was thankful that he couldn't see. Those yellow eyes were too horrible. He heard the shuffle and scrape of Kalmar coming closer, then another low growl. "Please, Kal. I love you."

The growl turned into a roar, and Janner's hand went to his sword hilt. He drew it halfway out, then slammed it back into the scabbard and waited for the end. He couldn't think of anything else to do.

A scream rose from Janner's belly and burst from his mouth as he prepared for the pain. But Kalmar's snarling turned into a mournful howl that filled the tunnel. When the howl faded, Janner realized the distant song had stopped too. Maybe the singer had heard them.

As this frightening thought came to Janner, he heard a whine, then the sound of Kalmar padding off into the tunnel alone. Janner had been holding his breath, and he let it out in short gasps, clutching at his chest and blinking away tears. He was so sure he had reached the end. But he wasn't dead.

No. This might be something worse.

Now he was all alone in the darkness.

61

Alone in the
Deeps of Throg

Alone.

Alone in the Deeps of Throg.

Janner felt the weight of the mountain, miles of stone reaching to the cold ceiling of the world, all of it pressing down on the tunnel where he sat in the damp darkness.

Janner called for Kalmar, but the echo only taunted him, his own lonely voice as frightening as anything else he might have heard. He was in the cellar of Anklejelly Manor again, or in the Strander burrows under Dugtown, or worse, in the coffin at the Fork Factory. Why did his road always lead into blackness?

Please don't let me die here. Please let me find my way out.

Janner opened his eyes, half hoping that it was as simple as that; maybe there would be some light, some magical messenger to lead him back to the surface. But there was nothing. He had his matches, along with the bone torch and the oil flask, but in the same way that his voice only made him feel more alone, he was afraid the torch light would only illuminate his isolation.

He was lost and alone in the worst place he could imagine. The place that had driven his father mad, his uncle mad, and made monsters out of nearly every Annieran—including Kalmar.

What was he to do? Crawl deeper into the mountain? Or turn back, though that only led to the Blackwood and a horde of angry cloven?

A word came to his mind: *Protect*.

Protect Kalmar, who couldn't seem to escape his shame. Kalmar, running through the tunnels with his yellow eyes. Kalmar, who had almost killed him.

How was he supposed to protect a Fang? Janner was angry, but his anger wasn't directed at Kal. His anger was aimed at the one who had allowed all this to happen.

So tell me, Maker, what am I to do? What other torments do you have in store?

The word came to him again, clear and bright as a jewel: *Protect*.

This time he imagined Artham's voice. Esben's voice, too. Suddenly he heard Nia, Podo, Oskar, and Leeli, all speaking quietly, urging him as he had been urged since he was born: *Look out for your brother. You're a Throne Warden. Kalmar needs you.*

But he left me! He attacked me! Janner thought. *The Throne Warden protects the king, but who protects the Throne Warden?*

Janner gritted his teeth and banged his fists on the stone floor. It was a childish thing to do, but he didn't care. He wanted his father. He wanted a home. He wanted to live for just one day without any fear of evil, within or without.

Rest. *That* was what he wanted. He was so tired of running, so tired of the constant fear that each day held some new danger, or treachery, or lie. He wanted a good meal, a good book, a little fire in the winter and a little shade in the summer. Could there be some world where such a thing existed?

Even before Gnag rose to power there were wars and skirmishes and threats to peace—Aerwiar was a terribly broken place. He didn't have to look far to see it, either. Podo's missing leg: because he was hunting young sea dragons for money. Artham's madness: because he had abandoned his brother. Grigory Bunge, the Fangs, the Kimerans who were so treacherous that Gammon had to work in secret. Was every heart so prone to deceit? Was there no one trustworthy in all of Aerwiar?

Sara Cobbler.

The name came to him like the strum of a whistleharp.

He remembered her bright eyes in the Fork Factory. He remembered her beauty shining through the soot on her weary face. And he remembered the night he left her, remembered his terror as he drove the carriage through the night. That night, *he* had done the leaving. He had wanted to go back, but he didn't. He had driven away and left her to the Overseer's coffin. Had sweet Sara cursed him as he was now cursing Kalmar? Had she lain in the dark that night in the coffin and wondered why Janner had sped away?

Janner was as weak as everyone else in this fractured world, and he knew it.

Protect.

The word came to him again and again, as steady as a drum beat. Indeed, it had been beaten into him since he was a baby. And now the rhythm of his mother's word, his uncle's word, drove back the anger— not completely, but enough that he thought less of his own misery and more of his brother's.

He remembered old tales, stories about self-sacrifice and the way a single, beautiful act done for the sake of another could shine out across the dark of the ages like a breaking dawn. When he was little, he and Kal had made swords out of sticks and defeated dragons, Fangs, and villains, and Janner had lain awake in his bed at the Igiby cottage *yearning* to be one of those heroes. Maybe now the Maker was only giving him what he wanted. Maybe the Maker was answering the prayer of his little boy heart by leading him here and giving him the chance to live one of those stories.

Janner bowed his head in the blackness and quieted the clamor of the angry voices in his head. When they persisted he told them to shut up. He drew in a long breath and thought of Anniera again, where he came into the world in the glow of a great love for some great purpose. He thought of green fields and soft rain falling in shafts of sunlight, of the laughter of children on the white shores of the Shining Isle, of the ancient dream of every soul for peace and good work and better rest. It was a dream he had nursed in Glipwood, in Ban Rona, and he discovered that it was a dream that still ran like a deep river even in the Deeps of Throg.

His heart grew quiet.

Janner pictured Kalmar, as alone in the dark as he was himself.

"Protect," he said aloud. And the echo of his voice brought him comfort this time. It was a defiant sound.

Janner felt around on the floor and found the matches, then he tied a strip of cloth to the end of the bone, soaked it with oil, and lit it, discovering that the tunnel was smaller and wetter than he thought it would be. He shouldered his pack and draped his muddy Durgan cloak over it.

"My name is Janner Wingfeather, Throne Warden of Anniera," he said, adjusting Rudric's sword on his hip. "Hold on, Kal."

He followed the Fang deeper into the mountain.

62

The Queue of Destruction

The tunnel ran straight for several arrow shots before it opened into a circular chamber where four other tunnels intersected. Janner swung the torch close to the floor and saw Kal's paw prints dampening the dry spots. They led into the tunnel on the left, and when Janner had gone but a few paces in he came upon a stair that climbed steeply upward.

He climbed for a long time, repeatedly stopping to catch his breath before reaching a landing where the passageway split again. The floor was dry, and there were no tracks to guide him. Each direction led to more stairs, so Janner closed his eyes and listened. All he heard was the flutter of his torch and his own breathing. He wanted to call for Kalmar again, but instinct told him to stay quiet.

He heard—or thought he heard—a faint shuffling sound coming from the left stairway, so up and up he went, ignoring the burning in his thighs, until from somewhere above he was certain that he heard signs of life other than his own. A snorting, grobbling sound. He eased his sword from the scabbard and crouched, trying to steady his nerves and control his breathing.

A furless, dog-like cloven flopped around a bend in the stairway, spilled down two steps, and came to rest in front of Janner. Its legs, as far as Janner could tell, had no bones. Its jaw flapped open, and the tongue lolled about, dampening the stone. Its pitiful eyes stared at him out of a mass of gray, wrinkled flesh and it managed to mumble something indecipherable in a voice that was disturbingly human. It was hideous and stood no chance of making it out of the Deeps.

It mumbled again, and Janner said, "I'm sorry." He uncapped his canteen and edged forward, pouring a few drops of water into its useless mouth. It lapped it up clumsily, then flopped down the stairs and out of sight.

Gnag, Janner thought, clenching his jaws. *We have to stop this.*

He started up the steps again, trying to ignore the gooey trail the doggish cloven had left, and came to a large, open chamber ringed with unlit torches. Janner lit one of them and tossed his bone-torch aside.

Here, at least, was some sign of progress. He was no longer creeping through a cave, but a dungeon. Such was his good fortune, he laughed grimly to himself, that a dungeon was an improvement.

In the chamber were seven rusty iron doors, all of which stood open. The doors led to hallways lined with cages where living things scuttled and rasped. He couldn't help but imagine Esben and Artham chained to the walls of one of those cells.

He tiptoed down the nearest corridor. He didn't want to look, but his torch flung light into each cell as he passed, and he saw chains on the walls, some of which shackled human skeletons. In other cells he saw animals hunkered in the corners, scrawny and listless. There were wolves, snakes coiled and watching him pass with cold eyes, flabbits and gugglers with noses twitching, and horned hounds and saggy hounds growling. Bats as big as goats clutched the ceilings of some cells, rustling their wings as he passed.

Some of the forms looked human, but with twisted or half-formed animal features—like Artham's talons, he thought. They lifted their sad eyes and moaned pleadingly as he passed. He came to the end of the hall and found another round chamber with another set of corridors. The cells held more of the same: people, or the remains of people, and animals, all in varying degrees of melding, most of whom seemed broken beyond repair. Who were these poor souls doomed to the Deeps?

On and on the dungeon stretched. Whenever Janner came upon stairs that led upward, he took them. Sometimes the corridors twisted and turned, sometimes they were long and straight. Some of the cells were so full of ordinary animals hissing, barking, hooting, roaring, gribbiting, and mooing that he felt like he was in a barn. And that led Janner to wonder what happened to all these animals after their melding. Did they shrivel up and die? Did the animal and the human actually combine somehow, forming one being from two? Or was there a wolf somewhere that was part Kalmar, just as there was a Kalmar that was part wolf? And if so, did that mean there might be a bear here that was part Esben?

Janner walked for so long that he grew careless. The dungeon was so noisy with chattering and mumbling and moaning that he didn't bother to hide the sound of his footsteps, and when he came to a door, he stopped listening before he opened it, stopped peeking around the corners before he stepped into a new room. Even surrounded by the half-living, he began to feel alone again. So when he came to the chamber where the Stone Keeper sang, he pushed through the door and nearly screamed in shock.

The room was so big it was difficult to see the ceiling. The steady glow of many lanterns illuminated the faces of a multitude waiting in a line that coiled around the room, filling the chamber. At the center of the room was an iron box, a bigger version of the Overseer's coffin, but standing on its end. It was crowned with spikes, with a little window in the door and a lever on one side.

Beside the box stood the Stone Keeper, a haunting figure draped in a robe and hood. Soothing music came from the shadows of her cowl, and the people in line swayed with the song. Janner slipped back into the passageway and stomped on his torch until it was out, then he peeked in at the throng, trembling with relief that no one had seen him.

On the opposite side of the chamber was a large door, flanked by Fang guards. They held spears and watched the people with lazy satisfaction.

Suddenly, the room flashed with yellow light that emanated from slits in the iron box. The door swung open and smoke poured out, then a creature emerged. It was glistening with some kind of fluid, and it blinked in confusion.

The Stone Keeper announced in a musical voice, "Your name is Raknarr!"

The creature spread two black, moist wings and shrieked. Another Bat Fang had been born.

The multitude answered with a muted cheer before quieting into a murmuring chant: "Sing the song of the ancient stones and the blood of the beast imbues your bones."

Two Green Fangs guided the new Bat Fang through the large doors as a young man stepped up to the dais. The Stone Keeper spoke to him quietly, then he stepped into the box with a chilling eagerness.

"Wait," she said, gesturing to a nearby Fang. "This bat is spent. Bring me a fresh one."

She reached into the box and removed a steaming, withered bat—a big one, like those Janner had seen in the dungeon. The Fang handed her a healthy, struggling one. She cradled it and stroked it like a baby, and the bat was calm when she put it in the box then ushered the young man in after it. When she closed the door, Janner heard the man sing, then came another flash of light, and he emerged damp and trembling like a baby from a womb.

"Your name is Murgle!"

He—or *it*—spread its wings and screeched.

Another Green Fang sat at a desk beside the dais, writing in a large book. Janner watched as more and more people stepped into the box, one by one. Again and again, they conferred with the Stone Keeper, sang the song, then emerged as Fangs. Every couple of meldings— depending on the size of the human—the Stone Keeper declared the bat spent and asked for a fresh one.

Janner watched all this with grim fascination. Kalmar had described what had happened in the Phoobs, but to see Gnag's machinations with his own eyes was another thing altogether. He couldn't under-stand why the people were so eager to become monsters. He wanted to stop them somehow, to snap them out of whatever evil spell had convinced them to give up their names. Children, women, and men of all ages seemed content, happy, even, for their turn to sing the song of the ancient stones and lose themselves for the twisted transformation.

He knew Kalmar had done the same; but he also knew that his brother, and Artham and Esben for that matter, had not gone will-ingly—not at first, anyway. They had been broken. They had been worn down by pain and loneliness so that melding seemed the better choice.

How long had Artham and Esben resisted? Months? Years? Janner doubted he would have lasted so long.

Janner's anger at Gnag the Nameless grew tenfold as he watched the way he had built his army all these years: first by capture, then by torture and isolation, then by this strange power he had discovered. Janner even felt sorry for the bats, who were drained of—he could think of no other word—their *batness*, then discarded like garbage.

Then he saw Kalmar.

63

The Making of Grimgar

Kalmar stood among the other Fang guards, watching the line of prisoners. Janner couldn't see his eyes, couldn't see the yellow glow that surely filled them, but there his brother stood, a willing Fang among many.

Before Janner could think or mourn or act, a Fang guard flung open the door and spotted him. "What do you think you're doing in here?" it said, snarling.

"Nothing, sir. Just—just looking around."

"Get back in line." The Grey Fang growled at Janner and jerked him by the arm.

Janner, thankful that his cape hid his pack and sword, kept his head low and joined the queue, pretending that he wanted to be Fanged. He shuffled forward with the crowd and lost sight of Kalmar.

Again and again came the flash of yellow light, followed by the emergence of a newly melded Bat Fang or Grey Fang or Green Fang and the Stone Keeper's announcement of the Fang's new name. The line moved in a circle, first around the outer edge of the chamber, then weaving closer and closer to the center dais. Janner felt more conspicuous with every melding. The people around him all seemed so darkly gleeful whenever the new Fang stepped from the box, but Janner couldn't hide his revulsion. He couldn't understand why anyone would be so happy to lose themselves.

And was it his imagination that the skinny, bearded fellow in front of him glanced his way too often? Did the woman and older boy behind him seem quieter than the rest? Were they were suspicious of the Annieran boy with the dirty black cloak that hid a sword and backpack?

A Grey Fang leaned against the wall, chewing on a haunch of raw meat, and Janner felt certain that someone would point him out to the guard. But the line edged Janner past the Fang, and it chewed on, slurping and grunting with pleasure. No one said a word, which was good, but Janner was inching ever closer to the dais, which was bad.

He slipped his hand under his cloak and rested it on the hilt of his sword. At first his mind raced, trying to work out a way to escape, but when he could think of no solution, his mind grew tired and he slogged along in a thoughtless trance. *Something* was going to happen, he knew that. He would reach the dais, and the Stone Keeper would realize he didn't want to be Fanged—but then what? And where was Kalmar? He'd lost sight of him.

Janner hung his head and shuffled forward, flash after flash, bat after bat, name after ugly name. He even hummed along with the song without realizing it. And then a thought fluttered through his mind like a moth: maybe it *would* be better to sing the song and be done with it. No more running. No more looking for a home that didn't exist. No more wondering if Gnag was waiting around every corner to gobble him up.

Shuffle forward. Flash. Cheers. Excited chatter. Shuffle forward. Flash. On it went, and the song sank into Janner's mind, deeper and deeper, until the people around him no longer seemed quite so foolish, or quite so evil. Who could blame them, after all? They had merely chosen the winning side. In a sense, they were choosing life over death. And what could be more sane than preserving one's own life? Even Podo said that it was better to fight on. Perhaps the melding was a kind of fighting for life, even if it meant a hollow life. It was better than nothing, wasn't it?

And then Janner found himself facing the dais and the iron box. It was almost his turn. Just a few paces away stood the Stone Keeper. The skinny, bearded man in front of him shifted his weight from side to side and rubbed his hands together with excitement. The woman and the boy behind him whispered to each other, wondering aloud which animal they might meld with. There were only two more people in front of Janner, and then he would be face to face with the hooded woman. He should have been afraid, but her soothing voice made him sleepy.

Then he saw Kalmar again.

Janner's eyes snapped open. The Stone Keeper's voice was no longer sweet but sinister, and it seemed suddenly laughable that Janner would ever give himself over. Kalmar stood a little behind the box and to the left, in the shadow of one of the larger Fangs—where it was impossible to see his eyes.

Janner was sorely tempted to shout his brother's name, to try and break the spell of his Fangness so they could fight their way out. But what if it didn't work? What if it only got them both caught? If Janner stayed quiet, maybe Kalmar would snap out of it and slip away undetected.

While Janner's mind raced, the bearded man in front of him clapped like a child and sprang up the steps. The Stone Keeper asked him where he was from.

"Yorsha Doon," he said in a thick accent. "A village in the southern hold of Hasini."

The Green Fang wrote it down in the ledger.

"Very good," the Stone Keeper said. "We Doonlanders make some of the *best* Fangs."

"Oh, yes," the man said. "The best."

She swung open the iron door and the man stepped into the darkness. "You know the song," she said. "Give your heart to it, and join the victor's army."

She pulled the door shut and the man sang along with her. She pulled a lever on the side of the box, the light shot out of from every crack, and she opened the door again. Steam and smoke poured out, then the man—the Bat Fang—hobbled forth on unsteady legs, grinning madly.

"Your name is Grimgar!" the Stone Keeper announced, and the crowd cheered as the Green Fang scribbled away in the book.

In a small way, Janner had come to know the skinny, bearded man as they had shuffled along, and in moments he had morphed into this monster. Janner knew enough of despair to pity him, but was horrified by the way the man welcomed his own destruction.

His mind was too full of these thoughts to do anything but stand at the foot of the dais like a dumb sheep and wonder what would happen when the Stone Keeper turned her attention on him.

64

The Ancient Stone

Go on," said the boy behind Janner, jabbing him in the shoulder.

But Janner's feet refused to move. His neck prickled with the feeling of hundreds of staring eyes, knowing that in moments he would be thrust into action. He pulled his gaze from the Stone Keeper, who led the newly melded Bat Fang down the steps, and looked desperately for Kalmar, but he was nowhere to be seen.

Janner had to fight her, of course. The woman who had midwifed so many into their doom, who held such sway over Fang and human alike, who must have been Gnag's right arm of power all these years and for all these years had ordered the kidnapping, torture, and death of so many free souls—the same woman who had destroyed Uncle Artham's mind and tormented their father—had to be stopped. And who else would do it? Who else had ever stood here in the Deeps of Throg, sword at hand, to defy her? If he died trying, Janner thought, it would be a good death. His Annieran blood sang in his veins.

Janner slipped his hand beneath his cloak and gripped the hilt of Rudric's sword. He tried not to look into the shadow of the Stone Keeper's cowl, afraid of the eyes that watched him, afraid that they would siphon away what little courage he had.

She pushed open the door to the iron box and asked, "What is your name, boy?" Her voice was just louder than a whisper. "Your name?" she repeated.

"My name is Janner Wingfeather."

Janner whipped out his sword and faced the woman, his skin cold and clammy, his head dizzy with the danger. He did his best to ignore the looks of shock on every face in the room, but there was one face he couldn't ignore.

The Stone Keeper reared back and shrieked, and under the cowl her pale features glowed like something undead and angry. Janner knew he wouldn't escape, wouldn't last long against so many, especially without Kalmar's help—but maybe it was enough to stop the Stone Keeper.

Though his instinct screamed at him to flee, he lunged forward and jabbed his blade at the woman who had killed so many.

With an unnatural speed, she dodged the blade, planted one of her bony white hands on Janner's chest, and shoved him backwards and into the iron box.

Janner crashed into the wall and crumpled to the floor as the door slammed shut and latched. Outside, the Stone Keeper cackled with glee and the Fangs howled.

"Well, *that* didn't go how I thought it would," Janner muttered.

A bat flapped weakly about on the floor beside him—as weak and helpless as he was. Janner stood up, knees still trembling with the rush of danger, and banged his fist against the wall. He wanted to call for Kalmar, but it was possible that the Fangs didn't know he was out there. It would do no good to give him away, not if he was Janner's only hope of escape.

"Let me out!" he shouted, feeling the foolishness of his words, as if the Stone Keeper would just shrug and open the door. But he didn't know what else to do.

Then he noticed a small compartment in the wall. Faint light emanated from the cracks, which was how he could see the shriveled bat at his feet. The chamber walls were grimy, smeared with filth and hair, but the light was as beautiful as a sunrise.

He peeked through the metal shutters at its source. It was a splinter of stone, no larger than a pebble. It glowed steady as the sun, a constant and lovely light that was bright enough to make Janner squint, but not so bright that it hurt to stare. He thought at first that the music had ignited the light, but now he saw that the stone couldn't help but glow, and the Stone Keeper opened the shutter just long enough for the melding.

Using the point of his sword, Janner pried open the shutter until he could fit his hand through. Janner swallowed, hoping the stone wasn't as hot as it looked, then reached in and removed it. It was cool and surprisingly heavy, tingling in Janner's palm. He wished he could stare at it for hours.

The bat squeaked. Then the door squeaked.

Janner looked up. The Stone Keeper stood beside a Grey Fang in the open doorway. "Seize him," the woman said.

The Fang snarled.

Then the Stone Keeper flung back her cowl, and Janner saw a face that would haunt him for the rest of his life.

65

Under the Keeper's Cowl

The Stone Keeper's face was old, but not the sort of old that Podo was, or Oskar, or even Bonifer Squoon, who was the oldest person Janner had ever met. The Stone Keeper was old in a stretched, unnatural manner, as if her skin had loosened and loosened with time, but she had sewn it up at the back of her head like a mask. Her hair was stringy and black, but from the look of the black smudges on her flaking scalp, it was clear that she had darkened the strands with some kind of dye. Her cheekbones were high and prominent, which made her eyes as deep as empty graves. Her head wobbled, perched on a broomstick neck.

When she saw Janner with the ancient stone, she screamed and hissed, baring her teeth. She had two long, black fangs: stout, round, and glistening in her mouth, and they protracted and retracted hungrily. She was no ordinary old woman, Janner realized, but a melded thing.

She stood beside the Fang with her arms flung wide—several arms, Janner now saw, because her robe had opened enough that movement was visible within its folds. As her scream died away, many fingers probed their way out of the robe and pulled it open revealing black, spidery limbs, all of which ended in hands that reached out for Janner.

Janner raised his sword and closed his fingers on the stone, which plunged the inside of the box into darkness. The Stone Keeper shouted something at the Fang and it stepped inside. Janner screamed as he raised his sword to strike.

The Fang moved swiftly. It grabbed his wrist and pinned him against the wall, and its voice pushed through the panic in Janner's mind: "It's me! Janner, it's me!"

"Kal?" Janner said between breaths, peering at the wolfish face. Thank the Maker, his brother's eyes were blue.

Kalmar grabbed Janner's wrist and dragged him out of the box and into the openness of the chamber. "Show them," Kalmar whispered out of the side of his mouth.

"Show them what?"

"The ancient stone!" Kalmar shouted, releasing Janner's arm and raising his own sword.

Janner opened his hand, and the stone's buttery glow filled the chamber. The crowd stared, dumbstruck, and the Grey and Green Fangs stationed throughout the room shielded their eyes, their weapons raised in alarm.

Kalmar swung his sword at the Stone Keeper. She skittered sideways to avoid it, and Janner realized she was directly in front of the open box.

He leaped forward and shoved the Stone Keeper. He felt her many arms wriggling and scraping him as he pushed, but she was spindly and light beneath her robes and she tumbled backward into the darkness of the melding box. Kalmar slammed the door and latched it shut.

All this had taken only seconds, but Janner felt years older as he and Kalmar turned to face the multitude in the chamber. The collective shock of the humans and Fangs alike faded, and the cavern erupted with howls and hisses and shouts of anger.

"I think maybe it's time to get out of here," Kalmar said.

Janner glanced at the door behind the bat cages. "I think you're right." Janner opened his fist and the light burst forth once more. The Fangs recoiled as if they had been stung.

The boys leapt from the dais and raced for the exit. They made it through the stunned crowd and slammed the door behind them. Janner slipped the stone into his pocket and held the door while Kalmar slid the lock into place.

"It won't hold them for long," Kalmar said. "Let's go."

They raced down the torch-lit corridor with the sound of chaos fading behind them. When they reached the end of the corridor it split into three passageways. The one on the right led to a stair and they bounded up, two steps at a time.

"I thought I lost you," Janner said as they climbed.

"I thought I lost me, too," Kalmar said, "until you said your name. It brought me back. I attacked you, didn't I?"

"Yeah."

"I'm sorry."

"I forgive you," Janner said. "And I forgive you for the next time, too, and the time after that."

They stopped to rest at the top of the stair. "But what if I really hurt you?" Kalmar's ears flattened and he stared at his hands. "Or worse?"

"You're my brother. I forgive you."

Kalmar's eyes met Janner's, then he looked quickly away.

Janner put a hand on Kal's shoulder. "Listen. You can't get rid of me. I'm the Throne Warden. Besides, I can't fight Gnag alone. We're in this together."

Kalmar nodded. "What do we do?"

"We climb these steps. We keep our swords ready. And we remember who we are. What's your name? Say it."

"My name is Kalmar Wingfeather."

"Wolf King of Anniera," Janner added. "And I'm proud to be your brother. You were amazing back there."

The brothers shared an awkward silence, then shook it off and bounded up the steps, closer and closer to the courts of Gnag the Nameless.

66

Vooming the Shaft

The brothers climbed as quickly as they could, but Janner's legs were burning, and he was breathing so hard he was afraid he might vomit. They heard sounds of pursuit behind them, a racket of howls and shouts that grew in volume with every step.

Kalmar, who wasn't winded in the least, stopped suddenly. "I smell something." His ears pricked forward, then he bounded up the steps before Janner could catch enough breath to say a word. Kalmar crept back toward him with one finger over his mouth, beckoning for Janner to follow. Just around the next turn they came to another big room, bigger even than the melding chamber. Torches burned along the walls, and the cavern spread so far to the left and right that the torches shrank into tiny specks of light. Where the ceiling should have been there was only airy blackness, and after a short distance the floor dropped away as well. The room was but a perch in the wall of a massive hollow, a shaft that seemed to reach from the peak of the mountain to its very roots. Then Janner saw what Kalmar had smelled.

A small group of trolls stood near the precipice, conversing in grunts that reminded the boys of Oood. But these trolls were full grown, twice Oood's size. They stood beside a wooden platform and an enormous spool of chain. The spool laid flat on its side and a number of poles extended out from its edges. It looked like a table with spokes. There was a great metal gear beside the spool, threaded with more chain. It rotated slowly, issuing an echo of clinks throughout the chamber. The chain ascended up and up, into the shaft.

"What are they doing?" Janner whispered.

"I don't know," Kal said. He looked back down the stairway and laid his ears laid flat against his head. "They're coming."

The trolls' conversation was cut short by a change in the rattle of chain. They lumbered over to the giant spool, each troll wrapped its massive hands around one of the spokes, and they heaved, rotating the spool. As they turned it, an iron gondola—like the Black Carriage, but without wheels or horses—floated downward out of the darkness above and came to rest on the platform. The door swung open and out stepped seven Green Fangs, hissing and laughing together. They crossed the room without a glance at the trolls and exited through a doorway. The trolls made cruel faces at the Fangs' backs, then one of them shut the gondola door and beckoned the others back to the giant spool.

"You're my prisoner," Kalmar whispered.

"What?" Janner said, then without explanation, Kalmar dragged him into the open.

"Wait!" Kalmar called out in his gruffest voice.

"Erp?" answered one of the trolls.

"The Stone Keeper wants this prisoner brought to Gnag."

The trolls all narrowed their little eyes.

"Quickly! She said there was no time to lose. She believes this"—he jerked Janner's arm—"is one of the Jewels of Anniera. The Hollish army has infiltrated the Deeps. Hurry, fools!"

The trolls' eyes widened, and when sounds of the Fangs below echoed out of the passageway, they grunted and waved Kalmar and Janner into the gondola.

"No! I'll never go!" Janner shouted dramatically.

"Quiet!" Kalmar barked, and shoved Janner through the door.

By the light of the lantern inside the gondola, Janner could see the floor was covered with maggots and grime, and he gagged. The door

slammed shut, the trolls heaved, and the gondola lifted from the platform and swung out into the shaft.

"Hurry!" Kalmar shouted at the trolls, banging on the side of the
box. Janner peeked through the window and saw the trolls move to
another gear. They each took hold of a chain and pulled. The gondola jerked upward and sent both boys tumbling about, and then they
began to slowly and steadily ascend.

"We'll never make it before the Fangs get here," Kalmar said.

"Tell them to go faster!"

"Faster!" Kalmar shouted. "They're coming, you fools!"

The trolls argued with one another and pointed from the passageway to the gondola. Then one of them shrugged and crossed to a
lever on the wall. There was a sign above the lever painted in a large,
sloppy and childish script, which spelled "VOOM."

Janner followed the length of chain from the lever, along the wall to
a pulley, then up to several dangling boulders. Just as the troll grabbed
the lever, Janner realized what was about to happen.

"Get down!" he shouted.

The troll pulled the lever and the boulders plummeted into the
deep. The gondola shot upward so fast that Janner and Kal were glued
to the grimy floor.

Below them, they heard the trolls laughing and shouting, "Voom!
Voom!"

When the delivery of Madia's second child was imminent, Bonifer rushed to the castle and stood outside the door of the midwifery. Ortham, as custom required, was at the other end of the castle pacing his bedchambers and praying to the Maker for his wife and new child. In agony, Bonifer listened to the cries of his true love as she labored in the birth of his truest enemy's child.

The struggle went long into the night, and the midwife, a fine old woman named Gineva, called for Bonifer. In great confusion he entered the delivery room and stared aghast at the profusion of blood. Madia was weary beyond words and lay panting amidst the bloodied blankets.

'She's going to die,' said Gineva sadly. 'Send for the king.'

'What of the baby?' asked Bonifer through his tears.

'It shall die as well,' answered the midwife.

At the midwife's words, Queen Madia gathered the last of her strength and gave a final heave.

'My queen!' Gineva cried. 'It is done!'

Casting propriety aside, Bonifer rushed to the midwife's side and beheld the fruit of Madia's womb. It was a pale, ugly, misshapen thing, and when it drew its first breath and squirmed, Bonifer cringed with revulsion.

Gineva gasped, handed the twisted child to Bonifer, and said, 'There is another.' A second child had emerged hale and whole, well-formed and crying—while the first was baleful and silent.

Bonifer and Gineva looked at one another, neither understanding the portent.

The queen spoke in a voice hardly above a whisper, 'Let me see.'

With a glance at the writhing, broken child in Bonifer's arms, the midwife passed the healthy boy to Madia.

'I shall name you Jru,' Madia whispered to the baby on her bosom. 'And you,' she said, reaching weakly for the pale one in Bonifer's arms. He handed over the baby, glad to be rid of it. Madia held the broken boy and wept with joy and pity and great love before she fell from consciousness.

Bonifer took the wretched child from Madia, then clutched the mid-wife's face in his hand. Squoon's eyes belied the evil in his heart, and Gineva shrank with fear. 'You will tell no one of this child.'

'My lord, do not kill it!' she pleaded.

'Do not fear, old one,' said Bonifer, his face twisting from a murderous sneer into a compassionate smile so quickly that Gineva felt she was looking into the eyes of evil itself. 'You will care for this creature,' he said. 'Madia needs not trouble herself with such a thing.'

With murderous threats, he secreted the old midwife and the child to his home.

While Madia slept, Bonifer came to the king and explained that there was indeed a twin, deformed beyond reckoning, who died soon after his birth. Ortham's sorrow over the dead child was quickly overshadowed by his joy over Jru's birth and Madia's survival. At Bonifer's urging, Ortham entrusted Bonifer with the child's secret burial and never laid eyes on its body. Bonifer convinced the king to spare Anniera undue sorrow by speaking not of the dead twin and rejoicing instead that Jru was born, and that the queen had survived the birthing.

The next night, Bonifer fled with Gineva and the baby under the cover of darkness. They sailed across the Symian Straits to Yorsha Doon, where he conscripted a wetnurse—a young and pregnant widow named Murgah—and sent word that he required audience with the mysterious Lord of Throg.

Long they journeyed across the wasteland, and though the Doonish nursemaid had cringed when she first beheld the baby she, like Madia and Gineva, came to harbor great affection for it. Bonifer, too, began to think of the child as his own, and considered it his reward for his long and secret love for Madia—more than that, though, he reveled in the evil he had done to Ortham by stealing away the king's own son.

—From *The Annieriad*

67

Outside Leeli's Window

The boys peered out the window of the speeding gondola. Wind whistled downward, and now and then they saw streaks of orange as lanterns and torches flew past and dwindled into dim specks far below. If it hadn't been for the stenchy goop on the floor, and the fact that Janner was doubtful they would survive, it would have been fun.

"This could take a while," Kalmar said.

Janner looked up, imagining what it would be like when the gondola slammed into the top of the shaft. "And it could end badly."

"So," Kalmar said after a pause, drumming his fingers on the seat. "Did you bring any games or anything?"

Janner smiled. "No, but I brought this." He pulled the stone out of his pocket and its glow outshone the lantern.

"It's so small," Kal said, squinting one eye. "Do you think it used to be bigger?"

"I don't know. According to legend, Yurgen the Dragon King bit into one of the rocks, cracked his teeth, and broke off two small flinders."

"The *holoré* and the *holoél*, right?"

Janner looked at Kalmar with surprise. "So you were paying attention in history class after all."

"Nah, I heard Oskar talking about it with Grandpa a few weeks ago," Kalmar said with a wave of his hand.

"I wonder if this means the other stone is in the Phoobs, with a different Stone Keeper," Janner said.

"Yeah," Kalmar said. "That wasn't the same woman I saw in the islands." He shuddered. "The one in the Phoobs was young—pretty, even. I'll never forget her voice."

"I wish we could have stopped her," Janner said. "Forever, I mean."

"Maybe we did," Kalmar said. "She can't meld without the stone. I'm just glad we got out of that room alive—otherwise, we wouldn't be together in this lovely, maggoty box of death."

They laughed, then sat in silence, Kalmar sniffing the air and Janner imagining, with a shiver of terror, how high they were above the Dark Sea by now. The shaft seemed to rise forever. It was easy to imagine that they were in some kind of flying carriage soaring upward into the blackness of the night sky. And somewhere, up there in the darkness, Castle Throg was waiting for them.

I SEE YOU.

Leeli awoke with a start.

Her leg jerked and nearly knocked Frankle to the floor. Even before she opened her eyes she was imagining Gnag the Nameless waiting to ambush the boys. She felt panic like a snake wriggling in her gut.

Since the battle had begun five days ago, she had thought of the Great Library as a stronghold. But now it felt like a prison. All she wanted in the world was to get out, to somehow run to the Deeps of Throg so she could help her brothers—or at least be with them when they fell into Gnag's hands. That they were so far away and she was stuck here felt wrong. She was angry at herself for falling asleep, angry at her mother for allowing it when there was so much at stake.

Leeli swung her feet to the floor and grabbed her whistleharp, determined to find the right song and stir up the vision again. She wanted to know where her brothers were, to make sure they knew Ban Rona was still under attack—and that a new fleet of ships was coming. There was a chance they had also heard Gnag's voice, but for some reason she doubted it—his words seemed aimed at her somehow, as if he was taunting her.

She took a deep breath and licked her sore lips, then raised the whistleharp and played. The magic didn't happen immediately, but she was getting better at mustering the emotion she needed to send the song out to her brothers, and by the time she'd played only a handful of notes, she saw them.

Janner and Kalmar sat up straight. Leeli's whistleharp rang in their ears, and the world around them shimmered.

Janner heard his sister's voice in his mind. *Are you safe?*

Not exactly safe, Janner thought. *But we're alive.*

He saw his sister, alone in a familiar room. It was the Great Library. He found that he could push his mind outside the walls of her room, and he saw Rudric there, weary and smeared with blood and dirt. Oskar was at the table reading the First Book with a look of desperation on his face, and Nia was kneeling on the floor to give water to a wounded Hollish warrior. Podo leaned against a wall of books and sharpened his sword; there was a scowl on his lips.

Where are you? Leeli asked.

We're almost to Castle Throg. To Gnag.

Leeli's music faltered and the image wavered.

Leeli, wait! Janner cried in his mind. Her song steadied and the vision solidified. *Pray for us*, he told her. *Tell everyone we love them.*

Then, through the haze of the vision, he saw Kalmar's face change. His brother's eyes grew wide with terror, his mouth fell open, his ears flattened, and he shook his head slowly from side to side.

Before Janner had time to ask him what was wrong, a dark laughter, dripping with wickedness, erupted and grew until it rattled Janner's skull. He heard a third voice in his mind, not Leeli's or Kal's; it was a ragged voice, guttural and wretched, a voice that made bile rise in Janner's throat.

JANNER, KALMAR, AND LEELI, it said, somehow whispering and screaming at the same time. *THE JEWELS OF ANNIERA. HOW I HAVE LONGED TO WELCOME YOU ALL TO MY CASTLE.* Gnag laughed again. *AND NOW THAT YOU HAVE ARRIVED, I'M SORRY TO SAY THAT I'M NOT THERE. BUT DO MAKE YOUR-SELVES AT HOME! LEELI WINGFEATHER, IT'S YOU THAT I WANT. AND IT'S YOU THAT I HAVE.*

No! Janner cried. *Leave her alone!*

LEELI, Gnag said in a sing-song voice. *LOOK OUT YOUR WINDOW.*

Still playing her song, Leeli stepped to the window. Janner saw the whistleharp fall from her hands. The music stopped, the vision vanished, and the connection broke.

But not before Janner and Kalmar heard their sister's long and piercing scream.

68

The Skreean Fleet

Outside Leeli's window, a woman in a black robe hung in the clutches of a Bat Fang. The wind blew back her cowl, revealing long black hair that framed a face both beautiful and white as bone. She smiled at Leeli and opened the window.

"Leeli Wingfeather," the woman said in a soothing voice. "Come with me."

Leeli tried to play her whistleharp, but she couldn't hold it steady. *Where are the Hollish warriors?* she wondered. Did no one see the Bat Fang? Right here outside her window? She wanted to scream for help, but her voice was caught in her throat.

The woman crawled through the window and placed her hand on Leeli's shoulder. "Come with me now, or those you love will suffer."

At the woman's touch, Leeli's scream broke free and rang through every corridor of the Great Library and out into the streets beyond. The woman jerked Leeli toward the window, wrapped an arm around her middle, and climbed out. Leeli whacked her crutch against the woman's legs, but it did no good.

The Bat Fang carried them both up and over the roof of the building. Leeli saw the confusion of the warriors on the roof as they shrank into the distance, saw as a few of them raised their bows to shoot then realized they couldn't risk hitting Leeli. The bulk of the warriors, however, were congregated on the opposite side of the roof, loosing arrows into the streets below. As the Bat Fang lifted them higher and higher, Leeli saw a great commotion on the harbor side of the city. Green Fangs slithered from the sea by the hundreds, and all the Hollowsfolk in the city rushed to the waterfront to repel the new invasion.

The Bat Fang carried Leeli and the woman with a surer flight than the one who had tried to kidnap Leeli before, and it was strong enough to lift them so high that Ban Rona looked like a toy city below.

Up over the Watercraw they flew, to where the Fang fleet was moored. The ships must have sped to the city that night. Leeli saw masses of Green Fangs leaping from the decks and swimming between the chains of the Watercraw. The surface of the water rippled with venomous life.

As she watched, mute with terror, the Bat Fang carried them out beyond the last stony reaches of land, and she saw Ban Rona from the sea. The cliffs flanking the craw teemed with trolls and Grey Fangs, while Bat Fangs launched into the sky to attack the city from above. Ban Rona—under attack from sea, from land, and from sky—was lost. Everyone Leeli loved was trapped.

"You have me," she said, tears streaming freely from her eyes. "Leave the city alone."

The woman only squeezed her tighter.

The Bat Fang swooped down to a ship at the rear of the fleet. It set them gently on the deck and bowed as it backed away. Leeli crumpled to the deck, weeping as the woman walked to the captain's quarters and turned.

"You know what to do," she said to a Grey Fang standing at the helm. Then she looked at Leeli and gestured at the door. "Gnag the Nameless will see you now."

The crew set sail and two Grey Fangs prodded Leeli toward the hatchway. She didn't want to go, but she was too weak to resist. They pushed her forward and she half-crawled, half-rolled into the chamber beyond, clinging to her crutch as if it were her only hope.

69

Bargaining with a Fang

W hat happened?" Kalmar cried, jerking back and rocking the gondola.

"I don't know!" Janner said. "What did you see?"

"I saw . . . him. Gnag. I saw him." Kalmar shuddered. "I've seen glimpses before, but this was different. He was right in front of me. Did you hear anything?"

"He said to look out the window. He's in—"

"Ban Rona," Kal whispered.

Janner felt like a fool. Braving the cloven. Losing Oood. Surviving the Stone Keeper. All these days on the run, he'd been driven by a mad hope that somehow he and Kalmar could help everyone in Ban Rona by stopping Gnag. But it was all for nothing if Gnag was already gone—and not just gone, but in the Hollows, where everyone they loved was probably about to die.

The gondola suddenly lurched and slowed. They looked out the window at a cluster of torches high above as the gondola floated closer. The torches were in the hands of Green Fangs, standing at the edge of the shaft and grinning down at them. The Fangs were in a chamber paved with flagstones of polished marble. The room was a large half-circle with an archway at the rear. They were no longer in the dungeons, Janner realized—this was the Castle Throg.

"What do we do?" Kalmar asked. The brothers stood side by side as the gondola drew level with the Fangs.

"Stick to the plan," Janner said. "I'm your prisoner."

"Right." Kalmar drew his sword and grabbed Janner's arm.

One of the Fangs slunk forward and guided the swaying gondola to solid ground. Janner took a deep breath and prepared to fight. But instead of opening the door, the Fang sneered and fastened a padlock to the latch. It jangled the keys at the boys, then retreated and bowed to a skinnier, older Fang—a Fang that looked familiar.

"Tell them I'm your prisoner," Janner whispered.

"I have a prisoner," Kalmar growled. "Let me pass!"

The older Fang stepped forward, tilted its head, and peered through the window with its flat, black eyes. It stank even worse than the rot on the floor. "The Igiby boys," it said. "I haven't seen you ssssince—where was it again? Ah. The Glipwood Township. Just before your fool of an uncle rode in on the dog. We've come a long way, you and I," it said with a flick of its tongue.

Kalmar growled. "I'm a Fang! I have a prisoner!"

"Oh? A prisoner! The blue-eyed mutt has a prisoner. Very good. And I have two. The Igiby brothers who eluded me in Skree will elude me no longer. The Nameless One said you'd be arriving ssssoon."

Janner's skin went cold. He remembered standing in the streets of Glipwood in a sea of Fangs. And he remembered General Khrak, the most feared Fang in all of Skree.

"I don't know how you made it past the Stone Keeper," Khrak continued, "but the voom all but announced your arrival. We only use it in emergencies, you ssssee, and there are never *emergencies* in the Castle Throg. And here you are, as the Nameless One said you would be."

"But—but," Janner stammered.

"How did he know?" Khrak laughed. "He sensed you in the Outer Vales. He heard your sister and knew that she was alone in Ban Rona. Once you were safely in the Deeps, he went to fetch her himself." He turned and paced the floor. "The Bat Fangs are stupid, but I must admit, they have many usesssss. They can fly to Ban Rona in a day and a half. I suspect you will know that soon enough."

Anger burned in Janner's veins, frustration at the futility of it all. They had come so far, only for Gnag to have left Throg. They were about to be caged like animals, and even if they made it out, how could they get to Ban Rona in time to help Leeli and the others?

"You don't know what happened back there, do you?" Kalmar asked. "You think we just happened to make it this far. You don't know about the Stone Keeper."

Khrak stopped pacing and turned.

"We have the stone," Kalmar said.

"You what?" Khrak made no attempt to conceal his surprise.

"We have it." Kalmar smiled. "And if you don't let us go, we'll throw it down the shaft."

"Lies."

"Show him, Janner."

"Ships and sharks," Janner said under his breath as he dug in his pocket.

"What does that *mean*?" Khrak snapped.

"Something our grandpa taught us," Kalmar said as Janner removed the stone.

"There's always a way out," Janner said, and he opened his hand.

The stone's light shone forth, beams shooting out from every crevice in the gondola. Khrak recoiled and the other Fangs hissed in surprise. The Fangs recovered quickly and pressed forward, surrounding the gondola and drawing their swords as they tried to block the windows.

"You wouldn't throw one of the ancient stones into the pit," Khrak said. "That little rock has more power than you can imagine."

"This stone," Janner said evenly, "has caused us nothing but trouble. It's the reason half the world has fallen to ruin. I would be happy to see it cast into the darkness." Janner squinted an eye at the window opposite the door. "Now. Let us out of here, or it's going over. Kal, stab any Fangs that try to block that window."

Kalmar nodded and pointed his sword at the window. The Fangs peeking in retreated.

"You won't do it!" Khrak shouted. "We'll leave you to rot in that cage!"

"Ah, but that's where you're wrong. Ships and sharks, remember?"

"What does that mean?" Khrak shouted.

"It means there's always a way out, like I told you." Janner smiled.

"Not always," Khrak said.

"Not for you," Janner said. "But we're in the Maker's keeping. Even if we die trying, death is just another way out. But you? You'll just turn to dust."

"You'll die," Khrak said. "Just like your father Esben."

"His death," Kalmar said, "was glorious. So be it."

Khrak said nothing. After a moment, he nodded at the other Fangs. They backed away, all but the one with the key. "Vark," Khrak said, "open the door, then back away. Don't let them near the cliff."

"Are you sure this is going to work?" Kalmar whispered.

"I have no idea." Janner took a deep breath. "Just stay close to the edge."

"You'd really throw the stone away?" Kalmar asked.

"Absolutely."

The Fang removed the padlock and opened the door.

70

The Crags at Castle Rock

Janner and Kal looked warily at General Khrak and his guards. If the Fangs attacked and Janner threw the stone into the shaft, there was a good chance that he and Kalmar might follow it over the edge to their deaths. But Gnag seemed to want them alive—and that was a strange comfort.

"Let's go already," Kalmar said. He stepped out of the gondola and raised his sword. "Get back! Do it, or my brother will throw the stone!"

The Fangs retreated several paces, and Janner followed Kalmar into the open. The boys stood with their backs against gondola, and behind them they heard the rustle of wind as it billowed down into the throat of the chasm. Kalmar stepped to the right and edged along the brink, beckoning for Janner to follow. The Fangs hissed and crouched, ready to spring at Khrak's command. The brothers stood at the edge of the black abyss, swords ready, the stone cradled in Janner's open hand.

But Khrak's malevolent eyes were fixed on Janner's face—not the stone. Then Janner noticed that the other three Fangs were squinting, averting their eyes from its glow as if they were afraid of it. When Janner lifted the stone level with his head, Khrak squinted too, then quickly shifted his gaze to Kalmar's face, then to the floor.

The light troubled the Fangs. Either its power was frightening or its beauty was repulsive. Janner took a quick step forward and waved the stone at them. They recoiled. Khrak hissed and bared his teeth.

"Stay close," Janner whispered to Kalmar.

They stepped forward, and the Fangs backed away.

"Sing something," Janner said.

"Huh?"

"Sing something—something Annieran."

"I can't sing," Kalmar said. "You sing something."

Janner racked his brain, but it was blank. "Leeli's always singing. Can't you remember something?"

"How about 'The Crags at Castle Rock'?"

"Perfect."

Janner didn't like singing any more than Kal did. Whenever they had been forced to sing, they usually let Leeli do all the work. But a moment later, the brothers clumsily sang the first verse.

The rain that rakes the ocean span
The sun that breaks and warms the land
The bows that bound from cliff to cliff
The grass that greens the stone and sand
The bells that ring in the tower clock
The swallows that sing to the swooping flock
And circle the mast of the sailing skiff
All hallow the Maker of Castle Rock

The Fangs clutched the sides of their heads and hissed.

"What's the next verse?" Janner inched forward, toward the distant archway. Kalmar began singing again, and Janner joined him.

When the waves march in and beat the brow
Of the headland stones I remember how
In the summer we stood on the windy dune
As the daylight broke and we made the vow
To return to Castle Rock someday

No matter how far was our home away
We would go there together and sing a tune
To sound of the bells in the light of the moon
For the praise of the Maker who gave us the boon
Of the summer we spent on the northern bay

One of the Fangs retched. Khrak whacked it with the flat of his blade. "It's only a song, you fool!"

It was the moment Janner had been hoping for. "Run!" he shouted.

Janner and Kalmar darted between the reeling Fangs and ran for the arched door. But as soon as the song stopped and Janner's fist closed over the stone, the Fangs recovered and gave chase while Khrak bellowed curses.

Kalmar reached the door before Janner and began pulling it shut. Janner could hear the Fangs at his heels and knew he wouldn't make it. One of the Fangs snagged his Durgan cloak and jerked him backward, pulling him from his feet. Janner felt pain in his throat where his cloak choked him, then a flash in his shoulder when he hit the ground, and then he saw a burst of light. The stone had flown from his hand.

"THE RAIN THAT RAKES THE OCEAN SPAN," Kalmar half-screamed, half-sang. "THE SUN THAT BREAKS AND WARMS THE LAND . . ."

Janner saw stars, felt claws on his arms and legs, and heard the hissing of Fangs as he struggled to his feet. He tried to grab his sword, but his hands didn't seem to work properly. When he finally had the hilt in his grip he thrust the sword blindly and heard a shriek. Clutching at his throat, he staggered to his feet, coughing from the bitter dust floating in the air as Kalmar sang at the top of his lungs.

"THE BOWS THAT BOUND FROM CLIFF TO CLIFF, THE GRASS THAT GREENS THE STONE AND SAND . . ."

When Janner's vision cleared, he saw that there were only two Fangs left. He had killed one, and Kalmar had killed another. Khrak and the other remaining Fang were hunkered over, shielding their eyes from the stone—which was now in Kalmar's hand—and clutching their ears. Janner was tempted to cover his ears, too, so awful was the sound of Kal's frantic, tuneless singing. Leeli would have been deeply offended.

Janner ran through the archway and helped Kalmar heave the huge oaken door closed. Khrak lunged toward them, and Janner thrust Rudric's sword through the door's narrowing gap. Khrak's lean lizard face pressed into the opening, snapping at the boys and spewing venom.

"Pull!" Janner screamed, and the boys struggled with all their might. Janner let go of his sword so he could use both hands on the handle, but the sword didn't fall—it was embedded in Khrak's chest. As the boys watched, the old Fang's eyes clouded over, his skin dried, his tongue cracked and hardened, and, with one final tug on the door, General Khrak's head exploded in a spray of dust.

Janner yanked his sword out of the breach and the door slammed shut. Kalmar shoved the crossbeam into place and locked it tight.

Janner slid to the floor, gasping for breath. Kalmar wasn't winded, but his eyes were wide with fear. He sniffed the air, clutching the stone in one hand.

They listened at the door, but all they heard was the worried muttering of the one remaining Fang. "General? Oh, maggotmeal. General Khrak?" They heard the Fang's footsteps as it ran away.

"You all right?" Kalmar asked, pulling Janner to his feet.

"I think so."

Janner's neck burned and his cloak was torn, but he wasn't wounded. He sheathed his sword and looked around. They were in a long, arched corridor of gleaming flagstones lined with white statues of many strange creatures. There were toothy cows, digtoads, chorkneys, bomnubbles and cave blats, all on pedestals in fearsome poses. Other than the statues, they were alone.

At least, they thought they were.

"That was a wonderful song," said a familiar voice that sent chills down Janner's spine. "Welcome to Castle Throg, boys." An old man hobbled out from behind one of the statues. "What a delight to see you again."

71

Spidifer

Squoon!" Janner's heart steamed with anger. "You're supposed to be dead."

Squoon chuckled. "A great many things were *supposed* to happen. I was *supposed* to marry Madia, but I didn't. Gnag the Nameless was *supposed* to make me into a spider, but he wouldn't, no matter how I begged. Though I served him for years, though I escaped your foul father, though I swam to shelter, though I made my way over rock and sand to Yorsha Doon, though I crossed the Chasm and rode the chains to Throg, Gnag wouldn't meld me! But he was *supposed* to."

Bonifer Squoon hobbled closer. He looked older than he had in Ban Rona, and wickeder, too. His eyes were wild and terrible, bloodshot and twitching. He was dressed in the same suit he had worn the night he had betrayed the Wingfeathers and all of the Hollows—the night he had kidnapped the children and aided in the death of their father. Gone was the sweet old man with the scholarly bearing. Now he looked like what he had been all along: a murderer, a treacherous shell of a man.

He took a step nearer and waggled his fingers at Janner. "I know you have the stone," he said. "Give it to me."

"Why?" Janner tried to take a step backward but thudded into the door.

Kalmar stepped forward and brandished his sword. "Get back, Squoon. And tell us how to get out of here. We need to get to Ban Rona."

"It's useless, boy. Gnag is gone. He's off to fetch your sister." Squoon stretched out his bony hand to Kalmar. "Now give me the stone!"

Squoon was carrying something under his arm. Janner could see a small rusty box the size of a brick, tucked up against the old man's heart. Then Squoon began to sing. He sang the song of the ancient stones, his raspy, old voice giving it a dark and sinister tone.

"Quiet!" Janner shouted.

But Squoon smiled and sang louder as he inched toward Kalmar. He sang the song wildly, scrabbling at Kalmar's fist and prying open his fingers. Janner tried to pull Bonifer away, but the old man was stronger than he looked.

There was one quick flash of the stone as Bonifer, still wildly singing, twisted Kal's fingers and at the same time opened the little box. Out crawled a shiny black spider the size of a small bird. It crawled up Bonifer's arm and onto his face just as the light flashed. Janner and Kalmar screamed and backed away.

Bonifer's twisted song turned into twisted laughter as an unnatural smoke swirled around him. He wiggled on the floor like a happy child. The smoke pooled on the floor and clouded around Bonifer.

"We need to get out of here," Janner said.

Then eight long, glistening spider legs unfolded from the smoke. Bonifer's torn clothing hung from them in shreds. The black legs flexed and then lifted the hairy, pulsating form to which they were attached. The triumphant face of Bonifer Squoon was fused to the spider's bloated abdomen, and on his cheeks were eyes, dozens of them, black and lidless.

The Squoonish thing lifted its front legs and admired them with happy wonder then slowly turned and fixed the brothers with a yellow-toothed smile. "There," he said in a scratchy voice. "That's better."

The brothers snatched their swords from the floor and ran.

"Put this in your pocket! I don't want it," Kalmar cried as they bolted along the corridor, dodging weird creatures that looked at them with surprise. Kalmar thrust the stone at Janner, who jammed it into his pocket. Janner glanced over his shoulder and saw the Bonifer-spider flexing its wobbly legs and turning their way.

The corridor led to a wide, ornate stairway that split at the top and led in opposite directions.

"Which way?" Kalmar shouted.

"I don't know! Go right!"

They took the stairs two at a time until they came to the top and found themselves in some sort of armory. The walls were lined with racks of swords and spears, all of which seemed utterly useless against a giant spider.

Janner and Kalmar sprinted to the opposite end of the armory and paused to catch their breath. "There has to be a way off this mountain," Janner said. "Do you smell anything? A way out or something?"

Kalmar sniffed. "I smell—him. Bonifer, or whatever it is." He sniffed again. "And I smell trolls. Lots of them."

"Which way?"

Kalmar closed his eyes, then pointed to the left.

"That's where we're going."

"Huh?" Kalmar said.

"They're probably guarding the way out."

"BOYS." Bonifer's corrupted, spidery voice rattled through the air. "I'M HUNGRY."

"Come on!" Janner grabbed Kal's arm and ran from the armory into a banquet hall littered with piles of rotten food. There were no Fangs in sight. At the far end of the hall, above the entrance and near the ceiling, was a row of narrow windows that opened onto the sky. The sight of those little patches of beautiful, clear blue brought a lump into Janner's throat, and he realized that he had come to believe that he would never see the sky again.

They dashed across the hall, slipping on rotten food strewn on the floor. When they reached the door, Kalmar whined.

"What is it?" Janner asked.

"Trolls. Just outside."

Behind them, the door to the banqueting hall burst into splinters. Squoon ducked through the archway and stretched to his full height. The Bonifer-spider scooped up a pile of rotting food and raised it to his mouth, smearing it all over his face as he slurped it up. He saw the brothers, smiled, and crept in their direction, legs clacking on the floor.

"It's either trolls or a giant spider that wants to eat us," Janner said in a trembling voice.

"Trolls," the boys said together.

They heaved open the door and bolted out into the bright, wind-blown world at the top of the Killridge Mountains.

72

Rain and Fire

Janner and Kalmar stepped out into a courtyard as wide as the Field of Finley. It was encircled by a stone wall at least twenty feet high, with snow heaped at the edges. The deep blue sky was cloudless and cold. Directly across the courtyard was an arched opening in the wall that framed countless snow-capped peaks marching off into the distance. The brothers were at the top of the world.

And the top of the world was crowded with trolls—*big* trolls—dressed in furs, which made them look bigger and more fearsome, like a herd of bomnubbles.

"Grrk," one of them said.

One by one, the trolls turned their attention to the boy and the wolf standing with their backs to the castle door. There was no way the brothers could cross the courtyard before the trolls seized them. Or ate them. Or smashed them flat. But Janner could see no other option. The wide world beyond the archway beckoned.

Janner pulled the stone from his pocket, but here in the daylight its glow seemed a petty thing. Besides, the trolls weren't melded; he doubted the stone's power held any sway over them.

The hulks grunted to each other and pointed suspiciously, moving closer to the boys.

"Should we run for it?" Janner asked.

Behind them, the spider scratched at the oaken door.

"Yes." Kalmar laughed nervously. "Yes, we should."

Janner crouched, trying to ignore the tremble in his tired legs. *If I die, it will be a good death*, he told himself. *Uncle Artham would be proud, wouldn't he?*

The spider scraped at the door again, then hammered it, and the old wood cracked.

"Ready?" Janner asked as the trolls edged nearer.

Kalmar chuckled. "You know, I could really go for some troll poetry about now. Know any?"

"In fact, I do," Janner said with a grin. "We run on the count of *squibbit*. Ready?"

"Ready."

"Grrk. Glog-glog ack woggy!"

Kalmar recited the second line. *"Grrk. Glog-glogacksnock-jibbit."*

"Ooog, wacklesnodspadgenoggy," Janner continued, tensing to spring. *"Nacketbrigglesweeeeeem! Grrk—"*

"—squibbit?"

Before they ran, Janner realized another voice had finished the poem. One of the trolls stepped forward and repeated the line: *"Nacketbrigglesweeeeeem! Grrk. Squibbit?"*

Janner was dumbstruck.

"You talk troll?" the troll asked.

"Um, grrk," Kalmar said.

"Grrk!" Janner blurted. "Glog-glogacksnock-jibbit!"

The troll grunted something to his companions. The rest of them murmured and broke into childlike smiles.

"How boys know troll talk?" a second troll asked.

"A troll friend taught us," said Janner, trying to ignore the pounding on the door behind him.

"Troll friends?" the first troll said happily, clapping his hands.

"Yes!" Janner hardly dared to hope that this was happening. "His name was Oood!"

"Oood?" said the second troll. "Me remember Oood. Oood, son of Glab and Thracky!"

"Glab my cousin!" said another troll in the back.

All at once the tension in the courtyard floated away, and the trolls fell into happy chatter, congregating around the boys and looking at them with hideously cheery faces. Janner's legs almost gave out. The door behind them shuddered with another blow and the trolls looked at the boys questioningly.

"Listen!" Janner said. "Oood was our friend. He was going to help us smash Gnag."

The trolls nodded and scratched their heads and bellybuttons.

"Smash Gnag good." The first troll beat his chest. "Yiggit want to go home to Glagron. It too cold here. No trees." The other trolls grunted their agreement.

"Will you help us?" Kalmar asked.

"Why help Fang?" Yiggit said, narrowing his little eyes.

"He's not a Fang!" Janner said. "He's the High King of Anniera. Gnag did this." He pointed at Kalmar's fur.

"Anniera," said Yiggit, nodding. "Gnag smash Anniera."

"Yes," Kalmar said. "Now, Anniera smash Gnag."

The trolls thought about this, then the whole congregation raised their giant fists in the air and shouted, "Smash Gnag!"

Bonifer banged on the door again and the trolls looked confused.

"There's a big spider thing on the other side of that door." Kalmar waggled his fingers. "A bad monster. Can you stop it?"

"Easy," said Yiggit with a shrug, and he grunted some commands at the others.

"We need to get to Ban Rona," Janner said. "Down from Throg."

"Come." Yiggit beckoned several of his fellow trolls to follow. The rest parted and allowed the brothers to pass, then grinned and gathered around the castle door, waiting to smash whatever emerged.

Just as Janner and Kalmar passed through the archway that only moments ago seemed impossible to reach, the door burst open. Janner glanced behind. Spidery legs shot out over the trolls' heads, the trolls descended on the giant spider, and Bonifer's voice rang out into the air for the last time.

"Yiggit help you down," said their new friend.

Janner pulled his eyes away from the courtyard and beheld the dizzying expanse of the Killridge Mountains spread before him. Beyond the wall, the mountain fell steeply away. At the brink of the cliff there was another gondola attached to another series of chains. The chains stretched over the precipice and descended to an iron tower built into a distant slope, then to another, and another, down the face of the mountain and around a stony ridge below.

Yiggit indicated with a grunt that the boys were to get into the gondola, then he moved to an enormous wheel and busied himself with a series of levers. Janner and Kalmar nervously climbed the stone steps to the gondola and ducked inside. It was as filthy as the other, but Janner wasn't going to complain. He peeked out the window, eyes watering in the cold wind, and waited as several other trolls joined Yiggit at the wheel.

"Oood is a good boy," Yiggit said.

"Yes." Janner didn't have the heart to tell them that Oood was gone.

Yiggit and the others heaved. The gondola lifted from the ground and swayed, then swung out over the open air.

"We're in a big hurry," Kalmar said. "Can you voom us?"

"Voom!" Yiggit waved the other trolls out of the way. He waited until the boys sat down, then he flipped a lever and the gondola shot out over empty air.

The brothers leaned back in their seats, heedless of the grime and their perilous speed. They were exhausted and out of words.

Janner looked behind them at the full height of Castle Throg for the first time. It was beautiful in its way, stone on stone, spired and silent in the freezing heights, a lonely place on a lonely mountain, where madness had made its home. Never before had Janner so longed for green, warm things, growing trees, rolling waves and smiling faces.

The gondola descended until the highest spire of Throg disappeared among the peaks.

73

Across the Chasm

Down they went, not knowing what had become of their sister, not knowing what lay at the bottom of the mountain, not knowing anything but hunger, thirst, cold, and weariness. They had come further and done more in their few years than most men ever would. They were living lives that would pass into legend.

Stories would be written about them—stories that would be read by children and parents at bedtime. Brothers and sisters would enact their favorite scenes, dressing up like Fangs or sea dragons or even Podo Helmer. Janner, Tink, and Leeli had done so themselves when they were children, Podo had done so with his siblings when he was young, and so it had been all the way back to the First Fellows, who heard tales from the Maker's own mouth about other worlds he had made.

Now, however, all the boys knew was the cold, the worry over their fate, their family's fate—the world's fate—and the noisy silence of the wind in the mountains.

Janner slept for a while, woke in the dark, then peeked out the gondola window at the vast steeps under a crescent moon. Kalmar dozed in the seat across from him, stirring and changing position whenever the gondola lurched past another tower embedded into the stony mountainside.

They had been descending for hours. Janner stuck his head through the opening in the door and scanned the foothills below for some an indication of how much further they had to go, but he saw nothing but darkness. He rummaged through his pack, then Kalmar's, looking for food, for crumbs, for apple cores to fend off his growing hunger, but found nothing. No water, either.

He reached out and strained for the gondola roof, and his fingers stabbed into hard snow. He broke off a chunk and carefully lowered it back inside. He munched on the snow and thought long about Leeli and his family, about Oskar and Sara Cobbler, and was soon lulled to sleep again by the interminable rocking of the gondola.

"Janner, wake up," Kalmar said.

Janner sat up with a jerk. Kalmar pointed out the window at the breaking dawn. They couldn't see the sun behind the mountains, but it painted the high clouds in the east in pinks and fair yellows. In the west lay a misty flatness that looked like the Dark Sea at dusk back in Glipwood. But it wasn't the sea. It was the barren desert of the Woes of Shreve.

The gondola was reaching its terminus. The mountainside was rocky and snowless, and Janner noticed that he wasn't as cold as he had been all night. The chain that carried them stretched down toward a tiny cluster of buildings.

"Do you see anyone?" Janner asked.

"Not yet. But someone's home. There's smoke in the chimneys."

As Janner studied the settlement, trying to judge the distance, he saw something that took his breath away. The buildings and the little platform where the gondola would come to rest were on the far side of a yawning chasm.

The gondola lumbered forward, lurched over another pole, and swung the boys out over a rift in the earth so deep that it seemed to swallow the sunlight. It stretched away on either side as far as they could see, as if the mountains had decided one day to detach themselves from the rest of the continent. The chain drooped across it for several hundred yards, connecting to another platform on the other side. Birds—hawks and falcons and at least one rare gryfendril—wheeled in the empty air below them like fish swimming in the deep.

Janner and Kal held still, as if a sudden movement might snap the chain and send them plummeting into the abyss. The gondola creaked forward, dipping lower and lower, and soon they were below the rim of the chasm, looking up at the platform instead of down on it. Janner could feel the great nothing below his feet and wondered how in Aerwiar anyone was able to get the chain across such a canyon. And who was crazy enough to ride the chain for the first time?

Neither of the boys spoke. There was nothing to say. They would deal with whatever met them when the gondola stopped. Janner couldn't wait to put his feet on solid ground again, no matter how many Fangs might await them.

The gondola edged closer and closer to the cliff as the sun rose. Smoke floated from the chimneys and Janner felt the familiar tremble of fear in his gut. Something was about to happen, and he had no idea what.

"Maybe everyone's asleep," Kalmar whispered.

"Maybe," Janner said, but he doubted it.

With a final lurch the gondola lifted, dragged across the platform, and came to rest. Just as Janner allowed himself to believe that their arrival would go unnoticed, the gondola shifted again and the top thudded into a mechanism that triggered a resounding bell. The sound shook the air and echoed off the opposite cliff.

"Great," Kal grumbled.

The boys sat frozen, as if their stillness might undo the alarm. Nothing happened, so Janner eased open the door and the brothers stepped out, joints aching, and tiptoed down from the platform. A rocky path led between the buildings and into an open space. With the chasm at their backs, there was no way to go but forward.

Kalmar sniffed the air and whispered, "Be careful. Fangs."

Then the door of the nearest building flew open and out of the darkness emerged the Stone Keeper, skittering across the ground on her many legs. Her hood was thrown back and her sickly, stretched face bore a triumphant smile.

She rushed forward so fast that Janner had little time to react. He fumbled in his pocket for the stone, thinking he might try the same bargain as before, but the Stone Keeper seized both boys by the wrists. She sent them sprawling to the ground with surprising strength, laughing all the while. Janner lay on his back in shock, dimly aware of another falcon wheeling in the pink sky.

The boys groaned as they tried to climb to their feet and draw their swords at the same time. Fangs, Grey and Green, streamed from the doors of the other buildings, all with sneers and swords and victory in their eyes. Humans were there, too, Wanderers of the Woes dressed in black, faces painted red with bloodrock dye. Their swords were curved and their faces dispassionate as they watched the Fangs subdue and disarm the boys. Janner felt his arms wrenched behind his back and held in an iron grip.

"Now," the Stone Keeper said, "you will return the *holoél* to me. I know you have it."

"But—but how did you—?"

"Bat Fangs have many uses." Her smile revealed her sharp black teeth.

Janner glanced over the Stone Keeper's shoulder and saw several Bat Fangs flapping about in the sky. They looked clumsy and ridiculous next to the gryfendrils and falcons circling in the chasm. One of the bats dove suddenly and Janner watched with dismay as it snatched one of the beautiful hawks and began to eat it in mid-air.

"It's not as pleasant a ride down from Throg as you two had," the Stone Keeper said, "but the bats are *much* faster."

Janner tried not to watch as the Bat Fang snatched other birds—the gryfendril among them—and glided over to alight on the roof of the nearest building, where it squatted and watched with its useless milky eyes as the birds struggled in its claws.

"Gnag told me you were coming," she continued. "And I was a fool not to recognize you when you first approached the melding box. I looked forward to meeting you, Kalmar, most of all." She smiled her horrid smile and stroked Kalmar's furry cheek. "You turned out quite lovely."

He struggled but the Grey Fangs held him fast.

"What do you want with us?" Kalmar asked through clenched teeth.

"That's for the Nameless One to tell you." The Stone Keeper turned her attention to Janner. "Now, boy. None of your heroics. I'll have the stone back. It still has some power yet, and I intend to put it to good use."

"You'll never Fang me," Janner said.

"Perhaps. But we'll lock you away and torture you for a few years once Gnag is finished with you." The Stone Keeper jammed her hand into Janner's pocket and removed the stone, then waved for the Bat Fangs to approach. "Bind them."

Janner struggled as the Fangs tied his arms and legs. Two of the bats loped over, clutched the boys, and lifted them into the air. The Stone Keeper drew her cowl over her head and climbed into a large basket with a rope at each corner. Four more Bat Fangs flapped toward her, gripped the ropes, and lifted her as the Woefolk and Fangs watched in silence.

"Where are you taking us?" Janner demanded as they rose.

"Home, of course."

Bonifer and the baby, along with old Gineva and the Doonish wet-nurse, crossed the Chasm, rode the chains up the Killridge Mountains, and came at last to Castle Throg. Far above the tree line, where the air was thin and the wind screamed, the castle rose like a cluster of knives aimed at the sky. The gate swung open and the travelers stepped from the howl of the wind into the vast silence of Throg.

The entry hall was dimly lit, and Bonifer saw only shadowy shapes skittering and creeping from pillar to tapestry to nook. 'Hello?' he called, and his voice echoed down through the dim hall.

Soon came the sound of slow footsteps, and Bonifer beheld an old man, old as the mountain. The man's beard dragged along the floor and he looked so frail that he might have been made of paper.

'Squoon?' said the man in a voice so deep and strong that it seemed uttered by another being entirely.

'Yes, my lord,' Bonifer said with a bow.

'My name is Will.'

Bonifer's skin went cold. 'Ouster Will?'

'The same,' said the man, and his laughter chilled Bonifer like the mountain wind. The rebel son of Dwayne and Gladys, older than epochs, haunt of scarytales and dark songs, stood before Bonifer in the flesh. 'It's a wonder what water from the First Well can do,' Ouster Will said. He hobbled to the nursemaid and tore the child from her arms. He held up the poor creature by one of its legs and turned it about as if he were inspecting a slab of meat. 'This is the best you could do? It will never be able to walk, and its face is hideous.' Ouster Will thrust the child back at Gineva. 'I asked for human children. Not monsters.' The old man made his way back down the long torchlit hall.

'Wait, my lord!' Bonifer said.

'Go, before I have my pets gobble you up.'

Bonifer and the women shrank back at the sight of creatures slinking out of the shadows. There were horse-like heads and oozing bodies heaving themselves along on insectile legs, snakes with boneless and useless wings flopping toward him like fish, a toothy cow with the upper half of a wolf growing from its ribs and both of its mouths snapping at the air.

'This is the child of the High King of Anniera!' Bonifer cried.

Ouster Will stopped and motioned for the animals to retreat back into the shadows. He hobbled back to Bonifer and the nursemaid, smiling wickedly. He took the baby again and asked, 'What is its name?'

'It—it has no name, lord.'

'Then I shall give it a name. And I shall make something of it. Go.'

'The gold, sir?' Bonifer said with a nervous laugh.

'At Yorsha Doon. Now go.' Ouster Will stroked the baby's twisted limbs and misshapen face. 'I have work to do.'

Bonifer and Gineva turned to leave, but Murgah the wetnurse bowed and said, 'My lord, let me stay and care for the child along with my own.'

So Bonifer and Gineva left the woman behind and stepped out into the howling wind. Squoon took a deep breath and smiled to himself. All that was left to do was to murder the old midwife Gineva. He had decided that she was a risk he wasn't willing to take, and cast her headlong into the Chasm.

Bonifer found his ship in Yorsha Doon laden with chests of gold, and when he returned to Anniera, Ortham greeted him warmly and introduced him to his newborn son, Jru. 'Where have you been these last weeks?' asked the king, and Bonifer explained that he had been called away because of a Hollish trade dispute.

Queen Madia was still recovering from her labor, still grieving the supposed death of Jru's twin. But when Madia saw her old friend she hugged him and welcomed him home, eager to speak of young Illia's reaction to her new brother. Even as he delighted in Madia's conversation, Bonifer watched her closely for signs of doubt or suspicion. Soon he was assured that his treachery had gone undiscovered.

Years passed. Bonifer continued to supply Ouster Will with animals and no longer doubted the ancient lord's purpose: he was melding animals, using old lore as well as the holoré and holoél to make new beasts. Bonifer often wondered why, and soon he gathered that Ouster Will was building an army. If that was true, Bonifer was glad to be his ally, not his enemy. He would continue to help Will any way he could—and not just because of money or alliance. Bonifer Squoon also wanted to be close to the child, whom Ouster Will had come to call "The Nameless."

The Nameless crawled the halls of Throg in the company of horrors. Bonifer Squoon visited a few times each year and told the child stories of Anniera, a kingdom where he said the weak were spurned and exiled. He lied to the child.

'Your real father, High King Ortham, was disgusted by your malformation and planned to kill you. Only I loved you. Only I rescued you from the clutches of Anniera and brought you here to Lord Will, who shall repair what the Maker has done to you.'

'The Maker?' asked the boy, his useless legs bent beneath him, his twisted visage peering up at Squoon.

'Yes. The Maker is the one who twisted your body. He is the one who willed your birth to a father who would kill you without even giving you the blessing of a name. He is the one who took my Madia, who has cut me off from love. If you would be whole, you must do so yourself. The Maker will not help you. Only Lord Will, who has worked these long years to perfect the Maker's shabby work, will help you. Men and women are weak. Do you know how long it takes an ordinary human child to learn to walk? A year! Do you know how long it takes a toothy cow to walk? Minutes. Do you know how long you would survive in the cold if I threw you outside tonight?'

'No, Bonifer.'

'You would be dead by morning. But any one of these beasts around you would live many nights, warmed by their blood and their fur and their superior constitution. Man is weak. Let Will make you strong. Let the blood of the beast imbue your bones. Rise above the Maker's foul work, and break the yoke of weakness. Let Aerwiar crawl with better beasts, and let Ouster Will rule them. Do you know that you are the rightful king of Anniera?'

'I am?' asked Gnag.

'And one day you shall crush it.'

Gnag smiled.

—From *The Annieriad*

Part Four:

ANNIERA

74

Gnag the Nameless

The portholes were closed. A single candle burned on a table.

When Leeli's eyes adjusted to the dim light she beheld a stooping figure beside the robed woman. He was bald and thin as a skeleton. His cheeks were sunken, and his mouth drew down in an exaggerated frown. Veins twisted across the surface of his skull like traces of red lightning. The thing—for it was hard to call him a man—wore a robe that pooled around him on the floor. But it was his eyes that struck the deepest terror into Leeli's heart. They appeared lidless, watching her dispassionately and protruding from a skull that was covered in milky flesh.

Gnag the Nameless looked profoundly old. He reminded her of a dead tree moldering on the forest floor, and his eyes were shiny white grubs bored into the flesh of the decaying wood.

"You have the whistleharp?" the woman asked Leeli.

Leeli clutched it without meaning to and scrambled away, pressing her back against the door. Gnag said nothing, but his gaze weighed Leeli down like a pile of stones.

"Good," the woman said. "You'll need it."

"I won't use it for you."

The woman smiled. "You will."

"What do you want with us?" Leeli asked.

"He wants what you have. Power."

"But we're only children."

"Children with power."

"I don't know what you're talking about."

His eyes never leaving Leeli's face, Gnag unfolded his arms and stepped closer, his robe dragging across the floor. He lurched and swayed as if he were still learning how to walk, and the sound of his footsteps was wrong somehow.

Gnag reached one of his long, bony hands toward her. Leeli pushed harder against the door, as if she might squeeze herself through a seam in the wood.

"Maker help me!" she pleaded.

The hull groaned as the sails filled with a sudden wind. The ship heeled to one side, and Gnag lost his balance. He tumbled across the floor and thudded into the wall in a tangle of limbs. Leeli saw that he had not two legs, but four—and not just four legs, but four squat, stout legs. Two of them ended in hoofs, and the other two had paws.

The woman gasped and rushed to help him up. Panting and snorting like a pig, Gnag stood again and shoved the woman away. He looked ill.

"Where are you taking me?" Leeli asked.

Gnag stared at her with his protuberant, milky eyes. When he finally spoke, his voice was deep and gurgling. "To my home."

Leeli forced herself to meet his gaze. "Throg?"

"Anniera."

Gnag was from Anniera? Leeli brushed the absurd thought aside, figuring that Gnag was trying to upset or confuse her somehow. She turned her attention to the woman, who seemed to be enjoying Leeli's confusion as she huddled against the wall.

"Who are you, anyway?" Leeli asked.

"My name is Amrah."

"What does he want with me?"

The woman glanced at Gnag but he only stood there, staring. He tore a chunk of bread from a loaf on the table and chewed on it in silence. Leeli was glad the woman was in the room, just to have something to distract her from Gnag's creepy eyes. He wiped the corners of his mouth and folded his arms again, licking crumbs from teeth that looked like burnt toast.

"We're taking you to Anniera," Amrah said, smiling again at the doubt on Leeli's face. "He is Annieran, as you are."

"That doesn't make any sense. He hates Anniera."

"Because it hated him," said the woman.

"I don't understand," Leeli said.

Gnag's face remained expressionless, but the woman rolled her eyes. "Show me your whistleharp."

Leeli pulled it from her coat and held it out suspiciously. The silver pipe glistened in the candlelight.

The woman stepped forward and snatched it from around Leeli's neck. "Do you know who this belonged to?" she asked, holding the whistleharp as if she were holding a dead fish.

"Madia Wingfeather. My great-grandmother."

"Madia. The great queen of Anniera. The great abandoner of children," Amrah said, and Gnag showed some emotion as a look of hatred passed over his face.

"What do you mean?" Leeli asked.

"I *mean*, girl," Amrah said quietly, hiding the whistleharp in her robe, "that she was the Nameless One's mother."

The thought was so bizarre, so impossible, that Leeli's mind reeled. "That means he's my—my—"

"Great uncle," said the woman.

Gnag watched Leeli, his nostrils flaring with each breath.

"Then why have you never heard of him? Why is his name not in the histories of Anniera? Why was he not coddled in the Castle Rysen as you were?" Amrah leaned closer. "Why is the Shining Isle a guttering ruin?"

"I don't know," Leeli whispered.

Amrah's voice grew sickly sweet as she crossed the room and placed her hand lovingly on Gnag's shoulder. "Shall I tell her, my lord?"

Gnag shoved Amrah's hand away. He clenched and unclenched his jaw before he spoke. "I am the elder twin of Jru Wingfeather. Behold the one who was cast out!"

He wobbled forward and removed his robe.

Gnag's four legs weren't his own, but were instead those of two pitiful cloven, bent over and straining beneath Gnag's weight. One of the little creatures had a goat's body and head but the arms of a man; the other was furry like a Grey Fang but had the head of a hogpig. Their shoulders were harnessed to a crude basket, which supported Gnag's real legs—legs that were malformed and crumpled beneath him like dead branches.

Of all the awful things Leeli had seen, this was the worst. Gnag the Nameless, subjecting these poor creatures to such humiliation; Gnag the Nameless, bony and leering; Gnag the Nameless, crooked and cruel. Gnag the Nameless—Leeli's great uncle?

Gnag dropped the robes, concealing the two cloven. He leaned to his left and they bore him over to the table so he could tear off another hunk of bread. He waved a hand at Amrah and turned his back to Leeli. "Lock her up."

Amrah pulled Leeli to her feet and led her out of Gnag's quarters and into the light. After her encounter with Gnag the Nameless, the Fangs on deck seemed of little concern—puppies by comparison. When the door closed, separating Gnag from the rest of Leeli's world, she drew a deep breath and exhaled it slowly.

"That story—it can't be true," Leeli said.

"When the Nameless One was born," the woman said as they crossed the deck, "Madia was disgusted. When Jru followed, she rejoiced. They deemed Gnag too ugly, too deformed to be a part of their precious family—*your* precious family. He was cast out. But Bonifer Squoon rescued him. He told Gnag everything."

"Bonifer was a liar," Leeli said.

"Everyone's a liar."

"Madia wouldn't have just—just *thrown* out her baby."

"Then why was Lord Gnag raised in Throg without a soul knowing there was another Wingfeather born? Because he was weak and ugly. And the Shining Isle, that land of beauty and strength," Amrah said sarcastically as she opened a hatch, "would not have him."

"But who cared for him in Throg? Bonifer Squoon?" Leeli asked, not just because she wanted to know, but because she didn't want to be locked away in the dark.

"Bonifer visited him often, and my mother cared for him for years. But an old man—a very old man—raised Gnag. He had lived there for epochs, seeking to unlock the great power of the *holoré* and *holoél*. Do you know what they are?"

"The ancient stones." Leeli glared at Amrah. "That's what you used to change Kalmar. But who was the old man?"

"He was a fool," Amrah said. "A fool who lacked the wisdom of the Nameless One. He melded and melded—but all he made were monsters. Slogging things, useless beasts—what you call the cloven. Many he kept in the castle or in the Deeps, and many he cast into the Blackwood. He tried to bend his subjects to his . . . *will*." Amrah stifled a smile that Leeli didn't understand. "But it was useless. His subjects had to choose. They had to *want* to meld. That was the Nameless One's revelation. It didn't matter if he twisted their bodies as long as their souls remained straight. The melding would only work if he first showed them what power awaited, what glorious strength might be theirs if only they sang the song in the stonelight. Gnag tried to tell him but he wouldn't listen. Then the old man banished my mother and I from Throg." Amrah prodded Leeli into the berth. "So he killed the old man in his sleep."

A shiver ran down from Leeli's shoulders and she stopped in the doorway. "He killed him?"

"He was your age at the time."

"But why?"

"The old man saw Gnag the way Madia saw him, as a useless and loathsome thing. He wanted to meld him with a rat or a thwap—something puny. Gnag refused. The true king of Anniera was not to be corrupted, but glorified. So he killed Ouster Will and brought us back to serve him."

"Ouster Will," Leeli said, struggling to believe it. "*The* Ouster Will?"

"I told you he was old. Kept alive by the Water from the First Well, all those years in Throg, trying to unlock the secrets of the ancient stones. That's why Ouster Will conspired to murder Yurgen's son, you know. He needed the Maker's power, hidden in the deep of the world, and he tricked Yurgen into digging for it."

"But how did he know the stones existed?"

"Because Gladys and Dwayne had walked the Fane of Fire."

"I don't know what you're talking about."

Amrah glanced over her shoulder at Gnag's door, then led Leeli into the room, lit a lantern, and shut the door. The berth was much smaller than Gnag's, but big enough for a cot and a small table and chair.

Amrah sat on the chair and studied Leeli's face. The lamplight warmed the woman's pale skin and made her look more beautiful and less wicked. She gestured to the cot. "Sit, Leeli Wingfeather."

Leeli leaned her crutch against the wall and eased herself onto the cot.

"I will tell you what I can." Amrah stared at the lantern and spoke softly, and Leeli was so enthralled that she forgot she was a prisoner on Gnag's ship. "The Fane of Fire lies beneath the castle where the First Fellows lived. It's a secret, sacred place where the king and the Maker commune. Legend tells that it is a golden hall where the Maker dwells, and the stones there glimmer golden. Those stones, according to the

First Books, keep the world alive. They hold unimaginable power. Do you know the tale of the sea dragons? How they sank the mountains?"

Leeli nodded uncertainly. This was Janner's territory, but she had a vague understanding of the old tale.

"In the First Epoch," Amrah said, "Ouster Will sailed to the dragon kingdom in the southern sea. He disguised himself as his brother Omer—a friend to the dragons for many years—and there on the shore, instead of communing with the young dragon as Omer did, he smote Yurgen's son with a fatal wound. Then, casting off his disguise, he rushed to the Hall of the Dragon King and told Yurgen of his son's wounding at Omer's hand. 'You can save your heir,' he told Yurgen, 'if only you dig into the deeps and harvest the stones that beat at the heart of Aerwiar.'

"You know the story. Yurgen and his dragons dug, they rent the earth, they trenched the sea, they sank the mountains to save the young dragon, and indeed Yurgen returned with two flinders of stone. But it was too late. His son was dead. Yurgen soon learned of Ouster Will's treachery, but Will hid himself away. He took the stones to Throg, where he lived a thousand years, heedless of the anger that raged between Yurgen and men."

"Using the Water from the First Well," Leeli said.

"Yes. But when the dragons dug, they bent the shape of the world. The forests throve, mountains shifted, Anniera itself was torn from the continent, and the Well was lost.

"But Will was fortunate. Before he slew Yurgen's son, he secreted a cask of the water and drank it whenever he weakened. A small amount, enough to keep his old heart beating. Gnag watched him do it. But little by little, the cask ran dry. Will grew frantic, reckless, mad with age. He melded carelessly, so eager was he to make some new thing. Then Gnag killed him and drank the last of the water himself."

"But what does any of that have to do with Anniera? Why would he burn the island?"

"So many questions," Amrah said with a smile. "Lie down. We can talk more tomorrow. You should sleep." The woman's voice softened, and Leeli's eyelids drooped as if on command. "Rest, Leeli Wingfeather."

She felt the woman's eyes on her as she drifted to sleep.

75

The Isle of Anniera

The ship thudded into a dock, and Leeli awoke with a scream. An acrid smell filled her nostrils. Smoke—but not the pleasant smell of chimneys or cookstoves.

The door opened and a Green Fang thrust his head into the room. "Welcome to Anniera."

She squinted up at the Fang silhouetted by sunlight. It was daytime, thank the Maker. She had thrashed in her dreams all night, waking occasionally and crying herself back to sleep in the darkness. It had been the longest night of her life.

She swung her feet to the floor and grabbed her crutch, feeling for her whistleharp out of habit. When it wasn't there she panicked, then remembered that Amrah had taken it the night before. Leeli felt powerless without it. She took a deep breath and reminded herself that Gnag needed her alive.

She pushed through the door and coughed her way across the deck in a haze of smoke. The sun was a red torch, low in the east. The Grey and Green Fangs were busy lashing the ship to the dock, drawing in the sail, and shouting orders to more Fangs on shore. No one seemed to notice her, and there was no sign of Amrah or Gnag.

She covered her face and squinted through the smoke at what was left of the Shining Isle.

The earth was charred, black, and muddy. Not a single blade of grass greened the ground. Stone walls and the remains of several structures, all blackened with soot, lay wasted near the dock. Black tree stumps crowded a distant rise like old fence posts and tombstones. There had once been a forest here. A forest and a village, it seemed. Only the dock remained unburned, but it was shabbily built, suggesting that the original dock had been destroyed and the Fangs had hastily constructed a new one.

The ship floated in a small harbor cut from the rock, but to the left and right stretched a craggy shoreline buffeted by waves. It reminded Leeli of the cliffs in Glipwood, only smaller. South of the harbor lay the estuary of a river that vomited ash and sludge into the sea. Everywhere Leeli looked, she saw destruction: ashes, smoke from smoldering stumps, piles of scattered stone, and in the distance the gentle mountains of Anniera, burning, burning, burning.

"The Shining Isle," gurgled Gnag from behind her. "Beautiful."

He stood on the dock beside Amrah, draped in his black robe, and Leeli shuddered at the knowledge that the two little cloven bore him up. His eyeballs gleamed in the shadow of his cowl. Gnag tilted forward, and he seemed to float along the dock to the shore.

"Good morning," said Amrah kindly, beckoning to Leeli with one of her white hands. "Come. We'll eat on the way."

Leeli took a deep breath, then crossed over the ashen waters and limped onto the island of her birth. The last time she had been here, she was a baby. She had been grabbed by a Green Fang, and her leg had been terribly twisted. It throbbed now as she imagined it. Then she remembered Wendolyn. Podo's wife. Leeli's grandmother, who had died at the hands of the Fangs as the Wingfeathers made their escape. Leeli had heard these stories, but now they were as real to her as the ground under her feet.

How she had longed for Anniera! She had imagined being welcomed by her mother and father's people, ushered into a new home where she had always belonged. It was never like this in her daydreams—never with Gnag the Nameless wobbling before her, surrounded by wolves and smoke. The worst of it was that she was alone.

Gnag stopped in front of a carriage, and two Green Fangs removed his robe. They unbuckled Gnag's tiny legs from his little platform and lifted him into the carriage while the two cloven gasped for breath, working their shoulders and bleating with relief. The two horses harnessed to the carriage were muddy, their manes and tails matted and clumpy, their eyes drooping with weariness.

"Come on, then," Amrah said, waving Leeli over to the carriage. "It'll be all right."

Leeli knew Amrah couldn't be trusted. The woman had destroyed many lives and was in league with Gnag the Nameless—and yet her gentle presence was Leeli's only source of comfort, even if it was a charade. What other choice did she have?

Leeli slogged through the black mud, slipping more than once while the Fangs looked on in dispassionate silence. She struggled into the carriage and pressed herself into the corner, as far from Gnag as possible. The door closed, the horses pulled, and Gnag stared at her with eager eyes.

They rolled over the hills, a bleak world barren of any color or life or movement other than that of the guttering flames sparking the hills. The land was sallow and silent, as dead as a corpse, riddled with deep holes and piles of dirt. The few Fangs she spotted in the distance meandered about purposelessly. Gnag, as far as she could tell, never once looked out the window, which probably meant he had made this journey many times before.

Gnag waved a finger at the black landscape. "Does it trouble you?"

"Yes," Leeli answered quietly.

"Good."

"But why? Why did you do this?"

Gnag grinned at Leeli, showing his brown teeth. "Because I could."

"That doesn't make any sense!" Leeli sniffled and hugged her knees.

"Tell her," Gnag said, rapping his white knuckles on the ceiling. "I'm hungry."

The two cloven clambered down from the roof and through the windows, bearing satchels of food and a waterskin. They tended to Gnag with little grunts and whines that were disturbingly affectionate.

"Once Ouster Will was gone," Amrah said, "Lord Gnag spent many years perfecting the melding, learning to reshape not just bodies but souls. He began to build an army. Green Fangs at first, but they were unruly, undisciplined, and weak—they couldn't take the cold. Not only that, we realized that if the Fangs returned too often to familiar places, they began to remember things from their former lives—and remembering drove them mad. So we keep careful records of their old names and cities. We move them around. Lord Gnag, in his great wisdom, also learned something else." Amrah looked at Gnag lovingly, but he was too interested in eating to notice. "He learned that if he wanted an army worthy of Throg, they had to be trained from a young age. He needed children. Children could be . . . *shaped*. And so he made the Grey Fangs."

"Smarter, quicker. Able to fight in snow or summer," Gnag muttered with a mouthful of meat. "And able to sniff you out, girl."

"But why? You already have Anniera. You've already ruined everything there is to ruin!"

Gnag dragged his forearm across his mouth to wipe away the drool and stared at Leeli with a sneer. His pale cheeks were splotched with anger. The closer the carriage drew them to their destination, the more agitated Gnag became.

"Because the ancient stones are too small," Amrah said. She placed a calming hand on Gnag's forearm. He shot a glance at her and relaxed as she continued. "Their power is waning. He needs more stones—for himself. He only wants to be healed, Leeli. Wouldn't you, if you could? You, at least, can walk with a crutch. But poor Gnag has never taken a step without the help of his servants." Amrah's voice sweetened. "Have you no compassion?"

Amrah's words made a strange kind of sense, but Leeli knew it was wrong. Gnag was evil. He was a killer.

"Just take your silly stones and leave us alone," Leeli said, tears springing to her eyes. "Take Anniera! There's nothing left for us here anyway."

Gnag leaned forward and clenched his fists. "Anniera is already mine, girl. It always was. I was born second, don't you see? According to your silly tradition, I'm the king! All this time, I've been the rightful heir to the throne of Anniera. Isn't that a delightful thought? It's *my* island! The Annierans are *my* subjects. Rysen is *my* castle."

Leeli wiped her nose. "Then why don't you just kill us and get it over with?"

Gnag leaned back in his chair. "Because, as much as it pains me to say it, I need your help."

"What?"

"For nine years I have tried to open the door to the Fane of Fire, but I cannot do it. I have rubbled the castle, my Fangs have pummeled the door, we have dug into the heart of the island and melted the very stone, but the way is shut to me. One thing I found, however, among your father's keepings—another of the First Books. It tells that the only way to open the door is with the Jewels of Anniera. And the key is word, form, and song. The king can't open it alone, though I've tried with all my cunning. Only when there were three children born to the king could the Fane be opened. I need the Song Maiden. I need the Limner and the Shaper, too. Only the three of you can do it."

"T.H.A.G.S.," Leeli said.

"What?"

"Nothing," she muttered. "And what if we refuse?"

Gnag rolled his bulgy eyes again. "Do you suppose I haven't thought of that? Do you think I went to all this trouble only to allow you to *refuse* in the end?"

"Lord Gnag," Amrah said soothingly.

"Quiet, woman!" He lunged forward and put his face only inches from Leeli's. She shut her eyes, feeling Gnag's hot breath in her face. *"You will open the Faneway,"* he whispered. *"I have spent my life bending wills to my own, and yours will be no different."*

For a moment more, Leeli felt his reeking presence hover just inches from her face, then he grunted and leaned back in his seat. Leeli wept openly, too frightened to move, wishing she could wake up and find herself in her bed at Chimney Hill.

"Shh," said Amrah. "We're almost there, child."

The driver reined up the weary horses and opened the carriage door. Leeli kept her eyes shut, trying to block out the sounds of Gnag's grunting and the cloven snorting as the Fangs strapped Gnag to their backs. Amrah gently pulled Leeli from the carriage and handed her the crutch.

Leeli opened her eyes and looked through her tears at the place of her birth.

The Castle Rysen looked like the skeleton of a giant beast, its ribcage open to the gray heavens. The roof had burned away long ago, and all but a few of the stone arches had collapsed. Heaps of rubble, the charred remains of rafters and timbers, broken glass, and blackened furniture were strewn in every direction. Leeli saw what used to be a courtyard, littered with the sodden splinters of chairs or tables where Annierans had once danced and feasted. Shards of pottery and tarnished silver cups lay half exposed in the mud. The castle had burned, and been rained upon, and had burned again.

More Fangs, both Green and Grey, emerged from the ruins. They carried pickaxes and hammers and looked haggard compared to the Fangs she had seen fighting in Ban Rona. When they saw Gnag, they bowed and held still.

Gnag ignored them. He forsook his robe and tilted forward, and the cloven carried him to the castle ruin. Amrah guided Leeli after him. She limped through mud, loathing the squelch of her crutch with each step. She tried not to wonder where her grandmother Wendolyn had died, where her parents had strolled, where her brothers had played as toddlers. Janner would have been three, Kalmar two, when Gnag's hammer of war had fallen on the island.

Leeli kept her eyes on the mud at her feet lest she collapse into tears. She summoned Nia's strength and fought to keep her back straight, her eyes fierce. She would not fall helplessly to the mud only to be wrenched to her feet and prodded forward by the Fangs. This was *her* home, not theirs.

Their way led to a corridor in the rubble, at the end of which was a well-traveled stair that sank away into darkness. Leeli paused at the top and looked up, wondering if this was the last time she would see the sky. Even sullied with smoke, it was beautiful. She bade it farewell and followed Gnag the Nameless into the dark below the Castle Rysen.

At the bottom of the stair was a torch lit room.

"Mother," said Amrah.

When Leeli's eyes adjusted she saw Amrah standing beside another robed woman. Beyond her, against the wall, were Janner and Kalmar, gagged and bound.

76

The Fane of Fire

Janner was as happy to see Leeli as he was frightened. She looked unhurt, if weary and a bit muddy. Her eyes widened when she saw the boys, and a silent fear passed between the three of them. Janner and Kalmar grunted and strained against their bonds—a pointless act. They had been tied and handled like bales of hay since their arrival on the island.

After the initial shock and relief of seeing Leeli, Janner beheld Gnag the Nameless in the flesh. No introduction was necessary. The pale, twisted old man wobbled closer on the clovens' backs, gazing at the brothers with a look of gleeful triumph.

"The Throne Warden and the Wolf King," Gnag said. His voice was dark and gurgling, like a muddy creek. "Limner, Shaper, and Song Maiden. I have you at last."

The two Stone Keepers held still, watching their master. Janner couldn't hide the revulsion on his face.

"You Annierans have such an aversion to ugliness." Gnag chuckled and turned to face an iron door. The older Stone Keeper opened it and Gnag wobbled through. "Bring them."

Two Fangs lifted the boys while the younger Stone Keeper led Leeli forward. "It's nice to see you again, Kalmar," she said. "You turned out beautifully."

Janner wanted to scream, wanted to chew through his gag and rend the cords binding his wrists and ankles, but there was nothing he could do. Leeli looked hopeless. Janner's eyes met Kalmar's, and the despair he saw there wilted his heart. Whatever Gnag had wanted of them all these years lay just beyond the door, and there was no stopping it now.

The room was round, like an empty well. The walls were ornamented with images of twisting vines, flowers, and depictions of stars, moons, clouds, hills, waves, and forests. Whoever painted it had possessed great skill, and in the flickering torchlight the scene seemed to breathe with life. The stones on the floor were laid in a circular pattern with three symbols carved at the center: a whistleharp, an eye, and a quill.

This was the chamber Esben must have written about in his letter to Janner. *Ancient secrets lie beneath these stones and cities*, he had written. *They have been lost to us, but still, we mustn't let them fall to evil.*

"Help me, Murgah," Gnag said to the older Stone Keeper. She skittered over to him and unbuckled the straps, then held him in her arms as if he were a child. "Out," Gnag said, and the cloven and the Fangs hurried from the room. "Amrah, cut their bonds."

The younger Stone Keeper produced a dagger from the folds of her robes and cut the cords and gags from both boys. Janner and Kalmar scrambled to Leeli's side.

"Are you all right?" Janner asked, though it seemed like a silly question.

"Wonderful," Leeli said.

Kalmar snarled and stepped in front of his siblings. "Let us out of here."

"Oh! Yes. I'll just set you free because you commanded it—since you're the king, of course." Gnag rested in the Stone Keeper's arms and quivered with laughter. "No, Jewels of Anniera, I have you just where I want you."

"We won't do it," Janner said. "Whatever it is you want us to do."

"You won't? Even if it means I send the order to slay your mother?"

"You don't have her," Janner said.

"Yes, he does," Leeli said. "Ban Rona has fallen."

"Then she may already be dead," Kalmar said. "Besides, she'd rather die than let you win."

"She's alive. I got word by crow just this morning, and they assure me she's in a great deal of pain. If you're so certain she'd rather die, then perhaps I'll just . . . keep her alive. I so enjoyed my time with your father. I broke him and your uncle both in the end. Your mother will break too, given enough time in the Deeps." Gnag smirked. "And don't try to do anything foolish. If anything happens to me in here, my Fangs outside have already been given instructions regarding poor Nia Wingfeather."

"What do you want from us?" Janner shouted.

"All I want, children, is for you to open this door."

"What's down there?" Kalmar asked.

"Give me the *holoré* and *holoél*," Gnag said to the Stone Keepers.

After a moment of hesitation they each removed a small pouch that hung around their necks and handed them to Gnag. He removed the two flinders and held them in his palm. The chamber pulsed with light.

"With these pebbles I melded armies. Below your feet lie hoards of the same. The power that heaves the tide, cycles the seasons, blossoms the trees—a whole cavern of glowing stones." Gnag's gaze drifted to the floor, and his face twisted into a mixture of deep sadness and terrible anger. "All I want is to be beautiful, don't you see? To unmake what the Maker has done, to straighten what he bent, to strengthen what he made weak." Gnag held out his arms and swept his hands across his wretched body. "Would you begrudge a crippled old man his only hope of healing?"

Kalmar shook his head. "There's more to healing than what the eye can see."

"Blather and rot," Gnag said with a sneer. His hand snapped shut and the chamber darkened again. "You'll open this door, or your mother will regret it for an age to come, *nephews*."

"What?" Janner said.

"Tell them, Leeli," Amrah said.

Leeli looked at him sadly. "It's true."

Had the Stone Keeper cast some spell over Leeli? Why would she believe such foolishness?

"We'll open the door." Leeli held out her hand. "But I'll need my whistleharp."

"Leeli, no," Janner said.

"We can't let him hurt Mama."

"But we can't just give him what he wants, either," Kalmar said.

"We don't have a choice," she said, looking urgently at the boys. "Just trust me. Please." Leeli limped to the center of the room and stood on the carving of the whistleharp. She pointed at the eye. "Kal, I think you stand there. Janner, you stand on the quill."

Gnag grinned eagerly and watched as the boys, dumbstruck, did as they were told. Amrah handed the whistleharp to Leeli.

"What do we do?" Leeli asked.

The old Stone Keeper reached into a satchel hidden in the folds of her robe and retrieved an old book. It looked like Janner's First Book but smaller. She handed it to Gnag, and he flipped it open to a page he seemed to have studied many times. He held it out in the torchlight so they could see.

"The Song Maiden plays this melody." He jabbed a finger at a string of notes. "The Limner recites these words"—he indicated something written in an old language—"and the Shaper traces this symbol in the air. Thus the Fane is only opened by the Jewels of Anniera, as it was from the beginning."

"Leeli, this is a bad idea," Janner said. "We can't let him in there."

Leeli's face was serene, and Janner was baffled. Kalmar stared at the symbol in the book and moved his finger, practicing the shape as if he were drawing on an invisible page.

Before Janner could say another word, Leeli raised her whistleharp and played a simple, lovely melody. The air shimmered with it, and the torches fluttered as if a breeze blew through the room. Shaking his head, Janner read the words aloud, though they were foreign and felt strange in his mouth—strange but *right* somehow, as if he had always been meant to speak them. While the melody rang and his words mingled with it, Kalmar raised his hand, extended one finger, and traced the symbol in the air. His finger left a trail of glimmering sparks that hung between the children.

The floor vibrated with a pleasant resonance, a deep accompaniment to Leeli's melody. The words Janner spoke, the song bouncing off the walls, and the sparkling symbol in the air seemed to exist in an exquisite union, filling Janner's ears, eyes, heart, and bones with the very life of Aerwiar. He had never felt anything like it. Out of the corner of his eye he saw Gnag and the Stone Keeper. Their faces were illumined and awestruck, but they seemed far away and irrelevant.

The symbol that floated between the children gathered to an exhilarating golden brightness, tilted until it was parallel with the floor of the chamber, then descended to the images around their feet. Warm light filled the carvings of the eye, whistleharp, and quill like liquid gold, then shot out along the seams of every stone in the chamber. The light surged, then vanished, leaving the chamber in an expectant silence.

Leeli lowered the whistleharp. Janner stopped talking and realized that he had been reciting the old words without looking at the page. Kalmar's hand fell to his side. The only sound was their breathing and the crackle of the torches, which now seemed dim and lifeless compared to the uncommon light that had flooded the room. Gnag panted hungrily.

Then the floor moved. There was a deep grinding of stone on stone, and the three children hurried back to the walls. Yellow light burst from the edges of the center circle where they had stood. The stone sank away, and the light so filled the chamber that they had to shield their eyes. The grinding ceased, and Janner lowered his hands from his face. The room glowed again, now with a steady yellow luminescence, as if the rising sun shone through the opening in the floor.

Gnag the Nameless squirmed out of the Stone Keeper's arms, splatted to his belly, and scooted forward, peering over the edge. He lifted his face to the children with a ghastly, trembling smile.

"The Fane of Fire," he whispered, nearly choking on his tears. "Murgah, help me down."

Gnag cast the two ancient stones into the Fane and held out his hands. The Stone Keeper glided forward, took Gnag's hands, and lowered him through.

"What have we done?" Janner whispered.

77

Stealing the Stone

The Stone Keepers were so intent on the opening that Janner was sure he and his siblings could have slipped away unnoticed. But he was as curious as Gnag, aching to see what the ancient chamber held.

The old books said the Maker walked with Dwayne and Gladys there. Did that mean that the Maker himself was there even now? Could they see him? And if he *was* there, what would he do with someone like Gnag the Nameless poking around in this sacred place?

Janner edged forward, and Leeli and Kalmar followed without a word. The entrance was like a well of light, but the light came from the stones themselves.

Gnag eased himself down, gripping the stones along one side of the shaft while his skinny legs dangled. He reached the bottom and looked up with a hideous, ecstatic smile.

"There are stones everywhere!" he shouted. He wriggled along the passageway and out of sight, then returned, clutching a stone the size of a loaf of bread in both hands. "Murgah, Amrah, look!"

"Bring it up!" Murgah said.

"It's too heavy."

The Stone Keeper pointed at Janner. "You. Go down and bring up the stone."

Janner looked at Kalmar and Leeli, who both nodded. He sat on the edge and marveled at the way the light tingled on his skin, even through his clothes. He climbed down, silenced by the beauty of the stones and the warmth and energy surging in his fingers where he touched them. Janner reached the bottom and looked up at the glowing faces of his siblings and the twinkle of the Stone Keeper's eyes deep in her cowl.

The passageway was littered with the stones, little ones and big ones piled against the walls—a million treasures heaped along the path. The passage led off into the distance, ever widening toward what appeared to be a large cavern. Janner heard the sound of running water and glimpsed the green of growing things mingled with the golden stones.

He wanted to explore, to see what lay beyond the entrance, but Gnag, ignoring the cavern in the distance, scooted on his useless legs from wall to wall, running his pale fingers across the stones and cackling with glee.

"Here!" Gnag said, shoving the brick at Janner. "Take this, and bring me up with you."

"Don't you want to see what's up ahead?" Janner asked without taking his eyes from the cavern. "This—this is where the Maker walked with the First Fellows."

Gnag caressed the stone. "Such power."

"But—that could mean that . . . *he's* in there." It was a frightening thought, but the kind of frightening that made Janner want to see if it was true. He took a step further down the corridor, his flesh prickling with wonder. "I mean—what if it's true?"

"Do what I tell you, boy, or I'll have Murgah break your sister's other leg. It'll be done before you know it."

With an effort, Janner pulled his eyes from the gold and green ahead. He looked back up at the entrance to where his siblings waited. If the Maker was truly in the Fane of Fire, and if he was who Janner believed him to be, then it was up to the Maker to stop Gnag. Janner didn't know what else to do.

He took the stone—it was much heavier than he anticipated—and cradled it awkwardly as he climbed out. When he reached the top, the old Stone Keeper took it. Her face was still shrouded in shadow, but he saw by the glint of her black teeth that she was smiling.

"Fetch the Nameless One," she said.

Janner paused. What was keeping them from shutting the door? If they repeated the ritual, then surely the door would shut, and Gnag would be trapped forever. Then the Maker could deal with him.

"Play," Janner whispered to Leeli as he heaved himself out of the opening.

She and Kalmar understood at once. She began the melody as Kalmar traced the symbol in the air. Janner remembered enough of the strange words to speak the first of them, then some ancient memory took over.

The Stone Keepers shrieked as the chamber sang with old power. Amrah lunged for Leeli's whistleharp, but it was too late. The circle of stone that had sunk away had begun to rise again.

Then Janner saw with a pang of defeat that Gnag hunched atop it, rising out of the Fane with a look of satisfaction.

Amrah jerked the whistleharp out of Leeli's hands as the door settled into place with a thud. "You little wretch," she said, all the sweetness in her voice replaced by seething hatred.

The light flashed, the music faded, and the children found themselves staring defiantly at Gnag and the two women in the gentle glow of the stolen stone.

"I thought you might try that," Gnag said with a smile.

"You have what you want. Now leave us alone," Kalmar said.

"I have one more chore for you. After that, I'm finished with the Jewels of Anniera."

"You'll let us go?"

"I didn't say that. I think I'd rather end you all. Or, of course, I could Fang you. All the way, that is," he said with a look of contempt at Kalmar.

"We'd rather die," Janner said.

"Good." Gnag squirmed across the floor and Amrah picked him up. "Call the Fangs. We need to get to the sea."

78

Gnag's Plan

The Fangs bound the children's hands and feet, then slung them over their shoulders just as Slarb had done with Leeli all those months ago in Glipwood.

When they emerged from the cellar, the sun was high, fighting its way through the smoke. It was Janner's first real look at his ruined homeland, and it, along with Gnag's possession of a new and greater melding stone, drove out what little hope remained in Janner's heart.

Gnag had the stone. They had helped him get it. And Nia! She was captured, which meant that Oskar and Podo were as well—if they were alive at all. Ban Rona had fallen. Uncle Artham was an ocean away.

Janner felt his anger rising against not just Gnag but the Maker himself. If the Maker was a speaker of worlds, a benevolent lord of all that was, then why would he allow such misery, such relentless destruction of all that was good and true? Janner wanted to cry, but the heat of his anger burned away the tears. Besides, bouncing along on the shoulder of a stinky Green Fang made it hard to think clearly enough to grieve the way he wanted to. He resigned himself to defeat and stared listlessly at the Fang's feet as they marched through the black mud.

"Take them to the ship," Murgah said.

They were gagged and placed in a ratty carriage and driven back to the sea. They rode in silence for a long while, until the smell of salt-water cut through the smoke and grime and Fang stench.

Once they were on the ship, they were consigned to a dark cabin. A Grey Fang untied them and pointed to a bucket of water and a tray that held a bowl of gruel and several hunks of stale bread.

"Eat if you want."

The Fang locked the door behind him, and for the first time since Janner's birthday party, the three children were able to talk. Leeli told them Gnag's story, about Bonifer and Madia and the twins. Janner remembered what Bonifer had said on the night Esben died. *I did it for love.* It was hard to believe, but all the puzzle pieces fit.

"What's going to happen?" Leeli asked.

"Gnag wins." Janner took a gulp of water and wiped his mouth. "And we helped him do it. Or *you* did, at least."

"What do you mean?" Leeli's voice was small and weak.

"You played the song. You said we should just open the door for him."

"He said he would torture Mama!" she shouted.

"He was probably going to torture her anyway. Only now he has exactly what he needs to do it right!"

"Janner—" The tone of Kalmar's voice was a warning to ease off. Kalmar scooted closer to Leeli.

Janner ignored him. "Why were you so determined to open the Fane?" he demanded.

Leeli blinked back tears. "Because I thought—I thought—"

"*What* did you think?"

"I thought that if it was true that the Maker walked in the Fane of Fire, then maybe he would stop Gnag. Maybe he would be waiting in there for him and he might help us."

Janner leaned his forehead against the door and sniffled. The Maker. Once again, he had failed them. "I thought the Maker would help us, too," he said quietly. "But it looks like we're on our own. If he's real, he doesn't care."

"Don't say that," Kalmar said.

Janner looked up. "Why not?"

"Because we're alive. And we're together. We don't know for sure what's happened to Ban Rona, or to Mama or Grandpa. Maybe—maybe there's still reason to hope."

"Maybe there's not."

"But maybe there *is*," Kalmar said.

Janner sighed and plopped onto the cot. It was a pointless argument. The Maker would do what he would, and they would suffer for it.

The children sat in an uncomfortable silence until the door opened and a Green Fang grinned at the three of them. "Gnag needsssss you, girl."

It grabbed Leeli by the arm and yanked her out of the room. The boys called after her and beat the door, but it wouldn't budge.

"What is he doing?" Kalmar asked.

"Whatever he wants," Janner muttered.

They heard voices and footsteps on the deck. The ship rocked, but it wasn't under sail. As far as Janner could tell, they were still at the dock.

Gnag's possession of the new and greater stone gave Janner a terrible feeling, worse than despair or dread or even fear. It was a feeling of vast and inescapable emptiness, as if Gnag had found a way to open a portal into a great nothingness where Aerwiar itself didn't exist, light didn't exist—where even, perhaps, the Maker didn't exist. He sensed in Gnag's scheming the end of all things.

Janner was sweating and shivering at the thought, as if a fever had ambushed him. Angry as he was with the Maker, he prayed to him, begging him to be real, to have some end in mind that would surprise them, Gnag most of all. But from his dark cabin on a ship docked on the shores of a blackened island, Janner couldn't fathom it. Whatever Gnag was planning would be terrible in ways the world had never seen.

Then the brother's heads whipped up. Leeli was playing her whistleharp. Janner and Kalmar held their ears to the door. After a few strains of the melody passed, Gnag's voice cut through: "That's not it. You can't fool me, girl." They heard Leeli crying.

Janner rattled the door handle in desperation.

"No! I won't do it!" Leeli sobbed.

Footsteps thudded across the deck and stopped outside the door. The lock clicked and a Fang flung open the door, then several more Fangs rushed in and dragged the boys, kicking and screaming, from the cabin.

Leeli leaned on her crutch at the stern, weeping in the wind. Amrah stood behind her, gripping her shoulders. Gnag was still in Murgah's arms, hugging a satchel to his chest.

"Now, Song Maiden of Anniera, you will play 'Yurgen's Tune,' or I'll have your brothers killed. Don't think I won't do it. They have served their purpose."

"No," Leeli cried. "If he comes he'll kill us all."

"I happen to know that he won't," Gnag said in a sickly sweet voice. "Now be a good girl. *Play the song.*" He held a hand out to the Fangs and Janner felt their grip tighten. A sword edge pressed against his throat.

"No! Wait!" Leeli screamed.

Leeli wiped her nose and looked at her brothers with a terrible sadness. She shook her head in resignation and raised the whistleharp.

"Good," Gnag said. "Call him."

She was trembling, so the whistleharp squeaked at first, but she found the melody and plucked the strings as she blew. The Fangs on the ship growled, and those not holding the boys covered their ears. The wind picked up and cleared the film of smoke away, allowing weak sunlight to bathe the deck of the ship.

Leeli finished the melody, but nothing happened.

"You," Gnag said to a Bat Fang that dangled from the boom. "Fly me up there. Hurry up."

The beast took Gnag from Murgah's arms and flapped up above the mainmast, circling slowly. Gnag dangled from its arms and peered out at the gray sea.

"Play it again, girl!" Gnag shouted.

Leeli sighed and sent the melody out across the waves again.

"Look!" Gnag shouted. The Fangs, still agitated by the music, dragged Janner and Kalmar to the starboard rail and scanned the horizon. Janner spied a disturbance in the waters. The sea piled up like a hill, foam spreading out in its wake, as a massive form beneath the surface drove toward them.

"He comes, Murgah!" Gnag cried. The Fangs murmured with excitement.

The swell of water sped their way, and it wasn't slowing. Janner braced himself for impact, thinking that Yurgen would ram the ship and kill them all.

"So much for Ships and Sharks," he said to Kalmar, who nodded without taking his eyes from the coming wrath.

At the last moment the old dragon burst from the sea in a foamy blast and towered over the ship. His great bulk glistened in the smoky sunlight and trembled with fury. He swung his head from side to side and roared at the sky with all the power of the deep.

In their terror, the Fangs cowered and ran for cover, releasing Janner and Kalmar. Even Gnag the Nameless cringed as his Bat Fang struggled to stay aloft. Seawater rained down around them, and the ship heeled over sharply before righting itself and rocking in the sea.

Yurgen's voice thundered in Janner's mind.

What business have you with me?

79

The Dark Alliance

The Bat Fang clung to Gnag and bobbed in the air, its leather wings working hard to keep it aloft, while the ship below rocked in the dragon's tide.

"King Yurgen!" Gnag cried. "I come bearing a great gift!"

The dragon turned his attention from Leeli and swung his head to inspect the withered old man dangling from the bat. Gnag's milky arms were outstretched, gripping the leather satchel. *Is he giving Yurgen the stone?* Janner wondered. That was what Yurgen had wanted, according to the legend—a healing stone to save his wounded son. But that had been epochs ago, and the young dragon was long dead.

What gift? Who are you?

"I am Gnag the Nameless! From the Castle Throg."

Throg. A deep rumble issued from the dragon's chest. Yurgen knew of Throg, then. And he didn't like it. *Gnag the Nameless. I've heard of you. This age owes you its ruin.*

Gnag bowed his head, as if it were a compliment. "Yes, King Yurgen. Yet it is not ruin I seek, but glory."

The dragon narrowed his eyes and moved his head closer to Gnag. Yurgen cocked his head and issued a huff of hot breath from his nostrils. *What glory do you seek?*

"The glory of power. Of dominion. Of beauty. I am the rightful king of Anniera. You are the king of the Sunken Mountains. There was once an alliance between my kingdom and yours, and I would . . . unify us once again."

"You're no king!" Kalmar shouted.

"Silence him," Gnag said, and a Grey Fang clamped a hand over Kal's snout.

He is an Annieran of royal blood, or he wouldn't hear my voice, boy. Yurgen glanced at Kalmar, Janner, and Leeli in turn. There was no question that the dragon remembered them. Janner suspected that Yurgen remembered everything.

There ignited in Janner's chest a sensation of anger—as if boiling water had spilled out of Yurgen's heart and burned his own. Kalmar whined, thrashing in the Fang's grip. His eyes were wide with shock, and Janner knew that Kalmar beheld some inner vision Yurgen had shown him. Leeli crumpled to her knees and covered her face in her hands, wailing.

Janner didn't understand what was happening. He strained to hear Yurgen's thoughts, but they were shielded from him somehow.

The dragon turned his attention to Gnag again. *I am weary of the affairs of men. They bring only murder and sorrow. I lost my son. My dragonkin have lost many young ones to men seeking GLORY. I want not glory, but the satisfaction of vengeance. Now that I have found it*—Yurgen glanced at the Wingfeather children again—*I would rest.*

The satisfaction of vengeance? As Janner struggled to understand the old dragon's meaning, a name floated to the front of his mind: *Scale Raker.*

Podo.

Images assaulted Kalmar's mind. Yurgen's memories became his own. He saw many sea dragons, lurking in the dark blue deep. Kalmar recognized Hulwen, the crippled young dragon they had met on the *Enramere*—the one whom Podo had wounded years ago—hovering nearby, her reddish fins gliding like wings in the water.

Far above, on the surface, there was some commotion that Yurgen didn't understand. Kalmar knew by Yurgen's memories that what he saw took place in the harbor at Ban Rona, where the dragons had long smelled Scale Raker's nearness. The Podo-scent sharpened in Yurgen's mind—Kalmar's mind—and, leaving the other dragons behind, the great gray dragon swam to the surface and eased his head out of the sea, just enough to see what was happening in the city.

Kalmar saw through Yurgen's eyes. Ban Rona was overrun with Fangs—Bat Fangs above, Grey Fangs in the streets, and Green Fangs slithering through the water and onto the shores. Hollowsfolk fought them bravely, but it was clear that the Fangs would soon destroy them all.

Then Yurgen's attention fixed on one man. The man had one leg, white hair, and wielded a bone in one hand and a sword in the other. Podo. He stood near the waterfront beside a fat man with spectacles, and the dust of dead Fangs swirled around them both as they fought.

Kalmar heard, through Yurgen's senses, the words shouted by the fat man.

"We have to summon the dragons, Podo! It's our only hope!"

"Where's Leeli?" Podo shouted. "She has to play the song!"

"They took her!"

"They *what*?" Podo roared, spinning around on his stump to face Oskar.

"She was taken from the window of the Great Library!" Oskar's chin quivered and he pushed up his spectacles. "Podo, I'm sorry."

"No!" Podo closed his eyes and hung his head. "No," he repeated. "My Leeli."

Oskar and Podo stood together amidst the battle, two tired old men beholding the destruction of their world. Hollowsfolk and Fangs strove about them, and the dogs growled and howled and fell by the hundreds, and above it all Rudric's voice bellowed for bravery.

But the Fangs were too many.

"It's over," Oskar said, leaning on his sword.

Podo lifted his eyes and stared wearily out at the Fang-fraught bay, then at the Bat Fangs overhead. He seemed to have aged a hundred years in the space of a heartbeat, as if all his days and all his sorrows had caught up to him at once. Podo dusted two Grey Fangs as they rushed him, then set his gaze on the sea. The old pirate raised his sword in one hand, his legbone in the other.

"It's not over," he said through gritted teeth. "There's always a way out."

As the Green Fangs bubbled out of the water, Podo Helmer hacked his way seaward, forming a path of dust and destruction through which Oskar struggled to follow.

"Podo, no!" he cried.

"Ye said there was no other way!" Podo shouted over his shoulder as he swung sword and bone. "The dragons are our only hope."

"Podo!" Oskar fell to his knees.

Podo Helmer, son of Skree, Strander of the East Bend, Pirate of the Symian Straits, husband of Wendolyn Igiby, father of the High Queen of the Shining Isle, and beloved grandfather of the Jewels of Anniera, waded knee-deep into the Dark Sea of Darkness to meet his doom.

"Help us!" Podo screamed, batting away Green Fangs as they slithered out of the sea. "Ye can have me if ye want, but for the Maker's sake, help us!"

Kalmar shook his head and whined, wanting to cut off Yurgen's memories, wanting to stop his grandfather from setting foot in the sea. But everything he saw had already happened. He was forced to watch as Podo strode deeper into the water, as he tossed his legbone and sword aside, as Yurgen roared and exploded out of the bay along with Hulwen and several more dragons.

Scale Raker! Yurgen's mind thundered.

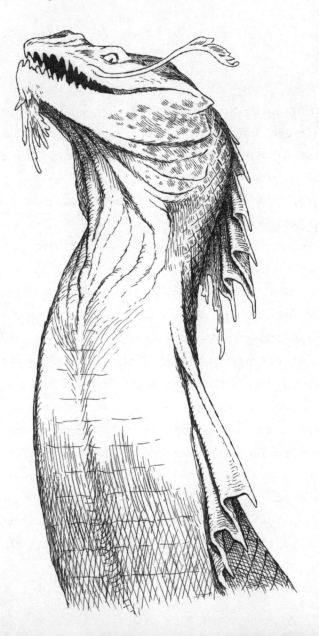

Kalmar looked down through Yurgen's eyes at his grandfather, noble and fierce and pointing at Ban Rona, shouting, "Help us!" as Yurgen's jaws widened and he thrust his great head at the old man.

"*Grandpa!*" Kalmar howled. He clutched the sides of his head and thrashed on the deck of the ship until Yurgen released his mind. Then he opened his eyes and looked at Janner, struggling to breathe through the weight in his chest. "Grandpa's gone."

Leeli crumpled to the deck and wept.

"You—you killed him?" Janner screamed. He felt the full, horrible weight of Yurgen's vengeance. The old gray dragon peered down at them with a smile in his eyes.

It was quick. Quicker and more merciful than the death that Scale Raker afforded my young ones.

Janner wanted to cry, but the air seemed to have been sucked from his lungs. He hadn't seen much, but he had heard every word between Oskar and Podo, down to the gritty determination in Podo's grunts as he strove for the water's edge.

Janner doubled over, thinking of his grandfather, thinking of the pain in the old man's eyes whenever he looked out at the sea or when he heard mention of the dragons. He didn't understand what Podo and Oskar thought would happen. There may have been an alliance with Anniera ages ago, but that didn't mean Yurgen the Dragon King would suddenly give aid to the Hollowsfolk. Obviously, he hadn't.

And yet knowing that Yurgen had seen the impending destruction of Ban Rona, had seen that Podo was trying to get him to help, and had still done nothing—it made Janner's soul smolder with rage.

Janner clenched his fists and met Yurgen's eyes with all the anger he could muster. "You didn't have to kill him!"

There was justice in his death, boy. Scale Raker would have agreed.

"He was only trying to get you to help! At least you could have stayed and fought the Fangs. Then his death would have meant something."

Now Janner joined Kalmar and Leeli in their weeping.

It meant something to me. It meant vengeance. And now I am finished with the affairs of men.

"But—" Janner said.

"Silence him, too!" Gnag snapped, and before Janner could say another word a Green Fang's cold hand covered his mouth.

Janner tried to order his thoughts, to demand of Yurgen a better answer, but grief stole his words and he could only cry. His tears ran down his cheeks and wet the scales on the Fang's hand.

"Yurgen the Mighty!" Gnag fumbled with the satchel and waved for the Bat Fang to fly him closer to the dragon. "I bring you proof of my goodwill."

What proof? Yurgen seemed disinterested. Gnag unlatched the bag and grinned at the dragon as he lifted out the ancient stone.

But it wasn't the stone.

Janner blinked away his tears. It was a skull. A white, clean human skull.

Gnag held it over his head triumphantly. "If it's justice you want, I deliver it to you in the name of our new alliance. This is the head of Ouster Will, betrayer of the dragons, slayer of your son."

Yurgen's old eyes widened, and his grey bulk quivered with emotion. His head rocked back on his long, sleek neck and swayed in the air as he opened wide his jaws and roared at the sky. Smoke poured out of the dragon's throat as from a chimney, and foam frothed the sea.

"I killed him," Gnag said with a bow of his head.

He threw the skull into the air, and Yurgen lunged forward, snapping it up in his jaws. He swallowed it with a moan of pleasure, and Janner shuddered at the thought of Podo's similar fate. Slowly, Yurgen's

quavering ceased, his eyelids drew open, and he gazed at Gnag with a
wickedly satisfied smile. He even licked his lips.

An alliance, you say?

"Yes, Yurgen. Let us reign together. Let us build the world as we
see fit. Let us subdue men and women and their vile cities. Let us hold
sway over the sea, air, and land. I have done so much already. But with
your help we will rule Aerwiar in defiance of the Maker who in his
foolishness gave dominion to man and his offspring. Never again shall
you lose a son or young dragon. Never again shall I be cast off like a
dead rat." Gnag stretched out his white arms. "Join me."

The water at Yurgen's sides churned as he rose higher from the sea
and stretched out his wing-like fins. The two faced one another like old
friends about to embrace.

All the grief in Janner's heart turned to white-hot terror. Who
could defeat such a force? Gnag with all his minions, and Yurgen with
the strength of all the dragons in the sea at his command. All the good
kings of Anniera must have groaned in their graves.

And yet the Maker was silent. Such evil played out under the Maker's gaze, and he said nothing, did nothing. *Why?* Janner wondered
with a despairing terror.

"Then let us seal our alliance with a song," Gnag said. Janner saw
him glance at the old Stone Keeper, and she gave a subtle nod.

Yurgen bowed his head toward Gnag. *What song shall we sing,
Slayer of Ouster Will?*

"I know just the one," Gnag said.

80

The Melding

Gnag the Nameless sang the song of the ancient stones.

Yurgen closed his eyes and swayed with the melody. He even raised his mountainous voice and hummed along, as if it were an old tune he was struggling to recall. Gnag's eyes widened madly as he grinned at Murgah and struggled to maintain the melody in his rapture. Janner was dizzy with fear, unable to move or to take his eyes away from the unfolding evil.

Kalmar whipped his head from the Fang's grip and screamed, "Yurgen, no!" Leeli tried to play her whistleharp but Amrah knocked it away and held Leeli's arms behind her back.

The Grey Fangs and Green Fangs all watched with their mouths hanging open, awestruck at the genius of their master's scheme come to fruition.

Murgah reached into her satchel and removed the ancient stone in a burst of light that cut through the smoke like the sun through a storm cloud. The golden beams bathed everything they touched with a buttery glow, but when they fell on one soul in particular—the one with a heart bent toward transformation, and that for the sake of its own power—the light infused the singer with whatever life lay nearest to it. Gnag shouted a command and the Bat Fang squealed and flung him onto the dragon's back. Gnag tumbled downward, arms and useless legs akimbo, a look of unbridled joy on his face as he thudded into Yurgen.

Then it happened.

Gnag's blood and bone comingled with Yurgen's ancient power. The old dragon's heart was also bent toward the promise of power, that of a dark alliance with Gnag, and though he knew not what was happening, he sensed the surge of the stonelight's melding and leaned into it wholly. He welcomed the melding, old as he was and eager to rend and ravage the world as he had done at the end of the First Epoch.

The ancient stone flashed so brightly that the Fangs and children alike shrank from it. Janner forced open his eyes. A whirl of steam engulfed Yurgen and Gnag, twisting upward like a waterspout, spewing its offense at the gray sky. Water bubbled and foamed. A sound like distant thunder pulsed from the vortex and rattled the ship's timbers and its passengers' teeth.

The Stone Keeper covered the stone again, and the world went dim, lit only by the red sun beyond the curtain of smoke.

Janner didn't want to look, but he couldn't help himself. If he was going to die, he wanted to see the monster that would kill him.

A silhouette emerged from the steamy haze.

The Gnag-Dragon stood knee deep in the sea, half-man and half-beast, taller than the ship's mast. Gnag's head had grown to the size of a boulder and remained bald and white, wrinkly and freckled with age. His nose and mouth were elongated just enough to suggest a snout without diminishing his human likeness. His eyes were closed as he worked his jaw and rolled his head to the left and right, adjusting to the feel of his new frame. The great head was mounted to wide shoulders. His chest glistened with gray scales that plated his flesh down to two strong legs as thick as trees. His arms, also sinuous and strong, flexed, his clawed fingers as long as oars closing and opening on empty air.

He looked, at first, merely like a giant, uncrippled version of the old Gnag the Nameless. That would have been bad enough. But then he spread his wings—wicked brown wings that worked in and out like the sails of a demon ship. There was no doubt that they were capable of carrying Gnag in flight. Then Janner saw the long dragon tail whipping about in a froth of seawater.

The Gnag-Dragon at last opened its eyes, which had become two black orbs with vertical slits for pupils. Those terrible eyes blinked and looked about at the sky, the burned island, the dock, the ship, and finally the frightened souls on the deck.

The Fangs had all fallen on their faces, along with the Stone Keepers, and Murgah hugged the satchel holding the ancient stone as if for survival.

Only Janner, Leeli, and Kalmar remained on their feet. They stepped over the backs of the prone Fangs and stood together, holding hands on the rocking ship.

"Bow to your king," Gnag said, and Janner also heard the words in his mind as he had heard Yurgen's:

BOW TO YOUR KING.

"Never." Kalmar stood between Janner and Leeli, looking up at Gnag defiantly. "I already told you. You're no king."

Gnag arched his back and roared, revealing the same broken, brown teeth (though they were now as big as doors). He angrily whipped the waves with his tail and spread his arms and wings as wide as he could—then he saw, floating in the sea, a shriveled husk of dragonskin—what was left of Yurgen. Gnag lifted it out of the water with two of his fingers and wrinkled his nose. Then with a chuckle he tossed the skin out into the sea, where what was left of Yurgen the Dragon King sank away.

Gnag turned his attention back to the children. "After I destroy Ban Rona and what's left of your family, you may not feel so bold." *AFTER I DESTROY BAN RONA AND WHAT'S LEFT OF YOUR FAMILY, YOU MAY NOT FEEL SO BOLD.* Gnag's voice, within and without, tore at Janner's mind as much as his ears.

The Gnag-Dragon folded his wings. He squatted in the sea, crossing his whitish arms over his chest, then launched himself into the air with a triumphant laugh. He beat his wings clumsily at first, but then they found a rhythm so hard and sure that it seemed a storm had descended on the world. The ship was torn from its moorings and careered out into the open sea.

The Gnag-Dragon rose higher and higher, his deep and wicked laughter sounding across the wide world. Then he swooped low, his tail skimming the surface of the Dark Sea, and flew north and east, in the direction of Ban Rona. He circled as high as the clouds, but his voice boomed clear and close:

"FOLLOW."

FOLLOW, he said in Janner's mind. *I WANT YOU TO SEE IT, CHILDREN. I WANT YOU TO KNOW MY POWER.* The voice was somehow Yurgen's *and* Gnag's—all of the old dragon's strength along with Gnag's hatred, doubled by the hunger for vengeance that each of them carried.

Murgah clambered to her feet. "Set sail for Ban Rona! Witness the victory of your king!"

The Fangs hurried about the ship, ignoring the Wingfeather children completely, and minutes later, the ship caught the wind and cut the waves in the wake of Gnag's flight. Murgah shouldered the satchel with the ancient stone, passed the children without a glance, and disappeared into the captain's quarters with Amrah on her heels.

It seemed to Janner that the Maker had betrayed them yet again, because a foreboding storm gathered behind them and the air howled with a steady gale, blowing them straight and swift to the shores of the Hollows.

"What do we do?" Leeli shouted over the wind, wiping tears from her cheeks.

"What *can* we do?" Kalmar said.

"What have we ever been able to do?" Janner asked bitterly. "Nothing."

He dropped wearily to the steps that led to the upper deck and sat with his head down. Kalmar and Leeli sat beside him, shivering in the blustering cold, damp with sea spray.

Behind them, the charred shores of Anniera shrank to a dim, dead shadow in the distance, while before them, beyond the reach of the driving storm, the hills of the Green Hollows rose from the sea like the backs of drowned giants, growing ever more vivid.

Gnag the Nameless reveled in the violent wind, looping and tumbling, gliding down past the port side of the ship only to flap his wings and rise again. His laughter dwarfed the thunder.

Janner had little doubt that whoever yet lived in Ban Rona heard Gnag's voice on the wind like the pealing of doomsday bells.

81

The Destruction of Ban Rona

Is he really dead?" Leeli asked.

Kalmar leaned against the forecastle steps with his eyes closed. He looked as sad and worn as a stray dog. "I saw it all," he said. "It *was* quick, at least."

Leeli stared into space, listless.

Janner put his arm around her and pulled her close. He wanted to cry, but he was too tired to feel anything but defeat. "Look," he said, pointing out beyond the bow. In the distance they saw the masts of dozens of ships. Gnag's armada was clustered at the mouth of the Watercraw.

Leeli wiped her nose. "I don't want to look."

Smoke clouded the air over the bluffs, much as it had over the Isle of Anniera. Janner hung his head. Everywhere Gnag went, smoke and ruin were sure to follow. And what had become of Nia? Oskar? Rudric and Danniby and the O'Sallys? Guildmaster Clout? Gnag's thundering laughter seemed to answer Janner's thoughts with mockery.

The Gnag-Dragon dove into the sea with a deafening explosion of seawater, then swam to the starboard side of the ship. His pale head rose above the ship's rail and he scanned the deck until he found the children. One of his giant hands lifted from the waves and beckoned almost playfully.

Come here, he said in Janner's head. When Janner didn't move, he repeated, *COME HERE. All of you.*

The three children stood and edged closer to the rail. Gnag stared at them with eyes like caves, deep and black and terrible.

I want this to be a surprise.

Gnag's hand shot out and grabbed the children, squeezing them together in his fist. Leeli's crutch pressed against Janner's back. Gnag's wet grip was cold and squishy, and though Leeli screamed and the boys grunted, they weren't crushed.

Gnag swam away from the ship, his tail slithering through the water, while the Fangs furled the ship's sails and lashed it to another outside the craw. The children struggled uselessly while the Gnag-Dragon pushed his way through the city of ships as playfully as a child in a tub of toys. Gnag raised a finger to his lips and said, "Shhh!" with a threatening squeeze.

The storm behind them billowed in the sky, blowing steadily though there was yet no rain. Janner heard little over the wind and the hollow thump of ship on ship while Gnag eased his way among them.

"My lord!" said Murgah from the deck. "Wait!"

"SHHH!" Gnag said, scowling over his shoulder.

"But we didn't name you!" Amrah shouted.

"Don't you remember?" Gnag asked with a grin. "I have no name! *Now be quiet!* I want my nephews and niece to watch as my Fangs behold Ban Rona's destroyer."

Murgah waved her arms. "But—"

Gnag lifted himself a little way out of the water and growled, just enough to see her shrink back, then he continued on his way. Janner tried not to think about how icksome Gnag's hand felt, and he tried to think even less about the awful sight that lay on the other side of the Watercraw.

Gnag swam to the southern side of the craw and drew himself out of the fitful sea, a monster from a scarytale creeping up the crags. His wings flapped for balance, then he opened them so that they caught the east wind and pressed him to the cliff.

When he reached the brink, he paused and held the children close to his face. If he had wanted to, he could have swallowed the three of them in one stenchuous gulp. Janner's eyes wandered across the fleshy white face, porous and veined. Hairs as thick as branches lined the inside of the monster's nose. Gnag saw Janner's disgust and smiled.

"Even now, you Annierans think me hideous. Mother Madia would be so proud of you. But I shall teach you of beauty. The beauty of power."

"There are different kinds of power," Kalmar said.

"Nonsense." Gnag curled his lip. "Behold, Jewels of Anniera, the great city of Ban Rona!"

Gnag flapped his wings and leapt over the edge of the cliff with a roar. He landed on the top of the cliff and struck a mighty pose. His wings fanned out to their full width, and he lifted the children over his head and whipped his tail in the stormy bellows while lightning scraped the sky behind him.

Janner didn't want to look, but look he did.

Broken planks and splintered hulls floated in the harbor where ship and dock alike had been crushed. Torn sails floated sadly in the flotsam. The shore was littered with armor and the remains of wall and pier and barricade. The gutted husks of all the buildings of Ban Rona smoked silently—and not a soul could be seen.

It was as if the battle had raged a month ago and was left to rot—but it was only yesterday that Leeli had been taken. Where was everyone?

Janner felt Gnag's hand tremble. His wings folded and his hands drooped to his sides as he turned left and right, looking dejectedly for someone or something to admire him.

What has happened here? Gnag asked. *Where is my army?*

He leapt from the cliff and glided down along the water's surface, then alighted on the shore and scanned the city. He paced the waterfront, kicking at the detritus like a spoiled child. There were no dead bodies, no army rejoicing at its king's arrival. Not a single Fang slithered or flapped or prowled about. There was only a film of dust that coated the muddy streets like brown snow, and the warsmoke that dissipated as the first gusts of the storm howled through the Watercraw.

The monster's grip loosened, and the children slipped to the muddy shore. Gnag seemed to have forgotten about them. Janner and Kalmar helped Leeli to her feet and then backed away to hide behind a pile of rubble.

Gnag trudged up the nearest street. His dragon feet squelched the mud, scraped the cobblestones, and snapped fallen roof beams like dried sticks. The sounds of his march echoed off the bones of the dead city.

Then a faint sound drifted out of the hills.

Leeli furrowed her brow. "I've heard that song before," she said.

Another wisp of music came, clearer and pushing toward them against the wind. Janner's heart leapt, for it was a song that trickled out of the hills, a song as green as the Hollows in full spring, a song as old as Aerwiar. Janner remembered it. He couldn't recall why, but he remembered it. And it was a beautiful thing, welcome and warm amid the wreckage of Ban Rona.

Kalmar sniffed and grabbed Janner's arm. "They're at the Field of Finley."

"Who?" Janner asked.

Leeli clutched her whistleharp. "The dragons."

"Everyone," Kalmar said.

"It worked," Leeli said. "He did it." A smile washed over her face and she looked at her brothers with shining eyes. "Grandpa did it."

Thunder shook the air. The storm was about to collapse on the bay.

"I'm so confused," Janner said.

"He called the dragons. Yurgen killed him, but Hulwen—the younger dragon, remember? She must have stayed and fought. I can hear her singing."

"That doesn't make any sense. She's a *sea* dragon, remember?"

"I'm telling you, that's Hulwen's voice."

"It's true," Kalmar said. "I can smell her. Not just her, either. There are several of them. And Hollowsfolk by the hundreds." Kalmar looked at Janner with a blaze of hope in his eyes. "We need to get to the field."

Several streets away, the Gnag-Dragon's head bobbed above the rooftops as he wandered through the city, kicking and stamping and muttering to himself. Janner sensed his thoughts, and they were all confusion and wrath and disappointment. He seemed a monstrous child in search of a lost toy.

But as they watched, he stopped in his tracks, canted one ear to the air and listened. Then he whipped his great bald head to the east with a grunt.

"No!" Kalmar howled. "Leave them alone!"

Gnag looked over the rooftops and fixed the three of them with a wicked glare. He bowed mockingly, then ran up the length of Apple Way toward the edge of the city. His tail smashed buildings as he sped past and gained speed, until he opened his wings and took to the air.

When he flew over the Great Hall, he swooped and shouldered its stout walls in an explosion of stone that mingled with the thunder overhead. The Great Tree shuddered and limbs cracked loose in splinters. Gnag laughed with the glee of his power and sped over the hill and down into the hollows, straight for the Field of Finley.

"We have to warn them," Kalmar said. Then he ran. He bolted like a gray arrow, arms and legs pumping with all the strength in his heart.

"Come on, Leeli!" Janner said, grabbing her elbow.

"Wait." Leeli stood her ground. "I still have this." She held out her whistleharp and arced one of her eyebrows just as Podo would have done. "Maybe they'll hear me."

Janner didn't want to disappoint her, but there was no way her little whistleharp's call could reach the field.

Then the storm descended on the city. The wind howled like Janner had never heard, and he and Leeli struggled to keep their feet.

82

The Battle Begins

Leeli had no song in mind. She reached deep into her soul, the music flowering from the rich soil of a hundred tunes she had sung or played over the years. The bouquet she gathered was simple and warm, glimmering with all the hope her love had planted.

Janner stood behind her with his eyes closed, abandoning all his resentment toward the Maker and praying boldly for the song to speed over the hills to the Field of Finley.

The storm was dark but not malevolent, a joyful blast of thunder and rain, wind and wildness. It scoured the town of every mote of Fang dust, every loose shingle, every fragment of waste. It lifted Leeli's song like a pebble and sent it skipping across the rolling, spring-green hills and hollows—but the storm also seemed to hammer the song into the ground, where Janner sensed it pulsing eastward, flowing like an underground river.

Janner shut his eyes and struggled to keep his footing as his Durgan cape whipped around him and Leeli both, snapping like a flag in the gale as Leeli gave herself over to the magic of the music, heedless of the stinging rain and crashing thunder.

"Your Highness, there's a storm coming," Oskar said.

"I see it."

Nia and the other weary survivors of the Battle of Ban Rona were gathered on the Field of Finley to pay tribute to their dead. Old and young, wounded and able, they came to the field believing the great battle—and perhaps even the war—was over. With the sea dragons' help, the last of the Fangs had been dusted, and it seemed there was no one left to fight.

Hulwen the Dragon Princess watched the ceremony from the eastern end of the field; the graceful, battered length of her amber body shone like a jewel in the valley's palm. Her front two fins, now that she was out of the water, looked more like wings, her rear fins like legs. Six other dragons, old and young, also rested at the edges of the field, and Hollowsfolk from every clan were scattered among them.

At the center of the field a bier blazed, and Rudric stood near the fire with his head bowed. Hulwen sang the lay for Yurgen's son, the same melody they always raised at the cliffs of Glipwood under the sundered summer moon.

"Wait! Quiet!" Nia said, and the dragons lifted their great heads to listen.

"What is it, Your Highness?" Oskar asked. He sat on the wet grass with the First Book in his lap and peered up at Nia. He heard the melody as the wind burst over the field and his eyes widened. "Is it—"

"Yes!" Nia cried. "It's Leeli!"

The Hollowsfolk murmured. The dogs whined and wagged their tails.

Then, against the black canvas of the sky, Gnag swooped over the rise and landed on the hill. He struck the same pose he had employed in vain at the Watercraw. Nia screamed. Rudric gasped and drew his warhammer.

Gnag heard Nia's scream and smiled down at the gathering on the field. Then his smile faded. He saw the dragons as they lifted themselves to their full height on their fins and stared at him with defiance.

The survivors faced Gnag, their courage wakened by Leeli's music as it had been when the city was under siege, and drew their weapons. At the sight of the monster, they might have cowered, might have cast themselves upon Gnag's mercy or fled, but with the melody surging through the air and earth, piercing their hearts with its great beauty, wounds were forgotten, strength was replenished, and fear only served to renew their fury.

A gray form appeared at the top of the hill, no more than an arrow-shot north of the Gnag-Dragon.

"Kalmar?" Nia whispered.

Kalmar answered with a mighty howl that mingled with Leeli's song, the whistling gale, and the shouts of the Hollowsfolk. He called them to battle with the authority of a high king of Anniera.

"Fight! Fight for the dead and the living! For the hills and hollows and the Shining Isle!" His ancestral blood spoke the words and his heart answered his own call as if he had been overtaken by a soul more courageous than his own.

Kalmar ran straight toward Gnag. He bared his teeth and attacked. With a fool's bright and reckless will, he leapt onto Gnag's scaly leg and scrambled to his back. Gnag grunted with surprise and clawed at Kalmar like a man swatting at a wasp.

The Hollowsfolk charged with the dragons and dogs and sped up the hill to aid their king. Gnag was distracted by Kalmar long enough to be caught off guard by the living wave that crashed upon him. Dragons snapped at his arms and legs, Hollish men and women hacked with sword and beat with hammer, and the hounds of the Hollows tore at his heels.

Gnag tottered and fell, a thrash of wings and white flesh struggling against their holy wrath.

Then came the rain. All creation was bent against Gnag's black soul as the storm descended and the warriors rose. It seemed for a moment that it would be as easy as that.

But Gnag's strength was great and his hatred greater. He burst from the cluster. Kalmar and the Hollowsfolk flew away like leaves in a gust; the dragons tumbled back.

Gnag snarled, bared his rotten teeth, rolled his bulging black eyes, and leapt into the air with a growl of triumph. He spread his wings and flapped free. The wind kicked him from side to side, but he gloated in the sky, feinting and diving amidst flashes of lightning, then swooping to batter Hollowsfolk, dogs, and dragons alike.

Kalmar stood at the center of the melee with a sword he had taken up from a fallen Hollish warrior. "Come down and fight!" he screamed, and his words roused the warriors again.

Gnag loosed a bestial bellow and dove again, aiming for Kalmar alone. Kalmar dove to the side, affording the dragons and warriors a chance to stab and bite at the monster. Gnag flapped into the air again. He was wounded, with blackish sludge running down his flanks instead of red blood, yet he was unfazed, and again he exulted. He circled above and laughed like the thunder that rumbled over the field.

"Kal!" Nia shouted, running up the hill with the others. "Where are Leeli and Janner?"

"They're alive," he answered without taking his eyes from Gnag. "They're at Ban Rona." Nia wanted to hug him and knew he wanted to be hugged, but this wasn't the time. He wasn't just her son—he was the king, and the people needed a king to follow.

"Kalmar," Rudric said as he approached. "Is that him?"

"Gnag the Nameless," Kalmar said, "but worse."

Nia stood beside Kalmar and watched Gnag, wondering how they would defeat such an enemy, even with the sea dragons on their side. She looked at Hulwen, who pushed herself up as well as she could, snapping vainly at the air. The other dragons did the same. For the moment, Gnag seemed content to taunt them as he circled them in the air.

"What is he doing?" Kalmar asked. Gnag's attention was drawn to the hills in the south, as if he were peering at the distant mountains, thinking of his lair.

"He's leaving," Nia said angrily. "We can't let him escape. This is our chance to end this forever."

"He's not leaving. Maker help us." Kalmar pointed to the south.

Gnag threw back his head and bellowed, "COME, MY MINIONS! SUBDUE AND DESTROY!"

Kalmar, Nia, and Rudric watched a tide of ridgerunners pour into the valley. Grey Fangs ran among them, shouting orders. Some of the ridgerunners whirled slings over their heads while others shot arrows— the first of which thunked into Hulwen's side. She roared with pain as she heaved her girth around to meet the onrush.

The Hollowsfolk gathered into a line and braced for the ridgerunners' charge. They were a skirmishing race, unaccustomed to open battle, so no eye had ever seen so many of them in one place.

Kalmar shouted for them to stop. They were enemies, yes, but were in truth only loyal to themselves and their fruit. Nia knew it was some empty promise of reward from Gnag that now drove them to their doom. Hollish warriors looked to Kalmar for orders; they didn't want to slay the ridgerunners, but there were thousands of them.

Ridgerunner arrows and stones wounded and killed Hollish brothers and sisters, mothers and fathers just as surely as if Fangs had loosed them. The first of the little creatures fell easily to the Hollish defense as Gnag wheeled and the storm shook the heavens. There was little to do but fight back. The uncertainty of the Hollowsfolk turned to desperation as they realized how outnumbered they were.

Then, as the Gray Fangs among the ridgerunners pushed through, howled and struck, another wave of Green, Grey, and Bat Fangs swept over the hill behind them. They had sent the ridgerunners first to take the brunt of the Hollish defense.

The sea dragons did their part, raking their fins and tails through the ranks of ridgerunners, roaring and chomping and pounding as if threshing wheat. Even Oskar N. Reteep had found a sword and swung it like an old woman swatting flies. Ridgerunners fell, but more came—and more streamed in from the hills. Every minute, more Hollish warriors and dogs died, and it was clear that soon there would be nothing to do but surrender or be crushed.

Everything Nia knew to be true of the men and women of the Hollows told her that they would never surrender; when the storm passed, the sun would shine on a field of death and defeat. The dragons might survive, but what of that? They would make their way back to the sea and live on in the silent deeps.

"Slay them all!" Gnag said as he swooped overhead.

Nia, jostled by warriors pressing into battle from the rear, looked behind them as if some unforeseen aid might sweep over the opposing hill, but none came. Who was left to fight? These were the last of the Hollowsfolk. There were no more Annierans.

Then her eyes were drawn to the west, toward Ban Rona, and she saw that Janner and Leeli had reached the field at last. They stood together in the wind and rain, looking on with shock. Their eyes met Nia's, and the strength of their love passed between them. Janner took a step nearer the chaos. Nia knew he wanted to fight, but she waved her arms and screamed, "Janner, no! Keep Leeli safe!"

Janner couldn't hear her, but he seemed to understand. He grabbed Leeli's hand and pulled her back, but Leeli jerked her arm away and lifted her whistleharp to her mouth. Nia fought back a shrieking ridgerunner that had broken the line, then she waved her sword in the air and shook her head. "Leeli, don't!" Leeli and Janner were helplessly exposed, standing where Gnag could swoop down and kill them in an instant. Her music would only draw his attention.

Then Nia saw Leeli pointing beyond the field and saying something to Janner. He peered into the eastern hills, and his jaw fell open.

Nia had no time to wonder what Janner had seen because Rudric shouted her name. She turned in time to face a wounded Gray Fang with a short sword. It snarled at her and lunged. Nia tried to dodge the blow, but two ridgerunners were tugging at her dress and threw her off balance. Just before the Fang's sword struck, Rudric's hammer slammed into the Fang's chest and sent it soaring backwards. It turned to dust before it hit the ground.

The six dragons—for one had fallen—writhed under a heap of stabbing ridgerunners, hundreds of the little beasts on each of them. Poor Hulwen moaned as she struggled. Everywhere Nia looked her people and allies were either wounded or dead—and above it all, glorying in his certain victory, was Gnag the Nameless.

83

Hulwen's Healing

Oood!" Janner shouted, all but dancing for joy. The troll was a long way off, cresting the opposite hill, but Janner knew it was him. He didn't understand how, but he didn't care. Oood was alive.

And he was riding something. That something had a mouthful of dangerous yellow teeth—and it mooed. The toothy cow turned its head to snap at Oood, and the troll thumped its jaw and waved a disapproving finger. The cow obeyed.

Just behind Oood, a throng of lurching, misshapen cloven appeared on the hill and spread out on either side of him. Elder Cadwick galloped up next to Oood and surveyed the chaos. He raised a sword and shouted, and his voice carried through the rain and wind to Janner and Leeli.

"I can't believe it." Janner laughed and pointed. "I can't believe it!"

"Who is it?" Leeli asked.

"The cloven," Janner said. "And one wonderful troll."

Cadwick charged down the hill, and the cloven followed with Oood among them. The Fangs and ridgerunners in the fray didn't see them until it was too late. The cloven cut into the enemy's ranks like a plough into a garden plot, and Gnag's army rolled like churned soil.

There were hundreds of cloven, small and large, long-limbed and skittering, furry and lumpy—every one of them grobbling or shrieking with battle rage. Oood, who seemed to have grown since Janner had seen him last, slung his fists like battering rams.

The Fangs' morale broke. They cowered and stumbled and wailed, and then they began to retreat. Ridgerunners shot away from the slaughter like bees from a hive.

The dragons, though nearly overwhelmed, had decimated the enemy's numbers—but they'd done so at great cost. Two more of the dragons were dead, and the remaining four lurched about the field, badly wounded.

From the hill, Janner watched Kalmar, Nia, and Rudric hurry over to Elder Cadwick as the Hollish warriors stared warily at the cloven. They spoke a few words then began gathering weapons from fallen comrades and readying themselves for the next attack. Cadwick barked orders at the cloven and they reinforced the Hollish line, which was arranged protectively in front of the battered dragons.

The battle lulled—but only for a moment. Gnag the Nameless was enraged. He bellowed from the sky, ordering his army to attack, and the Fang commanders rallied their forces and sent a new wave streaming onto the Field of Finley.

"Janner, we have to help," Leeli said, with Podo's fire in her voice.

"Mama told us to stay back," Janner said. "I have to keep you safe."

"Then keep me safe."

Leeli broke away and limped as fast as she could down the hill. Janner followed, but made no attempt to stop her. They reached the field just as the new wave of Fangs and ridgerunners smashed into the defense.

Leeli limped straight to Hulwen and knelt at her head. The dragon was alive, but her chest rose and fell unsteadily as she struggled to breathe. Her wounds bled freely. Hulwen's broken fin—the one Podo had maimed years ago—lay in the mud near Leeli's twisted leg as she stroked Hulwen's face and spoke soothing words, oblivious to the battle.

"Janner, stay with her!" Nia shouted as she dragged a wounded warrior from the fight. "Do you hear me?"

Gnag's laughter resounded in the sky and Janner's heart sank. *He must be winning*, Janner thought.

Yes. I am, nephew.

Janner looked over Hulwen's shoulder and saw Gnag grinning at him from the hilltop, watching the battle with his white arms folded.

"Get out of my head," Janner said.

Gnag reared back and laughed again. *I'll get out of yours if you get out of mine.*

Janner's nose stung with an odor that was both rank and comforting, and he turned to see Oood trotting toward him. Janner wanted to ask the troll how he was alive and how the cloven had come to their aid, but all he said was, "You've grown."

"Brother give Oood *gooooood* water." Oood thumped his chest. "Make Oood better. Want some?" He offered Janner a large canteen.

"No, that's all right," Janner said with a weak smile.

Oood pointed at Hulwen. "Oood give dragon good water? Make her better, too."

The troll knelt beside Leeli and patted Hulwen's jaw. She opened her mouth, revealing rows of sharp, white teeth, and he poured some of the water onto her huge, ruddy tongue. Hulwen worked her jaw and dragged her tongue across the roof of her mouth. She sighed.

Leeli laid her head against Hulwen's snout. "She's dying."

Song Maiden, Hulwen said, her voice seeming stronger in Janner's mind. *My fins hurt.*

Leeli scooted along the dragon's body, took one look at the glimmering red fins, and gasped. "Janner, she's changing! Look!"

The wounds along Hulwen's flanks steamed and sealed shut. Indeed, her whole body seemed to expand—but especially her fins. There was a cracking sound, and her bones straightened in short jerks.

"Dragon have wings?" Oood said, scratching his chin.

"Oood, where did you say you got that water?" Janner asked.

Oood pointed east. "When Oood was hurt by cloven, Kahmmer bring him water. When Oood wake up, he go to find more good water, find pool in middle of trees. Big, *fat* trees! Come back and brothers gone." Oood looked sad, then he patted his canteen and smiled. "Brother give Oood good, *good* water."

Leeli laughed. "Janner—Kal found the First Well!"

Hulwen groaned, whether in pain or pleasure Janner couldn't tell. But he *could* tell that her fins were changing. But not into something new. They were being restored after ages of disuse.

Janner remembered the medallion his mother had given Commander Gnorm, the one with the Annieran symbol of the dragon. The dragon with *wings*.

"Leeli," Janner said. "They can fly."

"What?"

"Before the dragons sank the mountains, I think they could fly."

I never knew, Hulwen said. *Yurgen kept us to the sea after the mountains sank.*

With a resounding grunt, Hulwen heaved herself over onto her belly and stretched out her fins—her *wings*. They crept outward, wide and gleaming in the driving rain, and the bones snapped into place. The rear fins had changed too. No longer were they sleek and slender, but robust and strong. The spikes that had jutted out from the tips now bent and flexed like claws. She had feet. She stood on her wobbly legs and worked her wings.

Song Maiden, Hulwen said, *I need a song. An old one. Help me to fly.*

Leeli flung her crutch aside and climbed onto Hulwen's back. The dragon rolled her neck to one side, situating Leeli between her shoulder blades, just in front of her wings. Leeli clamped her legs tight around the base of Hulwen's neck, her eyes wide. She took a deep breath and then played "The Flame of Anyara," one of the oldest Annieran tunes she knew.

When Hulwen flapped her wings and lifted herself from the muddy earth, Janner's knees went weak and he plopped to the ground in wonder. Leeli Wingfeather, Song Maiden of Anniera, was riding a dragon.

Throne Warden, Hulwen said as she rose, *heal my kin.*

"Yes ma'am," Janner whispered. He blinked away his tears and looked for the other three wounded dragons amidst the fighting.

The Hollowsfolk, cloven, and dogs alike had separated into several attack formations—and the Fangs and ridgerunners were weakening. Gnag waved his arms and shouted frantically at his army. Janner spotted Rudric and Kalmar fighting side-by-side, driving deeper into the enemy with every swing of their weapons. Oskar, meanwhile, had employed his finest tactic, which was to spin like a top with his sword outstretched, flaying anything and everything within reach. (Fortunately there were no hounds or Hollish soldiers nearby.)

Then Janner spotted the three other dragons, each of them surrounded by the thickest of the fighting. There was no way to reach them.

"Oood!"

The troll pulled away from the Fangs he was pounding and smiled at Janner.

"We need to get to those dragons." Janner pointed.

Oood lowered his head and ran straight into the Fang ranks with Janner at his heels. They skidded to a stop beside a green dragon's head. Janner asked it to open its mouth, poured a bit of the water in, then pointed Oood toward the next dragon. The troll drove his way through the battle and protected Janner as he administered the water again. Janner glanced back at the green dragon and saw its wings unfolding just as Hulwen's had.

"Go!" he shouted, and Oood ran to the final dragon.

By the time the canteen was empty, all three dragons were rising into the air to join Leeli and Hulwen. The Fangs grimaced and covered their ears as Leeli's melody rode the storm winds. Roaring with elation, the dragons rose, hearkening to Leeli's song. Ridgerunner and Fang arrows bounced off Hulwen's hide and fell to the ground as Bat Fangs flung themselves at the flying dragons and were swatted away like insects. Leeli's music disoriented the Fangs and Gnag alike, bending them to the ground with its beauty.

At last, the enemy fled. Terrified Fangs and ridgerunners scurried up the hill to their master, but they found no safety there. Gnag the Nameless was wild with fury, crushing them as they approached. "Fight!" he screamed. "Fight, you cowards!"

Some obeyed Gnag and ran madly back towards the Hollish line while others ran for the hills. Fang collided into Fang halfway up the slope, and they began fighting each other. The ridgerunners, shrewd enough to sense their folly, scattered like thwaps in every direction, disappearing as quickly as they had come.

The rain stopped. The air stilled, and the rear of the cloud-wrack drifted past them. A crisp gray sheen of high clouds softened the firmament, and the air felt clean and new as the Hollowsfolk and cloven banged sword on shield and rejoiced in their victory.

The only thing that sullied the sky was Gnag the Nameless. He winged a circle above his hilltop, paying no mind to his scattered army. The monster rose higher and higher until he looked as small as a bird, then he folded his wings and dove.

He gained speed as he fell, then aimed himself at Hulwen and Leeli.

84

Beloved

As Leeli played, Hulwen veered hard to the left to dodge Gnag's attack. Lceli was forced to let go of her whistleharp and hold tight to Hulwen's neck as Gnag zoomed by, clawing the dragon's right wing as he did.

While the other three dragons harried Gnag, Hulwen flew Leeli back to the Hollish army. She skidded to a stop and lowered one shoulder so Leeli could slide down into Nia's arms.

Hulwen took to the sky again as Gnag roared and swiped. He punched the green dragon squarely in the jaw, and it tumbled backward like a windblown leaf. Gnag growled in triumph before tackling the blue one in midair. They fell together as Gnag tore with his claws. The dragon bit Gnag's shoulder and black sludge oozed from the wounds. Just before they hit the ground, they broke apart and soared into the air again. Gnag wiped the blood from his shoulder and smiled, but as the dragon rose, its strength gave out, and it tumbled to the ground.

Now only three dragons remained: a green, a gold, and Hulwen, red as embers. They looked tired and wary, hovering in the air around Gnag as he taunted them.

"He's winning," Kalmar said.

Gnag scanned the earth until he spotted the Wingfeathers. He narrowed his eyes and was about to dive when Hulwen rammed into him.

"Why does he hate us?" Nia asked quietly.

"Because Queen Madia cast him out," Leeli said.

Nia looked with surprise from the battle to Leeli. "What do you mean?"

"He's our great uncle," Janner said. "The abandoned brother of King Jru."

Oskar sputtered, looking like he was choking on a berrybun.

Nia clenched her jaw and straightened. "That's absurd. Jru Wing-feather had no brother."

"In the words of—of—" Oskar blurted.

"Gnag told me they were twins," Leeli said. "One was deformed. Madia cast him out, but Bonifer saved him and took him to Throg."

Oskar fumbled with the First Book and flipped through the pages at the back. "In the words of—"

"She would never have done such a thing," Nia said.

"In the words of Madia Wingfeather, *she didn't!*" Oskar jabbed his finger at a few lines written on the final pages of the First Book. "She didn't cast him out! She loved him!"

"What are you talking about?" Nia asked.

"She wrote it right here!" Oskar jiggled with urgency. "The end of the First Book is a brief accounting of the kings and queens of Anniera. Each sovereign added their own words to these pages. I read it ages ago, but I didn't think it mattered!"

"So Bonifer . . . *stole* Gnag?" Kalmar asked.

"He must have," Oskar said, turning his eyes to Gnag. "And then fed Gnag the lie that he was unwanted. But Madia wrote here that she held the brothers in love before she lost consciousness. When she woke, Bonifer told her the twin had died. He convinced her and Ortham to spare the kingdom the sorrow of the boy's death, so they told no one there was a twin. Madia grieved for weeks. She even named him."

"What was his name?" Kalmar asked without taking his eyes from the battle in the sky.

"I don't even want to know," Janner said. It didn't matter anymore. Gnag was about to conquer them all anyway.

"This doesn't make any sense!" Nia clung to Leeli. "What does he *want*?"

"He wants to be king," Leeli said.

"No," Oskar said. "That's what he *thinks* he wants."

Nia shook her head again. "I don't understand."

Gnag broke away from the three dragons and flew straight toward the Wingfeathers. Hulwen and the other dragons flew alongside him and bit at his flanks until Gnag reared up and attacked them again.

"What are you saying, Mister Reteep?" Janner asked.

"What Gnag really wants," Oskar said as he held out the First Book and pointed at a line of script, "is a name."

Janner read the name, and all at once he understood. He closed his eyes and pushed his way into Gnag's mind. Deep in the darkness he saw a crippled little boy. A boy wandering through a castle of horrors, a boy who had been told every day of his life that he was unwanted and unloved—worst of all, no one had even bothered to give him a name. Gnag had, after a time, named himself, choosing one that sounded as hideous as he believed himself to be, and of course it brought him no peace.

He haunted the cold halls of Throg in bitter sorrow, hungry from an emptiness he couldn't explain. It left a cavity in his soul that had hardened his heart until it was as cold and silent as a gravestone. A gravestone as nameless and blank as Gnag himself.

He destroyed Anniera to repay his mother Madia's cruelty with a greater cruelty. If he had no name, then he would *make* one for himself. More than that, he yearned to make himself beautiful, desirable, a thing of such striking aspect that if Madia could see him, she would never have cast him off like a dead rat.

And then, after the Castle Rysen was sacked, Gnag learned of the Fane of Fire and the children—the Jewels of Anniera. Treasures to their parents and their people, protected, named, and loved. Gnag's bitterness had tightened to an unholy knot of contempt. The hole in his heart was like a whirlpool, sucking life and love and beauty into itself, not to absorb but to destroy, to wipe the world clean of what had become poison to his soul.

It all unfolded in Janner's mind like a terrible dream, and he gasped for breath. He looked up at Gnag through the storm of dragon wings. The white-skulled beast caught Janner's eye in the midst of the clash, and it was clear that Gnag knew Janner had invaded his mind.

Gnag thrashed against the dragons and drove his knee into Hulwen's ribs. She shrieked and tumbled toward the earth. When she landed, she slid down the hill, leaving a muddy gouge in her wake, and lay still. An eerie silence followed, broken only by the flapping of wings. Though Hulwen was younger and smaller than the other two dragons, her defeat shocked them.

As the two dragons—the green and the gold—stared at Hulwen, Gnag lunged forward and grabbed each of their necks and flung them straight toward the earth. They slammed into the hillside, broken and dying.

Janner felt a surge of emotion in his mind, sensing Gnag's elation. Tears leaked from the corners of Gnag's black eyes as he glided over the Field of Finley with an insane smile stretched across his face.

His eyes roved the Field for another enemy who might oppose him, but all that was left was a rabble of cloven among a rabble of weary men and women, all of whom stared up at him as if at the face of death itself. Their fear was to Gnag like perfume.

A coldness coursed up through Janner's legs when Gnag's eyes came to rest on him and his family. Gnag alighted on the Field of Finley and approached, dragging his tail through the mud and stepping over the dead dragons. None of the Hollowsfolk or cloven moved. They knew their defeat.

You see, boy? Gnag's voice in Janner's mind was calm now. *All I have set out to do, I have done. All that I want, I have.*

"No, you don't," Janner said.

"Behold the dead," Gnag said, towering over the Wingfeathers. "Behold the mighty dragons, slain by my mightier hand. Think on the ruins of Anniera. Think on the death of *Esben*." Gnag gestured grandly at the death-strewn battlefield. "Behold the beauty of my works!"

He crouched before the Wingfeathers, bringing his face close. When he breathed, Leeli's hair blew back from her shoulders. "You say I don't have what I wanted? I say there is nothing left to want."

"Davion," Janner said.

Gnag stared at him. "What?"

"That's your name."

After a pause, Gnag snorted. "I have no name."

"You always have," Kalmar said. "Your name is Davion Wingfeather. Beloved of Madia."

The muscles in Gnag's face sagged a little. He blinked slowly. His wings drooped and the veins in his arms diminished. He shook his head and narrowed his eyes again. "What do you mean?"

Oskar jostled his way forward with the First Book over his head. He cleared his throat. "In the words of Madia Wingfeather, 'I gave birth to two sons—one hale and whole, the other broken and so beautiful. I named the younger Jru, and the elder Davion, for I loved him with a special love. My heart burned for them both, fierce as sunfire. But when I awoke, Bonifer told me the elder—poor Davion!—had died. I wept for a fortnight. How I longed to see how the Maker would have shaped his lovely heart.'" Oskar held the book out for Gnag to see.

"She always loved you," Leeli said.

Gnag recoiled, staggering backwards. A thousand emotions washed over his face and pulsed in Janner's mind. He shook his head and his breaths came in gasps. "No," he muttered. "You *lie!*"

"Bonifer lied," Janner said. "Ouster Will lied."

"Quiet!" Gnag screamed.

Janner sensed Gnag's thoughts—a storm of questions and hopes and regrets swirling in a sea of confusion. "You have a name, uncle."

"It means nothing," Gnag spat.

"It means everything," Kalmar said.

Gnag bared his teeth. "Madia is dead. Whatever love she had for me is DEAD."

"She may be dead," Leeli said, "but her love for you was real. It happened, and it will always have happened. Whatever you do, you can never change the truth that a baby was born, was loved, and was given a name."

Gnag coughed and dropped to one knee. He shut his eyes and gritted his teeth. "But Bonifer said . . ." He doubled over and clutched his stomach.

"What's your name?" Kalmar asked.

"I have no name." Gnag's voice had lost its enormity. His gray lips moved, and he convulsed with a sob. *I have no name. I have no name. I have no name. I have no name—*

What is your name? Janner asked in his mind.

Gnag tumbled forward, lay on his side, and hugged his knees like a child. His wings splayed in the mud around him. *I have no name.*

Leeli, Janner, and Kalmar stepped closer to Gnag's head. It was as big as a boulder, white and wet and quivering. The Song Maiden reached out her tiny hand and placed it against Gnag's cold flesh.

"What's your name?" she whispered into his giant ear.

Gnag's hands covered his face. He sobbed, and it was the saddest sound Janner had ever heard.

In a wrecked, shivering voice, he answered at last, "My name is Davion Wingfeather."

85

Aftermath

Gnag the Nameless—Davion Wingfeather—rolled onto his back. His hands slid from his face and he opened his eyes. To Janner's surprise, they had turned to a soft blue, the same color as Kal's.

He stared at the sky as tears flowed back from the corners of his eyes and pooled in the mud. The black sludge that had oozed from his wounds was now bright red and streaming from a hundred cuts and punctures. And though his monstrous size hadn't changed, he seemed smaller somehow. All his soft white flesh had gone limp like an empty sack. It was easier to see the man in the monster now.

Davion drew a long breath and exhaled a rattling sigh. He didn't seem to know where he was, or what had happened, but Janner felt his thoughts.

My name is Davion Wingfeather, Son of Madia and Ortham. My name is Davion Wingfeather, and I am dying. My name is Davion Wingfeather, and I am sorry. My name is Davion Wingfeather, and I was loved.

Without a shudder, without a convulsion or a single twitch, his last breath seeped from his lungs and he died. Gnag's body turned gray and crackled, then a gust of wind sent clouds of his ashes billowing over the hills. He was gone.

Janner, Kalmar, and Leeli felt a mighty grief—grief that Bonifer's lies had created such a monster out of the boy Madia had loved, and for all the evil those lies had loosed on the world.

How many thousands had died because of Gnag's hatred and pain? Janner thought of the Annierans who fell in the invasion, the terror of all the Skreeans kidnapped and killed and melded, the death of so many Hollowsfolk on this day and every day since the war began. But despite all the destruction, Janner now felt more pity for Gnag than anger.

"Children," said Nia. She knelt and stretched out her arms. They sank into her embrace. As she cried, the promise of the coming peace dawned in Janner's heart and he cried with her. All that was left of the Wingfeather family sat in the mud, a pitiful but joyous sight.

"Ma'am, I'm sorry to interrupt, but there's little time," Oskar said as he removed his spectacles and wiped his nose. "It's Rudric."

Nia brushed herself off and climbed to her feet. "Where is he? What's wrong?"

Oskar led her through a somber throng of Hollowsfolk and cloven. The Keeper of the Hollows lay on his side among the slain, struggling to breathe. A Fang sword protruded from his back, along with seven ridgerunner arrows.

Rudric's face was pallid as he stared into the empty air. "Nia," he whispered. "I'm sorry. I didn't know."

She sat beside him and laid her head on his shoulder. His bleeding wounds and the weapons lodged in his body arrayed him with glory. He had defended his city, his country, and his kin to the last, and lived to see the dawn of restoration. His body was limp as a rag, but his right fist was yet clenched on the hilt of his warhammer.

"Let go," Nia said, peeling back his fingers with great care. The hammer slipped to the mud. "Your people are safe."

"I'm sorry. I didn't mean to . . . Esben—"

"All is forgiven, my love," Nia whispered.

Rudric closed his eyes. Nia placed a lingering kiss on his forehead, and when she drew back, he had passed through the veil to the welcoming song of his fathers at the Maker's Feast.

When Janner turned away from Nia's anguished face, the tragedy of war settled on his heart. Everywhere he looked, the fallen lay. They had given their lives, so there was a kind of beauty in it, but that beauty was only a blanket over a mountain of sorrow. There were slain cloven. Dogs nestled, breathless and still, against the bodies of their masters. There were dead ridgerunners, too. A lament rose to the heavens as the survivors mourned.

"Baxter!" Leeli knelt as the big dog ran her way. He slammed into her and she toppled backward as the dog licked her face and ears. She sat up and click-whistled something to him. The dog barked and bolted away.

"Where's he going?" Thorn O'Sally asked as he made his way through the crowd.

"Thorn!" Leeli pulled herself to her feet and jumped into his arms. Now it was Thorn who toppled backward with Leeli on top of him. She blushed and stood up, brushing off the front of her muddy dress. "Sorry. Baxter's, um, going to round up the other dogs to help with houndricks. We need to get the wounded to Ban Rona."

Thorn cleared his throat, too embarrassed to look her in the eye.

Leeli twirled her hair. "I'm glad you're safe. Where's your dad? And Kelvey?"

"They're all right." He pointed to Kelvey and Biggin, tending to two wounded dogs. "Hurt, but not real bad."

After the shock of Gnag's death passed, the survivors busied themselves with the wounded. With Rudric dead, the Hollowsfolk were leaderless and unsure of how to proceed. Nia gave orders, and soon the Field of Finley was a bustle of activity. Hollish warriors tended humans and cloven alike, and soon Oood and the able cloven joined them, carrying the maimed to houndricks or administering water. Janner was amazed to see how readily the Hollowsfolk accepted help from the cloven when only months ago they were ready to destroy any that crossed their borders.

Across the field, Hulwen groaned, rolled to her feet, and made straight for the other dragons. Of the seven, four were dead and the rest were injured. They spoke with one another using grunts and hums and huffs of air, nosing one another's wings with admiration as they flexed their new legs. Their musical speech was a welcome sound after the cacophony of battle. It quieted, however, when Hulwen directed them to help her move the slain dragons to the center of the field.

Guildmaster Clout and Olumphia Groundwich were among the survivors, as were Nibbick and Grigory Bunge. Danniby and many of the guildmasters and guildmistresses had lost their lives in defense of the Guildling Hall and the Great Library. Many of the guildlings had been protected from the worst of the fighting, however, so there were happy reunions, too. In all, Oskar reported that there were four hundred and sixty-two survivors, though that number dropped as the hours passed and wounds claimed more casualties.

Oood helped gather the wounded, but his odor was so severe that he sent many of the warriors into coughing fits. "Oood," Janner said as he trotted over. "How about taking a rest? I want you to meet my family."

At the word "family," Oood's face fell, then he grunted and followed Janner to Nia and the others.

"Mama, this is my friend Oood, a son of a poet from the Jungles of Plontst. He saved Kal and me in the Blackwood."

Without hesitation Nia embraced the smelly beast and pulled him down so she could kiss his cheek. "Thank you for taking care of my sons. I'm in your debt."

Oood's callous, warty cheeks turned red as apples and he grinned so wide that his eyes disappeared. Leeli giggled and Kalmar patted Oood's shoulder.

"Janner and Kal save Oood, too," he said with a bashful shrug. He played with his bellybutton absentmindedly and looked at the ground. "Oood think Janner's mama pretty lady."

Nia smiled. "Thank you. I'm sure your mother is pretty, too."

Oood's eyes twinkled and he nodded eagerly. "Oood's mama SO pretty, like a pile of grkkle smeegs." His face fell again. "Oood miss his mama and papa. Want to go home now."

"I think that's a good idea," Kalmar said. "I'm sure they miss you."

"Come to Oood's house in Glagron someday?" Oood asked. "Show you trees and castle and lobe the ocky vabs! Read poems!"

The Wingfeathers laughed and agreed that a visit would be nice.

Oood took a deep breath and looked around at the carnage. "Stay and help?"

"You've helped so much already," Janner said. "You can go home now. Gnag can't stop you. Tell your people not to smash us if we visit the Jungles of Plontst."

Oood grew serious and tapped the side of his head. "Good think. *Very* good think. Trolls smash boys they don't know." He held one finger in the air. "No worry! Oood's papa write poem about boy and wolf boy and GREAT battle. Make trolls everywhere love you."

The young troll looked around for his toothy cow, but someone— either Hollish or Fang—had slain it during the battle, which was a good thing. Without Oood to tame it, there was no telling how many people the beast might have chewed. Oood bade them farewell and set off in a jog toward the mountains, the *thud-thud-thud* of his footsteps fading slowly away into the great silence of the hills.

"He came to us after you entered the Deeps," said Elder Cadwick, cantering toward them with a hogpig woman and the backwards bear at his side. Cadwick's arm rested in a makeshift sling. Janner gasped when he saw four ridgerunner arrows protruding from his flanks. When he saw Janner's expression, Cadwick waved his good hand dismissively. "I'll be fine. Mother Mungry will tend to me soon enough."

Only then did Janner spot her bustling from warrior to warrior, fussing over their wounds but clearly more concerned with their feet than anything else. Her tail-hand scrabbled along behind her, which caused the Hollowsfolk to cringe.

"How did you know to come?" Kalmar asked.

"Oood returned, stronger than ever, which was a great mystery until he showed us the water he had recovered from the First Well. The next day our Pleaders spotted a multitude of ridgerunners and Fangs pouring out of the mountains, marching straight for Ban Rona. The troll boy convinced our queen to send us. She had already heard rumor from the spring birds and the earth itself that a great battle was coming." Cadwick took a deep breath and smiled. "I had forgotten how beautiful is the open sky over these hills."

"We thank you," Nia said.

"Of course, Your Highness," Cadwick answered with a bow. "You are as beautiful as I remembered. I was a blacksmith in the village of Pennybridge and met you and your mother Wendolyn once."

Before Nia recovered from her surprise, Mother Mungry bustled over and set to work on Cadwick's wounds. "Pennybridge?" Nia asked.

"Shoo!" Mother Mungry said. "Can't you see his foot is likely wounded?" Janner didn't bother to mention that Cadwick had hooves, not feet. "And these arrows!" Mother Mungry put her hands on her hips and shook her head. "Much work to be done on this one. If you're not either hurt or healing, it's best to stay out of the way, Your Highness. No disrespect intended."

Wincing, Cadwick knelt and muttered an apology to the Wing-feathers as Mother Mungry's hands (including her tail-hand) spidered across Cadwick's side to inspect his injuries. Kalmar yawned, which caused Janner and Leeli to yawn in turn. Janner couldn't remember the last time he had slept.

"She's right," Nia said to the children. "The day is fading and we're little help here."

The Wingfeathers and Oskar walked back to Ban Rona, but not to Chimney Hill. It was gone, Nia told the boys, burned to the ground along with hundreds of other homes and buildings. The city was all but leveled, first from the war and then the great storm and the Gnag-Dragon, but they found enough remaining shelter to house the living.

That evening as the last Hollish warrior on the field (a man named Paddy Durbin Thistlefoot) surveyed the scene from the crest of the hill, he saw the silent heaps of Hollish, cloven, and ridgerunner bodies at the center, and off to the south the dusty remains of the monster that had tried to destroy the world. He shook his head at the senselessness of it all, then trudged home in the dusk behind the others.

"Oy, Lennry!" he called to a man in the rear, helping to carry a wounded woman on a litter. "What was that thing's name again?"

"Gnag?"

"No, his *real* name. The one the Wingfeather kids told 'im."

Lennry Greensmith thought about it, then shrugged. "Don't remember."

"Me neither," said Paddy. "Let's go get some bibes."

86

Murgah and the Stone

The Wingfeathers and Oskar N. Reteep sheltered that night in what was left of the Orchard Inn. The proprietor was gone, and most of the building was gone, but there were two rooms left standing, one of which was the dining room where they had eaten on their first night in the Hollows, months before—the same room, in fact, where Janner had first met Bonifer Squoon. They swept the broken glass from the floors, gathered the driest blankets they could find, and hunkered down by the light of a candle.

Oskar lit a pipe, the scent of which made them think of Podo. Nia told the children of Podo's heroism, how none of them would have survived if he hadn't roused the dragons out of the water to fight. They all grieved for him, but the grief quickly led to the joy of remembrance, in which they told stories about him and laughed even harder than they had wept. Podo had been old, and he hated being old. "He wanted to die with his boot on," Nia said.

Then Janner and Kalmar told everyone about their adventures in the Blackwood, and Clovenfast, and about Arundelle the Cloven Queen who had sent Cadwick and the cloven to help. Nia broke into a smile when they mentioned her, because Arundelle was well known by the Wingfeathers. Everyone in the royal court knew that Arundelle and Artham loved one another, Nia said, though the couple thought their affection was a secret. "Most of the women in Anniera had their eyes on him in those days, but his heart was set on Arundelle." Nia shook her head with wonder. "So you're telling me some of the cloven are *Annieran*?"

"That's what Cadwick and Arundelle told us," Janner answered. "They seemed to understand who our father was, at least."

"They remember, then?" Oskar asked.

"That's the problem," Kalmar said. "The remembering drives them kind of crazy. Like Uncle Artham, only worse."

Uncle Artham. Where was he? Janner missed him especially, but until someone sailed to Skree or Artham sailed to the Hollows, there was no way to know what had become of him. Sara Cobbler's face floated into Janner's mind, but he didn't mention it.

When the boys described Throg, the prisoners there, and the death of Bonifer Squoon, Nia and Oskar listened in grave silence.

"They're still there," Kalmar said. "All those people. Still in the dungeon, and in that castle. What do we do?"

"We'll do something," Nia said. "But not tonight. We need to rest."

"I'm sorry about Chimney Hill, Mama," Leeli said.

"Me too." Nia pulled the covers up to Leeli's chin.

"We'll rebuild it, right?" Leeli said sleepily.

Nia smiled. "Even better than before."

Janner felt his eyes drooping. He yawned. "And this time I want my own room. Full of books."

"I can help with that," Oskar said.

"That's not going to happen." Kalmar didn't sound sleepy at all. He was lying on his back with his hands folded under his head, staring at the ceiling. Janner had seen that look on his brother's face before, whenever he was thinking about a drawing or something he wanted to build. "We're not going back to Chimney Hill."

Janner sat up. "Why not?"

"Because," Kalmar said, "we already have a home."

Everyone knew what he meant, but no one said a word.

The next morning was the warmest yet that spring. The sky was wide and high and blue with the breezy promise of new life. The rubble of Ban Rona was a terrible thing to see, but it didn't seem as insurmountable as it had the night before.

The children emerged from the Orchard Inn and heard the sound of singing echoing up the streets. The Wingfeathers and Oskar walked toward the center of town and discovered a group Hollowsfolk in a work line, passing broken timbers into a bonfire as another group sifted through fallen buildings and separated reusable wood from Fang armor and weapons.

The aroma of hot food drifted through the air, and Kalmar veered toward its source without waiting for the others. Janner's stomach growled, and he tried not to think about the last time he had eaten. The only thing he wanted in his head was the present and the future—the morning was too beautiful for bad memories.

He found Kalmar in a line of Hollish children waiting to be served plonkfish stew from a tent. Olumphia Groundwich stood behind the table, ladling soup into bowls and shooing the children away to eat in the street outside.

"Good morning, Your Highness," she said with a quick smile as Nia greeted her with a hug. Three more whiskers had sprung up since Janner had last seen her. "The sun came up today, thank the Maker."

Olumphia let the Wingfeathers sit behind the table, where they gobbled up their food without a care for their manners, and for once, Nia allowed it.

Janner wiped his mouth and looked around. "Where are all the cloven?"

"They left in the night," said a voice behind them. Guildmaster Clout walked in with one arm wrapped in a bandage. "No one knows why." He stepped around the table and kissed Olumphia on the cheek. "Hello, my lovely."

"Not here, you clubbard!" Olumphia swung the ladle at him. "Out!"

"As you wish, my bumpkin nibblet." He turned his attention to the children and resumed his gruff manner. "The cloven were a bit creepy for our tastes anyway. Few of them could speak, and they all stank like sod liver. Without that Cadwick fellow around, I feared they might go wild and hurt someone."

"Out!" Olumphia said again.

"My squeezle wants me to scram. I'll see you guildlings later." Clout stopped before he ducked out of the tent. "I almost forgot. The she-dragon has been loitering about at the quayside. Seems she might want to see you three. It's hard to tell." He blew a kiss at Olumphia and she answered by hurling a spoon at him.

"I'm glad you two are finally on speaking terms," Nia said to her friend.

"Oy. I liked him better when he ignored me."

When they had finished eating, the Wingfeathers went to find Hulwen. The streets were mostly empty, and the structures were mostly flattened, but the sky was so clear that it was impossible not to feel hopeful. Every broken building represented a restoration that was already underway. As they neared the waterfront, Hulwen emerged from the sea and bowed her head.

The Stone Keepers are leaving, Hulwen said, and Janner told the others.

They have the stone.

"Where are they?" Janner asked.

Sailing south, toward Yorsha Doon.

"We can't let them get away," Kalmar said. "The last thing Aerwiar needs are two crazy witches on the loose with an ancient stone."

"Will you take us to them?" Leeli asked Hulwen.

As you wish. Hulwen climbed out of the water. She had grown used to her legs, and the seawater seemed to have salved her wounds. She laid down on the stony shore, and Leeli climbed onto her back.

"Come on," Leeli said when Janner and Kal hesitated. The boys clambered up behind Leeli. The dragon's hide was soft and cool to the touch. "You too, Mama."

With a sigh, Nia climbed on behind the children. As soon as they were situated, Hulwen swam gracefully out to the Watercraw, keeping her four passengers well out of the sea. She ducked through an opening in the chain gate and weaved through the mass of empty Fang ships. It was eerie, like walking through a graveyard. Hulls bumped against one another, sounding as hollow as empty coffins.

When they were clear of the mass of ships, Hulwen increased her speed and swam toward a ship in the distance—the same one that had carried the children to the Hollows the day before, which already seemed an age ago.

When they reached the ship, the deck was clear.

They heard Murgah's voice before they saw her. "What do you want?" she shouted from the cabin on the foredeck. Her voice gurgled, as if she were talking with a mouthful of soup. Amrah and the Fangs were nowhere to be seen.

"What do *you* want?" Kalmar asked.

"What have you done with our master?" she asked. She sounded desperate. "Where is he?"

"He's dead," Kalmar said. "It's over."

"Don't come any closer!" she shrieked. "We have the stone!"

"And what do you plan to do with it?" Kalmar asked.

She laughed madly. "I'll throw it into the sea!"

Kalmar flashed a smile at Janner and the others. "No! Don't!" he said. "Whatever you do, don't throw the stone into the sea!"

"I will if you don't leave me be! I'll never let you have it."

"Bring us closer," Kalmar whispered to Hulwen.

"I see you!" the Stone Keeper screamed. "I'll do it!"

When Hulwen was close enough, Kalmar hopped over the rail of the ship and landed on the deck. Murgah and Amrah burst from the door—except it wasn't Murgah and Amrah. They were the two most wretched and hideous cloven Janner had ever seen.

The old one, who had been Fanged once already, was now lumpy and greenish and covered with gills. Many fins covered her cheeks, neck, and shoulders, flapping like moth wings as she squelched forward on translucent pods where her feet should have been. The only thing about her still remotely human was her terrible, sneering face.

Amrah, on the other hand, still wore her robe, but she dragged herself foward on her belly, using bright red crab claws. Where her legs should have been, a long fish tail flapped on the deck. The gills on her neck opened and closed as she gasped for breath and bared her teeth. The satchel that held the ancient stone was slung over her shoulder.

"Hurry, daughter!" the Murgah-fish-thing gurgled, and she lurched to the opposite rail. With a cackling scream, she flopped over the side and splashed into the sea. Amrah clawed her way to the top of the rail and turned. Janner saw fear on her face, but it was quickly replaced by a look of hatred. She followed her mother into the sea.

Kalmar stared over the edge with his mouth hanging open. "That wasn't exactly what I had in mind," he said. "Are they . . . ?"

Hulwen dipped her head under the water and lifted it out again a moment later. *They're alive. But the Dark Sea of Darkness is a dangerous place, even for a sea dragon*, she said. *They won't last long.*

"But what about the stone?" Janner asked.

I'll find it.

The amidships hatch popped open and the heads of several Green and Grey Fangs poked out. "Are they gone?" one of them asked. "They melded with a bunch of fish! Tried to get us to do the same."

"It was gross," another Fang said.

"Yeah, they're gone," Kalmar said as he retreated to the rail, ready to jump back to Hulwen if he needed to. "The war's over. Gnag is dead."

The Fang whispered to the others then spoke to Kalmar again. "Er, what do we do now?"

Kal's head cocked to one side. He looked at Janner, but Janner only shrugged. "Well, I guess you can go away."

The Fangs whispered among themselves, then the leader spoke again. "Where do we go?"

"I don't know," Kalmar said. "Just go away. Stop hurting people."

"I'm not sure we can do that. Not without our old names."

"The ones the Fang wrote down in the book?"

"Yes."

"You're telling me you *want* to know your old names?"

"Some of us do."

"I don't!" one shouted from below. "I like being evil!"

"I'm sick of it," said the first one. "But when I try to remember my old name, or where I came from, my head hurts. Everything gets squishy."

"What if I gave you new names?"

The hatch lowered and Kalmar heard them whispering again. The conversation rose and fell in heated murmurs, then abruptly the voices hushed and the hatch popped open again. "Will they be good names?"

Kalmar shrugged. "I don't know. I guess so. Why don't you come out so we can talk about it? I have a dragon, so don't do anything stupid."

After a brief pause the hatch flipped wide open and twenty-three Fangs climbed onto the deck. Hulwen lifted her head so the Fangs could see her. They shrank back and held out their hands.

Janner had no idea what Kalmar was doing. Did he think that he could just give them a random name and the Fangs would suddenly be good again? *Was* it that simple?

It wasn't.

87

Mercy

When word reached Ban Rona that there was a ship of Fangs heading into the harbor, there was little fear and much anger. Kalmar had asked that the chain at the Watercraw be lowered for the first time since the war began, and after some discussion with Guildmaster Clout (who had unintentionally become Rudric's replacement), it was done. Four Hollish men and women mounted the towers at either side of the Craw and sent the chains hurtling to the sea. Hulwen conscripted the other dragons to help her clear away the empty Fang ships from the mouth of the Watercraw, and once the entryway was clear, a gold dragon towed the ship of Fangs into the harbor. A crowd of Hollowsfolk waited on the shore, every one of them holding a weapon.

As Hulwen guided the ship into its berth along the quay, Kalmar stood at the prow and explained.

"Hollowsfolk! There are seventeen Grey Fangs, five Green Fangs, and one very big Bat Fang in the belly of this ship. I don't blame you if you want to execute them all right now." Several Hollish warriors affirmed this with shouts, and Kalmar nodded. "But I know what it feels like to be Fanged. I'm only myself because Artham Wingfeather rescued me before I was given a name. So I propose that we show them the mercy of imprisonment rather than death."

"Oy! What happens if they escape?" shouted Clout. "They've killed our countrymen. They'll kill again, and you know it."

Kalmar stiffened. "They've asked for mercy. We should give it—as the Maker has given it to us."

"These monsters killed our people," a woman shouted. "Our families!"

"I know," Kalmar said. "But these monsters—they used to *be* someone's family. They just—they lost their way. Maybe we can do more than just defeat Gnag. Maybe we can undo what he's done."

The Hollowsfolk shook their heads and muttered, and though they eventually agreed to send the Fangs to the dungeon, Kalmar could see they did so begrudgingly.

"That went well," Leeli said with a smile.

"This might be a terrible idea," Kalmar said, "but I've got to try."

A group of men boarded the ship and Kalmar opened the midships hatch. "We're taking you to the dungeon," Kalmar called down. "This won't be pleasant, I'm afraid."

In the dark of the hold, Janner could see the Fangs only by the sunlight reflected in their eyes. Even with Gnag dead, he couldn't shake the fear that they might leap forth with a snarl and try to kill them all. But they didn't. They crept out one at a time and were passive as the Hollish men wrenched their arms behind their backs and secured them with shackles.

One by one, the Green and Grey Fangs (and one tall, silent Bat Fang) were lowered down from the ship and led through the crowd. The Hollowsfolk watched in silence as the Fangs, heads down and arms bound, passed through the city their kind had destroyed. The sight evoked too many emotions for the Hollowsfolk to express anything but silent grief.

The walls of the Great Hall were damaged, but the old tree had held and kept it from total ruin. When the rubble blocking the doors to the lower level was cleared away, Kalmar and Clout led the prisoners to their cells. Janner followed, feeling an unexplainable need to be near his brother.

When they reached the lowest corridor, he heard the inhuman snarling of the Fang that had been there all along: Nuzzard. Kalmar stopped in the hall, ears twitching.

"What is it?" Clout asked.

"Nothing," Kalmar said.

Kalmar led the train of Fangs past the cell without looking inside it. But when Janner passed at the rear of the procession, he stopped and peeked through the caged window to see the thing that made such a racket. He looked on a shriveled, pitiful beast, in much worse condition than when Janner had seen it upon their arrival in the Hollows. Its fur had fallen out in patches and it crouched in a corner, whipping its head about madly. It was as if everything human in the Fang had evaporated, leaving only a mindless and soulless beast behind.

No wonder Kalmar was afraid, Janner thought. He was afraid of becoming *this*. Was this what lay in store for the other Fangs? Was this what lay in store for Kalmar?

Clout consigned the Fangs to individual cells and locked the doors. When he was satisfied that they were all secure, he led Janner and Kalmar out of the dungeon. "What's your plan here, guildling?"

"I don't have a plan," Kalmar answered. "I just don't want to kill them."

"But you know they'll only get worse. Like the other one."

"Yeah. Unless I can stop it."

"Why would you want to?" Clout asked.

"Because I'm not Gnag, I guess."

"And you really think they want to change?" Clout asked.

"Not all of them. But if some of them do, then maybe—I don't know. Maybe there's hope. There might be an Annieran or a Skreean or even someone from the Hollows in there who wishes they had never been fanged in the first place."

"It won't work." Clout pushed through the doors to the Great Hall and left the brothers alone.

Kalmar sighed and sat on a chunk of stone that had fallen from the ceiling. "Do you think I'm a fool, Janner?"

Janner sat beside him. "No. But I'd like to know what you plan to do."

"I need to get back to Anniera."

"Right. The beautiful Shining Isle," Janner said wryly, kicking a loose stone across the floor. "They say one gets used to the smoke after a while."

"And the ash-covered hills. So lovely."

"Don't forget the Castle Rysen. They say its ruins are beautiful in the spring."

Kalmar's smile faded and he toed at the rubble. "What a mess."

"Well, whatever it is you're planning, I'm with you." Janner punched Kalmar in the shoulder. "I have to keep you out of trouble."

The boys found Nia and Leeli near the Great Library, helping a distressed Oskar sort through heaps of wet books. The Hollowsfolk had resumed their cleanup and Janner heard them singing at their work several streets away.

"Mama, can we leave?" Kalmar asked.

Nia looked up from her book pile with surprise. "What do you mean, *leave*?"

Kalmar nodded. "I want to go home."

"You mean Anniera." Nia looked at each of her children, then at Oskar, who was buried up to his waist in books. "I was hoping you'd say that. Oskar, do you want to join us?"

"Books," Oskar said without looking up.

"You don't have to come. And if you want to join us later, it's a short sail away. There won't be any books in Anniera, I'm afraid."

"There's so much to do." Oskar removed his spectacles and gestured at the piles. "I'll come. Just wait a moment while I figure out where to place *Smoodge's Finest Plays, Poems, and Porridge Recipes*. There are so many options, you know! It could go in Poetry, of course. But it also belongs with Hollish Delectables. So much to do!"

"And you're the one to do it," Kalmar said. "They need you here."

"But—" Oskar said.

"That's a command from the king," Janner said.

Kalmar waved his hand at the scattered books. "Ban Rona needs a Head Librarian."

"And Anniera needs a king." Oskar nodded. "Hugs," he said with a sniffle. "I need to hug." He tried to extract himself from his pile but failed, so the children climbed over them and embraced the old man. He patted their backs and squeezed each of them, saying, "In the words of . . ." over and over without thinking of a single quote.

"We'll see you soon," Janner said.

"Please do," Oskar blubbered.

Nia leaned over and lifted Oskar's white stringy hair from his pate, then planted a kiss. Oskar was stunned, then bowed his head and wept as the Jewels of Anniera and their mother made their way to the water.

88

Sailing Home

The Wingfeathers told few people they were leaving. Leeli insisted that they find Thorn, which took only a few moments once she whistled for a dog and sent it to fetch him. He arrived at the quay with Baxter and Frankle on his heels.

"You're off, then," he said.

"Yes. But not forever. It's just that we—"

"I understand. Let me get my Pa."

Without another word, Thorn left the dogs with Leeli and trotted up the street to where the work was being done. "Where is he going?" Leeli wondered aloud. Thorn returned a few minutes later with Biggin O'Sally and Kelvey.

"Thorn said you was leaving," Biggin said.

"Were," Nia corrected.

"Thorn said you was leaving *were*." Biggin shrugged. "I figured that to be the case. I don't know much about sailing, but Kelvey does. He has a double guild in houndry and sailery, with a lesser in muffinry." He pointed to a small boat on the north end of the pier where the damage was less severe. "Ship's ready to sail."

Biggin left no room for argument, and Nia and the children followed them without protest. They soon found themselves under sail in a gentle wind, heading through the Watercraw and toward open sea. It was a small ship, but plenty big enough for the seven of them to fit comfortably on the deck. Thorn sat next to Leeli, chatting about Frankle's newfound obedience, while Kelvey took the helm and directed the boys.

After longing to see the Shining Isle for so many years, then seeing it as Gnag's prisoners for so short a time, Janner felt oddly unexcited. The seas were calm—especially so after the stormy voyage the day before—and Kelvey estimated that they'd arrive well before sunset.

Janner leaned against the rail and listened to the grownups talk for a while, then his eyes grew heavy and he made a pillow from his Durgan cloak and lay on the starboard bench. The feel of the wind and the warm sun, the sound of pleasant chatter, and the rocking of the boat sent him into a deep sleep in which he dreamed of his father and Uncle Artham at play on white shores.

Nia's whisper woke him. "We're almost there."

Janner sat up and yawned as Leeli handed him a hunk of sweetbread and a handful of shadberries. The sun stared at them from low in the west, glowing orange in a field of purple and blue. Kalmar sat at the bow, resting his chin on the rail. Beyond him, Janner watched Anniera rise from the sea.

Waves spewed up from the feet of the cliffs on either side of a little bay—the same one from which they had embarked the day before. He wasn't sure if it was his imagination, but there seemed to be less smoke, less desolation than there had been the day before. The land visible between the cliffs was still blackened, and smoke still rose in tendrils, but he was at least able to see the graceful shape of the island. It was easy to imagine how beautiful it would be if it were green and lush.

There was no shiver in his bones, no tingle in his spine as the ship floated into the bay's still waters where the River Rysen met the sea. He didn't feel the thrill he had always imagined when the boat thumped into the dock and he and his family set foot on the Shining Isle at last, without Gnag or his minions to defy them.

And yet, he wasn't disappointed. Janner wasn't interested in the feeling of being home as much as the actuality of it. He wanted to help his family build a life here. He wanted to roam the island unafraid, to see the seasons turn from year to year. Oh, how he wanted to be *still*. No more running, no more terror, no more anxiety or troubled dreams. Just this one place in all the world into which the word "home" would fit unlike anywhere else.

Janner, Kalmar, Leeli, and Nia stood together on the sand while the O'Sallys tended the ship. The only sound was water: waves tickling the shore and tears causing Nia to sniffle. She hadn't been home since Gnag had first attacked nine years before. Podo had said they floated down the River Rysen with a wall of fire on either side, weeping at the death of Wendolyn and the injury to Leeli's leg and the certain death of so many Annierans.

Janner could see those memories playing out on Nia's face and sending tears streaming down her cheeks. She took a step forward and collapsed to the sand. Janner and Kalmar helped her to her feet.

"It's over, Mama," Leeli said.

"Is it?" Nia wiped her nose with her sleeve and shook her head.

"Yes," Kalmar said. "And it's beginning, too. We're home."

Janner took Nia's hand and led her up from the shore, along a path carved into the rock. The O'Sallys and the dogs joined them. Baxter and Frankle bounded from stone to stone, trying to smell everything at once. When they all reached the crest of the sea cliff, they came upon the ruins of several buildings.

"This was called Lorryshire. There was a bakery there," Nia pointed at a pile of charred planks. "They had the finest sausage bread in all the island. Your father and I came here often in the autumn for the beanbrew." She smiled and wiped her cheeks. "There's so much work to do."

Biggin O'Sally grunted. "I could use some beanbrew about now."

"How far is it to the castle?" Kalmar asked.

"No more than an hour on foot." Nia looked out at the sinking sun. "If we hurry, we'll be there before dark."

Gnag's troops had used the road often enough over the years that it was well worn and easily traveled. Along the way Nia told them stories, awakened in her memory by the lay of the land and the ruins of buildings. Even in the smoky sadness of the place there was a sense of peace that made the journey surprisingly pleasant. As they walked, the joy Janner had anticipated simmered in his chest—a slowly and steadily rising warmth rather than an eruption—as he allowed himself to believe that this was actually happening.

They saw no Fangs prowling the hills, no sign of malice—only what was left in its wake. Leeli pointed at a sunbathed hillside where a flock of white birds picked their way through the ashes, evidence that not everything on the island was dead. The sun began to slide below the horizon and lit the high clouds in pinks and reds that set their faces and the very air aglow.

Then they saw the castle. The children had been there only the day before, but now Janner really *saw* it—and what a beauty it must have been! What was left of its walls rose out of the very stone, as if the castle had been a living thing, sprouted from the island's bedrock. Now those walls were jagged and broken, but it was easy to picture the large roof they must have once supported.

Nia stopped and gathered the children close. She pointed out where the highest spires once stood, where the courtyard once opened onto a grand garden in which the people rested after their days in the fields, where she and her court fed them feasts of game and the fruit of the forests and they sang under the stars and the rising moon.

"Speaking of stars," Nia said, "they're coming out. We need to find a place to sleep."

"Oy," agreed Biggin. "It'll get mighty chilly at night."

"I know a place," Kalmar said.

Frankle and Baxter trotted beside him as he led them up the hill and among the ruins to the cellar. He sniffed and confirmed that they were indeed alone, and then he led them down the steps.

Biggin and Kelvey lit the torches left behind by the Fangs while Nia and Leeli nested, clearing away the rubble to arrange a comfortable place to sleep. Janner and Kalmar laid out the food Biggin had brought, and soon the seven of them (and the two dogs) sat in a circle, eating in silence. Janner knew by the look on his mother's face that her thoughts wandered deep in the forest of the past, and he didn't want to interrupt her. The O'Sallys munched, muttering their amazement that they were sharing a meal in the Castle Rysen.

When the meal was finished, Nia told them about her first night in the castle many years ago, when, unable to sleep, she had crept out of her new bedchambers and wandered the grounds under the moonlight. She had fallen asleep on the soft grass in the garden and woke under a pile of dirt. The gardenkeeper and his crew had covered her in it from the waist down and planted an assortment of firebud and totato seedlings. When Nia had sat up, sputtering her disgust, she saw Esben and Artham doubled over, laughing like little boys.

"Your father promised to take the gardener and his family sailing on the *Silverstar* as payment for his mischief." Nia smiled at her children and asked Biggin to douse the torches. "In the morning, maybe we'll plant some new memories."

Janner and the others fell quickly asleep, even though Biggin's snore was clamorous. A few hours later, Janner woke with Kalmar's face just inches away. His wolf whiskers tickled Janner's cheeks. "Shh. I need you," Kalmar whispered. "Stay quiet."

Leeli knelt beside him, her outline faintly illuminated by the starlight floating in through the doorway above. Janner and Leeli followed Kalmar, trusting his wolf eyes as they crept around Nia's sleeping body.

"What are we doing?" Janner whispered.

"Hold on." Kalmar tugged the squeaky iron door open just enough for them to squeeze through. When they were inside and the door was shut behind them, Kalmar spoke. "I know you'll think I've lost my brain, but I need to go down there. To the Fane of Fire."

Janner rubbed his eyes and tried to clear the sleep out of his mind. Being in this room again unsettled him. He couldn't help but picture

Gnag the Nameless rising out of the shaft with the look of satisfaction on his face.

But his trepidation went deeper than that. He remembered being in the shaft, looking along the glowing passageway to the chamber and sensing a presence there. If the legends were true, and he had no reason to doubt them any longer, that presence had been the Maker himself. Janner was ashamed of all the anger he had flung at the Maker—when he was in the Deeps, when he was in the Fork Factory, when he was on Gnag's ship, riding the storm that had, in fact, carried Leeli's music to the Field of Finley. The thought of coming face-to-face with that presence terrified him.

"I don't think that's a good idea," Janner whispered.

"Why not?" Leeli asked. "The kings of Anniera have always walked with the Maker there."

"I don't know. I just—I don't want to go down there."

Kalmar started to say something but hesitated.

"What is it?" Janner whispered.

"Janner," he said, "you're not supposed to. I'm the king, not you."

Of course. The Fane of Fire was for the High King. When he had entered before, Janner was trespassing. He shuddered to think what might have happened if he had followed the passage to the chamber.

But now Janner felt a sting of jealousy. Why shouldn't they all be allowed to enter? It took the three of them to open the door. He had done as much to fight for Anniera as Kal had. His mind raced with all the trouble Kal had caused over the years, from their days in Glip-wood, to his cowardice in Dugtown, to his Fanging in the Phoobs. And now *Kal* was the one who got to walk with the Maker. How was that fair? The old familiar anger, which had only moments ago filled him with shame, now filled him with indignation.

"Janner?" Leeli said.

He let out a breath he hadn't realized he was holding. Janner shook his head, thankful that in the darkness they couldn't see the way his cheeks flushed. "I'm sorry," he said—not just to his siblings. What a tangle his heart was. "Of course. I know the Fane is for you. I just—"

"It's all right," Kalmar said. "I understand. Believe me, I'd trade places with you if I could."

Janner wanted to cry, though he didn't understand why.

Kalmar guided them to the circle on the floor. "Do you both remember what you're supposed to do?"

"Yes," Janner said. "I think so."

He had only spoken the words twice before, but by some strange remembrance in his blood he knew that once he started speaking, they would come easily. Leeli played the music quietly, and Janner recited the old script. Kalmar traced the glittering form in the air. At once the light blazed through the seams in the wall. The shapes carved into the floor glowed and twinkled with silver sparks as the floating figure rotated and descended over them. The shaft slid open and rays of golden light splayed forth.

Down Kalmar went, as if he were climbing into the sun itself.

89

The Maker

Janner didn't know what to feel as he and Leeli watched Kalmar descend. He was embarrassed at his jealousy, at the bitterness he had aimed at the Maker over the years; he was afraid to be so close to such power and mystery; and he was unsettled by the memories of Gnag in the same room only a day before.

Kalmar reached the bottom, looked up at them with a nervous smile, and walked out of sight. Janner and Leeli sat at the edge and listened for a long time. They waited without speaking, staring at dust motes that swam in the beam of light.

Janner's heart somersaulted with shame, embarrassment, envy, frustration at himself, contrition, gratitude, and then more frustration. As soon as he settled on one feeling, the next one crowded it out. He sighed, wishing he could rest and let things be as they were. He felt as if he were two people: one boy who saw the situation objectively, who knew the right answers—which were to be content with his lot, grateful to the Maker, humble to his calling—and another boy whom he hated, who felt things hotly and demanded attention like a child throwing a fit.

Even the good feelings betrayed him, because once he felt them he was proud of having them, which opened the door for the next multitude of conflicting emotions. *No*, he would think. *Gnag is dead. You're the Throne Warden. Be glad Kalmar is acting like a king; be glad the Maker is real; be glad you get to be a part of this.* He would settle for a moment, even breathe a sigh of relief. Then like a rat in the kitchen, a dark thought would skitter across the floor of his thoughts.

On and on it went, in the light of the Fane of Fire, while Leeli contentedly rested her head on his shoulder and waited.

Gradually Janner began to understand, deeper in his heart than any of these other thoughts or feelings, that what was happening inside of him was the Maker's doing. Just being this close to the Fane of Fire stirred the muck in Janner's soul so that every broken part of him floated to the surface and was drawn in sharp relief, just like those dust motes.

After more than an hour, with Leeli now asleep on his shoulder, Janner understood something about his own heart: he was deeply, blatantly *selfish*. In so many situations, from Glipwood to the Deeps to Gnag's ship, whenever he had unleashed his frustration at the Maker, he had been thinking more of himself than anyone or anything else. Even in the performance of his duties, he thought mainly of his own dutifulness; in his courageous moments he thought of his courage. Only in his pain and despair did he turn his attention to the Maker, and then it was only to demand answers or outcomes.

The light from the Fane of Fire illumined his heart and showed him who he really was: a weak, petty young man. Even in that realization he recognized his selfishness, because he was thinking not of the grace the Maker had shown him—*was* showing him—but of his own weakness and pettiness. There was no way out.

Be still.

"What?" Janner said aloud, looking around for the owner of the voice. Someone had spoken, but whom? When he tried to remember what the voice sounded like, its quality vanished from memory. Then he realized that, of course, the one who had spoken had also made the world. Janner trembled.

Be still.

"Yes sir," Janner whispered. He knew the voice and had always known it. It seemed to come from the Fane—but also from the floor where he sat, and from the sky and the water and the wind and the blood in his veins and the air in his lungs. His heart swelled, and something like a shout rose from his throat, but it came out as a whimper.

Be still.

"Yes sir," Janner repeated, and now he was crying. He felt in his heart a braid of pain and delight and longing that made his bones burn and his heart quake. All his attention turned from himself and he yearned for the speaker of those words so desperately that he wished he could die and be born again as a single spoken syllable from his mouth, just to know the pleasure of his presence.

He vividly sensed Leeli's sweet, gentle breathing and the music that wreathed her dear heart; he saw Kalmar's woundedness and ached to embrace the boy in the wolf; he even saw his own troubled, selfish soul: the scarred flesh and weary eyes, his conflicted emotions, and he loved the Janner that he saw through the Maker's eyes. He knew himself as he was known. He saw, and was still.

A great love enveloped him, and he thought of his father's bearlike embrace, only now he knew those arms were but a shadow of the bright love that beat the world's heart and held him now, as they always had, with an inescapable, indescribable tenderness.

Be still.

The voice repeated the words again and again, like a beating heart, until Janner was at last able to obey and to rest, rest, *rest*. There in the light of the Fane of Fire, Janner Wingfeather encountered— absorbed—an abiding peace that he would never forget all the days of his life.

He was still. And he was loved.

"Psst! Janner!" Kalmar said, poking Janner's shoulder.

Janner sat up, afraid at once that he had only dreamed the Maker's presence—yet to his relief he was still in the chamber, still awash in the golden light. Not only that, he sensed the change in his heart. It hadn't been a dream.

Leeli sat up and stretched as Kalmar knelt beside the two of them with an easy smile on his face. "Let's go."

Janner wanted to ask Kalmar what had happened, but he chose to wait. The room held a holy stillness that he didn't want to disturb.

The Jewels of Anniera took their places and repeated the word, form, and song, and the chamber was once again plunged into darkness. The children climbed the stairs and crept around Nia and the O'Sallys. They found their pallets and lay in the dark for a long time before drifting into a deep and healing slumber.

Sunlight and birdsong woke them. In the glow of a cool dawn, the Wingfeathers and O'Sallys climbed from the cellar, and when they looked out at the rolling hills, they beheld a resurrection of white flowers, sprung from the ashen earth overnight, called up by the previous day's rainstorm and the warming of spring. The flower petals blanketed the island and glimmered with dew, as if the stars themselves had floated down like snow while they slept. Little green vines adorned the rubble and the husks of all the shattered homes, blessing the wreckage with silvery blooms as glad as a wedding day. Honeybees zoomed from flower to flower like children in a candyhouse, as the River Rysen coursed through it all, laughing its way to the sea.

"I didn't realize," Leeli said, "that the Shining Isle actually, you know, *shone.*"

Nia laughed.

They ate a quick breakfast and the O'Sallys got to work, rummaging through the ruins for the wood to build a shelter. It was good work under a good sun, but they only managed to find a few suitable planks.

"It's worse than I thought," Biggin said with a shake of his head. "No use pretending. We have to go back to Ban Rona for supplies. We need tools. We need carpenters. And we need seeds to get into the ground before the planting season gets away from us."

"And that means we need horses, ploughs, hoes, and shovels," Kelvey added.

"You're right." Nia plucked a handful of the blossoms and smelled them. "But I think I'll stay. I couldn't bear to leave again so soon."

"Oy, I figured as much. Kelvey and I can manage the boat. We'll get help and be back in a few days. There's fish in the river or those birds wouldn't be diving. There's a net in the boat that Thorn knows how to use."

"Oy, I scored good in fishery," Thorn said, obviously trying to impress Leeli.

"And there's a sackful of dried fruities that we'll leave you as well. Firewood shouldn't be a problem." Biggin chuckled. "No time to waste. See you real soon."

"Janner and I need to go too," Kalmar blurted, as if he had been holding his breath. "I need to help the Fangs."

"Help the Fangs?" Nia asked. "What about your mother and sister? We could use some help, too, you know, and we didn't destroy the world. No. Absolutely not. Every time our family separates, terrible things happen."

Kalmar swallowed. "We have to go, Mama."

"The Maker told him so," Leeli said, scratching behind Frankle's ears.

"The Maker *what*?" Nia asked. "What do you mean?"

"It's hard to explain." Kalmar sighed. "Just trust me, I have to do this."

"If your boys are coming," Biggin said, "Kelvey can stay here. Right, lad?"

"Real glad to help."

"Really," Nia grumbled.

"Oy."

Nia smoothed the front of her dress and straightened. "Just hurry back."

"You don't have to tell me," Janner said once they were well out to sea. "I'll understand if it's, you know, between you and *him*."

Kal stared at the horizon for a while before he answered. "It's not that I don't want to tell you about it. It's just hard to explain. The Fane was beautiful. Just being in the room made my skin feel all swimmy. There were trees, and running water, and so much light that every color was more . . . I don't know, *colorful*. Then he said my name. But when he said it, it was more than my name." Kalmar scratched his chin and squinted one eye. "It's hard to talk about it. You're the one who's good with words. When I think about *him*, my brain gets all fuzzy. It's not that I can't remember. It's that when I remember I can't think of any words."

Janner imagined how hard it would be to describe the voice he had heard the night before—a voice heard with more than just his ears; a voice that was loud and quiet and beautiful and enormous and pristine; a voice as vast as the heavens yet small as a grain of sand, stirring yet calming, yet—well, he couldn't describe it. "But did he tell you anything?"

A look of sadness passed over Kalmar's face. "He helped me understand something."

"How to help the Fangs?"

"Yes. I think." Kalmar shook his head. "The more I talk about it the less I understand it. I just need to do something." He looked at Janner and shrugged. "Sorry I'm not making much sense."

"It's all right. Like I said, I'm with you."

The day was dying when they sailed through the Watercraw—but Ban Rona was coming to life again. Lamplight shone in the windows of the less-damaged buildings, and the Hollowsfolk sang in the streets. From the ship, the boys saw children and dogs playing on the waterfront, and the aroma of supper hung in the air.

Late as it was, the boys decided to sleep in the berth of the ship, and the next morning, while Biggin set out to find volunteers and supplies, the boys followed the smell of hot porridge to Olumphia's food tent.

"Back already?" Olumphia said.

"Yes, ma'am." Kalmar licked his chops. "I need to take care of some things."

The boys devoured their breakfast and walked up the hill toward the Great Hall. Janner felt Olumphia watching them go while she stirred the porridge. It seemed that all the Hollowsfolk looked at them differently now. Conversations paused as they approached, then resumed in hushed tones when they had passed. Now that the war was over, and the boys had reclaimed Anniera as their home, Janner felt detached from the Ban Rona and its people. He also suspected that the Hollowsfolk were leery of Kalmar's protection of the Fangs. When the brothers arrived at the keep and the Durgan guards all but scowled at them, his suspicions were confirmed.

"You'll have to wait for Guildmaster Clout," one of them said. "We're under strict orders not to open these doors without his permission."

"What a mess," the other one muttered.

"What do you mean?" Kalmar asked.

"You'll see."

Clout arrived a few minutes later, his face as stern as it had been on their first day of class. "Your Highness," he said gruffly. "Throne Warden."

"Is something wrong?" Janner asked.

"Yes. Something is definitely wrong."

"Is it the Fangs?" Kal asked.

"These Fangs? Hardly. They're locked up tight. It's all the others I'm worried about." Clout's voice simmered with anger. "They're all over the Hollows."

90

The Coming of the King

We went out to the Field of Finley yesterday morning to tend to the dead," Clout said. He stood in front of the dungeon door in his Durgan cape, his hand resting on the pommel of his sword, looking as if he had no intention of letting the boys in. "When we got there, we found a whole mob of Fangs gathered around the pile of Gnag's dust. Green ones and Grey ones and Bat ones, too, all standing around like lost children. None of them attacked, I'll give you that, but they did plenty of hissing and howling. I thought we were going to have another battle on our hands, but after a while all they did was stand there and watch us while we buried our comrades."

"How many were there?" Kalmar asked.

"I don't know." Clout curled his lip and looked away. "Hundreds. Maybe a thousand. The point is, we don't want them here. We don't want them in the dungeon, or in the hills, or in the harbor. We want them to *leave*, do you understand?"

The Hollowsfolk wanted their quiet lives back, and Janner didn't blame them. The Wingfeathers had more or less brought the war to their land, and the poor Hollowsfolk had paid a terrible price.

"We'll take them," Kalmar said.

Clout and Janner both looked at him like he was crazy.

"Son," Clout said, "I know you're the king. I respect your position. But you're also a boy. I'm not sure you know what you're saying."

"Their ships are still out there, past the Watercraw. We'll load them up and take them away." Clout narrowed his eyes with suspicion, but Kalmar met his gaze. "Do you want them to leave or not?"

"I suppose I do." Clout looked from Kalmar to Janner and back again. "You don't actually think these monsters can be controlled, do you?"

Janner didn't understand any better than Clout what Kalmar planned to do. He couldn't imagine life on the Shining Isle with a multitude of Fangs, even if the fight had gone out of them. But he also knew that Kalmar had walked with the Maker in the Fane of Fire; if this was what the Maker wanted, then Janner knew better than to argue.

Clout grunted. "Fine. You can have your Fangs, and good riddance. But if there's any trouble we'll fight, do you understand? I'll not suffer another drop of Hollish blood shed by these beasts."

"I understand," Kalmar said. "But I think they're done fighting. Most of them, anyway."

Clout gave the boys two houndricks, and they rode out to the field. Countless mounds of dirt dotted the grass where the Hollowsfolk had buried their fallen. But further up the hill, where Gnag had crumbled to dust, a congregation of Fangs had gathered. Some sat on the ground and stared at the horizon, while others milled about aimlessly.

"It's like they're waiting for something," Janner said.

Kalmar drove his dog team ahead and called over his shoulder. "Maybe they're waiting for us."

The brothers dismounted their houndricks and greeted the Fangs nervously. The houndrick dogs whined and flattened their ears, which was exactly what Janner would have done if he were a dog. But with Gnag disposed of and Kalmar so confident, he found his courage.

The Fangs made no move to attack, but they turned their full attention on Kalmar.

"Fangs of Dang!" Kalmar said, climbing atop Gnag's ash heap. "My name is Kalmar Wingfeather, High King of the Shining Isle. I've come to offer you peace." The Fangs only stared at him as if he were speaking a foreign tongue. "Do you understand what I'm telling you?"

"Peace?" one of the Green Fangs hissed, as if it were a word it had never heard.

"Yes. No more fighting." Kalmar waited while the Fangs puzzled over the idea. "And that's not all. I'll give you new names if you want them. Gnag convinced you to trade your old names for power. This," he said, kicking at the ashes, "is where that ends. I'm asking you to trade your power for new names. Some of you want that, don't you?"

A Bat Fang hobbled forward and said, "I do."

"But where can we go?" the Green Fang asked. "Throg is empty. With no lord to feed us and lead us, we'll either starve or be bored to our bones, and with no Stone Keeper to meld anyone, there's no point in kidnapping more humans. There are no more Jewels to seek out." The Fang shrugged sadly. "We don't know what to do."

"What about building? Or, um, farming?" Kalmar asked.

"Kal, are you serious?" Janner whispered.

"What's farming again?" one of the Grey Fangs asked from the back. "I kind of remember that word."

"We'll teach you," Kalmar said. "You can come with me to Anniera. But you have to sing the song again—this time for peace and not power."

Whispers fanned out among the Fangs and many heads nodded.

"But listen," Kalmar continued, "if you don't come with me, I can't help you. The people of the Green Hollows have the right to protect their land. The way I see it, you have three choices. You can stay here and deal with the Hollowsfolk. Or you can go back to the Castle Throg and stay there. Or," Kal said, sweeping his eyes over the Fangs and taking a deep breath, "you can lay down your weapons and come with me." He allowed this to sink in, then he climbed back into the houndrick and sat down. "Think it over. If you want peace, meet me here in three days and we'll sail to Anniera."

Kalmar nodded at Janner, snapped the reins, and drove the dogs—but not in the direction of Ban Rona. He headed east. Toward the Blackwood.

"Do you know what you're doing?" Janner asked when he had caught up. His head, as usual, was brimming with questions. "Is this what the Maker told you to do? Where are we going?"

"Clovenfast," Kal said without looking back. "To bring our people home."

Janner raised his eyebrows and asked no more questions. Whatever Kalmar was doing, he was determined to do it.

They drove the dogs hard and reached the Outer Vales by nightfall. They made camp near a stream, tended the dogs, and spoke little. Janner woke the next morning to the smell of roasted wexter and two diggles Kalmar had caught sometime in the night.

They fed and watered the dogs, then harnessed them to the houndricks and pushed on, arriving by nightfall at the border of the Blackwood, near the place where the toothy cows had chased them into the forest. They made camp and spoke of Oood, wondering how he was faring on his long journey home and laughing about the trollish poem he had promised to write about their adventures. The brothers fell silent in the light of the fire, and Janner detected another flash of sadness on Kalmar's face. He wanted to ask about it, but was afraid to.

When the sun rose, they rode to the edge of the Blackwood and called out for Pleaders. No one answered, so they unharnessed the dogs and walked cautiously into the trees, ducking under branches and listening for toothy cows and cloven.

After an hour they heard a garbly voice in the trees. "What you want?"

"We seek Elder Cadwick!" Janner shouted.

Out from the brush stepped a tall, skinny cloven with a cat-like face and crumpled wings. It might have been beautiful if not for the insect legs jutting out from its torso. "He's been expecting you."

They followed the creature through the brush, encountering more and more cloven that scooted, loped, and squelched as they passed. At last the wooden wall of Clovenfast loomed above them, and the gates swung wide to reveal a mighty throng of cloven. A cheer shook the treetops when the Throne Warden and the Wolf King passed through the gates. Elder Cadwick trotted out to greet them. His flanks were bandaged and his arm was still in a sling, but he appeared otherwise healthy. His children clung to his horse legs and peeked out at the boys.

"My friends," he said with a warm smile. "My king."

"Elder Cadwick," Kalmar said. "If the cloven hadn't come to our aid, Gnag would still be out there flying around."

"And we'd probably all be dead," Janner said.

"We thank you, boy," Cadwick said to Janner. "Your arrival here began a great unraveling of our bonds. There was pain, but peace followed closely on its heels." Cadwick placed a hand over his heart. "For only when we left Clovenfast for the field of battle did our better memories rise to bless us. We returned only to discover that it was no longer our home." Cadwick leaned forward and smiled. "But that's not all. I want to show you what we found upon our return."

They followed Cadwick through the whispering throng of cloven and between the rows of dwellings. Shimrad was still there, admiring his fenceposts. The backwards bear stood near a firepit, warming his face and his rump at the same time.

Then the brothers drew up short at the sight of a multitude of ordinary humans—men, women, and children—gathered in the yard, looking hopeful and afraid, like a rabble of lost orphans. Their faces were filthy. Many of them hung their heads in shame.

"Who are they?" Janner asked.

"We saw you," said a man at the front of the crowd. "In the melding room. After you fought back, the Stone Keeper and the Fangs just left us there. And when no one returned for us, we left."

"We figured that if you could get in," said a young man about Janner's age, "then maybe we could find a way out."

"Where are you from?" Kalmar asked.

"All over," the man answered. "The Outer Vales. Yorsha Doon. A few of us are from Skree."

Janner couldn't believe these were the same people who had been so eager to be melded. He knew that if he allowed himself he might feel some superiority, some righteous judgment of their behavior in the dungeon—but the peace the Maker had breathed on him was a gentle reminder of his own despair, his own bitterness just before he had happened upon them in the Deeps. Would he have done any different, given enough time in all that darkness?

Janner's gaze fell on a woman whose muddy face was streaked with tears. "We want to go home," she said.

"As do we all," Cadwick said. "We have longed for our king to come."

"Then—you *want* to come with us?" Kalmar asked. "To Anniera?"

"It is our fondest hope, my king." Elder Cadwick bowed. "If you will have a broken people."

"I thought I was going to have to convince you."

Cadwick reared back and laughed. "We thought the same of you."

A murmur began at the rear of the crowd and washed forward, then the shimmering green of Arundelle's leaves appeared over the heads of the cloven. Her roots snaked their way across the leafy ground till she stood beside Cadwick, her strange and lovely face aglow with hope.

"Will you have us, my king?" she asked.

"Of course!" Kalmar said, laughing. He stepped closer to her and lowered his voice. "And I think I know how to heal you."

Arundelle's smile vanished and she stared at Kalmar for so long that Janner feared he had offended her somehow.

Kalmar cleared his throat. "If you want it, that is. You have to want it."

"This is the Maker's will?" Arundelle asked with a look of wonder.

"I think so," Kalmar said. "Though I don't really know what I'm doing."

"Elder Cadwick, will you tell them?" Arundelle whispered, her leaves quivering.

Cadwick trotted to the center of the congregation. "Clovenfast!" His gaze swept over the crowd, from his children and wife, to Mother Mungry, to the most bizarre cloven perching on the rooftops. "Your king has come with the hope of healing. Will you follow him to the Shining Isle?"

The joyous shouts sent flocks of fendril and gulpswallow bursting from the treetops.

Janner and Kalmar feasted with the cloven in Arundelle's courts as the sun smiled on the greening trees. While the cloven prepared to leave, Kalmar and Janner ducked into Esben's den. They read their names, saw their faces sketched on the flat stone, and stared long at Esben's carving of the Annierans at work in the harvest fields. Janner wished he could unearth the boulders and bear them all the way to the island where he could look at them every day. He ached to feel his father's arms again, to hear that warm, bearish voice speak his name. The brothers lingered there until Cadwick's shadow darkened the entrance.

"My lords," he said quietly, "we are ready."

Janner and Kalmar bade a silent farewell to the last images their father ever drew, then joined the cloven at the gates of Clovenfast. Kalmar gave the signal, and the city of the twisted and broken was emptied in the strangest procession the epochs of Aerwiar had ever known.

When Janner and Kalmar rode their houndricks away from the forest with Cadwick and Arundelle on either side, the trees swayed and rattled behind them. Out poured hundreds of odd creatures, men and women among them, smiling in the afternoon sun as they traveled west toward the sea.

91

The King's Offer

The next morning, Kalmar issued the order for Elder Cadwick to rouse the camp, then he led the multitude to the Field of Finley. They marched hard over hill and hollow all day, driven by the promise of Anniera's white shores, and arrived at the field under a dusky sky.

Janner was stunned when they crested a hill and looked out on the battlefield to behold what appeared to be all the Fangs in Dang, waiting on the hillside. The Grey Fangs howled—respectfully, somehow—when the houndricks rolled over the crown of the hill, but when the cloven poured into the valley, the Fangs drew back and tightened their ranks. Kalmar rode ahead and spoke to the Fangs, while Janner ordered the cloven and humans onto the field.

When they were all assembled, Kalmar motioned for everyone to sit, and the throng obeyed without hesitation. Janner was astonished by the strangeness of it—and not only by Kalmar's commanding presence. The cloven were scarytale monsters that had haunted the forest; the Fangs had been the wickedest brutes in Aerwiar; the humans with them had been ready to give themselves over to the Stone Keeper's bidding. Yet now they all sat together like obedient schoolchildren, waiting for a word from the only person in Aerwiar to whom they would listen.

"You don't have to be afraid anymore," Kalmar said, standing on the seat of his houndrick. He smiled at the Fangs who had congregated on his left. "You have a choice now. Just as you had a choice when you sang the ancient song and melded. Then, you didn't see much hope." The cloven and humans nodded, but most of the Fangs looked confused. "When the Stone Keeper gave you a new name, the *you* that existed in your blood and bones—died. And it left a hole."

Some of the Fangs poked at their arms and legs, as if they might discover a cavity they hadn't noticed before.

"What about us?" one of the digtoad cloven belched. "She never gave us no names."

"But you sang enough of the song to begin the melding. Maybe, like my father and my Uncle Artham, you changed your mind and stopped singing before the change was complete. And now you're stuck in the middle, torn between animal and human. Neither fully melded nor named. Just . . . twisted."

Janner was as intrigued and confused by his brother's words as everyone else on the field.

"But you can be healed," Kalmar said. "If you want it."

The cloven nodded and whispered excitedly among themselves. The Fangs, however, were divided. Some cried, "Heal us!" while others narrowed their eyes and growled.

"What if we don't want to change?" one of the Green Fangs hissed.

"Aye, what if we like being mean and flappy?" screeched a Bat Fang.

Kalmar cocked his head and shrugged. "Then I guess I'll leave you here. I'm not Gnag the Nameless. You can do what you want. But you'll have no place either here in the Hollows or on the Shining Isle. You'll have to contend with the Hollowsfolk—and trust me, they would like little more than to turn you all to dust." Kalmar pointed east. "You could always head to the Blackwood, to Clovenfast. Or to the mountains again. But you won't have the ancient stone to restore you when the madness comes. And when it does, it will only get worse. You'll die out there."

Kalmar stepped from the houndrick and moved among the Fangs. "I'm offering you a life on the Shining Isle, with fields to plow and homes to build. I'm offering you beauty and music and peace."

"Ugh," said one of the Grey Fangs.

But another stepped forward. "What do we have to do?"

"Come with me," Kalmar said. "If you don't want what I'm offering, I'll leave you here and you'll die anyway—either at the hands of the Hollowsfolk or the ridgerunners or each other. Or you can come with me. If you do that," Kal spread his hands, "then all I have is yours."

A fendril sang in the distance. Kalmar kept talking about healing, but Janner didn't think it was possible to un-Fang the Fangs. Did he think that giving them names would make them more human—like Kalmar and Artham were? Janner tried to imagine the Shining Isle teeming with Fangs and cloven, but in all his dreams of Anniera, he never pictured it the way Kalmar proposed. Even if the creatures were tamer somehow, it was still offensive. Nor did Janner believe a single Fang of Dang would willingly lay down his life at Kalmar's feet. Looking out at the hairy, scaly, and bat-winged horde that stank up the Field of Finley, he began to worry that Kalmar had lost his wits.

Kalmar climbed back into the houndrick and raised his voice. "If you accept my terms, then follow me to the ships. If not, I leave you to your own ends."

He shook the reins and drove the hounds up the hill toward Ban Rona. Janner followed, wanting to look over his shoulder but keeping his eyes on his brother. He heard the cloven close behind, snorting and whispering among themselves. When they crested the hill, Janner could stand it no longer. He reined up the hounds and turned.

Most of the Fangs were still in a cluster on the field, but every few seconds more of them broke away and made their way toward the city. One of the Grey Fangs howled and gestured mockingly at those who were leaving, then led the rest of the Fangs away in the direction of the Blackwood. In the end, fewer than half the Fangs joined them.

By the time the first stars appeared, the Field of Finley was empty. A gust of wind breathed on the valley and scattered the remaining ashes of Gnag the Nameless. The ashes settled among the new grass and clover, where they would lie silent for all the epochs to come.

92

Sailing Home
(Again)

When the boys led the procession past the Guildling Hall, they found Clout waiting with a contingent of Durgans. The men each held a torch in one hand and a weapon in the other. Clout's face was red with anger.

"Keeper Clout," Kalmar said with a nod as a contingent of cloven shuffled by.

"What do you think you're doing?" Clout demanded.

"I told you I would take them, sir."

"But," Clout said, looking from Janner to Kalmar to the cloven and Fangs moving silently by. "But—"

"I need the Fangs in the dungeon, sir," Kalmar said. "All of them. We'll be gone as soon as we can." Kalmar dismounted the houndrick and walked with the Fangs down the hill to the first streets of the city.

"What does he think he's doing?" Clout asked Janner.

"I honestly don't know, sir," Janner said.

"He's just going to—to set them free? To let them live? They killed thousands! They killed your *father*."

"I know who killed my father," Janner said evenly. "But I also know that Kal is building a kingdom."

"A kingdom of monsters," Clout muttered.

Janner climbed out of his houndrick. "They say that the people of Anniera were a people of song. They say that Annierans sang in the fields, that joy flowed through the land like the River Rysen."

"Oy. What of it?"

"If Kalmar can make them whole again," Janner said as he watched a young man shuffle by with a digtoad cloven at his side, "maybe he can give them something to sing about." Janner joined the procession and walked down the hill toward the city.

"Wait!" Clout called. "Is that all of the Fangs?"

"No, sir. A few hundred of them headed for the Blackwood and the mountains," Janner said over his shoulder. "Enough to keep the Durgan Patrol busy."

Janner caught up with Kalmar at the Great Hall and followed him into the dungeon. The guards gave them no trouble and watched, dumbstruck, as Kalmar opened the cells. He gathered the Fangs together and explained his offer, and every one of them agreed to follow the Wolf King to Anniera.

"Janner, wait," Kalmar said, as the Fangs filed out of the dungeon in silence. "There's one more."

Janner knew whom he meant. The boys made their way deeper into the dungeon and peered into Nuzzard's cell. The ragged beast crouched in one corner, watching the boys with malice.

"Kal, I don't think this is a good idea. It's too dangerous."

"I have to try." Kalmar unlocked the door, and it swung open slowly.

Janner backed up and drew his sword. But the thing's eyes never left Kalmar's face, and it made no movement other than its papery panting. Kalmar crouched in front of the Fang and reached out his hand. Nuzzard cringed, then held still as Kalmar touched its shoulder.

"I want to take you home. Is that all right?"

The Fang's stillness was its answer. As Janner watched, Kalmar knelt and slowly, slowly gathered the creature into his arms. Frail as the old Fang was, Kalmar carried it easily out of the dungeon. He passed the Nuzzard Fang to the first Grey Fang he saw. "Keep this one safe. Please see that it gets food and water."

The Grey Fang looked down at the shriveled beast in its arms and nodded with what Janner thought looked like pity. The Hollowsfolk hid in their broken houses and peeked out of windows as the boys walked with the solemn parade to the shore where Biggin O'Sally waited. Biggin looked as confounded as Clout.

"Oy, King Kalmar," Biggin said, eyeing the Fangs warily. "I tried to find help, but no one wanted to leave Ban Rona so soon with so much to be done. I have to admit," he added, "I'm not real keen on leaving, either."

"We have all the help we'll need," Kalmar said.

"I didn't say I wasn't coming," Biggin said. "I'm only staying long enough to get you settled in. This is all for you." He indicated a pile of supplies: sacks full of totato, clumpentine, sweetberry, greenion, and zingrid seeds; a wagonload of hoes and rakes, saws, hammers, bags of nails; and several more crates full of dried winter fruit. There was also a pack of dogs. "People mean to help Anniera as best as they can, but I'm afraid they're staying put for now."

"We're grateful," Janner said. "But Leeli will be heartbroken without Thorn."

"Oy, I wouldn't worry about that," Biggin said. "He aims to marry her as soon as their age befits. He loves her real bad."

Since it was clear that the Hollowsfolk were eager to get the Fangs out of the city, Elder Cadwick suggested that they waste no time boarding the ships. Janner helped divide the passengers into groups and figured out which of the Fangs knew enough to crew each boat. By dawn, every Fang ship was loaded and sailing out of the harbor. The last ship carried Janner, Kalmar, and Biggin O'Sally, along with Elder Cadwick and his family, Queen Arundelle and several of her tiny thwappish and gulp-swallow courtiers, and a crew of Green and Grey Fangs.

Janner gave the order to push away from the quay, and only then did the Hollowsfolk emerge from their homes to watch the fleet sail through the Watercraw and into the Dark Sea of Darkness. Janner didn't blame the Hollowsfolk for their distrust. Their wounds were deep and would be slow to heal.

The Fangs, to Janner's surprise, seemed less evil that morning than they had the night before. He suspected it was because they were used to following orders. Their leader had been wicked, so they had been trained in wickedness. Now that they had submitted to Kalmar's authority, they reflected his goodwill, even if unintentionally.

There was growling from time to time, and more than one fight broke out; a few of the Fangs even had changes of heart and jumped ship to swim back to their comrades. Kalmar didn't try to stop them; even if they made it back to shore, there would only be angry Hollowsfolk to greet them. But after a few hours on the open sea, their restlessness faded and even the Fangs who had second thoughts realized there was no point trying to go back.

Kalmar kept to himself. He spoke when spoken to, and smiled at Janner's occasional expressions of concern. Something was surely wrong, but whatever it was, Janner couldn't deny that it seemed *right*, too. Kalmar was at peace in a way that Janner had never seen, even if it was a peace marked by a strange sorrow. When Kalmar retreated to the captain's cabin, Janner followed. He wanted to be near his brother, and though they said few words, Kalmar welcomed his company.

Several hours later, Cadwick knocked on the cabin door.

"Your Highness," he said. "We have spotted land."

The boys stepped out into the bright sun and stood at the rail beside Cadwick and Arundelle. Her leaves had grown greener by the hour, rustling in the sea breeze. Her branches blew back from her face like long strands of silver-green hair.

"I remember it all," she said. "The cliffs. The white shores. The green hills. Music running out on the wind to greet us."

"Listen," Kalmar said.

A low melody rose from the sea and circled around them like a mist. As the harbor came into view, Janner caught glimmers of red and blue, gold and green, sparkling in the cove. The sea dragons whirled and spun over the water. They sang as they danced, just as they had each year below the cliffs at Glipwood—except that now, when they burst from the water, they soared on gilded wings, twisting and whirling in spirals high above the waves, before diving into the sea again.

Hulwen led the dance. When the she-dragon spotted the coming ships, she sang out, higher than the rest, and flew toward them. As she glided overhead, Janner noticed another sound woven through the strands of dragon song: a whistleharp.

"Leeli!" Janner shouted, and the two brothers waved as Hulwen flew over them with Leeli on her back. Their sister called back, but the dragon song was so deep and close that it drowned out her voice.

The dragons escorted the fleet—some of them swimming, some flying—under bales of billowing, sun-shot clouds. The cloven on the decks clamored and grunted happily, doing their broken best to sing along, while the Fangs plugged their ears and grimaced.

Hulwen landed at the water's edge and lowered Leeli to the dock. Hardly able to contain her glee, Leeli slid down and hopped to where Nia waited.

When the boys approached, Nia hugged them as if they had been gone for years. "I hope you know what you're doing," she said quietly as the first of the Fangs disembarked.

The dragons fell silent and floated in the sea, watching with curiosity as the Fangs and cloven began the slow, clumsy process of docking their ships and coming ashore. Some jumped overboard and swam, while others held back, still unsure of their decision to come.

Kalmar waved Hulwen over to the end of the dock and she raised her head till it was level with his. Janner couldn't hear what Kalmar said, but Hulwen's voice filled his head.

Yes, King Kalmar. I'll bring it in the morning. Hulwen nodded, then swam away.

Kalmar jogged over to Nia and Janner as Cadwick approached.

"My queen," Cadwick said. "It is good to be home."

"This is Arundelle," Janner said as the tree woman approached, her roots caressing the soil, burrowing for water.

"Arundelle," Nia said with a smile. "You, I remember."

"Your Highness." The gray bark of Arundelle's cheeks stretched to a smile. "I would bow, but—" Her leaves quivered as she laughed and bent her trunk a little.

"My boys tell me you're the Queen of Clovenfast."

"I *was* the queen," Arundelle said. "I would rather serve you and yours the rest of my life than rule in Clovenfast for another day."

"Elder Cadwick," Kalmar said, "tell the cloven and the Fangs to gather in the morning at the Castle Rysen."

"What shall I tell them is to happen?"

Sadness flashed over Kalmar's face again before he spoke. "I'm going to keep my promise."

Nia and Janner exchanged a worried glance as Thorn ambled over to them.

"Here you go," Thorn said, handing Leeli her crutch.

"Thanks," Leeli said with a blush. She had done a lot of blushing lately. "Are you coming back to the castle with us?"

"I think I'll stay and help Pa and Kelvey with the supplies. We'll sleep on one of the ships tonight." Thorn grinned, and Janner realized it was the first time he had ever seen it happen. "See you tomorrow, Song Maiden."

Leeli turned a deep shade of red as Thorn and the dogs headed to the docks.

"*I'll see you tomorrow, Song Maiden*," Kalmar said in a high-pitched voice, and Leeli punched him in the shoulder.

"We should get moving if we want to be back at the castle before dark," Nia said. "On the way, Kalmar, you can tell me what in Aerwiar is going on."

The Wingfeathers walked back to the Castle Rysen through fields of white flowers as the Fangs and cloven amassed on the shore.

93

Morning at the Castle Rysen

After Janner and Kalmar told Nia about the gathering of Fangs on the Field of Finley and the trip to Clovenfast, the Wingfeathers walked in silence along the River Rysen. The white flowers turned pink as the sky blazed, and fish splashed on the surface of the river from time to time. Janner's heart was more content than it had ever been, leaping with joy whenever his eyes fell on some new beauty of the Shining Isle. Little skonks darted under logs, nibbling on the flowering vines; fendrils soared overhead; owls hooted and swooped silently among blackened trees, snatching mice from the riverbanks. The island had burned, but it was far from dead.

The land rose gently from the river and the sea to the knoll where the Castle Rysen had stood. Already little paths were visible around the castle, trails threaded through the white flowers where Leeli and Nia had walked, as if their footsteps had begun to write a new story into the island's book. The shape of the land, too, was pleasant and soft, with hills not so dramatic as those in the Green Hollows, but wide and easy and visible for miles as it spread to the sea.

"I still don't understand what's happening," Leeli said as they settled around a lantern on the floor of the cellar that evening. "I mean—you're just going to give them all new names?"

"Sort of," Kalmar said. "It's hard to explain. The Maker—" He looked at Nia bashfully. "The Maker said I would know what to do when the time came."

"How can you be sure the Fangs won't change their minds and attack?" Nia asked.

"I can't. But you saw them," Kalmar said. "They're lost. They don't know what to do without Gnag bossing them around."

"And what if they go crazy?" Leeli asked. "You told us that it happened to you, just like it does to Uncle Artham."

"I think that *will* happen if we wait too long." He sighed and stared up at the lamplight flickering on the ceiling. "All I can tell you is that the Maker told me to bring them here. I know what goes on in someone's head when they're Fanged. It's terrible. It's a dark, bottomless feeling in your gut, and it seems like the only way to survive is to sing the song and accept the melding. I'm ashamed I didn't fight harder back in the Phoobs, but I was confused. And hopeless." He closed his eyes. "And to be honest, a part of me really *did* want the power the Stone Keeper promised. It seemed better than torture or death. When you run out of hope, everything is backwards. Your heart wants the opposite of what it needs."

"So you think these Fangs can just turn *good* again?" Nia asked.

"I don't know." Kalmar shook his head in frustration. "Actually, I do know. But I can't explain. You'll just have to trust me. Please?"

"I trust you," Janner said. "But to be honest, I'm dreading tomorrow."

"Me too," Kalmar said.

"Well, I think you're very brave," Leeli said matter-of-factly as she lay down. "No one else would have thought twice about trying to help all those Fangs." Leeli yawned. "I wish Grandpa was here."

"Me too," Kalmar said again.

Nia blew out the lantern and lay down beside the Jewels of Anniera. "I love you three," she said after a while. "There's nothing to do but sleep. Tomorrow, we'll see what tomorrow holds."

"Breakfast," Kalmar mumbled in a sleepy voice.

Janner lay awake for a long time. He thought about the Fane of Fire, just on the other side of the ancient door, where the world was made of light. He wished they could open that door and let the light out.

He wondered what was going on in Kalmar's head. Most of all, he wondered why Kalmar seemed so troubled, and why his own heart was so heavy with worry over whatever would happen in the morning.

They were home at last, but in a way that he never would have guessed: sleeping in the ruins of the Castle Rysen with a thousand Fangs and cloven gathered on the island.

Janner woke before dawn, troubled by a dream he couldn't remember. He sat up and knew somehow that Kalmar was gone. He tiptoed over Nia and Leeli and climbed the stairs out of the cellar.

The sky glimmered with stars so close he was tempted to try to touch them. The air was cool and still, and all the world was hushed with the anticipation of the coming sun.

Janner wandered the ruins of the castle, trying in vain to be quiet in all that stillness, and eventually climbed atop a broken wall where he could see the land below glowing faintly with the starlight caught in the flowers' open palms.

Then he spotted Kalmar, a shadow drifting along the slope. Janner didn't call for him but watched for a while, wondering what Kalmar was doing but not wanting to disturb him. Then he realized Kalmar was moving his way. Of course. Those wolf eyes and that acute sense of smell had probably sensed Janner's presence the moment he had climbed from the cellar.

Kalmar came near, quiet as a cloud, and stood beside Janner, looking out at the array of starry flowers. "I'm scared," he said.

Since Janner had no words, the best he had to offer was his presence. The two of them leaned against the remains of a wall. Janner's mind was too full of questions and confusion to sleep, but

Kalmar's head nodded. It hung low, his snout nearly resting on his chest, then Kal changed positions and rested his head on Janner's shoulder. Normally, Janner would have shoved him away, but Kalmar's furry warmth was welcome. Besides, the Wolf King, for all his bravery and newfound leadership, was still just an eleven-year-old boy. Janner eased his arm around his little brother and held him close.

The flame of dawn spread across the sky and warmed the Shining Isle of Anniera. When the sun's rays broke the horizon, they fell soft and golden on the two brothers, fast asleep and leaning against one another on the stony hill.

Janner opened his eyes with a shivery stretch, then nudged Kalmar. "Kal, wake up. They're here."

"Hmph?" Kal asked, smacking his lips.

Janner stood and pulled Kal to his feet. "Look."

Gathered at the foot of the castle mound was the whole multitude of Fangs on one side and cloven on the other. The few humans stood between them. There was hope on every face.

Then the boys spotted a winged shape, silhouetted by the rising sun, flying their way.

"Hulwen," Kalmar said. "Good."

The dragon circled the ruins of the Castle Rysen and then alighted beside the boys in a rush of air. She folded her wings, craned her gleaming neck, and lowered her head. She nodded at the brothers, and Janner heard her voice in his mind.

I have recovered the stone. What would you have me do with it?

"Did she bring it?" Kalmar asked with a yawn.

"She said she has the stone."

Kalmar touched Hulwen's snout. "Thank you. You can leave it here. Then go back to the sea. Hide. Until you know it's safe."

Hulwen paused, studying Kalmar's eyes. *What do you mean to do, Wolf King?*

"She wants to know what you're going to do," Janner said, his anxiety growing by the minute. What did Kal mean, telling a *dragon* to hide? What about Janner? What about their family? "Kal?"

"Everything's going to be all right," he said to the dragon. "But whatever you do, don't sing a note. Not till you know it's safe."

Hulwen huffed a burst of warm breath. *Very well. Maker help you.*

Hulwen lowered her head to the ground at Kal's feet. At first Janner thought she was bowing, but then he saw her jaw working and out slid the brick of shining stone from the Fane of Fire.

Hulwen took to the air and flew over the heads of the Fangs and cloven, on her way back to the sea.

"Now what?" Janner asked.

94

The Seed Is Planted

Janner and Kalmar stood in the ruins of the Castle Rysen before a multitude of monsters. There were cloven of all shapes and sizes (Elder Cadwick and Arundelle at the fore), along with Green Fangs, Grey Fangs, and Bat Fangs—all of them hissing, growling, and snorting as they shuffled closer to the boys.

Kalmar held the ancient stone in the crook of one arm, and the nearest creatures shielded their eyes from its light.

"This thing's heavy," Kalmar mumbled, and he shifted the rock to his other arm.

"Want me to hold it?" Janner asked, though he didn't really want to. The stone was beautiful, but its power frightened him.

"Kalmar, what are you doing?" Nia asked as she and Leeli hurried out of the cellar and joined the brothers.

Leeli rubbed her eyes and yawned. "He's healing them, Mama."

"But how?" Nia took one look at the stone and said, "Kalmar, that thing is dangerous."

Kalmar nodded and shifted the stone again.

A Grey Fang stepped forward, carrying Nuzzard in its arms. "I brought this one, as you asked, sir."

The emaciated creature's limbs dangled as if it were already dead, but its eyes were open and its breath came in quick gasps.

"Thank you." Kalmar bent closer to Nuzzard. "Can you sing?"

Nuzzard grunted weakly and nodded its head.

Arundelle glided closer and looked down at Kalmar. The stone lit the underside of her leaves and branches like a campfire in the woods. "The cloven are assembled, King Kalmar. What would you have us do?"

"Sing the song," Kalmar said. "Sing the song of the ancient stone, and the blood of the beast imbues your bones."

The cloven and Fangs whispered among themselves, some of them excitedly repeating the phrase.

Nia knelt in front of Kalmar and grabbed his shoulders. Fear whitened her face. "Son, what did the Maker ask you to do? Tell me!"

Kalmar looked his mother in the eye. "He said that I would know what to do. And I do, Mama. The stone will heal them."

"But that's not how it works, Kal," Janner said. "There was always another animal in the melding box. They have to meld *with* something."

"I know," Kalmar said. He lifted the stone over his head and shouted, "Sing the song of the ancient stone, and the blood of the beast imbues your bones!"

He pushed his way into the crowd until all Janner could see was the light of the stone floating through the beasts like a second sun about to rise.

Cadwick and Arundelle looked at one another nervously as the first Fangs began to sing, and then they too began to sing the old melody.

Janner remembered the steaming, shriveled husks of bats left in the melding box once their essence had been drained, and he imagined the same happening to Kalmar. His brother was going to die.

It made sense—Kalmar's strange sadness since he had emerged from the Fane of Fire, his promise to heal the broken ones—but the Throne Warden heart beating in Janner's chest compelled him. He couldn't stand by and watch as his little brother gave himself up, let himself die.

Protect. That was Janner's only duty as the elder brother. That was the calling of a Throne Warden. Protect the king. Protect him from the Fangs, from Gnag—even from himself. *Protect.*

Then a memory of Arundelle's words surfaced in his mind. *I was told in a dream that a boy would come to Clovenfast, and he would be the seed of a new garden.* This was what she'd foreseen—but Janner wouldn't accept it. Kalmar wasn't a boy. It wasn't going to work. It was only going to kill him. He was a Fang—or a cloven, or whatever they wanted to call him.

Protect, Janner thought. *Protect the king.*

Then a warm and powerful voice swept through Janner's mind. *Sing the song of the ancient stones, and the blood of the boy imbues your bones.*

The blood of the *boy?*

"Kalmar, no!" Janner screamed, and he ran.

He shoved past Elder Cadwick, past the smelly Fangs, and through the lumbering cloven as their voices unified into a single melody and the light of the stone pulsed and grew. Janner strained closer and closer to the light until he spotted among all the twisted and misshapen forms his little brother's fur and saw his weeping face as he struggled to hold the stone overhead.

"Kalmar, sing the song!" he shouted as he pushed through the crowd.

"What?" Kalmar said, blinking at Janner in confusion.

"Sing it!"

Kalmar's lips moved as he joined his voice with the others. The stone burned brighter and brighter. Golden beams shot from the ancient stone, spraying out through Kalmar's fingers.

Janner reached Kalmar at last and looked firmly into his bright blue eyes. "I love you," Janner said.

Then he tore the stone from Kalmar's hands, astonished by its weight and warmth, and hugged it tightly. He fell to the ground and curled his body around it.

The last things Janner saw were Kalmar's feet and the living light that washed over them. It flowed upward like water from the stone and the earth and the white blossoms and from Janner's heart, too—a pure and cleansing glow that blazed like the word that made the world.

Janner felt himself emptied of life, of air, even of thought, and his bones burned with a terrible and ecstatic love. He sensed the Maker's presence and pleasure like a roll of thunder, a crashing wave, a cool rain, a newborn's breath, all unfolding like the joy of spring from the earth's wintry grave.

95

The Price of Healing

Leeli held Nia back when Janner rushed through the singing mass. The ache she felt in her soul was bone-deep, but she had no doubt that whatever happened, this close to the Fane of Fire, it would be the Maker's doing. She clung to her mother's arm, though Nia screamed and fought, and when Nia fell, Leeli fell with her. They clung to one another and hid their eyes as the light enveloped them.

All at once the ancient song ended.

An unnatural fog enshrouded the mount and blocked the sun's light. Leeli grabbed her crutch and climbed to her feet, fully expecting the very thing she saw when the wind stirred and the fog thinned.

Hundreds and hundreds of men and women, glistening with dew and draped in ill-fitting Fang cloaks and armor, stood together in the silence of the dawn. A tall, beautiful woman, whom Leeli knew to be Arundelle, admired her arms, turning them this way and that, as if she had never seen arms before. The man beside her draped his cloak around her shoulders and turned to face the sun as three little children hugged his legs. Slowly, like the sound of a coming rain, laughter and gasps of delight swept through the throng, followed by joyful weeping.

"He did it," Leeli said.

And then a voice that Leeli hadn't heard in a long time shouted, "Janner!" It was Kalmar, but gone was the wolfish growl—and his voice alone among all the multitude was sorrowful.

"Janner, no!" he cried. "It was supposed to be me!"

Nia leapt to her feet and Leeli followed her through the crowd. When it parted Leeli saw Kalmar—Kalmar the boy, older and without a trace of fur—on the ground beside the glowing stone, with Janner in his arms.

Janner's body was as thin as a skeleton and steaming, and though all the life had gone out of it, the look on his face was one of abounding peace. The old scars on his neck and cheeks adorned him like badges of honor.

Nia and Leeli fell to their knees beside Janner's body. Nia's wail raked the sky, and she cradled her son, rocking him as she had when he was a baby. "My boy," she said. "My little boy."

Kalmar and Leeli laid their heads on their brother's sunken chest and wept with their mother, and soon the men and women all around joined them in a lament made sweeter by their gratitude.

A shadow fell across the Wingfeathers, and Leeli squinted up at a winged figure gliding overhead. Artham Wingfeather landed among the crowd without a word and looked at Janner, and the stone, and the restored Kalmar, seeming to understand at once what had happened. He spread his wings over the children and Nia, and placed his hand on Janner's forehead.

Artham looked around at the silent crowd. "This is the price of their healing."

"I didn't mean to," Kalmar said. "He told me to sing and I—"

"He didn't leave you," Artham said, smiling through his tears. "He never left you."

Kalmar sniffled and shook his head. "Until now."

They wrapped Janner in his Durgan Cloak, then Nia, her back straight and her chin high, carried him to the cellar. Kalmar carried the stone. Leeli was too sad to play a single note, watching as Nia laid Janner's body gently on the floor.

"Open the door," Nia commanded, pointing at the door that led to the Fane of Fire. "Take him down there. Tell the Maker to do something."

"We can't," Leeli said.

"It takes all three of us to open it." Kalmar gazed at Janner's form under the cloak.

"Artham's a Throne Warden," Nia said. "Get him to help."

"Even if we could open the Fane, it doesn't work like that," Kalmar said. "You can't just tell him what to do."

"Why not?" Nia's angry tears glimmered in the stone's glow.

Kalmar shook his head. "I'm sorry, Mama."

"And where were you?" Nia asked, narrowing her eyes at Artham. "You were too late."

"I came as soon as I could. I was so lost, Nia," Artham said. "But Sara found me."

"Sara?" Nia asked.

"Sara Cobbler. A girl Janner met in the Fork Factory. She found me in the forest and said if there really was such a place as Anniera, then she and her orphans wanted to live there. We sailed the *Enramere* straight from Skree, five days ago—it should have taken longer, but a storm sped us on. The ship will be here soon." Artham sighed and looked at Janner's body. "It was a fine voyage. He would have loved it."

He took Nia's hand and waited until she looked him in the eye. "Nia, what Janner did was magnificent. It was the only way."

Nia's shoulders slumped and she bowed her head. "The only way to what?"

"To seed the new garden," Kalmar said. "That's what Arundelle told us would happen."

Artham's jaw went slack. "Arundelle?"

He sounded so confused that Nia laughed in spite of herself. She looked up and smiled through her tears. "Yes, Arundelle."

"She's—"

"Alive. And she's right outside." Nia's anger turned again to grief, and she joined Kalmar and Leeli beside Janner's body. "Oh, Janner," she said. "You *were* magnificent."

"Mama," Leeli said, "let's go see the new garden."

The Wingfeathers emerged from the cellar under a bright blue sky and looked out on the new citizens of Anniera, all standing respectfully among the ruins of the castle as if they were waiting for something.

Arundelle drew Cadwick's cloak tighter around her shoulders and stepped forward. "Artham Wingfeather," she said, her long hair flowing in the breeze. "Will you still have me?"

Artham forgot to hide his claws and his reddish skin. He forgot to stutter or bob his head, and he forgot to listen to all the accusing voices in his mind. He completely forgot his shame. Then he lifted Arundelle in his arms and kissed her, and it was several minutes before he realized that they were flying high over the heads of the cheering crowd.

96

The Former Fangs
Have Passed Away

In the histories of Aerwiar, it was reckoned that the death of Janner Wingfeather and the rebirth of the Shining Isle of Anniera marked the first day of the Fifth Epoch, an age of peace and provision—a lasting repose that was known, in some measure, by every living thing that walked the land, swam the sea, or soared the sky.

While Janner's body rested in the cellar of the Castle Rysen, High King Kalmar Wingfeather blessed the new citizens of Anniera with new names. The former Fangs bowed before him one by one, and he gave them the finest, strongest, most graceful names he could imagine. They received their new names with humility and joy, because they understood the price that had been paid. Even the cloven who remembered their old names, gladdened by the hope of their lives to come, asked for new ones. The men and women who had never been Fanged did the same, welcoming the citizenship Kalmar freely offered.

Even as Kalmar blessed his people, some of the newly named Annierans formed an encampment in the fields below the Castle Rysen, while others began piling stone on stone, already rebuilding the walls of the castle. With Biggin O'Sally's tools, men and women marked out fields for planting, and by the end of the day new seeds were buried in the furrows, awaiting rain and resurrection.

Near the end of the line, a girl of Kalmar's age approached and fell at the king's feet. "My king! The Stone Keeper named me Nuzzard," the girl said, "but you carried me out of the dungeon."

Kalmar took the girl's hand and lifted her to her feet. She was beautiful. "Your new name is Galya. How does that sound?"

She took a deep, trembling breath and whispered, "I like it, Your Majesty."

"Just call me Kal," he said, and he watched her depart for the encampment in the company of a married couple who had rediscovered one another after many years of darkness.

Sara Cobbler arrived at sunset with all of her orphans, as well as Armulyn the Bard. He kissed the ground, then walked barefoot around the island in a daze, saying, "The stories are true," again and again to whomever would listen.

Sara wept at the news of Janner's death. Artham introduced her to Nia, who remembered her from Glipwood and delighted in Sara's affection for Janner, promising to raise her as her own daughter, to Leeli's great joy. While Artham and Arundelle strolled the fields around the castle, Sara told them all about Maraly and Gammon—also known as Shadowblade and the Florid Sword—and how happy they were, riding the rooftops in the moonlight to protect Skreeans from the scoundrels of the Strand.

That night Sara stood with the Wingfeathers as Artham placed Janner's body, still wrapped in his Durgan cloak, on a bier in the courtyard of the Castle Rysen.

Leeli played a lay for Janner, a melody that lodged in the hearts of the Annierans. Many years later, Armulyn the Bard added words—words of redemption and courage, vouchsafing the tale of Janner's honor for many Throne Wardens to come, so that all children, whether Annieran, or Hollish, or Skreean—or from some other faraway land—would know the glory of servanthood and sacrifice and selfless love.

"Janner Wingfeather," they would say, "never left his brother's side. He loved him to the end."

The world is whispering—listen, child!—
The world is telling a tale.
When the seafoam froths in the water wild
Or the fendril flies in the gale,

When the sky is mad with the swirling storm
And thunder shakes the hall,
Child, keep watch for the passing form
Of the one who made it all.

Listen, child, to the Hollish wind,
To the hush of heather down,
To the voice of the brook at the stony bend
And the bells of Rysentown.

The dark of the heart is a darkness deep
And the sweep of the night is wide
And the pain of the heart when the people weep
Is an overwhelming tide—

And yet! and yet! when the tide runs low
As the tide will always do
And the heavy sky where the bellows blow
Is bright at last, and blue

And the sun ascends in the quiet morn
And the sorrow sinks away,
When the veil of death and dark is torn
Asunder by the day,

Then the light of love is the flame of spring
And the flow of the river strong
And the hope of the heart as the people sing
Is an everlasting song.

The winter is whispering, "green and gold,"
And the heart is whispering, too—
It's a story the Maker has always told
And the story, my child, is true.

—Armulyn, Royal Bard of the Shining Isle

Epilogue

At dawn the next morning, Kalmar lit a torch in the castle cellar and cleared his throat.

"What are you doing?" Nia asked. She sat up and rubbed her eyes—eyes that were still red with sleep and weeping.

The sound of her voice woke Leeli and Sara, and they all squinted at Kalmar, who smiled at them with a look of mischief in his eyes. He was dressed in his Durgan cloak and had strapped Rudric's blade to his hip.

"It's time to go," Kalmar said. "Everybody up."

Artham peeked his head through the opening at the top of the stairs. "The sooner the better," Artham said. "Are they coming?"

"Yeah, they're awake and grumpy," Kalmar called up to him.

"What's going on?" Leeli asked with a yawn.

Kalmar helped her to her feet and handed her the crutch. "We're going on an adventure."

Nia, Leeli, and Sara were greatly confused as they climbed out of the cellar and into the cool morning. Hulwen the sea dragon was there, along with two other dragons. One of the dragons slumped under the weight of a very chubby man in spectacles.

"Oskar?" Leeli asked.

"In the words of Skeglin the Questionable, 'I'll organize the Great Library when I return.'" Oskar wiggled his haunches to keep his balance on the dragon's back. "I'm exceedingly happy to be in your company again, Wingfeathers."

Nia was the first to notice that Janner's body was no longer on the bier in the courtyard, but was wrapped in cloths and strapped to the green dragon's back.

"Kalmar, what are you doing?" Nia asked.

"Uncle Artham and I were talking," Kalmar said, "and we realized that there's this well, deep in the Blackwood—a well that's been lost for years and years."

Nia looked slowly from Kalmar to Janner's body and back again.

"And I know where it is," Kalmar said.

Leeli squealed, then scrambled onto Hulwen and hugged the dragon's neck. "Sara, sit with me!"

"Wait—what? On a *dragon*?" Sara was fully awake now. "Where are we going?"

"They say the water does amazing things," Artham said as he lifted Sara and situated her behind Leeli. "They say it heals—and maybe even more. I've wanted to taste it for a long time."

"It's worth a try," Kalmar said. "Either way, it's going to make a great story." Kalmar mounted the other dragon and held out his hand to his mother. "Are you coming?"

Acknowledgments

My undying gratitude goes to Pete Peterson, editor and confidant. It's no coincidence that brotherly love is a central theme in this story. Thanks also to my editor Jessica Barnes for her cheerleading and drill-sergeanting. My love and gratitude to Jamie (stronger and lovelier than Nia herself) and to Aedan, Asher, and Skye (my precious jewels), for caring more about this story and your father than I would have dreamed possible. Joe Sutphin perfectly captured the spirit of this book with his illustrations—not only that, he shaped a few of the characters and some parts of the story just because his drawings were so very cool. He's a kind soul and a consummate professional. Thanks to Justin Gerard for the map which now hangs over my mantel, and to Brannon McAllister for your excellent and tasteful design work. Thanks to Brian Rowley for making me the perfect pipe for spinning tales, and to the Rabbit Room community for reminding me what is true. Finally, I owe my undying thanks to the few thousand patrons who trusted me to follow through. Your enthusiasm for these books was an assuring voice and the perfect motivation when the task seemed too great.

Joe Sutphin would like to thank:

Gina, for your strength, faith, love and patience.
Tony, for being the finest mentor I could have ever imagined.
Andrew, for taking a chance on me.

RABBIT ROOM
—PRESS—
Nashville, Tennessee